MW00937213

An Eternity of Four years

—〰—

Book Two – The Catahoula Chronicles

A Novel By Lane Casteix

This is a work of fiction. Any references to historical events, real people, or real locales are used fictitiously. Other names, characters, places, and incidents are the product of the author's imagination, and any resemblance to actual events, locals, or persons, living or dead, is entirely coincidental.
Copyright 2014 Allen Lane Casteix

All rights reserved. No part of this publication may be reproduced, stored in a retrieval system, or transmitted in any form or by any means—electronic, mechanical, photocopying, recording, or otherwise—without the prior written permission of the author. The only exception is brief quotations in critical articles or reviews.

Sazerac and Sazerac Cocktail are registered trademarks of The Sazerac Company, Metairie, Louisiana

ISBN-13: 978-1512254730
ISBN-10: 1512254738

Acknowledgements

This book would not have been possible without the help of Janis, my wife of 45+ years, who encouraged me and tolerated me spending long hours at my faithful Mac to bring to life what was in my head. She was also my chief critic, challenging me when she saw something in the story that did not seem right to her. I value her input and love her dearly.

TABLE OF CONTENTS

Catahoula Genesis

December 2013
New Orleans, Louisiana

The old camelback trunk in my mother's attic had always intrigued me. When I asked about its contents, she said it contained just some old books and papers. It originally belonged to my grandmother and had belonged to her mother before that. Past those generations its provenance was uncertain.

With my mother's passing, the old trunk belonged to me. Unfortunately, it was locked, and there was no key to be found. Not wanting to destroy such a fine old trunk just to satisfy my curiosity, I tucked it into a corner of my attic with the expectation I would eventually find the key somewhere in my mother's possessions. There it sat, forgotten for nine years.

That changed when I was cleaning out some files that included my parent's old income tax filings. A strange lump at the bottom of one of the folders turned out to be a key, and my first thought was this is the key to the trunk!

I went immediately up to the attic and pulled the old trunk out of its corner. I was more than a little apprehensive about what I might find when I opened it. Did it contain some dark family secrets that should remain locked away? After mustering up my courage, I inserted the old key. It fit, and the lock loosened its hold on the old trunk's secrets.

My mother was right. It did contain some old books and papers. The "books" were the personal diaries of a woman named Rachel. The "papers," nearly two thousand handwritten pages, were secured

1

in four neat bundles with red ribbon. They turned out to be a manuscript written by a man named Ethan. I also found a portfolio of drawings by Rachel and bundles of letters they had written to each other. The documents dated from five years before the Civil War through its end in 1865 and a few years after.

With only a cursory examination of the trunk's contents, I realized I was in possession of something very special. The diaries and the manuscript, though written by two different people, were companion pieces, telling the same beautiful story from two different perspectives.

Catahoula Book One – The Last Day of Forever tells how they met, how they fell in love, and how their love was challenged. It carries their story up to the start of the American Civil War.

In *Catahoula Book Two – An Eternity of Four Years*, Rachel and Ethan are separated by a lie that destroys all they hold dear. She runs from the pain, and Ethan must search for her while the war rages around them.

Catahoula Book Three – The Avenging Angel follows their story after the war into Reconstruction as the young couple begins their life together at Catahoula Plantation in the shattered economy of the postwar South.

Here begins *An Eternity of Four Years*, a story told by Rachel and Ethan in their own words.

CHAPTER 1 – THE DUEL

12 April 1861

The sun was just peeking over the eastern horizon. Its feeble rays stabbed fitfully through the dense morning fog to give the gray monotones of dawn an ethereal glow. The chilling mist that hid the features of the so-called Dueling Oaks along Bayou St. John restricted my visibility to but one hundred paces or so. The oak's massive branches, touching the ground in places, had the appearance of being overly burdened and unable to lift up to reach the sun. Spanish moss dripped from those branches like ghostly fingers probing toward the earth.

I was exhausted, melancholy, and drunk as I stood upon the Field of Honor that morning, awaiting the arrival of my opponent. My clothing was damp from the fog, and my head throbbed from the copious amounts of absinthe I had consumed the previous night and well into the morning. With numbness of heart, I stared unseeing into the morning fog and marveled how one's fortunes can so suddenly and so completely change. A mere four days earlier, I was home at Catahoula Plantation along the Red River eagerly anticipating my marriage to Rachel Whitcomb that very day. Now, four days later …

I heard a voice repeating my name, each time more urgently and becoming louder. "Ethan. Ethan! ETHAN, are you listening to me?"

The voice drew me from the depths of my melancholy, and I turned slowly to its source. "You say something?"

My second, Jean DuBassey, held up his hands in exasperation. He seemed irritated that I had sent for him to act in that capacity and had arrived in a bit of a huff. "Did I say something? I have been talking to you for the last ten minutes. Obviously, you were not hearing anything I said?"

I shook my head. "Forgive me. Wha—what did you say?"

"I asked what is this all about? The last time I saw you was five years ago at your father's plantation in Catahoula Parish, and now you send for me to act as your second in a duel? And you do realize dueling is illegal in New Orleans?"

"As I recall, Jean, you said if I needed anything just ask, or words to that effect. Besides, you are the only person I could think of."

"You're drunk!"

I dismissed that accusation with a wave of my hand. "Maybe a little."

"Maybe a lot! How do you expect to fight a duel while drunk?"

"Actually, I was hoping you might help with that. You did claim you were an accomplished duelist, did you not?"

"You want me to teach you how to kill someone in ten minutes?"

I nodded. "Personally, I have not found killing someone anymore complicated than that—but all these Code Duello rules how to properly conduct a duel— that is rather complicated."

"Who have you killed?"

"Just a few renegade Indians out west when I was in the Army."

He leaned in and smelled my breath. "What have you been drinking?"

"Absinthe. Say, do you know there is a saloon on Bourbon Street—oh wait, you call them 'coffee houses'—yes, Aleix's Coffee House—and it sells mostly absinthe, and you drip water from these marvelous, little, marble fountains over lumps of sugar?" I paused and considered what I had said. "Well, I guess you do know; you live here, don't you?"

Jean shook his head again. "You dragged me from my bed, which I was sharing with a beautiful lady, by the way, to help you fight a duel? Who did you insult?"

"An arrogant fellow by the name of Toutant."

"Emile Justin Toutant?"

"The same. Friend of yours?"

"Not hardly. There are two people in this city you do not want to get into a duel with. I am one, and he is the other. What did you say that caused him to take offense?"

"He called me a coward."

"And why did he call you a coward?"

"Because I said the South will likely lose this war."

"And he took offense at that?"

"That—and maybe, I called him a name."

"This is like pulling teeth! What did you call him?"

"An ignorant buffoon, and maybe, I punched him."

"Maybe? Did you or didn't you?"

"Very well, I did punch him."

Jean sighed in resignation. "Not good. What's the choice of weapons?"

"Pistols."

"Not ten pound mauls in five feet of water on a sandbar in the Red River?" he said sarcastically to remind me of our "almost" duel five years before.

"That worked for you because you are only just over five feet tall, but the buffoon is as tall as I am."

Jean paused then looked past me and said, "The buffoon is here."

I turned and saw nothing at first but heard the trod of the horses, the rattle of the harness, and rumble of the carriage wheels. It appeared like a specter drifting out of the swirling fog and came to a stop under a gnarled and sagging oak thirty paces or so from where my second and I stood.

A gaudily dressed black man of immense size drove the rig. He was well over six feet tall and weighed 250 pounds or more. He was dressed in sky-blue, silken, knee-length pantaloons and matching swallow-tailed coat, vest and cravat, with a ruffled shirt, white silk stockings and black pumps. He wore a matching blue, ostrich-plumed turban on his head. Costumed so, he looked like some eunuch from the *Arabian Nights*. He jumped down from the driver's seat with a grace that seemed in stark contrast to his huge size and opened the door for his master.

A man, I assumed correctly to be my opponent's second, stepped out of the carriage. The surgeon followed, identified by his black bag.

Then Monsieur Toutant stepped arrogantly up to the carriage door and stood there for a moment smiling sardonically before dropping to the ground, alighting like some bird of prey. He drew a dainty, lace-trimmed handkerchief from his sleeve and dabbed his lips, then with a flourish, returned it to its place. He was handsomely dressed in a very fine, white linen suit and a ruffled shirt, a white silk brocade vest, and a maroon, silk cravat. He carried a silver handle cane, using it more as an extension of his arm and part of his costume rather than for any assistance while walking.

He stabbed the ground with his cane and, with his other hand upon his hip, struck an arrogant pose. His head thrown back, he looked down his long slender nose at me and said, "Bonjour, Monsieur Davis." He took a deep breath and pursed his lips before saying, "A good day to die, is it not?"

I suppose that was meant to unnerve me. It did not, because I was in an absinthe-induced daze. Quite frankly, I was so distressed as the result of other matters, matters of the heart that is, that I really didn't much give a damn if I lived or died. As a result, I stood upon this so-called Field of Honor to answer my insult to this finely dressed, pompous ass, and I was totally unafraid of the outcome. In retrospect, that attitude likely saved my life that morning. Events that had brought me to this state of melancholy were out of my control. I was, therefore, forced to place the whole miserable affair into the hands of the Lord—along with my life. As it were, He had plans for me but had not seen a need to take me into His confidence concerning them.

"Bonjour, Monsieur Toutant," I replied with a sweeping bow intended to mock him.

"Ethan!" snapped Jean DuBassey in a whispered tone. Then he turned to my opponent. "Monsieur Toutant, Monsieur Davis wishes for me to convey to you his apology for whatever insult you feel he has given. He assures me he meant no harm by his comments."

I looked at Jean, a frown on my face. "I said nothing of the kind!"

"Shut up! I'm trying to save your life. As your second, it is my job to prevent this fight," he replied. "Look it up. It is in that Code Duello you find so confusing."

The peacock fairly barked his rebuke. "Bah! He called me an ignorant buffoon and he punched me!" He stood there, one hand upon his hip, his other gesturing with his cane. "I am not accustomed to being insulted so, but I will accept your apology and spare your life," he paused for emphasis, "if you kneel at my feet and beg for it."

"He wants a fight, Ethan," whispered my second. "Nothing you can say will change that."

"Very well," I replied in whispered tones to Jean before addressing Monsieur Toutant, "Go to hell!"

"You sure know how to pick them. Toutant has only recently returned to New Orleans from an extended stay in France to avoid an unpleasantness he had with the law here. He killed two men before he left five years ago, in duels, of course, and one since he has been back. Thankfully, you did not choose swords. He is an expert and would likely cut you up into steaks."

"Are you suggesting I am not good with a sword?" I asked indignantly.

"The absinthe is talking now. You're a planter's son and hopefully a good shot since you choose pistols. He is, by the way, also an expert marksman."

"Well, I'm not."

"Not what?"

"I'm lousy with a sword, nearly failed it at VMI."

Jean shook his head. "You had best get to concentrating on the task at hand if you wish to live through this."

"I'm not sure I even care if I live."

"Oh, dear Lord, but you have no business being here." Jean sighed then grew serious. "Now listen to me, Ethan. I don't trust the man. He is too quick to take insult."

"As I recall you were quick to take insult once."

He nodded. "True, but I have grown wiser and less sensitive in the last five years. He has not."

"Are you ready, Monsieur Davis?" said Toutant.

"Any time."

He smiled. "Then let's get on with it." With that, he slipped his coat from his shoulders, expecting his blue-clad servant standing behind him to catch it. The poor devil was distracted, and Toutant's fine, white linen coat fell into the mud.

Furious, Toutant turned on that black and laid into him with his cane. I have witnessed only one beating of a slave that matched the savagery of what I saw that morning, and he died from it. His second protested, but Toutant only brushed him off and continued to rain blows on the Negro. The poor man could only cower and cover his head to fend off the blows one after another. He was nearly twice the size of Toutant and perfectly capable of snapping his head off with one hand, but he made no aggressive moves. Instead, he only took his beating and whimpered, "Please, Monsieur Toutant, please. Old Blue's sorry. Please!"

But Toutant did not stop. I'd had enough! I marched over and snatched the cane from his hand, tossing it into the nearby bayou.

"You'll kill him!"

"My only regret," he said to me in a very low, menacing voice, "is that I can kill you only once.

"Not going to happen. I propose a wager, sir. If I win this contest, the Negro is mine." Before all the words were out of my mouth, I wondered why I was even uttering them.

He looked at the whimpering, blue heap on the ground, his head bleeding in several places. "He has proven to be stupid and worthless as a servant. But what have you to wager, sir?"

I gestured over my shoulder. "That fine gray." As I later thought over the events of that day, why I offered to wager my trusty mount for a Negro, I am not rightly certain. I must conclude it was the absinthe and my anger at seeing a man so abused.

Toutant looked at Pepper, my big, dappled-gray horse and smiled. "Done."

And I thought, *What—have I done?* "Write the agreement down and have these men sign it. Then give it to the Negro to hold."

"You do not trust me?" sneered Toutant.

"Hard for you to sign a bill of sale if you're dead."

Toutant nodded to the surgeon.

The papers drawn up and signed, the still somewhat shaken surgeon stepped forward and began the proceedings. "Gentlemen, I must warn you that dueling is illegal in New Orleans." He got no response from either of us. "Very well. Monsieur DuBassey, will you assist in the loading of the pistols?"

Jean nodded and stepped up and took one of the two dueling pistols from the case as did Toutant's second. Out of sight of either of the two antagonists, each second was in turn handed the powder flask and a ball. Once the pistols were loaded, each was handed a percussion cap to prime the charge. Set on half cock, the loaded and primed pistols were returned to the case. Out of sight of the rest of us, the surgeon had the privilege of switching the places of the pistols, or not. Therefore, none but the surgeon knew which pistol had been loaded by which second.

Monsieur Toutant and I were called forward. "Choose your weapon, sir," the surgeon said as he presented the case to me. I made my choice; Toutant took the other. "Take your places, gentlemen."

Pistols raised, we stood back-to-back. "You will take ten paces on my count. On the ninth count you will cock your weapon. On the count of ten you will turn and fire. May the best man win. Are you ready, gentlemen?"

We both nodded.

"One, two, three . . ." We stepped off our paces in cadence to the surgeon's counting. At "nine," we cocked our weapons. At "ten," I spun and leveled my pistol at Toutant. Before I had him in my sights, he fired, and the ball whistled passed my left ear. I felt the heat and wind of its passage; it was that close. With my pistol pointing at his chest, he stood there facing sure death. His lip trembled as he took a deep breath and lifted his chin.

I raised my pistol skyward and discharged it. "It's finished," I said as I let the pistol fall to the ground at my feet. "Come, Jean, I need a drink. You're buying."

"Stop where you are!" yelled Toutant. "It is not over! No blood was drawn. I demand satisfaction! We shall finish it now!"

"What is he talking about?" I asked of my second.

"He's right, Ethan. No blood was drawn, and what you just did is called 'dumb shooting' and strictly not allowed under Code Duello. It was a further insult to his pride. He can demand satisfaction. You'll have to fight him again. You should have killed him when you had the chance."

I turned back to Toutant, who was pacing angrily. "I gave him his life. He is an idiot."

"Indeed, and a dangerous one. He was only arrogant and angry before. Now you have humiliated him, and he is completely unpredictable."

Toutant's eyes were aflame with anger, and his face was flush. "Sir, I declare this duel will be à l'outrance!"

I understood the French but not the meaning and looked to my second for an explanation. "To excess?"

"Literally, yes, but it means to the death. The duel will not end until one of you is dead."

"Well?" yelled Toutant, and for emphasis, he kicked the Negro still on the ground.

I turned to him. "I don't like killing fools, but I'll make an exception in your case."

Once more we went through the loading ritual. As I was about to step forward to choose my weapon, Jean stopped me and whispered, "Look at him. He's shaking with anger. If I yell, you turn and fire no matter what the count is. Understand?"

I nodded as I recalled the advice of Tom Sullivan, a sergeant I had as a mentor and close friend out in New Mexico Territory when I served with the 1st Regiment of Mounted Riflemen. He said anger distorts decision-making, and Toutant was *very* angry.

We took our positions back to back, and the surgeon began counting. "One, two, three..." We slowly paced off our steps, and I thought about what Jean said to me. I shook that off and tried to concentrate on the task at hand. "...eight, ni..."

"Ethan!" yelled Jean.

I spun, cocked my pistol, and fired the moment my front sight crossed Toutant's chest. He fired that same instant. His ball entered the loose shirtsleeve of my extended right arm near the wrist and exited near the armpit. I felt it pass, and for a brief moment, thought I was hit but soon realized it had not touched flesh. We both stood there as the gunsmoke slowly drifted away. I knew I wasn't hit, but he was also still standing. Then his head bobbed, and that was when I noticed the red stain slowly spreading from under his brocade vest. His knees gave out from under him, and he slumped into the mud. I tossed the pistol away and turned to my second.

Jean was shaking his head. "He turned on nine. I knew he was going to do it. It was in his eyes."

"You saved my life."

He slapped me on my back. "It is a bit early for a drink now. How about some coffee instead? But you buy, and you can tell me what this is all about. The last time I saw you it was I who challenged you to a duel." He laughed. "Which I am thankful to say did not end as tragically as did this incident. I still laugh when I think of that. Mauls you chose for weapons, ten pound mauls on a sandbar in five feet of water in the Red River, and I am such a little fellow barely over five feet and you are over six feet tall. Not a very fair match."

"Fortunately, you saw the humor in my gesture."

"Had you not had a cool head back then, one of us might not be alive today. And from what I just saw of your shooting, I might have been the one in the ground."

I smiled as I recalled our last meeting, but as we walked to our horses, I heard the thunder of hooves coming toward us. Five New Orleans policemen came from out of the fog, pistols drawn.

"Halt! Stand fast there!" one yelled. The leader dismounted and stepped over to the surgeon attending the dead Toutant. After asking the surgeon a few questions, he turned and approached me. "You were dueling?"

I did not answer.

"It is against the law to duel. What will it take to get you hot-tempered Creoles to give this stupidity up? I have never seen such arrogance, not even back in Ireland. You are under arrest, sir."

"For dueling?"

"For murder."

An Eternity of Four Years

Chapter 2 – A Change of Plans

I found myself in the New Orleans jail, not a very pleasant place to be, and spent the first day in a large holding cell. The next day, I was transferred to a smaller cell with an Irish fellow.

As the cell door creaked closed behind me, I took a quick look around before I tossed my coat on the bunk, which was little more than boards with a filthy, straw-filled mattress on top. That mattered little, for I had slept on worse during my service with the Regiment of Mounted Riflemen in New Mexico Territory. That was in the Old Army before the recent surrender of Fort Sumter. I had resigned my commission when Louisiana seceded from the Union, and like many other southerners, "gone south."

My cellmate was reclining in the other bunk with his hands behind his head. He was a rough-looking fellow several inches shorter than I am with a crop of curly dark red hair. His clothing was soiled and well worn. It turned out he was a refugee from the Great Famine in Ireland who had immigrated to America and worked as a common laborer on the New Orleans levees. He found himself in jail because he had beaten another fellow to within an inch of his life over a spilled beer. We spent a long moment staring at each other as we each took the other's measure.

He broke the silence. "And what have we here? A right, dandy-looking fellow, eh? What are you in for?"

"I killed a man," I said as I sat down on the filthy mattress and leaned back against the wall. Several large roaches scurried to safety.

"Ya don't look like a murderer. Ya look more like a Creole gentleman."

"Whatever I look like doesn't much matter. I killed a man in a duel, and it was self-defense; he was cheating. The authorities, however, call it murder."

He nodded knowingly. "Going ta hang ya, huh, lad?"

"That's what they tell me."

He swung his legs around to a sitting position and extended his hand, "Sean, Sean O'Hara, pleased to make your acquaintance."

"Ethan..." I paused as I considered my response. "My name is Ethan—Joubert."

"Sorry to hear ya might be hung, what with a war on and all. Sumter surrendered yesterday, and that changes everything. We got us a real fight now. As for me, I'm out of here. They agreed to drop the charges, because I'm signing up."

"You sound anxious to get into this war."

He waved a finger at me. "Glory, sir! It's a chance for some glory instead of tossing dirt from a shovel on a levee gang. I'd rather be a soldier than a digger."

"Ever soldiered?"

"Nay, sir, but it can't be any worse than being a digger. And the ladies love a handsome soldier."

"I was a soldier until a month ago, out west in New Mexico Territory. Soldiering isn't all that easy, and it isn't all glory, either. It's hot, miserable, and dangerous work that can get you killed. After a few months of soldiering, you may find yourself wishing you were back on that levee gang."

"I'll take my chances. At least, it isn't jail."

"What outfit are you signing up with?"

He beamed. "The Tiger Rifles. It is a militia company, part of Wheat's Battalion. And if anyone can get us into the fight, Major Wheat can. Maybe you can come along. The major is coming for me today. War beats jail any time, especially if you are facing the noose like you are."

"I'm not interested in the war just now. That's a fool's party. Besides, I have business in the North."

He looked at me disapprovingly. "A northern sympathizer?"

"No. I'm a southerner, but I have other priorities just now."

"We are about to be invaded, man. Have you no honor?"

I laughed as I leaned forward to make my point. "Honor? Seems to me the real reason you're signing up is to get out of jail."

"And glory," he reminded me.

"Oh, yes. Must not forget the glory," I replied sarcastically.

He nodded. "About your trip up north, you're wasting your time, lad. I hear they're arresting southerners. They'll put you in jail, unless you take a loyalty oath. Whatever business you have up there, ya best forget about it. Ya might as well join up. Better 'an hanging."

"They won't hang me for defending myself." I said that, but I had my doubts. Jean was trying to get the charges dropped. I was, in truth, only defending myself.

"Come along, O'Hara," said the turnkey as he opened our cell. "Your ticket out of here has come to pickup your worthless hide. As for you, Davis, you have a visitor."

My cellmate grabbed his hat and coat and looked at me. "Davis? Thought you said your name was Joubert?"

"I did."

He shook his head as if confused. "Think about what I said," he called out to me as he left.

With the cell locked again, Jean stepped up to the bars. I did not like the dour expression on his face.

"How are you, Ethan?"

"Tolerable. When do I get out of here?"

"It looks bad. I spoke to the judge myself. He intends to make an example out of you. He's taking this all the way and expects to get a conviction for murder."

"But it was self-defense."

"I know that, but the other two witnesses are friends of Toutant. They're saying I yelled for you to turn before the count of ten, and Toutant was only responding to my warning when he turned before the full count. They're calling that murder, and I may also be charged as an accomplice." He swallowed hard. "Ethan, they intend to hang you right after the trial, no appeal, no waiting. The judge's wife wants the dueling stopped. It offends her delicate nature, you see."

My head was numb. I had not thought my fortunes could get worse, and now this! "There is nothing that can be done?"

My friend sighed and glanced to his left. "There is an option." He gestured to someone outside of my view.

Up to the cell stepped a giant of a man. He was six foot four and 280 pounds, a most imposing looking fellow. Though his head seemed too small for his body, he was handsome with dark hair and eyes and a neatly trimmed mustache.

"Ethan, this is Major Chatham Roberdeau Wheat."

The major nodded and shook my hand through the bars. "Monsieur."

"Rob, why don't you tell him why you're here?"

Wheat nodded. "Jean tells me you served with the Brave Rifles."

"In New Mexico."

"Any action?"

"Some. Several skirmishes, and I commanded a patrol in a running three day fight with renegades."

"Who won?"

"We did."

He smiled. "VMI, too? Your military training and experience will be valuable. So few signing up have any. We could use a man like you. Will you join us? Your friend Jean has already agreed to."

"What about my hanging?"

"I spoke to the judge in your behalf, sir. Let's say he owes me a debt. He agreed to drop the charges, but only if you enlist in my battalion and leave New Orleans immediately."

"The Tiger Rifles?"

"That's one of my companies. We will be mustered into service in the Confederate Army as the 1st Special Infantry Battalion. We expect to leave for Virginia not many days later."

I sighed. "In what capacity will I be serving?"

"We've already elected the officers, but because of your training and combat experience, I am confident I can secure for you a lieutenancy as my adjutant, until we can work something else out."

Service in the Confederate Army was something I had hoped to avoid just then. I felt obliged to serve, to protect my home, family, and my state and was willing to do so, but I had more pressing matters to resolve at the moment. However, service was preferable to hanging, and my "more pressing matters" would have to wait until this war was over. Either that or hang.

"Your offer is most generous, sir. I accept."

Jean was beaming. "Wonderful, Ethan. You won't be sorry. This whole affair will be over in a few months."

"I certainly hope so. I have other business to attend to."

Wheat summoned the jailer and showed him the judge's order for my release. "He's coming with me. Let him out."

"Another one? Soon you'll have emptied the New Orleans jails, and good riddance to the lot of them," said the jailer as he unlocked my cell.

"Your boy is outside," said Jean. "He's been there waiting like a faithful dog all the while you were in jail."

"What are you talking about," I asked as I put on my coat.

"That huge Negro you won in the duel. His name is Blue."

"I forgot about him."

"He's yours now. He might come in handy while you're in Virginia. Some of the boys are bringing along their servants."

"I don't own any slaves, and he isn't my servant."

"Well, you own one now," replied Jean.

"Not for long." I stopped at a desk and scribbled out emancipation papers for Blue.

When we got outside, that big Negro rushed up to me. He was still dressed in that silly outfit, and it was soiled with blood and mud, though it looked like he had tried to clean himself up a bit. His face was swollen, one eye was almost shut, but he was so black you couldn't see the bruises. He had that stupid turban in his hand as he came up to me and bowed at the waist. "Oh, Massa Ethan, I'm so glad they let you go free. Old Blue has been worried about you, but they wouldn't let me come inside to see you. They treat you well?" He took a much-needed deep breath. "We all goin' to Virginia now, sir."

He was a pitiful sight, and I felt sorry for him. "I'm going to Virginia, not you."

"But you own Old Blue now. I go where you go."

"I don't own you."

"But you won me when you kilt Monsieur Toutant. Look, I have the papers right here. Says you own me."

"Listen, Blue. I don't want a servant. I don't need one, don't want the responsibility." I handed him the emancipation papers and twenty dollars. "If I own you, then I'm giving you your freedom. This paper says you are free. I'll have it proper registered before I leave. Use this money to live on until you can find a job. I expect you can find work as a servant or a laborer now that many of the Irish from the levee gangs have joined the army. Use your freedom well, Blue. Good luck."

He looked at me as if I was crazy. "I don't understand, Massa Ethan."

"You're free, Blue, and I don't want you with me."

His confused expression turned to one of hurt, and he pleaded, "But I have to go with you."

"And why is that?"

"Because you saved my life. That Monsieur Toutant would have kilt me sooner or later; I know he would've. I've been praying for someone to deliver me from that hateful man. The Lord sent you to do that. I have to go with you now."

I looked to my friends for help. Wheat shrugged. O'Hara seemed amused. Jean said, "He has a mighty convincing argument there, Ethan. If God is involved in this matter, you best do as he says."

"What are you talking about? Even if, by the providence of God, I was sent to deliver him, that job is done." I turned to the big Negro. "Blue, you can't come with me."

He stood there for a moment, deep in thought with a perplexed expression on his face. "You say I'm free now, Massa Ethan?"

"That's right."

"I can do anything I want?"

"That's correct."

"Go anywhere I want?"

"Yeessss, Blue. That paper I gave you says you can make your own decisions now."

"Then Blue is going to Virginia with you," he said with a determined nod of his big head. He had set me up, and I didn't see it coming.

Wheat and O'Hara both chuckled. Jean tried to hold in a laugh but failed miserably and fell into stomach-holding guffaws. "He got you, Ethan. Got you good. You had better watch out for this big, black fellow. He isn't as dumb as he looks."

Blue beamed. I frowned.

I no more wanted a servant than another belly button, but I was at a loss as to what to do about him. "Very well, Blue. You can go where you want. I can't stop you, but if you follow me, that silly outfit you're wearing isn't coming with you."

His grin grew even larger, flashing white teeth that seemed even brighter against his black skin. "Monsieur Toutant got this for me right after he bought me. I don't much like it either, Massa Ethan."

"Then take this money I gave you and go buy something else to wear. Know anything about mules?"

"I know all about mules!"

"Here is another fifty dollars. Buy yourself a good mule to ride—and bring me the change. And one more thing, I'm not your master, so stop calling me that. You can find me at the Sazerac Coffee House when you're done."

Jean slapped me on the back. "Now you are talking! Let's get a drink and celebrate!"

"Gentlemen," said Wheat. "I must beg off. I need to get back to camp, and you three need to report by sundown tomorrow. Don't make me come looking for you."

We made our way to the Sazerac on Exchange Alley and ordered a round.

"Now, tell me," said Jean after a sip of his drink. "What happened to that sweet little thing that was so in love with you five years ago? What was her name? Rachel? Yes, Rachel."

That was a subject I did not care to discuss just then. "She's gone," was my non-committal answer.

"Gone?"

"Gone, as in I do not wish to discuss it!" I snapped.

Jean nodded thoughtfully. "Well then, perhaps you will tell us how you came to be in New Orleans and in a duel?"

I looked at the faces eager to hear my tale. "That's not important."

"Very well. The last time I saw you, your name was Davis. Why have you changed it to Joubert? Any connection with Pernell Joubert?"

In my present state of mind, I was unprepared and unwilling to answer these questions. "No comment," was my terse reply.

"I see," said Jean with a knowing nod. "And why do I get the feeling the answer to the third question is connected with the answer to the second question which is connected to the answer to the first?"

I bolted down my Sazerac and ordered another. "Think what you wish, but it's none of your business."

Sensing he had stepped over some boundary, he became remorseful. "My apologies, Ethan. I did not realize I was prying into something very personal."

"Accepted. Shall we move on?"

The conversation quickly turned to the war, and I was glad of it. Three more Sazeracs, and I was feeling some relief from the pain in my heart.

Blue purchased suitable clothing and a mule with the money I gave him and was waiting for us outside the Sazerac when we came out. He was grinning as if he were the happiest man alive. "I'm ready, Massa Ethan!"

"So you are. And stop calling me master!"

"We all goin' to Virginia now?"

That night in the hotel, I tried to write my mother a letter and tell her all the things I needed to tell her. In the end, all I was able to say was I had enlisted and was eventually headed for Virginia—and that I had taken Joubert as my last name.

The next morning, with my saddlebags packed and Pepper saddled and ready to go, I looked over his back to Blue standing beside his mule watching me. "Something troubling you?"

He seemed reluctant to answer at first. "I'm free, you say?"

"Yes, Blue," I replied with exasperation in my voice. I knew he understood that and was testing me for some reason.

"Then I'm gonna speak the truth, sir."

"Usually a good policy. Speak up."

"I'm worried about you."

"Worried about me? Why?"

"Something is weighing heavy on your mind. I kin see it in your eyes. Seen the same look on you at the duel a few days ago. I'm thinking you're not acting like yourself right now. Somethin's hurting you inside."

Blue was a very perceptive fellow. I was indeed hurting inside, and I didn't know how to deal with that hurt. All of my life I had been able to solve my own problems, think my way out of trouble or fight if it came to that. I wasn't afraid of dying, and I wasn't afraid of killing, either. I had done that in New Mexico and at the duel. But *this*! This was so much larger than me. I knew there was a solution; there is always a solution, but wallowing in my self-pity, I wasn't ready to accept it.

"Saddle up, Blue. We have to get to Camp Moore before sunset."

He took that as my answer and said no more on the subject.

We arrived at Camp Moore in Tangipahoa Parish where the battalion had been in training and was waiting to muster into service. The 1st Special Battalion, Louisiana Volunteers consisted of five companies: The Walker Guards under Captain Robert A. Harris; the Old Dominion Guards commanded by Captain O. P. Miller, Henry Clay Gardner's Delta Rangers, and the Catahoula Guerrillas under an old acquaintance of mine, Captain J.W. Buhoup. The Catahoula Guerrillas were made up mostly of planter's sons from Catahoula Parish, many I knew, and the only company in the battalion not from New Orleans.

But the most colorful of the lot were the Tiger Rifles under the command of Captain Alex White. They adopted the uniform of the French Zouaves and wore baggy stripped pantaloons with white leggings and red shirts under short blue jackets decorated with gold braid on the front. Around the waist they wore a red sash. An Algerian-style fez with a bright yellow tassel hanging on the side was their headgear. They were a colorful lot and in more ways than just their costumes.

I purchased my uniforms, which were traditional in style, being gray and styled much like those I had worn while with the Brave Rifles in New Mexico. I chose a kepi for my hat, and my shell jacket was fitted and short in the waist. I purchased an infantry officer's sword made by Griswald in New Orleans and belt with accouterments for my Colt New Model Army .44 given to me when I graduated from VMI.

Wheat's Battalion, as we were most frequently referred to, had already established a questionable reputation as drunkards and thieves. Many of the recruits were Irish and German levee workers and laborers from the New Orleans area, and it was said that so many of those were recruited directly from the city's jail that Wheat had a recruiting desk in the jail. That was only partially true as I can testify.

The battalion was not only a mixed lot of nations and tongues, but its members were from all walks of life: lawyers, planters, merchants, laborers, and pimps. I immediately realized Wheat was going to have a discipline problem. Fortunately, he was a very stern disciplinarian. Not only was he feared but he was also well loved and respected by the men. He seemed to hold a spell over them.

Camp Moore was located well north of New Orleans and away from towns of any consequence that might have bars to tempt the men. Drunkenness, however, became such a problem it was necessary to require the signature of a company officer for any enlisted man to buy whiskey from the sutlers. This proved to be only a minor inconvenience. Officers were bribed for their written permission, or their signatures were simply forged. The sutlers were not terribly diligent verifying the signatures were genuine.

On 9 June the 1st Special Battalion mustered into service. Four hundred and fifty men strong, we left for Virginia four days later, but not before we had a good and proper riot. Some men from another unit went on a rampage, destroying their tents and burning the wooden floors. With some 12,000 men confined to a small area and about to go off to war, it is not surprising there would be some problems, and soon the whole camp was involved. Drunken brawls sprang up and spread, sending men to the hospital with broken bones and cuts. Some from our battalion were the worst of the lot, namely the Tiger Rifles. Even before we left Camp Moore, the battalion was labeled as troublemakers, and controlling the men required Wheat's constant vigilance.

The morning we departed for Virginia, Blue came to me. "Lieutenant Ethan?"

"Yes, Blue."

"Sir, I believe these boys is crazy. What have we done got ourselves involved with?"

I shook an accusing finger at him. "I told you not to come. I'm stuck here, but you can leave anytime you want. We're leaving for Virginia now, and this is your last chance to get out of here."

He shook his big head assertively. "No, sir. I go where you go, an' that's a fact."

I sighed. "Then who's crazy? Them or you?"

"All of us is crazy, Lieutenant Ethan, the whole mess of us."

As I write this tome many years after that day, I believe Blue was right. We were all crazy.

Chapter 3 – Off to See the Elephant

Both the North and the South went to war with grand illusions of honor and glory filling their heads. Few had any notion of what war was really all about. Most had never "seen the elephant," which, in the parlance of the soldier, means he has not yet experienced combat and all the horrors associated with it. Everyone assumed the war would be over quickly, lasting a year at most, more likely just a few months, with one large and decisive battle convincing the other side of the foolishness of it all. The North believed the South would be defeated and would give up its silly notion of secession. The South thought they would be victorious, and the defeated North would let us go our own way to establish a new nation. Both sides were wrong, and neither side was really prepared for the hell about to be unleashed.

The summer of '61 found both armies scrambling to fill out muster rolls, arm the new volunteers, train them and get them into the field as quickly as possible. Only small engagements characterized this period, but Confederate units in Virginia were within a short day's march from Washington and, thus, threatened the capitol. This was something Lincoln could not tolerate. Were Washington to somehow be captured, it is likely that France and England would be forced to recognize the Confederacy as a legitimate nation and not simply a part of the United States in rebellion as Lincoln insisted. Either nation could have conceivably come into the war on the side of the Confederacy; Napoleon even hinted as much. Such recognition would have opened a floodgate of supplies from Europe, supplies we badly needed to fight a war.

"Old Fuss and Feathers," the "Grand Old Man of the Army," otherwise known as General Winfield Scott, Lincoln's general of his armies, was 74 at the start of the war and too overweight to even mount a horse much less lead men in battle. He initially offered that job to Robert E. Lee, but when his home state of Virginia left the Union, Lee went south rather than fight against his own.

Scott found someone else, General Irwin McDowell, to lead the Army of the Potomac. Scott got his orders from the President, and McDowell got his from Scott, and he was ordered to remove the southern threat to the capitol. McDowell protested to Scott that his army was not ready, but his protests fell of deaf ears. Scott had his orders, and McDowell had to execute them, so General McDowell made his plans to march on Manassas Junction and submitted them for approval. The stage was set for the first big scrap.

By the time we arrived in Virginia in late June, Wheat's Battalion was being called "Wheat's Tigers." Eventually, the Tiger moniker would be applied to all the volunteers from Louisiana. For a spell, things were quiet as we settled into something resembling a routine. We continued drilling and training and chaffed to engage the Federals, little realizing that we were about to do so. The men were understandably restless and quarrelsome. Fights were frequent between individuals and even units.

The Louisiana volunteers very quickly gathered an unsavory reputation for themselves, Wheat's Battalion and Coppens' Battalion of Louisiana Zouaves in particular. On the way up to Virginia from Pensacola, where Coppens' battalion had been training, the officers left the men unattended and rode in their own car on the train. At one stop, the men uncoupled the officer's car, hijacked the train and left the officers at the station. By the time they caught up with the rest of the battalion in Montgomery, Alabama, the Zouaves had embarked on a drunken spree of looting, robbery and harassment, which lasted better than an hour, until city officials called out the 1st Georgia Volunteers to bring the drunken Zouaves under control with loaded muskets and the point of the bayonet. The Zouaves' officers arrived with drawn pistols and proceeded to regain control of their men. It took another hour to get them to give up their plunder and get back on the train. In the process, an officer shot and killed one man.

The 14th Louisiana Regiment earned a reputation nearly as unsavory as Coppens' men. On the trip to Virginia, the train stopped in Grand Junction, Tennessee, and they got hold of two barrels of whiskey and proceeded to have a drunken riot that resulted in numerous fights. Their officers had to shoot several men to restore order, but the men turned on them and forced the officers to retreat to a hotel, which was quickly set afire. Pistol in hand, the regimental commander, Colonel Sulakowski, waded into their midst and demanded that the mutineers return to their quarters immediately. But they did not move fast enough for him, and he shot two. The riot moved to the streets and lasted for another hour before they were subdued, but not before seven men were killed and nineteen were wounded. Sulakowski denounced several of his officers for allowing the men to get out of control. He disbanded one company, the instigators of the riot, and cashiered their officers.

We had not yet been in a fight with the Yankees, and we had garnered for ourselves a reputation of being poor quality soldiers that no one wanted in their brigades. Oh, we were a handsome lot on the drill field in our smart looking Zouave uniforms, fancy drill and commands shouted in French, but everyone desired to be rid of us, especially some of us. I must confess I also had doubts as to how well the Louisiana volunteers would perform under fire.

I complained to Wheat about the thefts of civilian property, and to his credit, he attempted to keep the men under control, but he was not always successful. "This is a war, Lieutenant. Some of this cannot be stopped. We are poorly supplied by our own government, and the men must subsist some way. We will pay for the damages when we can be sure it was our men who were responsible, and you must redouble your efforts to see that we are provisioned properly."

"I've done my best, sir. But the commissary is disorganized, and supplies are limited or non existent."

"I am well aware of the problem. We have whole regiments here and no equipment for them, not even muskets or uniforms. They are being sent back home until the supply problems can be sorted out. Until then, we must make do with what we can. The men are counting on you."

"Yes, sir."

With our reputation for pilfering and general loutishness, when the Tigers showed up, Virginians bolted the doors and windows—

not a very auspicious beginning for us. I, for one, was disgusted with the whole lot of them and regretted my decision to join up. But I had given my word and meant to see this through to the end, then as quickly as possible, put it all behind me and get on with my business. In July of '61, I still harbored hope, small as it was, that this war would be over before the year was out.

I had also hoped my enlistment would lead to a command of a company eventually, but it looked like I was destined to be nothing more than the aide to a major. Wheat had me do his every bidding. I transcribed his letters and took care of the reports as was expected in my capacity as adjutant, but he also used me as his scrounger, and I have never known a man to be desirous of so many unusual things as Wheat was, especially food. He fancied himself a gourmet cook and loved to show off his skills to the other officers, keeping me busy procuring all manner of exotic foods for him to cook. It is true that he was a good cook, and he loved to eat. One look at him would was proof of that.

Thank goodness for Blue! He turned out to be a consummate battlefield scrounger. Whatever I needed, Blue would somehow find it. He proved to be a tremendous help in securing all manner of things for our mess and the battalion.

Blue had a related trait that could sometimes be frustrating. He often professed the knowledge of all things. Back in New Orleans, I had asked him if he knew anything about mules, and he replied he knew all about mules. And he did. He purchased a good one and at a good price.

"Know anything about where we can find replacement ramrods, Blue?"

"I know all about ramrods!" he confidently answered. "For the Mississippi Rifles? How many you need?"

"How about getting some quail for our dinner?"

"I know all about where to find quail. Can't get 'em for tonight, but I can for tomorrow. That be good enough?"

Then I tried to trick him. "Can you get us some fulminate of mercury?" thinking he wouldn't know technical terms.

He frowned, and I figured I had him stumped. "I know all about fulminate of mercury, but what you need that for? Planning on making your own primer caps? How much you want?"

He settled in and found his own place in the greater scheme of camp life and turned out to be a very fine cook.

One night when we were alone around the campfire, I asked him about his background. He was somewhat secretive but did tell me some of his life up to the time we met.

"My mother was owned by a Creole family in New Orleans. Her name was Adel, and she was a beautiful woman of pure African descent, a tall, proud woman. She was their cook and one of only four slaves. My father was another, their carriage driver. I never knew him. They sold him before I was born. My momma told me a little 'bout him, that he was a big man like me. His name was Luke, like in the Bible, but that's all I know 'bout him.

"The folks that owned me had no need of someone like me. When I was jes' fourteen, they sold me as a field hand to a plantation on the west bank of the river across from New Orleans. After a couple years, my new massa discovered I could cook and added me to their kitchen staff. That lasted a few more years until they had to sell me to settle some debts. That's when Massa Toutant bought me."

"The day of the duel, he treated you badly. Was he always like that?" I asked.

"That man was mean, pure mean! He beat me for anything. It wasn't that way at first. He made me his pet and dressed me up in that blue outfit and made me his carriage driver, but I wasn't trained to be a carriage driver or a body servant, but I tried to learn fast. It got bad after he brought me into his bedroom one night and made me get undressed, an' he was touchin' me—and he asked me to—do things. I had a big bowl of gumbo for dinner that night, and I throwed up all over him at jes' the thought of what he wanted me to do. He beat me bad that night! I thought he was goin' to kill me." He turned and looked me in the eyes. "And that's when I started prayin'. Lord, send someone who can buy me away from this evil man! Then you showed up."

Tears were running down his face then. "When we arrived by the Bayou St John that morning, first thing I noticed was you. Somethin' about you standing there in that fog made you look like an angel, and I was thinking, *Lord, is this the one?*"

I smiled. "Blue, you're making the story up now."

He shook his head violently. "NO, sir! Not one word of it! Something else, too, I could feel your pain. Before I even stepped down off that carriage, I knew you were hurting inside jes' like I was. When Massa Toutant dropped his coat, I was praying for you. I was saying, 'Lord, if this be the one you sending, you have to put your hedge of protection 'round him. You cain't let no balls touch this man today.' And that's when that beautiful white coat went right into the mud—and Massa Toutant went to whipping me with that cane."

"Why have you never told me this?"

"You never axed. When you stepped up and took that cane away from him and throwed it in the bayou, I was sure it had to be you the Lord sent. Then the wager you proposed, and he agreed to, absolutely convinced me. That's when I *really* went to prayin' for you!"

I thought back on that morning. It is amazing how you can see things and at the same time not see them. "Well, it worked. I felt the passage of both balls barely an inch from me, and I have long wondered how someone with his reputation as a marksman could possibly have missed—twice?"

"The Lord was wit you, Lieutenant Ethan."

"What now, Blue?"

He shrugged before answering. "Doan know. What I do know is our futures are now connected, an' eventually, the Lord will show me what I'm to do for you. The Lord has plans for you an' me. For now, I am thinkin' you strike me as trouble jes' lookin' for a place to happen, an' I aim to see that it don't."

There was a long period of silence around the campfire after Blue's story. He was the first to break that silence. "Lieutenant Ethan, we come to Virginia to see the elephant. I ain't never seen no elephant and always wanted to see one and that big nose. When we gonna see him?"

I started laughing and couldn't stop. Blue looked at me like I was crazy.

In the beginning, back in New Orleans and before he told me that story, I didn't want him around, but I had became attached to him even before that night. As a freedman, he didn't need to follow me, but he claimed he was a bondservant of Christ, and I was his responsibility. Nothing I could do or say would dissuade him from that mission, and in retrospect, I am glad I was unsuccessful in those efforts.

Because of his cooking skills, he became the preferred cook for our mess, which seemed to suit him just fine. His haversacks, as he had two not one like the rest of us, seemed almost bottomless. He could reach in and draw out the most amazing things. Ask for something, and he would fish around in one of his haversacks and usually come up with it. One haversack was mostly stocked with spices in little leather bags. Since he was our cook, we very much appreciated that one. The man was good enough as a cook he could have been a successful chef at any New Orleans restaurant. He could take some of the most disagreeable ingredients and turn them into a tasty meal.

Since he was not a soldier, Blue was not on the army payroll and drew no pay. Our mess chipped in to provide him with what he needed to buy what food we didn't draw from the quartermaster and pay him a small amount for his services. But Blue was enterprising. He almost always had some "Blue bidness," as he called it, which he used to make money. It was usually food related, like compounding spices and selling them to other men in the battalion. Some of what he used to make his spice blend was easy to acquire, either in nature or from the sutlers, but some of the ingredients needed to be purchased in places like Richmond. He used the profits to reinvest in his "Blue bidness" and make even more money. Later in the war, he would go into Richmond and buy brogans and bring them back and sell them to the poor souls who were shoeless. He would make nearly a dollar a pair. Knowing this war would end someday, and expecting the Union to be the victor, he converted his Confederate money into Yankee dollars whenever he had the chance. By the time the war was over, he was wealthier than most of the rest of us.

Blue was a believer. While he was in the service of his second owner, another cook had seen to that, and he was baptized when he was eighteen. His mother had previously taught him to read and count his numbers. He acquired a Bible after his baptism and read it daily. He still had that same Bible in Virginia, but by then, it was well worn and barely holding together. He carried it wrapped in soft leather in the haversack he kept his spices in and called it his "spice of life." When the aromas of various spices filled the air, you knew Blue was either cooking or reading his Bible.

As a black man, he was usually looked upon as my servant, even though I made every effort to explain that he was a freedman and should be treated as such. That didn't stop some from attempting to verbally abuse him and treat him poorly. While Sean and Jean were not slave owners, both came from a culture that treated the Negro as beneath them. I made it clear to my messmates that Blue could leave anytime he wanted and was to be treated with respect. He was not my servant, and he certainly wasn't theirs. If that was not acceptable with them, they could leave, or we would. That set the tone for our mutual relationship, and Blue was eventually accepted as an equal, at least in our mess. I think his easy-going manner and cooking skills helped grease that skid.

Blue became my conscience. Whenever I slipped into one of my melancholy moods, he was always the first to notice and take steps to bring me out of it. If I started drinking, and he could not distract me in some way, he would make subtle comments about my abuse of alcohol. This was often annoying at the time, but he was right. He did his best to keep me out of trouble. Sometimes he was successful and sometimes not. He was genuinely concerned about my welfare, and it showed in his caring for me. Blue became my true friend and companion, someone I could always count on to be there in times of difficulty.

Chapter 4 – The Truth Comes Out

My work for the day done, and the camp settled down around campfires, I found my trusty bottle of brandy and pulled a hardtack crate up to the fire. Sean, Jean, Blue and several others were enjoying the cool of a summer eve with a pipe and a drink or two. Something about a campfire that gets you to thinking, and I was doing a lot of that as I took a long pull on the bottle, feeling one of my melancholy moods coming on.

I did not join in the conversations. Instead, I sat quietly and drank myself into a stupor, which relieved the pain, at least for a while. It was late and some of the men made their way to their beds, leaving my three messmates and me sitting around the fire. They knew what I was doing, having seen me do it before back at Camp Moore and since arriving in Virginia. They were afraid to even say anything to me because of my hostile responses on previous such occasions.

All except Blue. He pulled his crate closer and asked if something was wrong. I did not, at first, answer because the weight on my shoulders had become unbearable. I was thinking it was time to unload some of it.

My friends were quiet, respecting my misery, when I finally said something. "You want to know what happened to me?"

I got no answer, and they looked about at each other, unsure how to respond. Blue spoke first. "Maybe you ought to give your friends some of your load, Lieutenant Ethan."

I took one more pull on the bottle. Empty, I tossed it aside, picked up a stick and commenced to scratch in the dust with it. I was drunk, but I needed to be drunk to tell this story.

"Yes, I was in love with Rachel, and she was in love with me. It happened that first summer we met five years ago when Morgan—my father—brought her into our family as his ward after her mother died. We planned to marry after I finished my schooling at VMI. My mother was in favor of the union, but Morgan was not. In fact, he spent the next five years trying to keep us apart, first by intercepting our letters in an attempt to make each of us think the other no longer cared and what we had was merely a summer infatuation. Then he moved Rachel to a school in Boston, but we reconnected and picked up the pieces of our love and moved on. He found out and moved her to another school in England. This time, he arranged it so we could not correspond with each other. But Rachel is smart; she figured out a way around that through my VMI roommate's father's business in Baltimore."

I looked around at their faces in the flickering campfire light. I had their attention, so I continued. "Then Morgan took it one step further and arranged to have me posted with the 1st Regiment of Mounted Riflemen in New Mexico Territory when I graduated, thinking, with Rachel in England and me out west, we were about as far apart as he could get us. But he didn't know we had been communicating or that I had sent her money to come home. I told her if Louisiana seceded from the union, she was to immediately book passage, because I would be resigning my commission and returning to Catahoula. Louisiana did, and Rachel left England, and I left the Army. "

"Why was he so bent on keeping you two apart?" asked Jean.

I looked up from my dirt scribbles. "Said he had plans for me that did not include her. Said she would only hold me back from reaching my full potential. He figured I could marry the daughter of some general or some senator to enhance my career. He thought I had a future in politics. He had plans for all his kids. I think he was trying to live vicariously through his children after his eventual death. He had this grand notion of building an empire in Louisiana by marrying off his children to the right people, someone wealthy or politically powerful. He had plans for Sarah and Peyton, my stepsister and stepbrother, and even Brandy, a slave who was mostly white and his daughter by our mammy at Catahoula. He even had plans for Rachel, too. Said he had promised her mother on her deathbed he would help her find a suitable husband."

I went back to scribbling in the dirt. "But all his plans fell apart. Brandy ran away and went north. We haven't heard from her since, and that was a year ago. Peyton had a fight with him and joined the Army to get away from him; he hated him that much. Sarah, well Sarah went crazy because of him and hung herself. I guess that was the only way she knew how to escape from him. That leaves Rachel and me. The war was only days from starting when we arrived back at Catahoula. Morgan wasn't there and didn't know we were home, much less together against his will."

I paused in my narrative to consider how I might tell the rest. There was no good way to explain it, so I simply continued, "That night—that night, I made Rachel my wife with the expectation we would be married the next day and be together forever, but that was the last day of our forever. The next day—well, it was a day that changed everything for us.

"I remember it as if it all took place only this very morning. As I made my way to the Big House for breakfast, the sky was dark with rain-laden clouds, and the first of the raindrops fell to the dust as thunder rolled ominously across the river. But rain or not, I was getting married. Despite the threatening weather, breakfast that morning was a joyous one. Rachel sat beside me, her cheeks glowing rosy red, and my grinning mother sat across from us. Three sharp blasts of a streamer's whistle signaled Morgan's unexpected early return, and just as the rain began falling in earnest. He was already gloomy over the fact we were about to go to war, and the rain further dampening his mood. Seeing Rachel and me waiting arm-in-arm at the front door only made it worse. My mother took his wet coat and threw a woolen shawl over his shoulders, and he growled, 'When did you two get home?' My mother offered him breakfast, hoping a hot meal might tame his mood. He announced he and I needed to talk—in his study.

"Rachel followed us, but I left her outside with assurances we would go find a magistrate and get married as soon as this conversation with Morgan was finished. She took a seat on the bench in the dogtrot hallway outside the door. I entered and closed the door behind me. He poured himself a brandy and waved the bottle at me by way of offering me a drink, which I declined. I had decided it best to be forthright with him and announced that Rachel and I were getting married. He bolted down the brandy then stood up straight as a ramrod and said in his deep booming voice, 'I'm afraid you can't do that!' I, of course, asked why, and he muttered something about her age, which was absurd, seeing as she was nineteen.

"I assured him we were indeed getting married, and he could not stop us. His reply was simply, 'I can and I will, but I beg of you not to make me do it! You will not; you *cannot* marry Rachel.' By then, my patience was exhausted, and I was having a difficult time controlling my anger. That's when I told him our marriage was already a reality, and we had consummated it the night before.

"He sprang to his feet and screamed at me, 'You did what?' To which I replied, 'You heard me!' He sat down heavily into his chair. His elbows on his desk, he rested his head in his hands as if weary and remained that way for a long moment. Finally, he opened the drawer of his desk and took out his strongbox and retrieved from it the letter from Rachel's mother he had received five years earlier. Without looking up, he casually tossed it across the desk at me. 'You might want to read this,' he said in a labored voice. Rachel's mother was dying and had written to ask him to take Rachel and raise her as his own. The letter explained why Morgan was asked to take that responsibility—because she *was* his daughter. That letter was how he found out he had left a child in Virginia fourteen years before."

I stopped to observe the reactions of my friends. Jean shook his head slowly while looking down. Sean said nothing, and Blue was frowning. I continued.

"My knees very nearly buckled under me, and that's when I called him a few choice names. Then I asked why he had not told us sooner? He said something about his honor and my mother. You see, he was worried she might leave him. He had this need—a need to possess and control everything in his life. Her leaving would have proven his control was all just self-deception, and he could not admit that to himself. It would have been embarrassing to him that someone close to him could reject him—like the voters had when he lost his bid for reelection to the House.

"What came to my mind next was what this news would do to Rachel? He had this crazy idea we could keep it from her, knowing if she found out she would hate him for the lie and what it had done to us. That was something else he could not tolerate. He had already lost two daughters and a son. He loved Rachel and needed her to love him back. He could not tolerate her rejecting him, too. And he knew she would once she discovered the truth—another hit to his pride and his honor—and the grand plans he had for all his children. It didn't really matter, because she already hated him.

"I was yelling then but stopped when I remembered Rachel was just outside the door and had likely heard every word that had passed between us! I turned and ran to the door and threw it open, but she was gone. Mammy was there in the hall and told me Rachel had been listening at the door. Then she started weeping and ran upstairs! I took the stairs three at a time and met my mother at the top, and she told me Rachel had come up sobbing and locked herself in her room. I ignored her and marched down the hall to Rachel's room and found the door bolted. I knocked. Called to her. I listened, and all I heard was her sobbing on the other side of that door.

"Meanwhile, my mother knew something terrible had happened and wanted to know what it was. I ignored her and asked her to get Rachel to open the door. That didn't work, either. Having my mother crying in my ear wasn't helping me get Rachel to calm down, so I ordered her into her room and grabbed her by her arm and fairly dragged her down the hall. She wanting to know what had upset Rachel so, but it was not my place to tell her what Morgan had done. I sat on the bed beside her and put my arm around her and asked her to calm down and help me get this straightened out. I thought about what I had just said and realized there was no acceptable solution to this problem. Morgan had just told me Rachel was my sister. How do you change that?

"A steamer sounded its whistle three times out on the river, momentarily distracting me, but my mother's weeping demanded my attention. I tried to tell her this hurt could not be undone. It had destroyed two lives already, and it just might destroy two more before it had run its course. Then I went to go see to Rachel again, hoping she would let me into her room. I knocked softly at her door and called to her. This time I heard no weeping and took that as a good sign. On the chance she had unlocked it, I turned the handle, and the door opened. Her armoire was thrown open, and her clothes were strewn about the room. Cochon, her dog, was there and whimpering for her, but Rachel wasn't anywhere about. The dog broke for the door and down the stairs.

"Then I heard a whistle blow twice out on the river and recalled the three I had heard before. What that meant suddenly hit me: He was picking up a passenger. I spun and ran past my mother and down the stairs to the front door and found it ajar! I ran outside and, through the driving rain, could see the riverboat as it backed away and out into the current. I ran down the steps and out to the river. Cochon was already halfway there. By the time I got there, the riverboat was already headed downstream and nearly obscured from my sight by the rain. I stood helpless and watched as my precious Rachel disappeared from my view and from my life. In agony I sank to my knees and pounded my fist in the mud and bellowed her name like some wounded animal. After a moment, I looked up to the heavens and, in my anger, cursed God for allowing this to happen to us. He must have heard me, because lightning struck a tall cypress directly across the Red River. The bright flash was followed by a deafening clap of thunder, and like the sound of a hundred cannons, it echoed up and down the river.

"I went back to the house and was thinking how much I wanted to kill Morgan Davis, when a gunshot rang out from the direction of his study. I ran down the hall to find Morgan sprawled out in his chair with a bullet hole in his forehead. Mammy stood over him with his Pocket Colt in her hand and a horrified expression on her face.

"She looked at me and said, 'He needed killin'. He hurt too many people. He raped me! He killed Cornelius, the man I loved, because he was jealous of him. He drove off my daughter when he told her she was to be sold to some old Creole up around Cane River, and I'll never see her again. And he's the one who caused Miss Sarah to kill herself. Then he drove off Massa Peyton, and he did something terrible that broke yours and Miss Rachel's hearts. I couldn't let him hurt anyone again. His desk drawer with his pistol was open. I had enough. I took it out of the drawer when he wasn't looking. I cocked it.'

"Behind me, I heard my mother coming down the hall and enter the study. She gasped when she saw her husband.

"Mammy continued in a slow even tone devoid of emotion, 'When he heard me cock it, he turned to face me, and he was looking down the barrel of this pistol. And I pulled the trigger. Yes, sir, I pulled the trigger.' She looked at Analee and said, 'And I'm not sorry I did it, 'cause he needed killing.'

"I asked her to put down the pistol. She replied, 'They're gonna hang me, aren't they, Baby?' She was right; they would surely hang her for killing a white man. I took a step closer with my hand out and asked for the pistol again. She smiled at me as she put it to her temple and pulled the trigger! My mother screamed and fainted dead away…"

From Rachel's Diary
15 June 1861
Gettysburg, Pennsylvania

This is the first time in two months I have found the courage to make an entry in my diary. Even with the passage of those two months, I find writing about what happened so painful I cannot put pen to paper without my tears staining the pages. But someday, the truth must be known. The child that grows in my belly must eventually learn about his father. If I should die before I can tell him, he will have this journal to explain it all. These words are put down as much for his edification as for my own soul cleansing.

The events leading up to that night in April of this year are well documented in these pages. All my feelings are laid out here for my progeny to read about and, hopefully, appreciate the great love I have experienced. But now, I must tell the rest of the story, painful as it may be.

As the words here testify, I loved Ethan Edward Davis with all my heart and soul—and may God forgive me, I still do. Nothing will ever change that fact. And he loved me with equal passion, and I do not believe anything will ever change how he feels about me. That is why I did what I did when I learned Ethan and I shared the same father. I knew, feeling as we do about each other, we could never live in the same house. I knew I would not be able to look upon his face ever again without all the feelings I have for him coming forth uncontrollably. I could never look upon him as my brother, not after what we were to each other. Nor do I believe he can ever look at me and think of me only as his sister. Such is simply not possible for either of us. Therefore, I left Catahoula without even saying goodbye, for to do so would have made parting impossibly difficult for both of us.

Perhaps, some day after our child is grown, I will be strong enough to face him again. I know it is wrong to keep secret the fact that I will bear his child, but by doing so, I can spare him the burden of knowing the results of our impetuous act. I know he and his child must someday meet; it is only right for the both of them. But for now, I must shield all of us from the pain that will be associated with that meeting. This will be my burden alone to carry.

As I sat outside my father's study that fateful day, I could quite clearly hear Morgan and Ethan arguing over our pending marriage. When Ethan announced that our marriage was already consummated, and out of that came the revelation that Morgan Davis was my father, it shocked me to the depths of my soul, and I very nearly fainted. In that instant, I knew what I had to do, and the rain covered my escape from Catahoula.

I knew Ethan would come after me, and I could not rest even for a moment. After I withdrew my funds from my account in New Orleans, using a forged letter from my father, I took the first ship I could find leaving for the North.

I arrived in New York and made my way to Gettysburg and the home of my roommate from school in England, Miriam Hupmann. Her father was kind enough to take me in as a border, for which I am very thankful. There was no one else to turn to. My biggest fear now is that Ethan will figure out where I am and come for me. I cannot recall that I ever told him where Miriam was from. I believe I am safe.

Now, I have only to wait for the arrival of our child in January. I feel so terribly alone, and the guilt of what we did weighs heavily on my soul.

After a few moments to calm my spirit, I continued my story. "I spent the night tending to the business of getting my father's affairs in order. With my stepbrother gone, that regrettable duty fell to me. All the while, that comforting bottle of brandy was near at hand, and I considered getting rip-roaring drunk. In Morgan's big desk, I found bundles of letters between Rachel and me, letters he had intercepted and we had never received. At the back of the drawer was his strongbox, and in it was the heart locket I had given Rachel the Christmas we spent together in Boston. Morgan had stolen it because it contained a picture of us together. I burned the letter from Rachel's mother, lest mine find it. I reviewed the plantation's books and balanced the accounts. I was leaving, and my intention was to leave Catahoula in a condition such that my mother could run it with the help of a few loyal slaves. Early the next morning, I sent for our family lawyer and told him all that had happened, what I intended to do, and made arrangements for my wishes to be carried out even in my absence. He reluctantly agreed and drew up the necessary papers to be signed.

"I called my mother, Big Jake, and Old Zeke, two of our most trusted Negros, to my cabin. I sat them all down and tried to explain what I wanted done to save Catahoula in my absence. I handed my mother a stack of papers to sign—emancipation papers for all the slaves. I also figured to offer land I inherited to any slave that stayed to help my mother keep the place running, but they had to stay through the war I knew was coming. Some would leave once they had their freedom papers, but they would have been a burden to her anyway. I expected our ports to be blockaded, and they would not be able to get the cotton to market, so I instructed them to grow food crops and no cotton. And all transactions should be done in cash— no credit. Then I asked to speak to my mother alone.

"She asked again what had caused Rachel to run away? I think she already knew but was unwilling to accept it until I commented that the problem was created twenty years ago. She calculated that would have been about the time Rachel was conceived and realized— more accurately accepted the truth—that her husband was Rachel's father. Frankly, I was relieved it was finally out, but sorry my mother had to find out just then.

"My mother went to weeping so hard her body was shaking like she had the fever. I sought to console her, but she jumped to her feet and pointed to the door and yelled for me to go find Rachel and marry her immediately. At first I thought she might not have understood what I had said about Morgan being Rachel's father, then she said something that shocked me, 'Rachel is not your sister, Ethan! There's no common blood between you! Not one drop!'

"I did not, at first, understand, but she explained that she was in love with another man before her arranged marriage to Morgan. When her father died, Morgan was in Washington, and she returned alone to New Orleans to handle the funeral arrangements, and well— Morgan was not my father. She told me I looked so much like my father that all these years, every time she looked at me, she saw *him* and was reminded that she had done to Morgan exactly what he had done to her that she so hated him for."

"Pernell Joubert," said Jean softly.

"Correct. I had been mistaken for him more than once. I looked at my mother and saw in her the tremendous burden she then carried. Though her confession had made it possible for Rachel and me to marry, it carried the full responsibility for what had happened away from her dead husband and placed it squarely on her own shoulders. I knew she felt that burden weighing heavily upon her, and I pitied her, but there was nothing I could do to lift that weight from her; we both knew that. I knew it hurt her that her failure was now known by me, the one person she most wanted respect from. I also knew she felt responsibility for Rachel and me being separated now because of her previous silence. I tried to explain how her confession had given me hope where none existed before, and I was grateful for that.

"I left Catahoula that day and went straight to New Orleans as fast as Pepper could carry me. I arrived only hours behind Rachel to discover she had already drained her bank account, using a forged letter from Morgan, and was on a ship headed for New York. That's when I went and got blind, stinking drunk and ended up killing a man in a duel. And no, I don't know where she went or how to find her. Now, I'm stuck in the Confederate Army and can't even start looking until this war is over. I sure hope all of you are right, and it is a short one. The longer it lasts the colder her trail becomes."

There was silence around the campfire after I finished. Blue took out his handkerchief and wiped his eyes. I tossed my stick into the fire, and the dying flames sent up a shower of sparks as I staggered off to my bed and my nightmares.

Chapter 5 – First Blood

---

1 July 1861

Herr Hupmann is a tyrant! I see why poor Miriam was sent away to school in England. He trusts no women, not even his daughter and certainly not me. I am sure the only reason he is allowing me to stay in their spare bedroom is because of the room and board I pay. Though wealthy, he did send his daughter to an expensive school in England, he is tight-fisted. Miriam must account for very penny of the household budget.

With both her brothers in the army, she must run the household. She is allowed no freedom and no male visitors. She is twenty years old! She should be considering marriage by now!

Herr Hupmann keeps asking me questions about my past and why I find myself here in Gettysburg and not back in Louisiana with my other secesh friends. He seems to imply I may be of low moral character. I am nearly three months pregnant and will soon be showing. I fear what he will say and do when it becomes obvious I am pregnant and have no husband!

The Tiger Rifles were the first to draw blood when they skirmished with the Yankees at Seneca Dam on the Potomac. It was not much of a fight, but it built morale. White claimed he killed at least three Federals and suffered only one wounded Tiger. I was in the rear with Wheat when the fight took place, and by the time we arrived, it was all over. The rest of the battalion was jealous of the Tiger Rifles after that, but their time was coming with a fight the Yankees would eventually call "First Bull Run" and we would call "First Manassas."

General P. G. T. Beauregard had taken command of the Confederate forces in northern Virginia. I had been told earlier my father was serving with him, so I sought him out only to discover Pernell was recovering from malaria back in Charleston. I did find Peyton and told him what had happened. He already knew his father was dead, as my mother had written and told him some of the details. He was most unhappy that I had freed the slaves, but came to agree it was the only way to handle the problem with Morgan dead and the two of us gone. He told me of the fight he had with Morgan before he left. He'd had enough of Morgan's meddling in his life. There was a lady in Alexandria he was sweet on, but Morgan strongly disapproved, because her family had no wealth or power. I suggested he follow his heart in this matter.

On the 12th of July, Beauregard pulled all his advanced units around Manassas back behind a sluggish little creek called Bull Run. Wheat's Battalion took up positions on Beauregard's extreme left near Stone Bridge. Sensing weakness, General Irvin McDowell advanced in the wake of Beauregard's withdrawal. McDowell was under orders to engage the enemy, whereas Beauregard was ordered to avoid any offensive action, but I suspect Beauregard pulled back to draw McDowell out, not realizing that McDowell was coming out for a fight, anyway.

Beauregard arrayed his units along Bull Run, expecting McDowell to naturally be drawn to the most obvious crossings at Mitchell's Ford guarded by Bonham's Brigade, or Blackburn's Ford where Longstreet's Brigade stood ready, or McLean's Ford guarded by Jones' Brigade. Early's Brigade stood to the rear as reserves to be thrown into any weaknesses in the line. Another mile and a half downstream was Ewell's Brigade guarding Union Mills Ford, thus no less then five of the army's seven brigades were holding the right half of the line. On the left, Beauregard planned only a defense should McDowell attempt to turn his left flank. If McDowell did come out for a fight, Beauregard intended to move his army across the fords on his right (McDowell's left) and outflank him, cutting him off from Washington.

Only two pieces of artillery along with the 4th South Carolina and Wheat's Tigers, all under the command of Colonel Nathan G. Evans, were defending Stone Bridge on the Confederate left. Evans had at his disposal only about 1,100 men including the Tigers.

Early in the morning of 18 July, Brigadier General Daniel Tyler demonstrated against Longstreet at Blackburn's Ford. A right spirited fight ensued, which we could hear from our positions to the northwest. The Tigers complained of being stuck off on the extreme Confederate left and far away from the fight. Tyler got in over his head and was forced to withdraw with some of his units routed by a vigorous Confederate stand.

The humiliated Yankees retired to Centreville to formulate a new plan of attack. McDowell decided the Confederate center and right flank were too strong and the ground too heavily wooded, so he intended to maneuver around our left flank. He planned a masking maneuver against Stone Bridge, but his main attack would come at Sudley Ford.

On Saturday, 20 July, the men of General Johnston's brigades from the Shenandoah began arriving at Manassas Junction, including the Virginia Brigade led by an old acquaintance of mine from VMI, General Thomas J. Jackson. Though Johnston was senior, he deferred command to Beauregard, who was far more familiar with the situation. Johnston agreed with Beauregard's plan to flank the Federals on the lower Bull Run, so Beauregard deployed the new arrivals accordingly, thus none of these new reinforcements were sent to the Confederate left. Sudley's Ford remained vulnerable.

In the early morning hours of Sunday, 21 July, McDowell moved his units into position for the attack. We got a wakeup call at 6 a.m., when Federal artillery at Stone Bridge fired three shots to signal they were in position. That got our attention right smartly, and we were roused to the long roll of the drums. The officers and sergeants ran among the men, yelling. "Get up! Fall in! The Yankees are a'comin'! Fall in on me!" That is all it took to get the men moving. The fight we had been waiting for was upon us, and that realization quickened our movements.

We formed up without further encouragement. Wheat trooped the line, and I followed. "Look at my boys, Lieutenant Joubert. Aren't they fine looking? We're going to whip the Federals all the way back to Washington this day, I promise you that." The men heard that and let out with a whoop and a cry enough to send shivers up and down your spine.

"They do look ready for a fight, sir, and I think this is a good day for one," I replied, caught up in their exuberance.

"Very well, Lieutenant, inform Colonel Evans the Tigers are formed and ready."

I saluted. "My pleasure, sir!" I hurried off to present the major's compliments to Evans. The colonel had us take up positions on a hill overlooking the bridge where we formed up in line-of-battle and waited McDowell's pleasure. I sent Blue to the rear with Pepper. He was reluctant to leave me but eventually did as he was told.

With Tyler on our front, Evans kept his small command hidden in the trees behind the rise south of the bridge. He had only a small squadron of cavalry, two field pieces, his 4th South Carolina Regiment and Wheat's Tigers standing against a numerically superior force of Federals, and unknown to us, a large helping of McDowell's army moving around our left flank toward Sudley Ford, not much more than a mile away. McDowell was attacking the weakest point in our line with little more than a re-enforced regiment to stand against his eight brigades.

Evans called for reinforcements then sent two companies of the 4th South Carolina out as skirmishers and wisely refused to show his main force. The South Carolinians traded fire with the Federals for about an hour, but the rest of us remained hidden in the woods.

Wheat paced the line. "Where are they, Joubert? Why aren't they crossing the ford?"

"Is this a feint, sir?" I asked him. He ignored my question.

"What do you think, Ethan?" whispered Jean Dubassey from behind me.

I turned to my friend.

"We going to get into this fight?"

I shrugged. "Before this day is done, we're likely to have more than our share of fighting."

"But what if they go back to Washington before we get into it?" asked Captain White.

"I think they've come out for a fight and aim to give us one. They aren't going back to Washington until we send them there."

As if I were some sort of soothsayer, that seemed to allay their concerns. I was no expert in the art of war, but logic told me the Federals wouldn't give up that easily. Our withdrawal gave the impression of weakness, inviting McDowell to exploit it.

It soon became obvious to Evans that the Federals had no intention of crossing Stone Bridge. Word came from our pickets at

Sudley Ford that Yankees had been sighted marching in the direction of the ford. We were also warned by observers in a tall tower of the threat to our left flank.

When Evans was informed that the Federals were on our left, threatening to flank our positions, and we were facing overwhelming odds, he ordered the Tigers to move about a half mile to our left on the double quick to defend the flank. We arrived at our new position huffing and puffing, as much from the excitement as from the run, and were soon joined by six companies of the 4th South Carolina and both artillery pieces. The other four companies remained at Stone Bridge. The South Carolina boys anchored our left near Sudley Road, and the Tigers held the right near Bull Run. The two cannons were placed on each end of the line. By 9 a.m. we were in position hidden in the woods overlooking the open fields around Sudley Ford.

The men were in high spirits, and we anticipated Yankees to come pouring from the woods to our front any moment. "Come on, Blue Belly," yelled one of the Tigers. "We a'waiting fer ya right here. Come and get some a' what I got fer ya'!" Laughter rippled up and down the line.

"Hold your tongue!" ordered Wheat. "No sense tellin' them where we are! Let 'em find out the hard way."

The men quieted down a mite then, but it was hard for them to remain so. We waited in the woods, thankful to be shaded from the hot July sun, but McDowell failed to show. Soon the men were disenchanted with the whole affair. "They done turned tail and run when they heard they was facin' the Tigers." yelled a man in the second rank pointing to the huge dust cloud thrown up by the advancing Federals on the far side of the creek.

"Settle down!" ordered one of the company officers. "Check your primers." He did that to get them to thinking about what was at hand rather than cracking jokes and alerting the enemy to our position.

"Where do you think they are?" Wheat asked me. "We're all turned out for a fight, pretty as can be, and they turn tail on us?"

"They're out there, sir. I reckon they're getting into position right now," I replied as I watched the wood line along the ford for movement.

While Colonel Ambrose Burnside moved his Rhode Island Brigade into position across the way, Wheat moved us to our left closer to a grove of trees near the center of our line. That is when disaster struck. Some South Carolina troops hidden in the trees mistook us for Federals and opened fire, and some of our men returned fire. We had a right dandy scrap going on between two Confederate units, before the officers could sort it all out. The Tigers suffered three killed and several wounded before we were able to get the shooting stopped. We had spent the last three hours anticipating a fight and ended up killing each other instead. I hoped this day would turn out better than it had started.

There is an old saw that says to be careful what you wish for, you just might get it. At about 9:45, the Rhode Islanders under Colonel Burnside encountered the boys from Catahoula Parish who were deployed as our skirmishers. The Catahoula Guerrillas opened fire, and individual shots merged into long rolling volleys. The Catahoula boys took what cover they could behind trees. The rest of us soon joined in, and we got off five or six volleys before the South Carolina regiment advanced and joined the fight. The action got right quick and furious then. The Tigers were a whooping and yelling as they fired and loaded and fired again at the Rhode Islanders pouring from the woods. But we stopped them in their tracks and pinned them down on the slope. Burnside brought up the rest of his brigade, and we mauled them too, shooting Burnside's horse right out from under him. Burnside must have thought he was facing at least six regiments of infantry and two batteries of artillery. Not bad for one little old regiment plus one battalion and two piddling cannons. Colonel Matthew Porter brought his regiments up on Burnside's right. We then faced more than a brigade of Yankees.

"Keep at 'em, boys!" yelled Wheat. "Cut 'em down!"

I had little to do in this fight as I was without any command. I stuck close to Wheat to act as his bodyguard and his runner if necessary. I had my pistol drawn, but the Federals were not yet in range for me, so I held my fire rather than waste shots.

Wheat pranced up and down the line, and like a puppy, I followed, feeling about as useless as a teat on Old Bull. "Give 'em hell, boys!" he yelled. "Prepare to charge. We'll give them the bayonet!"

I did not, however, think that prudent. The Federals were holding and showing no sign of weakness, but that did not stop Wheat. "Charge!" he yelled as he held his sword above his head. And with a chorus of Rebel yells, we hurled ourselves at them. Even I joined in, screaming at the top of my voice.

Porter and Burnside were adjusting their lines and must have been surprised to see a Rebel swarm coming down the hill at them. The Tigers plunged headlong into the Federals and threw them into confusion, but the cost was high. The Rhode Islanders and the Tigers fought, our lines mixed and surging back and forth. Three times we charged, and each time they fell back, but our own lines were taking a beating. The Federals brought in reinforcements and recovered the initiative. Then we had to hold against the charge, standing against twenty times our number for more than an hour until we were forced to fall back.

We withdrew, drifting to our left in a fairly orderly retreat. Wheat attempted to rally his boys to make a stand around some haystacks. He was dismounted and waving that sword of his, calling for his men to rally around him. We responded to his call and formed ragged lines before returning fire into the advancing Yankees.

Wheat was to my left and still waving his saber when he was hit. The sickening thud of a lead hitting flesh attracted my attention, and I saw Wheat go down. The ball entered his chest under his up-stretched arm and passed through his lung and on out his back.

Buhoup rushed to his side and called for some of his men to carry him from the field. I stood dumbfounded, not believing any mere ball could harm this indomitable giant of a man. Some Tigers rolled him into a blanket and began to carry him from the field only to have two of their numbers shot down. Wheat tumbled to the ground and gasped, "Lay me down, boys, you must save yourselves." They, of course, ignored him and took up their burden once more. Someone placed the Old Dominion Guards' flag over Wheat as they rushed him to safety.

We continued to withdraw, our eleven companies facing thirteen thousand Yankees and effectively slowing their advance. But the wounding of Wheat seriously threatened our good order, and the battalion quickly disintegrated as we continued to withdraw under heavy fire. With the air alive with the angry buzz and whine of balls, the Federals saw our confusion and pressed the attack.

One of our fallen comrades lay on the ground with a shattered leg. His face was so blackened with gunpowder I didn't recognize him. "Tigers, go in once more!" he cried. "Go in my sons, they can never whip the Tigers!" Some of us rallied and turned on the advancing Federals, holding them until two brigades under General Bernard Bee and Colonel F. S. Bartow arrived and joined the fight.

The tide began to turn as we plunged back into the advancing Yankees, and for the next hour, the battle went back and forth. Some of the Tiger Rifles and Catahoula Guerrillas threw down their slow-firing Mississippi Rifles and charged into the Yankee host with drawn knives, cursing, yelling, cutting and screaming! It was here that the Tigers earned their justly deserved reputation as fierce fighters, but we were still outnumbered and merely buying time until more reinforcements could be brought up.

The Yankees moved still more units into the fight, extending their lines to our left in an attempt to turn our flank. Sherman's Brigade crossed Bull Run near Stone Bridge and fell upon the four companies of South Carolinians left to guard it. Keyes's brigade soon joined them. Both flanks were being turned, and we were in danger of being double enveloped. Our retreat turned into a rout, and we fell back in great haste to get away from the charging Federals. Units fell apart and intermingled in the wild withdrawal to Henry House Hill. There, we attempted to make a stand with perhaps 5,500 men facing nearly 20,000 Federals. We charged once more and threw them into confusion but only for a short while.

I was reloading my Colt, when I heard a familiar voice beside me and found myself standing next to my friend Jean Dubassey as he loaded and fired his musket at the advancing hoard. "Have enough Yankees to go around?"

"There's a mite more of them than we asked for," I commented as Jean rammed a ball home.

"Oui, my friend. The Lord has been overly generous this day!" he replied as he threw his musket to his shoulder and shot a charging Blue Coat in the chest. Jean dropped the butt of his musket to the ground as he reached in his cartridge box and pulled out another round. Two more Yankees were closing on our position as he tore off the end of the paper cartridge with his teeth in preparation for loading. I threw up my freshly loaded Colt and shot them both dead, one right through the head though I was aiming a bit lower.

"Nice shooting, Ethan," said Jean dryly as he threw his musket to his shoulder and fired into the Yankee ranks.

Burnside had two divisions across Bull Run and another in the process of crossing. We were soon thrown off Henry House Hill in great disarray, withdrawing to the northeast and Young's Branch. McDowell's target was the Manassas Gap railroad where he could cut us off from reinforcements from the Shenandoah Valley. He must have been certain that victory was within his grasp, and I would have been hard pressed to argue the point.

The brigades of Barnard Bee, Francis Bartow and Thomas Jackson arrived at the front and joined the fight. Jackson and his Virginians moved to the left near Henry House Hill and took up positions. The fire from the Federals was terrific as we fell back unable to hold. Colonel William Pendleton had four batteries of artillery on the hill and was pouring canister shot into the Federals. An Episcopal Minister, Pendleton shouted the order, "Fire, boys! And may God have mercy on their guilty souls!"

The 4th Alabama under Bee was taking a beating and being pushed back. Bee rode up to Jackson and announced, "General, they are beating us back!"

Jackson's reply was terse, "Sir, we will give them the bayonet."

Bee returned to his brigade and pointing to Jackson and the Virginians and said, "Look at Jackson and his Virginians standing there like a stone wall." There is some question to this day as to exactly what Bee meant by that, but General Bee had just given Jackson his famous nickname. After that Old Tom became known as "Stonewall Jackson," and the Virginians of Jackson's Brigade became known as the "Stonewall Brigade." Bee led the 4th Alabama forward and over the crest of Henry House Hill.

Beauregard had been indecisive all morning, continuing to expect the real blow to come at Mitchell's Ford. Johnston took the initiative and announced that the battle was on our left flank and ordered the brigades of Holmes, Early and Bonham to move to the left.

All morning Early's Division had been marching from ford to ford to respond to Federal threats when he was ordered to move to his left toward the fighting. Under his command were the 7th Virginia, 13th Mississippi, and the 7th Louisiana under Colonel Hays. They arrived much blown and were told to find and attack the Federal right flank. Early found it positioned along a ridge and pounced on the unsuspecting Federals.

The shattered remnants of Evans's Regiment and Wheat's Battalion regrouped and moved back up to the fight, taking up positions along side Bee's Alabamians. With fresh units added, our lines began to stabilize along Henry House Hill.

McDowell, still thinking he had the better of us, prepared to finish the job by pounding us with close range artillery. The batteries of Ricketts and Griffin were brought to the hill and left unsupported by infantry, making the gunners and artillery horses tempting targets for our sharpshooters until the 11th New York Zouaves and a battalion of Marines arrived to give the artillerymen support. Jackson's men held their fire until the Yankees were on the hill, and the Rebel line stood and delivered a crushing volley. The New Yorkers and Marines dropped to the ground and attempted to return fire. Many broke and ran.

Colonel Cummings and the 33rd Virginia charged the hill. The Confederates were dressed in blue uniforms, and the Federals hesitated, thinking they were their own infantry support. Too late the mistake was realized, and the Virginians were upon them, killing Ricketts and many of the horses, stampeding the rest. That was the end of them; their guns were ours!

Jackson immediately charged, and Beauregard committed units to the right as well. Confusion reigned for the next two hours, and the Federal guns on the hill exchanged hands several times. Fresh Confederate brigades joined the fight, and McDowell was finished. By 4:30 he accepted the fact that he had been handily defeated and ordered a withdrawal, but it was too late for that. Federal units were already falling back in a stampeding rout, the men throwing aside their weapons and equipment as they ran back to Washington. Beauregard sent some units in pursuit, but our troops, battle weary and hungry, were in no condition to continue the fight. Beauregard called off the pursuit around 7 p.m.

A drenching rain began to fall during the night and continued to the next morning. Blue found us cold and hungry huddled under gum blankets in the rain. Many of the boys had gunpowder blackened faces as dark as his. "Lordy, Lieutenant Ethan, but that was a fight! I ain't seen nothing to match that in all my days. Those boys in blue was about to send y'all back to Richmond."

"Never happen in a thousand years," said an exhausted Tiger.

Blue nodded. "Well, I brung you some food," he said as he fished in his bulging haversacks and bags tied to his mule and came up with biscuits and ham.

"Where did you get this?" I asked about to cram a biscuit into my mouth.

"Never mind, just eat it," he replied as he handed out the food to the others.

Major Wheat lay wounded in a hospital near the battlefield. I found him later that evening. As I approached, I heard the surgeon say, "Major, I will answer you candidly that you cannot live 'til day."

This was obviously not acceptable to Wheat. "I don't feel like dying yet," he defiantly announced.

Taken aback, the surgeon replied, "But there is no instance on record of recovery from such a wound."

That did not impress the major. "Well, then, I shall put my case on record."

An almost continuous string of dignitaries visited Wheat in the hospital after the battle, and it was predicted that he would surely be promoted to brigadier general and given a brigade to command if he lived. And true to his word, Major Wheat eventually recovered.

Wheat and his Tigers were treated as bona fide heroes after the fight at Manassas. We were justly credited with holding back the Federal onslaught until a defense could be organized. Southern papers carried romanticized accounts of our gallant stand against the numerically superior Yankee forces, especially the incident when some of our number attacked with Bowie knives. In spite of the heavy fighting, we lost only eight men killed, thirty-eight wounded and two missing.

That night, exhausted but exuberant, we huddled around sputtering campfires in the rain and licked our wounds. With the dawn, I counted two bullet holes in my uniform and one nasty bruise on my right thigh where a spent ball had grazed me. Until then I had not even been aware of my "wound," so to speak.

Other Louisiana commands that missed the fight were envious of Hays' Regiment and Wheat's Tigers. Richard Taylor's 9th Louisiana heard of the impending fight while still in Richmond and procured a train to carry them to the front. The locomotive was so worn out they had to get out and push it over some of the grades as they listened to the sound of the distant battle. To their chagrin, they arrived at Manassas after the battle was won.

Most of us in the fight, however, had gotten over the notion that war was romantic. Another notion that died at Manassas was that this war would be over soon. It became obvious that both sides needed time to turn their armies into a real fighting force. The blood spilled at Manassas sealed the fate of a nation and committed both sides to fight until one side was completely vanquished. And that would not happen anytime soon.

I tried to reconcile myself to the fact that I would not be able to continue my search for Rachel in the near future, perhaps not for years, assuming I even survived this disaster, and she did not, during that time, marry another still believing we were brother and sister.

18 July 1861

The papers are full of stories of the great battle near Manassas in Virginia along a creek called Bull Run. They speak of the part played in the battle by a unit from Louisiana called Wheat's Tigers. The papers said they were mostly rowdies and criminals from the New Orleans' jails, but one company in Wheat's Battalion is said to be planter's sons from Catahoula Parish. If Ethan is in the army, he is likely with Wheat. I am trying to get a copy of a southern paper with a list of casualties to see if Ethan is on it. I had hoped not to have this burden added to the one I already carry.

Oh, how I long to see him, to hold him in my arms, to tell him how much I love him, to share with him the blessed news that I am to have his child, but I cannot. I fear I will not be strong enough to carry this alone. If I could but speak to him, hear his voice to know he is alive! I cannot endure this war not knowing of his fate.

22 July 1861

Tragedy struck the Hupmann household today. They received word Miriam's younger brother, Eric, was killed at Bull Run. Herr Hupmann went into a rage when he heard, directing his anger against the South, and by my association with that region, I was also included.

I do not believe he was ever comfortable with me here, and it seems less so now. He barely speaks to me, and when he does, his words are sharp and his tone accusatory, almost as if I had fired the musket whose ball took Eric's life.

Herr Hupmann has gone into deep mourning for his son. Miriam says Eric was always his favorite.

25 July 1861

I have a copy of a Richmond paper with a casualty list from the Battle of Bull Run, which the South is calling the Battle of Manassas. I can find no Ethan Davis listed as killed, wounded, or captured. Thank God!

The paper says Major Wheat was wounded and very nearly killed. The Tigers are being called the heroes of the battle because they stood against many times their numbers and charged into the Federals with only knives.

The Richmond paper makes the battle sound like the Union Army was soundly defeated at Bull Run. The papers here were not so negative, but the truth is coming out. I spoke to a soldier, a private from Pennsylvania come back to Gettysburg to convalesce from his wounds, and he told us it was a terrible defeat for the Union. The poor boy wept as he described how they ran back to Washington. He said Wheat's Tigers were on the Confederate left flank and met the Federal flanking movement head on, inflicting heavy casualties. He says they are devils and described an animal-like scream the Tigers gave out when going into battle that was enough to curdle fresh milk. The lad says all the men are talking about this Rebel Yell, as he calls it, and how frightening it was. I once heard Ethan give out with a screaming yell on a hog hunt when the chase was on and he was excited. I wonder if that was the sound those boys heard.

All the Louisiana units around Manassas were formed into the 8th Brigade under General W. H. T. Walker of Georgia. General Walker was a stern disciplinarian and realized our lack of any real training. He promptly set about to change that and began the process of getting us into shape as a cohesive brigade and bring order where something resembling chaos had existed before.

Once we had recovered from the battle, I visited Beauregard's headquarters to inquire as to the whereabouts of my father. I was informed by one of Beauregard's aides that Captain Pernell Joubert had returned to New Orleans soon after his recovery from malaria to recruit more volunteers for the Louisiana regiments, and it was expected, he would return once that mission was completed. My father did not, however, return to Virginia. Instead, he joined Beauregard in Tennessee when the general was transferred to take command there, and command of the Army of Northern Virginia passed to Joe Johnston.

With Wheat in the hospital, Lieutenant Colonel Charles de Choiseul took temporary command of the Tigers, and he immediately set about taming us. True to form, the Tigers resisted his strict discipline. Several nasty incidents involving some of our more disreputable members led to a confrontation between Tigers and our temporary commander. As usual, liquor played a major part. Though the ranks were forbidden to have whiskey that never seemed to stop them from acquiring whatever they wanted.

It all started when a drunken Tiger twice snapped his musket at de Choiseul's orderly. Both times the weapon misfired, and the orderly subdued the fool. Later that day, several others beat and robbed a washerwoman. The miscreants were thrown into the guardhouse, and de Choiseul retired for the night. He was awakened later that night by a free-for-all at the guardhouse. Seven Tigers were trying to free their friends. De Choiseul had them confined as well.

The next morning, our very frustrated battalion commander caught several men leaving camp without permission. When de Choiseul approached them on horseback and questioned them, he got an impudent answer. Ordered to report to the guardhouse, the Tigers refused. De Choiseul angrily snatched one man up by his collar and threw him to the ground. He still refused to leave, and de Choiseul knocked him down a second time. Several other Tigers surrounded the colonel and were threatening him. He drew his pistol and informed the Tigers surrounding him that he would shoot the first one who raised a finger toward him. One man stepped forward and dared the colonel to do as he said. De Choiseul was not a bluffer; he shot the man in the face. The soldier turned his head at the last moment, and the ball only cut his tongue and not so neatly removed three teeth. That confrontation further sullied the reputation of the Tigers of Wheat's Battalion, but this ugly incident was not yet completely over.

20 June 1861

As I took a leisurely walk today, a neighbor from across the street bid me good afternoon and introduced himself. His name is Doctor Maxwell Johnson, a longtime neighbor of the Hupmanns. I had noticed him before as he seemed always interested in the goings-on at the Hupmann house.

I asked Miriam about this, and she explained, "Doctor Johnson is a very old friend of the family, but we no longer speak.

At least my father doesn't speak to him. My brothers and I do but only without Papa's knowledge, or he would be angry with us."

"What is that all about?" I asked.

"We were friends until my mother died many years ago. Papa blamed Doctor Johnson for her death and has never forgiven him. He has not spoken to him since, unless it is to exchange harsh words. There was nothing more Doctor Johnson could have done for my mother. He lost his own wife a few years later. They had only one daughter, Jenny, born very late in life."

"Where is Jenny now?"

"She died a few years ago just before I went off to school in England. In the absence of his wife, Jenny was the light of his life, and her loss devastated him. She would be about 25 now."

"How dreadful! How old is he?"

"Must be close to seventy?"

"And he lives alone?" I asked as I looked across the street and saw Doctor Johnson tending to some flowers in his yard.

"He has a housekeeper who comes in and cleans and cooks for him, but they barely get along. He is a very bitter man, much like Papa. It is sad because both of them used to be much happier."

That was all I knew about Doctor Johnson when he stopped me and introduced himself that afternoon. He struck me as a kindly man and perhaps not as bitter as Miriam said. He walks with a silver handled cane and a slight limp, but he carries himself proudly, standing upright, unbowed by age. His hair is as white as snow and not a lot was visible when he tipped his hat to me. He has a bushy moustache that is just as white as his hair. His face is heavily furrowed with age lines—or perhaps worry.

I introduced myself, "Good day to you, sir. I'm Rachel Whitcomb."

"Maxwell Johnson, and I know your name. I asked about you in town."

"Indeed?"

"Forgive me for being so forward, but you remind me so much of my daughter, Jenny. I have watched you from afar, and you seem to carry yourself the same way she did. She's deceased now. I again apologize for being so nosy."

"No need to apologize. I understand how the loss of a loved one can play upon one's mind." Then I added, "My mother was named Jenny. I love that name."

He nodded and seemed unable to speak at first but did not comment on my mother's name being Jenny. "I have seen you in the store in town and sometimes on the street taking your leisure, and it occurred to me that you looked sad as if you had experienced some great loss yourself?"

"How very perceptive of you. It is true. I have experienced a loss." I chose not to say more on the subject, even though he was clearly looking for me to do so.

"Perhaps we could have tea someday, Miss Rachel?"

"Yes, I would like that."

Chapter 6 – Rachel's Crisis

With Wheat still in the hospital, I had little to do and requested a furlough. My idleness had allowed me to spend too much time contemplating losing Rachel and my inability to go search for her. I saw the lull as a chance to make some progress in that effort. I recalled that Rachel had mentioned she lived near Culpeper, Virginia before coming to Louisiana and thought I might look into the possibility she had gone back there. Culpeper was but a short day's ride from where we were camped.

I arrived in Culpeper and made inquiries about Rachel with the local Post Master. If she was there, he would likely be aware of her presence.

"No, Lieutenant, I know of no Rachel Whitcomb here 'bouts. There was a Jenny Whitcomb, but she died years ago."

"Anyone still around that may have known Miss Jenny?"

"Yes, I believe so. You might ride out Sperryville Pike a few miles out of town. Look for a two-story farmhouse on a hill with a rail fence around it. The Dalton sisters, both widows, live there. The younger sister, Mildred, has been living there for at least twenty years. She may be able to help you."

I did as directed and soon found the farmhouse as described. I knocked on the door, and an elderly lady answered. "And who might you be, sir?"

"I am Lieutenant Ethan Joubert from Louisiana, currently serving in the Army of Northern Virginia. I wonder if I might have a word with you. I am searching for someone from these parts."

She smiled. "Why yes. We don't get many visitors, especially handsome young men, much less an officer in the army of our glorious Confederate States. Do come in," she bade me enter and called to her sister, "Rebecca, we have a guest!"

She introduced herself and her sister then offered me tea, which I gratefully accepted. "Well, Lieutenant Joubert, who might you be looking for?"

"Miss Mildred, Miss Rebecca, do either of you recall a Jenny Whitcomb or a Rachel Whitcomb?"

"Indeed," replied Mildred, "they lived just up the road from here. But Jenny is dead now."

"And Rachel," I replied, hoping she would tell me something that would be helpful.

"She left and went to Louisiana, as I recall. That was—maybe six years ago."

"Rachel has not come back here, has she?"

"Not that I know of." Mildred turned to her sister. "Becca, you remember them?"

"Indeed, I do."

"What do you recall of them?" I asked, feeling as If I were making some small progress in my search.

"Nothing much. Jenny Whitcomb's husband died and she had that child, Rachel."

"And you're sure Rachel hasn't come back here?"

"Well, she hasn't as far as we know," replied Mildred. "Why are you looking for her?"

Not wanting to go into details, I lied, "She has come into some money, part of an inheritance, and I would like to see that she gets what is rightfully hers." That seemed to satisfy them, and I stood to leave, "Ladies, I'm most grateful for your hospitality and help. It has been a pleasure."

My ride back to camp was a gloomy one, and I became all the more depressed over my circumstances. I had held a small hope my trip to Culpeper would help in some way in my search for Rachel, but that hope was dashed, and I was again plunged into the depths of despair. I bought a bottle of whiskey along the way and proceeded to get drunk, once more finding solace in the bottle.

15 August 1861

My small world once more closed in to compress me. Herr Hupmann confronted me about my pregnancy. My morning sickness must have given me away. He was not in the least pleased to have an unmarried woman with child under his roof, especially one that was also a southerner. He called me some unpleasant names, a bad influence on his daughter, and demanded I leave immediately. I think he has been looking for an excuse to force me from his home, and the pregnancy was the final straw for him. Miriam defended me, but she is under her father's complete control. It is, after all, his house.

So, I packed my bags and set out for the hotel. To make matters worse, it was about to rain, and I struggled with my bags to get to the hotel before it started.

"Going away?" a familiar voice asked.

I looked up, and it was Doctor Johnson returning from the square where he had gone to purchase a newspaper. "The hotel," I replied

"What on earth for? I thought you were living with the Hupmanns?"

"I was, but I overstayed my welcome, I suppose." That's when the rain started.

"You will get soaking wet before you get there." And he snatched up my two largest bags." You'll come to my house, and we'll talk about this." And he was off. Since he held my bags hostage, I had little choice but to follow him.

We still got wet before we got there, and he offered me a soft towel to dry off. "Please have a seat, and I'll make some tea."

While he was preparing the tea, I looked around his parlor. It was neat, and everything had its place. I noticed two portraits on the wall. One was obviously his wife and the other his daughter.

"I see you noticed my portraits?" He said, startling me, as he brought in the tea set and placed it on a table.

"Your wife and daughter? They are both lovely."

"Indeed, they were. I understand you also paint portraits?"

"Now, who told you that?"

"Miriam. She spoke of you, her roommate, and that dreadful school she was sent to by her father. Somehow, I knew I would eventually meet you." He poured the tea and said with a sigh, "You do look like my Jenny, and I sense that you have the same kind of spirit she had."

I took my seat and pointed to her portrait. "But I only resemble her in hair and eye color."

"And spirit," he corrected me. "What about you? Tell me what happened? I am thinking Hupmann discovered you are pregnant and tossed you out?"

"You know I'm pregnant?"

"Miss Rachel, I was a doctor for nearly 50 years. I know a pregnant woman when I see one. I knew you were when I introduced myself nearly a month ago."

"Very perceptive of you."

"So, Hupmann evicted you, and you were going to the hotel—to do what?"

I looked down at my cup of tea. "I'm not sure."

"You have nowhere else to go? What about home?"

"No, I cannot go home again."

He studied me. "That sounds rather final."

"It is, at least for now."

"Because home is in Louisiana?"

"It's more than that."

"Drink your tea before it gets cold." He waited for me to take a sip before speaking again. "And the father?"

"We were to be married, but those plans were altered by—circumstances." I began to weep as the memory of it all flooded up to the surface again.

"I am sorry," he said. "I should not have pried."

I composed myself as I felt a strange sense of security with this elderly gentleman. "No, for I am going to tell you everything. I need to talk about it with someone, and you don't seem like the type who would be judgmental."

"My word!" he exclaimed when I finished. "No wonder you looked distraught."

"It's I who must apologize now, for perhaps I should not have burdened you with my problems."

"Nonsense. What are friends for?"

I dried my tears with my hanky. "I don't know what to do now."

"Well, I do. You shall stay here for as long as you wish. I have plenty of room, and I would welcome your company."

"But I cannot do that? People will talk."

He took a deep breath and sighed. "Miss Rachel, I'm too old to much care what people say about me, and I would think you are in a position where you really can't afford to care what the gossips think. Some people will always find some fault to criticize. Besides, your presence here would certainly brighten this dreary place. I insist! There, it is settled!" he said as he poured more tea into my cup. "The room on the back of the house faces north with large windows, and do not you artists value north light? You can use that room as your studio. Paint your pictures and bring color, beauty, and laughter back into this house and make it a home again."

I thought about his offer. I really was in no position to refuse, and they would indeed gossip anyway, especially once my condition became known. "But you must let me pay you room and board. Herr Hupmann required it. I have money."

"I am not Herr Hupmann," he retorted almost angrily. "No money! Your presence will be payment enough for me. As I said, it is settled!"

---

23 August 1861

I have gotten settled in Doctor Johnson's house. He gave me a room of my own and offered the back room to use as a studio when I am ready.

I met his housekeeper, Delphine, an elderly Negro who cleans for him, washes and irons his clothes and cooks a few meals. She comes in only three times a week and has been working for Doctor J since before his wife died, so she knows him well. She reminds me of Mammy, although a bit feistier. She doesn't take any of Doctor J's guff.

She says Doctor J is a lost soul in need of someone to help him find his way again. He seems to have no focus in life, and she thinks he is slowly dying in his misery.

"You, Miss Rachel, may be just what he needs."

"Me?"

"You! He has not been happy since his Jenny died. Even though he denied it, I caught him singing the other day, and he hasn't done that since she passed away. I can see the change in him since you came to live here. Yes, ma'am, I think you make him happy again."

I never dreamed my mere presence could have such an impact on anyone, much less almost a complete stranger. Perhaps, it is because I resemble Jenny, or maybe it is because I am as lost as he seems to be. Both of us need someone to help us through our difficulties, and maybe we are good for each other.

I enjoy his company and the discussions we have well into the evenings after dinner. He has a sharp mind and is most inquisitive of all manner of subjects. He was very interested when I told him about my dog back in Louisiana. He had not heard of Catahoula Curs.

"They sound fascinating. So they wind scent rather than follow a ground spore? That would be a valuable trait in a hunting dog."

I told him how Ethan flipped the sow and got her to adopt Cochon as one of her piglets. He said he had never heard of such a thing. "That is a sight I would love to have seen!"

I have spoken to Miriam only once since her father expelled me from his house. She apologized profusely, but there was little she could do to change his mind. She fears he may be slipping away mentally, and I am inclined to agree. He is so easily angered and such minor things set him off. She says he has never struck her but he seems capable of that to me.

25 August 1861

Two nights ago I retired early without dinner, because I wasn't feeling well with some cramping in my belly. I awoke around midnight in excruciating pain and discovered I was bleeding. I called out for Doctor J, who came immediately, still in his nightshirt.

"What is it?" he exclaimed as he entered my room holding a lamp.

By then I was weeping. "The baby! The baby!"

"My goodness!" was all he could say as he came to my aid, but it was already too late, and there was nothing he could do. I had lost my child and I wept bitter tears.

I eventually fell asleep exhausted around one in the morning and awoke two hours later. Doctor J was sitting in a chair next to my bed, watching over me. "Feel any better?"

"Physically, perhaps?" Then I started weeping again and couldn't stop. All I could think was I had lost a baby, Ethan's baby, my baby! "What have I done to cause this?"

Doctor J sought to console me. "Rachel, you did nothing. It isn't your fault."

"But it must be!"

"No! Don't blame yourself. In my near fifty years of medicine, I have seen many such cases. It is all too common, and why does it happen? Well, we physicians aren't as smart as we would like you to believe. We rarely know, and your case is not one where I could say with some certainty why. Perhaps, the stress you have been under? It was your first pregnancy? But it wasn't because of you or anything you did, and you must not blame yourself."

That did not help the loss I felt deep inside, and I continued to weep. "It has been one thing after another! Will it ever stop? I lost my family and the man I love, now I must endure the loss of my baby?"

"Jenny, what you are feeling is normal, and you should mourn the loss of your child. Grieving is natural, and it can eventually bring relief from the pain." He reached out and grasped my arm with his hand.

But the tears would not stop. He remained with me and comforted me the rest of the night. At dawn I regained some control over my emotions. Perhaps I had cried my loss away?

"Can I get you anything?"

"Perhaps some tea and toast?"

"I'll be right back."

As he stood to leave, I grabbed his arm. "How bad was it? Can I ever have children?"

He smiled. "You are young and healthy, and I expect you will be able to get pregnant again."

I was much relieved. I do so want to have children.

An Eternity of Four Years

Chapter 7 – Winter 1861-62

Military operations ceased with the coming of winter, and we went into winter camp. Most of us began the construction of sturdy quarters to protect us from the cold Virginia winter. Our little mess built a snug log cabin with two bunks on each side, a table in the middle and a stick and mud fireplace at one end for warmth. On the outside of the end with the fireplace, we built a closed shed "barn" for Pepper and the mule to have shelter from the weather and some warmth from the fireplace. Our quarters were tight, but we would be warm in the coldest weather.

Wheat had returned to duty, and as part of the reorganization of the army, we got a new brigade commander. Davis desired for brigades to be composed of regiments from the same state and led by officers from that state. Thus the brigade was taken away from Walker, and he was given command of a brigade from Georgia. Richard Taylor of the 9th Louisiana Infantry Regiment was promoted to brigadier general over three more qualified and senior colonels, and the brigade was officially designated the 1st Louisiana Brigade.

Those passed over for command were not happy. Even Taylor was embarrassed by it and went to see Davis in person to ask him to reconsider his promotion, but he stood by his decision and wrote personal letters to the three passed over colonels to smooth ruffled feathers.

As was the custom of naming brigades after the general in command, ours became known as Taylor's Louisiana Brigade and included the 6th, 7th, 8th, and 9th Louisiana Infantry Regiments. To that was added Wheat's Battalion in spite of Taylor's efforts to be rid of us. By then, because of the famous and infamous exploits of a few Louisiana troops, all Louisiana volunteers were being referred to as "Tigers."

Dick Taylor was a wealthy planter with a plantation just upriver from New Orleans and the son of former President Zachery Taylor. He was also the brother-in-law of President Jefferson Davis, who had been married to his sister, then deceased. That fact figured heavily in the resentment the passed-over colonels felt when Taylor was promoted. It was also the reason the 9th elected him regimental colonel back in April of '61. They had labored under the hope that his close ties to Davis might get the regiment moved to Virginia and into action quicker.

Dick Taylor never attended any military school, having been educated at Harvard, Yale, and Edinburgh in Scotland, nor had he ever served in the military except as an aide to his father when he was campaigning in Mexico. Dick Taylor was, however, a well-educated man and a prolific reader, especially of books concerning military matters. Though technically unschooled in the art of war in the traditional manner, he knew something of the subject from his association with his famous father and his personal studies. More importantly, General Richard Taylor, though yet unproven, was a born soldier and a born leader.

He was a handsome man in his thirties and wore a heavy black beard. Something of a dandy accustom to running with the social elite of New Orleans, he was not well thought of by some of the men at first. That would soon change. He was prone to seizures of rheumatism that often rendered him paralyzed with pain. Taylor healthy was a charming man, but Taylor sick was another matter as his illness often left him ill tempered.

Our brigade was placed in General Richard Ewell's division, another strange fellow with as many quirks as Taylor. An 1840 graduate of West Point, Ewell had served in the cavalry and claimed knowledge of that service and none other, not exactly an attitude that instilled confidence in him since ours was an infantry division. His very appearance, however, drew sympathy. The man was bald, and his head was shaped like a bomb. He had a prominent nose and bulging eyes, and was said by many to resemble a bird. Ewell was also extremely nervous and had the peculiar habit of sleeping curled up around a campstool. He spoke with a lisp, often with his head cocked to one side. Even by the strange standards of the Tigers, we found Ewell an odd fellow, indeed.

Dick Taylor was a man who would abide no nonsense—and certainly no insubordination. The ugly incident that occurred to de Choiseul came back to haunt us soon after Taylor assumed command. The men responsible for the riot at the guardhouse were court martialed, found guilty and condemned to death by firing squad. Wheat pleaded for the two Tigers, saying that their company commander, the normally very strict Captain White, was on furlough at the time. To make the situation even more difficult for Wheat, one of the condemned men had helped carry him from the field when he was wounded at Manassas. Taylor ignored Wheat's pleading and ordered the firing squad to be composed of men from the condemned's own company, the Tiger Rifles. Wheat was beside himself and requested to be excused from the execution.

At 11:30 a.m. on 9 December, the entire brigade formed a square for the execution. Taylor chose twelve men from the Tiger Rifles to form the firing squad. The condemned Tigers were tied to two posts and blindfolded. The charges were read as a priest attended to the condemned. They kissed the crucifix held by the priest, and he stepped aside. Captain White gave the orders to the firing squad, and in a few moments, with the crack of twelve Mississippi Rifles, it was over. One Tiger broke ranks and rushed up to cradle in his arms the head of one of the condemned men, his brother. This brought tears to the eyes of some of the most hardened veterans among us.

Wheat did not attend, having been given permission by Taylor to remain in his tent. There he stayed and wept softly for his men. Unknown to the rest of us in Wheat's Battalion, Taylor had ordered a company from the Kelly's 8th Louisiana to stand behind the firing squad with loaded muskets, prepared to execute the executioners should they balk at doing their duty.

Taylor had made his point. He would tolerate no more of the behavior that had brought so much shame upon the Louisiana volunteers. We had fought well and gallantly at Manassas, and that is what Taylor wanted the brigade remembered for. The men from Louisiana calmed down a bit after that, but were never pillars of society.

We slipped into an easy routine in winter camp and tried to put the past behind us. Not a day passed that I did not think of Rachel, and I either pulled out my watch or her heart locket I wore around my neck to gaze upon her once more. Even though he was dead, Morgan still stood between us. I had no word of her and I feared the war, by its growing length, would keep me from ever finding her.

During that first winter, the war still had something of a romantic appeal for many of the soldiers, especially those not heavily engaged at Manassas. Food and supplies had finally reached the army in sufficient quantity. That first winter would be fondly looked back upon as a time of plenty. The officers and men entertained themselves with elaborate parties and what amounted to cooking contests. Priding himself on his culinary skills, Wheat was not to be outdone in this contest. As chief forager for the battalion, I was called to his quarters one morning and presented a special request. Blue, as usual, tagged along.

"Lieutenant Joubert, what did you think of Colonel Skinner's filet of sole last night?" he asked with a twinkle in his eye.

"Right tasty, sir. Best fish I've had in a long while." I replied. "That will be a hard one to beat."

Wheat smiled mischievously before he replied. "True, but I shall rise to the challenge."

"What do you have in mind, sir?"

"Cabeza de buey ai ranchero," he replied with a flare for the language.

I speak fluent French but know very little Spanish, and that was picked up when I was in New Mexico Territory with the Brave Rifles. "Cabeza is a head in Spanish, and buey is an ox? Ox head?"

"Yes, ox head," he replied as he pulled on his boots. "Think you can get one by tonight?"

Being from Louisiana, I have eaten many strange things in my life, but I had never had ox head. A request from Wheat, however, was as good as an order, and if he had wanted the other end of the ox, I would have been obliged to find one of those, too.

I glanced over at my able assistant who I was sure "knew all about oxen." Blue nodded in the affirmative. "It's as good as done, sir," I replied to Wheat.

"Excellent! Then see to it."

Blue found an ox head easily enough, and I never asked him anything about it except to ascertain that it was fresh. I brought the big ugly thing to Wheat. He seasoned it with some spices he bought from Blue and sewed the loose skin of the neck closed with horns still attached. He buried it in a pit of glowing coals at tattoo that night to slowly cook. Both Blue and I stood nearby and watched, thinking Wheat might be pushing the limits of this contest a bit far. The next morning, we dug the repulsive looking thing up and dusted off the dirt and ashes. Wheat deftly removed the skin and horns and discarded them. The ox head looked even uglier than before, but it smelled absolutely heavenly! And it tasted as good as it smelled! Colonel Skinner was forced to declare Wheat culinary champion.

15 September 1861

I am very happy that I accepted Doctor J's offer to move in with him. I am sure some tongues in town are wagging over it, but they would have, anyway, once it became more obvious I was pregnant—and not married.

We get along famously and spend long hours playing chess or cards, or simply talking. I have told him things I have told no one else, and he has revealed things about his wife and Jenny he has likely told no other.

He was a doctor for almost fifty years before he retired, the arthritis in his hand making surgery difficult. He studied at the famous Paris Clinical School, the finest medical school to be found. He still has all his instruments and keeps them clean and stored properly. He could open an office tomorrow if he so desired.

He often speaks of his daughter and Jenny, and he frequently slips and calls me by her name as he did the night of my spontaneous abortion. I don't mind if it brings some joy to this aged and lost soul.

He is a Methodist and was baptized as a teenager, but he now questions the existence of God because of the loss of his wife and Jenny that left him alone and so broken.

"How can a loving God allow such things?" he asked.

My responses are never satisfying for him. He says he admires my faith that this terrible thing that has happened to Ethan and me will somehow work out for our good.

Last night he asked if anyone back at Catahoula knew anything of my situation since leaving. He reasoned they must be worried about me.

"I've wanted to write to Ethan and his mother and tell them my reasons for leaving, but I was afraid such might give away my place of hiding.

"It is possible to get mail into the South easily enough. And there are ways your location can remain unknown. I have a doctor friend living in Richmond. I can arrange to have a letter sent by him; that is if you would care to write your

family. If you were my Jenny, and even if you never wanted to see me again, I would want to know you are safe."

I thought about his offer, and it was just the encouragement I needed. "Perhaps you are right" I took pen in hand that very night and wrote a letter to Ethan and another to Analee.

Our winter huts were cozy and comfortable, but we were packed inside in close quarters. That closeness helped spread the diseases that plagued us, mostly measles, mumps, and pneumonia. These took a toll on the men. At one point, less than half of the 8th Louisiana could muster for duty as so many men took sick, and many of those died. Had we been called to battle we would have been hard pressed to muster enough healthy men to fight off a regiment of determined Yankees.

It was during that first winter that I heard from my mother that my stepbrother Peyton had died of pneumonia. My stepfather and stepsister, and now Peyton were gone.

On 2 October, I received a letter addressed to Ethan Davis in care of Wheat's Battalion with no return address and postmarked Richmond. Someone who knew my history had scratched out the "Davis" and replaced it with "Joubert." The handwriting on the envelope was very familiar to me. It was in Rachel's hand! I shouted for joy, startling my fellows lounging around the campfire.

All looked at me, but Jean was the first to say something. "Well, that must be good news!"

"Rachel!" I exclaimed. "It is from Rachel!" My eyes filled with tears as I began reading it to myself.

16 September 1861

My dear Ethan,

I am writing this letter to let you know I am safe and well. I cannot tell you where I am, because I am sure you would come for me. I cannot allow that. I cannot face you just now, perhaps some day, but not now. This letter was mailed from Richmond by a friend of a friend. I am not there, so please do not assume I am and look for me.

Forgive me for not writing sooner, for I could not bring myself to do so. I pray you will understand why I had to leave as I did. I heard all you and Morgan were saying, and when I heard him admit I was his daughter, it felt as if someone had punched me in the stomach.

I knew then I could not remain at Catahoula and look upon your face every day, reminded of what we meant to each other and knowing we must remain apart. Such, I could not bear to live with. I decided I had to leave but knew you would stop me. I am sorry I could not even say goodbye.

I feel I should also tell you I was pregnant when I left. Unfortunately, I miscarried and lost the child, a boy. I am fine and was assured I could still have children. I am so sorry to have to deliver this news to you!

This will be my last letter to you, but you should know I will never stop loving you, and I know you will never stop loving me. Perhaps, someday we shall meet again.
With all my love,
Rachel

My hands drooped as if the letter weighed a hundred pounds, and my head fell forward with my chin against my chest—and I wept.

"Lieutenant Ethan, what happened?" asked Blue as he knelt beside me with his arm around my shoulders.

I could only sob quietly, and the big black man pulled me against his chest, his head upon my back. My other messmates looked on silently, respecting my grief.

I finally gained control of myself and tried to explain what was in the letter but could not get the words out. I stood, touched Blue on the shoulder in acknowledgement of his caring, and silently walked away from the campfire.

Three weeks later, I got a letter from my mother. In it was the letter Rachel had written to her. It said much the same about why she left without saying goodbye. My mother was particularly upset about the spontaneous abortion. That boy would have been her first grandchild. But at least we knew Rachel was safe and well.

Winter weather only served to deepen my depression, and I drank heavily, enough that my messmates, all three, Jean, Sean and Blue, chided me for it.

"I drink too much? Maybe you haven't had to deal with what I have?"

"You're just wallowing in self-pity," snapped Jean. "You're the one who spoke of having faith in God. Where is it? Looks to me like you are finding your faith in a bottle."

They were right, of course. As long as I was busy, I was fine. But when things got quiet, I slipped into my melancholy again, and that usually meant its relief was found in a bottle, not God where I should have been looking.

That first winter in Virginia was dull, especially when compared to those to come after it. We passed the winter with plenty and in relative comfort, not knowing that this would be the last such winter we would experience. There was ample food and clothing, and the days we were confined to our huts by snow and rain were passed snug and warm usually by reading or playing cards—or in my case, getting drunk.

Increasingly, I had come to terms with the fact that this "short war" would not be short after all. I knew in my heart it would go on—and on and on. And it had become the obstacle that stood between Rachel and me. Searching for her would not be possible anytime soon. Morgan, I could fight against and even beat, but how do you fight against a war? It has no shape, no strategy to discern and plot against. It is just there and standing in the way! Always standing in the way! This only deepened my misery and became even more of an excuse to "wallow in self-pity" as Jean had said—and drink even more to drown my misery.

28 October 1861

I have been sketching Doctor J and he wants to see what I'm doing, but I do not show him. That makes him furious, and he stomps around sputtering and mumbling about my secretive ways. I only laugh at him, which makes him all the more angry.

"In due time, I'll show you. Until then you must be patient."

That only seems to make him more interested in what I am drawing. I have to hide my portfolio, as I'm certain his curiosity would lead him to peeking if he has the chance.

He is such a lovely man, and though he fusses, I know he is all bluster and no bite. It's clear he loves me as if I was his Jenny, and he often calls me by her name. I remind him I am Rachel, and he apologizes, but in truth, I don't mind if it makes him happy.

5 November 1961

Doctor J and I made a trip to Baltimore to purchase art supplies and canvas. I wanted to go alone, but he insisted I should have an escort.

Traveling with him was most interesting, and he kept a running dialog pointing out features in the passing countryside. Our stay in Baltimore was only two nights, and we ate dinner at a fine restaurant near the hotel.

Upon our return to Gettysburg, we set about arranging the sunroom for me to use as my studio. We emptied it of much of the furniture and put it in storage to make room for my easel and taboret.

When all was in place and made ready, he turned to me and said, "All you need now is a subject. And I will be your first customer. I have always wanted my portrait done."

"You had portraits done of your wife and Jenny. Why didn't you have yours done at the same time?"

"I was too embarrassed," he replied with a shake of his head.

"But you are not embarrassed now?"

"Because I know you won't think me vain." I laughed, and he smiled. "When shall we begin?" he asked.

"I have already started. I have been sketching you for weeks, and I'm about ready to put paint to canvas." I opened my portfolio and showed him my many sketches of objects around the house, the chickens outside, a carriage, and those I had done of him. "It was to be a surprise, but you are so impatient you ruined it. Now you know why I wouldn't let you see what I was sketching."

He looked contrite as he picked up one of the sketches I had done of him and examined it most carefully. "Indeed, and a very fine likeness it is." He paused. "But do you think you can take about fifty years off me?"

I shook my head. "Doctor J, you are a character, you know that?"

He laughed. "I have been called a lot worse."

Packages from home saved many of us from complete boredom. In December I received one from my mother. In it were two sets of long underwear, four pair of woolen stockings, four pair of drawers and two warm blankets. Also in my package were canned pears, blackberries, and honey, a new pocketknife, and some stationary. I shared all the clothing with Blue and passed the food around among my messmates.

Christmas left me feeling even more melancholy as I remembered the one Christmas Rachel and I spent together my second year at VMI. That was when we had the pictures made for the watch she gave me and the gold locket I gave her.

As I lay on my cot in our hut, I took my watch out and opened it. Then I took Rachel's locket from around my neck and opened it, placing it beside my watch. She was lovely even then, so full of life, daring, exciting, and so loving. The two pictures were not the usual stiff poses seen in tintypes. That was her doing. She posed me on a settee and sat beside me laid back against my chest, her head beside my cheek with my arms around her. And we smiled because we were happy. As I looked at the picture, I could almost feel her in my arms again, and my eyes watered.

Ever vigilant to my needs, Blue asked, "Something wrong, Lieutenant Ethan?"

"No, Blue. I was just looking at my Rachel and remembering her."

He knocked the ash from his pipe and put it on the crude little mantle over our mud and stick fireplace. "I ain't ever forgot that story you told us. I felt so bad for you that it made me weep. She must be a pretty lady."

"See for yourself," I said as I handed him my watch.

He took my watch in his big rough hands as if it were the most delicate robin's egg. "Lordy, but she is pretty, Lieutenant Ethan, about the prettiest thing I ever did see."

"Yeah, I think so, too."

He continued to look at her as if she were some goddess. Finally he looked up and said, "I once told you the Lord sent you to save my life, and I expect He wants me to repay that debt. For a long time now, I've prayed for an answer. What does He want me to do for you?" Blue looked at Rachel once more. "Now, I know. He wants me to find her for you, and that's what I'm gonna do. I don't know how yet. I expect He'll tell me in His own good time, but I'm gonna find your Rachel for you, Lieutenant Ethan. Yes, sir, I'm gonna find her."

I smiled. "If anyone can do it, you can. You can find anything, Blue."

"Until I do, you just remember one thing, difficulties makes us better or bitter. The choice is yours."

That was one of Blue's truisms. He never told me where he got those little sayings, but most were Biblical in origin.

24 December 1861
The portrait of Doctor J is finished and I presented it to him as a Christmas gift.

"*My, my!*" *he said.* "*It is an excellent likeness. I didn't realize I was so handsome.*"

"*I think you are indeed a handsome man, and you will always be my beau, Doctor J.*"

"*It was not supposed to be a gift. I commissioned you to paint it and was expecting to be your first paying customer.*"

"*It is my small way of thanking you for your kindness. I could never accept money from you for it. It is my gift of love to you.*"

He seemed a bit unsure what to say and nodded his head before taking out his handkerchief and blowing his nose. Recovered, he said, "*Jenny, I have a gift for you, and I hope you will accept it.*" *He handed me a small box neatly wrapped.*

I smiled as I took it and carefully opened it. Inside was a pearl necklace. "*It belonged to my Jenny. I gave it to her when she turned eighteen.*"

I was overwhelmed. "*I cannot accept something so personal.*"

"*No, you have brought laughter and sunshine into this dreary house, just like my Jenny did, and I know she would want you to have it.*"

We celebrated alone that Christmas Eve, and how much I missed Ethan and how so very much I wanted to spend all my Christmas Times with him came back to haunt me.

"*You're thinking of Ethan, are you not?*"

"*Yes. We shared only one Christmas together, and it was wonderful. I do miss him.*"

"*It is obvious that you do. Why don't you write him again. I'm sure he's thinking of you and would love to hear from you. And maybe give him a return address this time?*"

"*No! I cannot do that. He would be here within the week, and I cannot face him.*"

"*Then just write the letter. I'll have it mailed for you.*"

In early January the battalion mail clerk entered our snug little cabin and looked around at the cramped, smoke-filled quarters.

Jean stirred first, "Who're you looking for, mailman?"

"Lieutenant Joubert." Then saw me in my bunk attempting to read a book by candlelight. "There you are. You need to tell whoever wrote this that your name ain't Davis no more, sir."

I came out of my bunk with the sound of that and fairly snatched the letter from his hand. "Yer welcome," the startled mailman said as he backed toward the door.

I grunted without even looking up as I tore into the envelope.

"That be from Rachel, Lieutenant Ethan?" asked Blue.

"Yeah, another of those mysterious letters?" added Sean.

By then I had the letter open and reading it, ignoring them.

25 December 1861
My dearest Ethan,

It is Christmas Time and I found myself thinking of you and that wonderful Christmas we spent together in Boston. My friend suggested I write to you ...

"Friend? What friend?" I muttered to myself.

... to at least let you know that I am well. So, I take pen in hand to write these few words. I pray this letter finds you in good health.

Again, there is no return address as I do wish for us to remain apart, at least until I can get over what has happened if such is even possible for me. I remain deeply in love with you, and I imagine I will always be so.

I have started painting again! I hope to gain a few commissions to help find some financial security. And it gives me something to do to occupy my time.

I will close now. I just wanted you to know I am thinking of you.
All my love,
Rachel

I did not have to answer my anxious friends. They knew by my expression the letter was from Rachel and how much it affected me.

22 February 1862

After Christmas, Doctor J hung his portrait beside those of his wife and Jenny. Unknown to me, he then began meeting with all his friends of any financial means and attempted to gain portrait commissions for me. At first he met only resistance. I am sure much of it centered on me, an unmarried, formerly pregnant woman living with a widowed man. Never mind he was three times my age. For some that only made it worse, but it didn't seem to bother Doctor J.

One day I found the painting missing, but he soon returned with it wrapped in cloth and tucked under his arm. Having caught him, he looked trapped and felt a need to explain himself. "I was showing it to some friends and bragging how good you are. They loved it! Said it looked just like me!"

I only nodded, knowing he was up to something.

It took nearly a month, but he convinced the local banker that he simply had to have a portrait of himself to hang in the bank. It took me almost three weeks to complete the portrait. Doctor J collected the commission and paid me. I suspect he actually paid for the portrait himself to get the banker to agree to it, but he strongly denied it, of course.

The banker loved his portrait. Soon all his depositors were commenting on it. That was the beginning. Before long, I had three more commissions.

I am now a professional portrait artist!

Chapter 8 – Into the Valley of Death

Lincoln found himself a new general to lead his Army of the Potomac, George McClellan or Little Mac as he was called. Little Mac saw an opportunity to flank the Confederate Army at Centreville and threaten Richmond from the east by a route up the Peninsula, a body of land north and east of Richmond between the York and James Rivers. Little Mac intended to land his army of 130,000 near Fort Monroe and march on Richmond. That action would surely draw the Army of Northern Virginia back from positions threatening Washington, and it did. In early March, we torched our winter huts, and the Tigers formed up to serve as rear guard for the army as it retreated south to meet this new threat.

We marched in a cold drizzle, and the roads quickly turned into mud quagmires entrapping the wheels of gun carriages and the feet of horses and men alike. Such a march is when a soldier discovers just what is really important to him and what is not. The heavy pots and pans, extra clothing, tents, extra canteens, axes, shovels, books, and all the other items we had accumulated in winter camp, and were absolutely certain we could not live without, were unceremoniously cast aside as the march grew more grueling. We were down to our weapons, the clothes on our backs, one blanket, one gum blanket, and our haversacks with a little food and tobacco in them.

The army crossed the Rappahannock and bivouacked. After several weeks, Ewell's Division, which included Taylor's 1st Louisiana Brigade, was ordered to move southwest to Gordonsville to be in position to support General "Stonewall" Jackson in the Shenandoah Valley, while the rest of the army marched to Richmond.

Jackson had been promoted to Major General and commanded a corps, which was operating in the Shenandoah. In April we received orders to join Jackson, who was under orders to prevent Federal units operating in the Shenandoah from joining in the campaign to take Richmond. We marched west to Swift Run Gap in the Blue Ridge Mountains and waited for instructions from Jackson.

A gloom fell over the Tigers when we received word that New Orleans had fallen to the Federals. We were in Virginia, and the families of many of our number were now in enemy territory and at their mercy of their captors. General Butler proved to be all that we feared in his administration of occupied New Orleans and would eventually come to be called "Beast Butler" for the heinous things he inflicted upon the citizens of the Crescent City. He was so disliked, some enterprising soul took to making and selling chamber pots with his likeness on the inside bottom.

The Shenandoah Valley is often called Virginia's breadbasket, and it was thus considered strategically important to the Confederate cause. Jackson warned very early in the war that if the Valley was lost, Virginia was lost, and it was assumed that if Virginia was lost, the Confederacy was doomed.

Busy again with the affairs of the battalion, I was able to focus on my job and less on myself. Blue was the first to notice. "You feeling better, Lieutenant Ethan?"

I had not noticed the change at first. "Yes, Blue. Having something to do helps."

The Shenandoah Valley runs roughly southwest to northeast and is defined by the Blue Ridge Mountains on the east and the Alleghenies to the west. It is about 135 miles long from Lexington at the south end to Harpers Ferry at the north end and varies some 15 to 25 miles wide most of its length. Three principle features define the Valley: the Shenandoah River, which flows north to empty into the Potomac at Harpers Ferry, Massanutten Mountain, which runs down the center third of the Valley, and the Valley Turnpike, a macadamized road that begins in the south at Staunton, running northward on the west side of Massanutten to Kernstown, then Winchester, terminating at Harpers Ferry at the north end. The Luray Valley Road runs on the east side of Massanutten and is much inferior to the Valley Turnpike. One pass cuts through Massanutten Mountain between New Market and Luray. All the rivers in the

Valley flow north, so the northern end of the valley is considered the lower end and the southern end is considered the upper end of the valley. Much of the lower end is north of Washington, and an army emerging from the valley at Harpers Ferry would be in a position to flank Washington from the northwest.

In the spring of '62 with an army that barely numbered 16,000 muskets, facing a Federal army that totaled over 90,000, Jackson intended to use these same features to campaign against the enemy. Outnumbered or not, the very fate of the Confederacy rested squarely upon his skill as a general and how well his small army preformed. All this was expected of a man that many, including Ewell and Taylor, thought was insane, and was called "Fool Tom" by most of his army.

Though Jackson had been campaigning in the Valley with some success during the winter of '62, the campaign began for the Tigers at the end of April of that year. Ewell's division of 8,500 muskets arrived at Swift Run Gap in the Blue Ridge on the night of 30 April, and in the darkness, we picked our way through Jackson's slumbering army to make camp. We awoke the next morning to find that Jackson's camp was empty and his army was gone! I was somewhat accustomed to Jackson's secretive behavior from my experience with him when I was a student at VMI, and he was one of my instructors, but neither Ewell nor Taylor could comprehend what Jackson was up to.

We sat at Swift Run Gap while Jackson marched out to, in his words, "mystify, confuse and deceive" the enemy as he described his manner of waging war. He marched southwest to Port Republic in a pouring rain that turned the roads into mud. On 3 May, he marched his army through Browns Gap and left the valley! The following day, they boarded trains and returned to the Valley he had abandoned only the day before. It was all Jackson's elaborate charade designed to deceive the Yankees into thinking he had departed the Valley for good. That afternoon he arrived in Staunton and eventually joined up with General Edward Johnson, and the two of them promptly defeated General Malory at the Battle of McDowell.

Meanwhile, we sat at Swift Run Gap and awaited orders from Stonewall. Both Ewell and Taylor fumed. Jackson was off gallivanting around the upper Valley with Ewell's division sitting idle at Swift Run Gap. Neither Ewell nor Taylor had any idea what the secretive

Jackson was up to, and both were convinced Jackson was mad. Taylor even attempted to have his command removed from under Jackson, but his request was denied.

I was summoned to General Taylor's tent on the night of 10 May to find the general at his field desk. "Sir, Lieutenant Joubert reporting as ordered."

Taylor looked up and returned my salute with a touch of his fingers to his brow. "Yes, Joubert, of course. Have a seat, Lieutenant."

I took the offered campstool and made myself as comfortable as those alleged seating devices allowed. "Major Wheat said you wished to speak to me, sir."

"Yes. That's true. Wheat tells me you were very close to Jackson at VMI?"

"Sir, I know the man. He was my instructor at the Virginia Military Institute."

"Wheat tells me you and Jackson were on friendly terms outside the classroom as well. Is that not true?"

"It is, sir. Jackson and I often met and discussed religion, among other things. As you are no doubt aware, he is a devout Christian and a student of the Word."

"Yes, yes. I know that much, but I know nothing of this man himself, and he baffles me. General Ewell seems to know little more. I was hoping you could help me to understand him. Quite honestly, sir, I think he's mad as a March hare."

I could not help but smile at that remark and well understood how Taylor could think Jackson was crazy. "I assure you he isn't mad, sir. He's eccentric, but hardly mad." I had no sooner made that statement, and General Ewell marched into Taylor's tent unannounced.

I immediately stood as did Taylor. We both saluted, and Ewell nodded. "Forgive me, gentlemen. General Taylor, I would like a word with you, sir."

"Of course. General, this young officer is the man I was telling you about."

Ewell looked at me with a confused expression on his face.

"Lieutenant Joubert. At your service."

Taylor hastened to explain. "Lieutenant Joubert is a good friend of Jackson."

"Good friend, huh?" said Ewell as he cocked his head.

"Perhaps not a good friend, sir, but I am acquainted with him."

"Interesting. Tell me. Is he mad, sir?" lisped Ewell, his head cocked to one side, as was his manner of speaking.

I tried to keep from smiling, lest he take me wrong. "No, sir. As I just told General Taylor, eccentric perhaps, and I suspect misunderstood. I think all of us are just a little mad. It is that part of our nature that allows us to be creative, and in a sense, helps us cling to the remainder of our sanity."

"I never thought of it that way, Lieutenant," said Ewell as he pulled up a stool. "Oh, be seated, gentlemen, please."

Taylor and I resumed our seats. "I think he might be a genius, and genius is often confused with insanity. He is deeply religious and has some strange ideas about health. As you know he has a chronic peptic disorder."

"I hear he sucks lemons for it," added Taylor.

"Yes, sir. He also sits ramrod straight up whenever possible. Says it helps digestion by keeping his internal organs properly aligned."

Ewell thought about that for a moment then said to Taylor, "Maybe I'm crazy too, but that makes sense. However, I confess that I do not understand the man. He tells me nothing, and I'm second in command. Were he to die tomorrow, I would know nothing of his plans for this army. Nothing I tell you! What is he up to, Lieutenant? Have you any notion?"

Like every other man in this army from the top down to the lowest private, I had an opinion based on my limited knowledge of the strategic and tactical situation, but I never expected, for even a moment, that two generals would seek my opinion. "Sir, I do have an notion, but—"

"Well spit it out, sir," demanded Ewell. "You likely know more that I do."

"Sir, as I see it, Richmond is threatened by two large armies, McClellan on the Peninsula and McDowell near Fredericksburg. Johnston was forced to retire back to Richmond with his smaller army and prepare to fight on interior lines. He has two choices regarding Jackson and his small army in the Valley: He can pull him out of the Valley to aid in the defense of Richmond or leave him here. I submit that Jackson is more valuable to Richmond's defense here in the Valley than with Johnston at Richmond."

"Very good, Lieutenant," said Ewell. "Explain yourself."

"Were Jackson gone from the Valley, Lincoln would be at liberty to pull most of his forces out to join in the attack on Richmond. By recalling Jackson to Richmond, Davis will have added some 16,000 to his army, and in doing so, will have allowed Lincoln to add perhaps five times that number to his own armies around Richmond. No advantage is gained for the Confederacy. In fact, the situation around Richmond would be worse than before. I believe Davis, Lee, and Johnston should leave Jackson right here, with the hope that his army will keep that 80,000 from joining McDowell."

"You are a very astute tactician, Lieutenant. We believe that is exactly what Davis and Lee intend. We aren't sure of Johnston's intentions, however. But here is the problem: Jackson, even with my division, will have only 16,000 men as you suggest, and he is facing Fremont, Shields, and Banks with not 80,000, but over 90,000. The odds are impossible."

"In a conventional sense, yes. But Jackson will not fight a conventional campaign. He cannot, for as you point out, he is manifestly outnumbered. For the moment, their forces are scattered, but if they ever succeed in massing and trapping him, he will be crushed by the enemy's numerical superiority. Stonewall cannot allow the enemy to mass against him. He will fight a campaign of deception and maneuver. He will attempt to hide his true weakness from the enemy, deceive him into keeping his forces divided, and strike only when he can bring superior mass to bear against an inferior force. We can expect to march all over this valley, hit the enemy here one day and somewhere else the next, but always attacking a weaker force, never the enemy's main army. In doing so, he may convince Lincoln that he has many more men at his disposal than he actually does and is, therefore, a threat to McDowell's rear and even Washington. If Jackson can do that, he will prevent Lincoln from pulling his army out of the Valley, and if Jackson can give him the impression that he intends to march on Washington, then Lincoln will be forced to abandon his Richmond siege to defend his own capitol. Sir, I believe that is called a 'check' in the game of chess," I replied confidently.

Ewell looked at Taylor for a long moment. "If that isn't what Jackson intends it ought to be."

Taylor nodded. "Indeed, sir, indeed."

Ewell looked at me in an almost suspicious manner as if taking my measure. "Am I to understand that you are only an aide to Wheat?"

"Yes, sir."

"Sir, if you are right you should be promoted. In fact if you're right, you'll likely make brigadier before this war is over." Looking to Taylor, he said, "General, you had best keep this man handy for a while. His services to the Confederacy may prove to be most valuable, certainly more so than if he remains only an aide to Wheat."

By 16 May, his division still sitting idle at Swift Run Gap and nearby Conrad's Store, Ewell was placed in an untenable position. He had exchanged dispatches with Jackson and was receiving confusing orders from Jackson, Lee, and Johnston. We had reports from our scouts that General Banks was threatening to leave the Valley to link up with McDowell at Fredericksburg. Ewell was under orders from Johnston that if Banks attempted to leave the Valley, he should come to Johnston's aid, but Jackson had ordered him to pursue Banks. Half of Bank's force under General Shields had already crossed the Blue Ridge. In that move, both Ewell and Jackson saw opportunity. Their combined force now outnumbered Banks by 2 to 1. Ewell wanted desperately to engage the weakened Banks, but his orders were to join Johnston on the other side of the Blue Ridge. He decided that as long as he was in the Shenandoah, he was within Jackson's Valley District and, therefore, under his command. Lee had also suggested that anything Jackson and Ewell could do to keep Banks in the Valley would help their desperate situation at Richmond. Though a bit of a stretch, he reasoned that he had Lee's approval to move against Banks.

On the night of 18 May, I was summoned to Taylor's tent once again, and as I entered and saluted, the general greeted me with a smile on his face. "Looks like you were right, Lieutenant. We march in the morning. Jackson ordered Ewell's division to march north along the Luray Valley and pursue Banks. This brigade is being detached and is to march around the south end of Massanutten Mountain to join Jackson at New Market."

I smiled. "That's good news, sir."

"It gets better. My adjutant is drawing up orders to transfer you to my staff. If we are to march with Jackson, I want you right there with me. I'm also promoting you to captain effective midnight tonight. Congratulations, sir." Taylor stuck out his hand. It was difficult for me not to grin broadly.

"Thank you, sir, for your confidence in me."

"Ewell was right. You have potential, and your talents were being wasted with Wheat. The major has already been informed. Go back to your battalion for tonight, but report for duty with my staff at five in the morning."

I walked out of General Taylor's tent barely able to contain my glee. In a short period I had gone from being Wheat's gofer to the confidant of generals, plus been promoted in the process! My star was rising at last.

Wheat and the rest of the battalion officers were waiting for me with a bottle of cognac to toast my promotion. "Couldn't have happened to a better man," snorted Rob Wheat with a slap on my back. "But where will I find my ox heads now?" The group roared with laughter.

"A toast," said Alex White. "To Captain Joubert *and* his lovely lady, Rachel, wherever she may be."

We bolted down our cognacs, but I was nearly overcome with sadness, because Rachel was the one person I most wanted to share my good fortune with. After a few more rounds and toasts, I retired to gather my things and write a letter to my mother. I suspected I would be very busy very soon and probably for an extended period of time. For the Tigers from Louisiana, Jackson's Valley Campaign was about to begin.

As the sun rose on the morning of 19 May 1862, we marched out of camp. Ewell went north, and the Louisiana Brigade went west. Taylor had me ride along with him so he could question me about Jackson. Blue rode along with Taylor's servant, Tom Strothers, a strapping black man.

As we drew near New Market and Jackson's camp, Taylor had his regimental commanders tighten up the formation. The men of Taylor's Louisiana Brigade, 3,000 muskets strong, marched smartly down the Valley Turnpike and into Jackson's camp that evening with regimental bands playing, the drums beating the cadence, and bayonets and polished gun barrels glistening in the warm glow of the setting sun with our blue Louisiana pelican battle flags flapping in the breeze. It was a sight to stir the hearts of even the most hardened.

Taylor and his staff were in the vanguard, followed by Wheat's band playing *The Girl I Left Behind,* then the Tiger Rifles in their fancy zouave uniforms following close behind the band. The Virginians and Marylanders of Jackson's command poured out of camp and lined the road on either side, hooting and cheering us on. That only served to make us prouder. The bands played louder, and we put even more snap into our step. I am here to tell you that there was no grander sight than this magnificent brigade marching proudly up the turnpike under our blue pelican battle flags. My heart fairly wanted to burst from my chest!

Jackson watched from a distance as his fresh new brigade trooped smartly by. He soon sent a member of his staff to greet us and instruct us to march through his whole army to camp on the north side. We didn't realize it at the time, but the Tigers were being positioned in camp so we would march in the vanguard of Jackson's army when we broke camp the next day and moved north.

We marched into the fields designated for us, and our officers shouted commands in French to the amazement of Jackson's troops gathered around to watch the show. Our bands continued to play, and some of our boys joined in pairs and danced in gay abandon as if their partners were the most beautiful Creole belles of New Orleans. Once more the battle hardened veterans of Jackson's Valley Army cheered.

Taylor laughed at the amazed Virginians then turned to me. "Where is he, Captain?"

I looked about for Jackson. I had seen him earlier when we marched down the pike but had lost him in the crowd. I soon spotted his lanky figure sitting on a rail fence overlooking the camp and road. "That's him, sir, there on that fence," I replied, pointing.

"Come along, Captain. I expect you will want to tell him hello."

"Yes, sir." I followed Taylor as he made his way through camp to Jackson.

Stonewall was sitting on the top rail, sucking on a lemon to ease his stomach problem as was his habit. He wore high cavalry boots that seemed oversized even for him, and his uniform was faded and weathered looking. I soon realized it was the same one he had worn back at VMI. He had a dark heavy beard, and brooding eyes peeked out from under the bill of his kepi, which he wore rakishly low over his brows so as to almost hide his eyes. He looked weary and much older than when I had last seen him.

I held back, and Taylor stepped up and reported. Jackson nodded and glanced over at me for a moment. Then turning back to Taylor, he asked in a low even tone, "By what route did you march today and how many miles?"

"Keazletown Road. Six and twenty miles."

Jackson gestured with his lemon to our brigade. "You seem to have no stragglers."

"Never allow straggling, sir."

Jackson nodded knowingly. "Then you must teach my people. They straggle badly."

One of our bands struck up a tune, and the men began dancing again. Stonewall watched for a few moments then said softly, "Thoughtless fellows for serious work."

Taylor turned and looked over his shoulder at his brigade then turned back to face Jackson. "I expect the work will not be less well done because of the gayety, sir."

Stonewall nodded but made no reply. Turning once more to me he said, "I believe I know you?"

"Yes, sir," I replied. "I was a student at VMI, class of '60."

Jackson smiled. "Of course," he replied evenly. "You're Ethan Davis, aren't you? The moustache deceived me. How are you, Captain Davis?"

"I'm fine, sir." I wasn't sure how to handle my name change, as it was something of an embarrassing subject. I decided to face it forthrightly and honestly. "General, you knew me as Ethan Davis in school, but my name is Ethan Joubert now." Taylor looked askance at me as he was not aware of my name change, but Jackson seemed unmoved by the news.

"I don't understand," Stonewall replied after a suck on his lemon half.

I sighed. "It—ah—well, I am a bastard, sir. My real father's name is Joubert," I replied, obviously embarrassed.

"Was that any of your doing?"

"No, sir."

"Then you needn't be embarrassed by it," he said as he tossed the spent lemon away. The interview was ended, and Jackson said nothing more. After a period of silence, Taylor excused himself, and we departed.

Once out of earshot, Taylor turned to me. "Strange fellow."

"He seems a bit distracted just now," I replied.

"You have a lot of respect for him, don't you?"

"Yes, I do. I think he is a much misunderstood man."

Taylor stopped and turned to me. "Captain, who is your father?"

"Pernell Joubert," I replied.

"I didn't know he had a son. He never spoke of you."

"My mother never told him. You know him, sir?"

"Yes. I know him well, and I always thought you resembled him. Played cards with Pernall many times. Fine gentleman. I expect he will be pleased to learn he has a son. He said he was in love once, often spoke of his desire for a family but never married, though he could have had his choice of any of the belles of New Orleans. I always thought that strange."

That night as we sat around our campfire and talked, Jackson quietly walked up and took a seat on a log, saying nothing as he did so. He seemed immersed in his thoughts and stared blankly into the flickering flames of our campfire before he calmly announced that we would march in the morning but gave no direction. He questioned Taylor about the methods he used for marching long distances. Apparently satisfied with the answers, he sat there silently, lost in his own thoughts for several hours. He was so deep in concentration that our conversations and even Taylor's famous camp stories seemed not to distract him. I do not believe I have ever known any man who could so completely concentrate as Jackson could. Some thought he was in prayer when he did that, and likely he was some of the time, but I think he would simply shut out the rest of the world as he sorted out all the possible scenarios he would face in a coming battle and all the possible options at his disposal for dealing with them. He would formulate his entire battle plan in his head, never committing it to paper, a dangerous practice should he be struck down on the field.

5 May 1862

McClellan has attempted to flank the Confederate Army and threaten Richmond. General Thomas J. "Stonewall" Jackson, Ethan's instructor at

VMI, is operating in the Shenandoah Valley. It is rumored the Louisiana Brigade is with him, and that would mean Ethan is there.

I am thinking the Valley will be the place to watch for a spell.

Chapter 9 – On to Winchester

We formed up the next morning, and with the Tigers leading the way and setting a brisk pace, moved north as if to engage Banks at Strasburg. As we marched through New Market, Jackson called for a turn to the east on the road leading to Massanutten Mountain. He sent only a cavalry detachment from Colonel Turner Ashby's command toward Strasburg to shield our movements. Instead of attacking Banks, we marched across the mountain and down the other side into the Luray Valley and across the South Fork of the Shenandoah. We arrived late in the day just south of Luray where Ewell was waiting for us. The Tigers had marched in a circle. Two days before, we had left Conrad's Store, marched around the south end of Massanutten and then over its center to camp near Luray. Jackson had a tendency for deception that mystified even me, and I was one of his admirers.

The following morning, 22 May, we moved north toward Front Royal where there was a small Federal detachment. We marched fifty minutes, stacked arms, and rested for ten. The Tigers were leading the column, and Taylor was ordered to keep up a grueling pace of thirty miles a day. The new rules reduced straggling, and fewer men dropped out of the ranks from exhaustion, stomach cramps or foot problems. That night we halted only ten miles from Front Royal.

Banks's army was much reduced with the departure of Shields with 11,000 men, leaving him only 7,600 men at Strasburg, 850 infantry and 600 cavalry at Winchester, 100 men at Buckton, and only Colonel Kenley's 1st Maryland's (U.S.) 1,100 men at Front Royal. Jackson now had an army that consisted of 16,000 men and possessed overwhelming odds in his favor as he moved on Kenley at Front Royal. Turner's cavalry screen was designed to convince Banks that he was the target. Instead, Jackson intended to crush the vulnerable Front Royal garrison.

At sunrise on 23 May, Ashby and some of his troopers crossed the South Fork of the Shenandoah and rode to capture the small Federal detachment at Buckton where he cut the telegraph wires, severing communications between Banks and Kenley. The rest of Jackson's army moved up the road toward Front Royal and found Kenley completely ignorant of the southern host about to fall upon him.

We moved on closer to Front Royal and emerged on the heights overlooking the town to find Kenley's tents pitched near the confluence of the North Fork and South Fork of the Shenandoah River, and on our side. His only escape was across the two bridges of the South Fork and then a single bridge on the North Fork. From our vantage point, it was obvious to the dullest soldier that this fight was going to be a race for those three bridges.

It was early in the afternoon when Jackson deployed his army in line-of-battle, placing Wheat's Tigers in the center along side Colonel Bradley T. Johnson's 1st Maryland Regiment (C.S.A.). Johnson's Marylanders were to be given the chance of drawing first blood from the traitorous Yankee Marylanders of Kenley's command. The 6th Louisiana was to follow as support. Taylor and his remaining three regiments were sent to our left flank near the river.

I was with Taylor as he formed our brigade in line-of-battle. From our position near the river, we could see the enemy on the opposite bank a ways down the river. Taylor moved to the river's edge to get a better look. As he sat upon his mount and scanned the river with his field glasses, his horse eased down to the waters edge for a cool drink. Yankees hidden in the bushes down river began taking shots at Taylor, and the balls sent up little geysers of water around him. This was Taylor's baptism under fire, and he intended to show no fear in front of his men. He knew they would be watching him carefully. He sat motionless as his mount drank, seemingly oblivious to the danger. After what seemed like an eternity, the horse, his thirst quenched, turned and walked back up the bank. As if nothing had happened, Taylor spurred him back to our lines to the cheers of the Tigers.

After he had returned to his position in the line, I leaned over in the saddle, and with a mischievous smile, said to the general, "You think he got his fill of water?"

Taylor looked at me with a cocked eyebrow. "A provident camel on the eve of a desert journey would not have laid in a greater supply of water that did my thoughtless beast," he replied dryly. I laughed, as did several of the others within earshot.

Soon a Federal battery on Richardson's Hill overlooking the South Fork and the town opened fire on our brigade. We moved down through the fields toward the town. Wheat and the Marylanders already had some of Kenley's men in flight and headed for the two bridges, but some of Wheat's Tigers stopped to loot the abandoned Federal camp, allowing them to escape across the bridge. But they were still within cannon range, so Jackson called for his guns only to discover that the long-range rifled guns were still well in the rear. "What an opportunity for cannon!" He exclaimed. "Oh that my guns were here! Order up every rifled gun and every brigade in the army!" he ordered.

Taylor suggested to Jackson that he move the Tigers to the nearby railroad bridge to cross. Jackson nodded his approval, and we moved out on the double quick. Taylor sent me to Kelly to deliver his orders for the 8th Louisiana to lead the charge. Kelly promptly moved his regiment forward, and I remained with the 8th, knowing they would be the first to cross. We dismounted and charged across on foot. Some of our fellows lost their footing on the cross ties and fell into the dark waters of the river swollen from recent rains and drowned. We made the other side and were quickly followed by the rest of the brigade. This forced the Federals to abandon their positions, which we now threatened to flank, and they withdrew across the North Fork's single bridge. But as they retreated, they set it on fire. This would force us to find another crossing down stream and allow the Yankees to escape, ruining Jackson's carefully laid plans and alerting Banks to our presence on his flank. Taylor saw only one course of action, and that was to take his brigade across the flaming bridge as quickly as possible before it was completely enveloped! Jackson approved, and we charged with Wheat's Tigers in the lead.

We hit the flaming bridge on the run, yelling to the top of our voices. Smoke obscured us from Yankee sharpshooters, which helped some, but the flames were threatening to envelop the bridge.

We kicked and shoved burning brands into the water in an attempt to save the structure. Many of our boys had burned hands for their efforts. As we moved forward through flames and smoke, we heard a groan and a loud crack above the crackle of the flames as a section of the bridge collapsed into the river. I grabbed the rail just before I would have been dumped into the swirling current and managed to hang on until strong hands pulled me back onto the bridge.

Enough of the bridge remained standing for us to continue to cross but only single file. Some of Kelly's men jumped into the river to form a vertical bucket brigade and passed canteens and hats full of water to those of us on the bridge to throw into the flames. We got the fire under control enough to continue the charge to the opposite shore and emerged from the smoke to see the Yankees skedaddle to safety. As if out of nowhere, Jackson was among us. How he got across that bridge so choked with Tigers I will never know. Seeing the escaping Federals, he ordered up Colonel Thomas Flournoy's 6th Virginia Cavalry to take up the pursuit.

Personally led by Jackson, the cavalry caught up with the Federals after only a few miles near Cedarville, and after a series of charges into the face of overwhelming odds, Flournoy's cavalry finally broke through and captured the rest of the confused and exhausted Yankees.

We had won the Battle of Front Royal handily. Kenley lost 904 of his 1,100 men, of whom 750 were captured. Jackson lost only thirty-five. The Tigers had unquestionably won the day with our two charges across the bridges. That night Jackson once more honored us when he joined our headquarters group around the campfire. I was cleaning my Colt as he stepped into the circle of light and took a seat on the log beside me, saying nothing as he did so. As before, he sat there quietly and stared into the flickering campfire absorbed in his own thoughts.

Sitting silently before our campfire that night, Jackson had much on his mind. I figured he had few options. Banks sat to the west of us at Strasburg just 10 miles away, evidently, still under the impression that Front Royal was merely a diversion, and the main attack would come from the south. The strong showing of Ashby's cavalry demonstration against Banks at the same time we were taking Front Royal likely helped him reach that conclusion.

Two roads led to Winchester only twenty miles away, the one from Front Royal and the Valley Turnpike from Strasburg. If we took the Front Royal road in a race to cut Banks off from Winchester and the Potomac, he might move on Front Royal and attack our flanks or our rear, or cut through the Blue Ridge at Manassas Gap and escape to join McDowell at Fredericksburg. Neither scenario was desirable, because Jackson wished to crush Banks or at least prevent him from escaping. Stonewall formed a plan based not on the two roads just mentioned but another that ran diagonally from Cedarville on the Front Royal road over to Middletown on the Pike. He planned to leave the bulk of his army near Front Royal until Banks made his move and issue his orders accordingly.

Very early the next morning, some of Wheat's more adventurous troops put on Yankee uniforms, commandeered a train and took a ride to Markham where a small Union outpost was unaware of our capture of Front Royal. The blue-clad Tigers were accepted by the Markham garrison and mingled among them, even persuading them to return to Front Royal with them. The Tigers and their new "friends" took the train back to Front Royal where the unsuspecting Yankees were promptly made prisoners.

Two regiments of Ewell's cavalry under Brigadier General George H. Steuart were dispatched to watch for Banks at Newtown four miles north of Middletown. Ewell was ordered to take the bulk of his division up the Front Royal road toward Winchester while remaining close enough to offer assistance if necessary. The rest of Jackson's army, including Taylor's Brigade, marched to Cedarville and halted, waiting for Banks to make his move.

At about eleven that morning, Steuart sent word by courier that the Valley Turnpike was choked with Federal supply wagons retreating to Winchester. Such a prize, Jackson could not ignore. We formed up and marched for Middletown. Jackson put Colonel Robert P. Chew's horse artillery with two rifled guns in the lead and ordered Wheat to keep close to the guns with his battalion. Taylor sent me along with Wheat with orders to report back to him as I saw fit. The rest of the brigade followed, but the fast moving artillery with Wheat's Tigers jogging along side soon left them behind.

With Federal cavalry slowing our march on Middletown, we finally arrived at around three in the afternoon at a rise overlooking the Valley Turnpike and found the Federal column spread before us.

The Pike was choked with wagons and men in both directions as far as the eye could see.

Chew quickly unlimbered his guns, and from less than a thousand yards, unleashed the fury of hell on the unsuspecting Federals. What resulted can only be described as a slaughter. They were trapped on the Turnpike by stone walls along both sides with no place for them to go. Chew's gunners cut huge holes in their ranks, bringing on complete confusion and disorder, and a rout quickly ensued. Screaming horses and panic stricken men ran about the Pike, running over their wounded and dead fellows, crushing them under the wheels of the wagons. It was a sickening bloodbath to the eyes of many of us watching from above. And as if that were not enough, the Tigers were then unleashed upon them.

Screaming the Rebel yell like mad banshees, we poured down off the heights and fell upon the panicked mass of Yankees, shooting, bayoneting and clubbing them with musket butts. To our rear, Taylor heard the sound of guns and quickened his march, arriving to find the fight virtually over. With a quick volley, he threw his lead column into the fight and rushed the town of Middletown. He found the Tigers had stopped to loot and were having a right merry time. But upon seeing Taylor approach, they fell into line, and looked as virtuous as deacons at a Sunday service.

We took some 200 prisoners, and when we captured some of their cavalry, we found them such poor horsemen that they were strapped to their mounts to keep them from falling off. Some even wore iron vests to protect themselves from musket balls, but a vest was laying nearby with a neat hole punched through its center where the Minié ball had drilled right through it and the wearer's heart.

Cannon fire from the south caused Jackson to believe that he had cut the front end of the column. He took Wheat, part of the 7th Louisiana, and Ashby's troopers to clean up the remains of the advance elements to the north, sending Taylor and the rest of his army south. We charged the Yankees and sent them scampering southward about a mile where they took up positions on a ridge overlooking the Pike to block our advance. We formed in battle lines and prepared to attack when several cannon shots cut through our ranks. A shell exploded right under Taylor's mount, showering him with dirt and cutting away his saddle blanket on both sides.

Amazingly, neither horse nor rider was even scratched. Artillery fire from our guns sent them retreating south again.

To the north, Jackson met with stiff resistance, and it became obvious that he was engaged with the Federal rear guard. Most of Bank's column had slipped passed us! The Louisiana Brigade reversed its march and joined Jackson, catching up to him near sunset, only to discover he wanted us to pursue Banks with all haste and press forward to Winchester some thirteen miles distant. We were exhausted and hungry, and this order seemed extreme, but we had no choice but to obey and press the enemy's rear as he retreated. The weather had grown cold, and our stiff and spent muscles troubled us. The rest of the army had been campaigning for weeks and were even worse off than the exhausted Tigers. The army was broken down and spent, but Jackson would hear none of it and demanded we continue the pursuit. He wanted to occupy the heights overlooking Winchester when dawn came. He had no intention of giving the Federals the high ground even if it meant killing some of us on the grueling night march before us.

So we stepped off and marched for Winchester with thirteen miles to cover in the darkness, no food or rest, and the Yankee rear guard intent on making every one of those thirteen miles bloody agony for us. All too soon it became obvious that there was little left in us, and our boys began to fall out from exhaustion. Unable to take another step, they fell out along the road sound asleep to be awakened by officers and sergeants and made to march again. We stumbled along in the dark, and some of our number fell dead asleep while marching, supported by their fellows on either side. Some were so tired that not even the rattle of muskets from the skirmishing with the Federal rear guard would wake them. I trailed along behind the brigade and walked leading Pepper and tried to keep the stragglers moving. I carried muskets for those so exhausted they could barely walk and gave rides on Pepper to others who could do little more but sit in the saddle and sleep. My strong steed was also spent and trudged along wearily, and I'm sure, asleep as he walked.

Onward we marched into the darkness, and some of Jackson's staff urged him to let his army rest, lest he have no army left when he reached Winchester, but Stonewall refused. "We must command the heights at dawn. Press on!"

I staggered and fell against Pepper's side and dropped to my knees. Strong hands lifted me up. "Ride for a while, Captain," said a man whose musket I had been carrying as he took it from me. He helped me into the saddle, and I slumped over and nearly fell out again. I caught myself and held on as Pepper stumbled forward as exhausted as I was. Men were falling out, and no amount of prodding could get them moving again. They were dead asleep in the road and had to be pulled to the side, lest their fellows trample them.

Pepper was staggering, and I knew I would kill him if I remained in the saddle. I climbed down and gave him a drink of whiskey from a canteen I had taken off a dead Yankee at Middletown. That seemed to give him some renewed strength and vigor. With my few short minutes of rest in the saddle I felt a mite refreshed and gave my trusty steed a rest as I walked, leading him along behind with no burden to carry but my saddle. I took a pull from my canteen and drained the last of the whiskey.

We pressed on through the night, Jackson's army giving everything it had left, and still he refused to give us rest, insisting that he must reach Winchester before dawn. While we struggled along the Valley Turnpike, Ewell and his division were making a similar forced march up the Front Royal Road, and his men were as tired as we were.

As the night passed, I too began to wonder about the sanity of Jackson. Was he really Fool Tom as we sometimes called him? Was he pushing us passed our limits because of his own driven ambition? Was he totally unconcerned for the condition of his troops?

A few hours before dawn, we drew closer to Winchester at what was still a grueling pace, especially for spent troops. I doubted if any of us would be in any condition to fight even if we got there before dawn. That would make this entire agonizing nightmare a waste.

The army was faltering badly and threatening complete breakdown on the road. Jackson finally called a halt only a mile from Winchester and gave us two hours rest. His exhausted army fell to the ground into blissful slumber right where they stood. A few miles to the east Ewell's division halted on the Port Royal road just two miles from Winchester. Jackson sent him a single sentence order: "Attack at daylight."

Some officers attempted to post pickets, but Jackson stopped them. "Let them rest," he told them, "Their commander will stand watch over this gallant army." As we slept, only one man stood watch to protect us from surprise attack, Major General Thomas J. Jackson.

I tied Pepper's bridle to my ankle and fell to the ground at his feet. My eyes closed before my head touched the ground, and sleep was instantly upon me.

The dawn came that Sunday, 25 May, shrouded in a chilling fog, and the army was roused from its brief rest. Bleary-eyed veterans staggered to their feet with stiff and sore muscles and found their companies and regiments to push on to Winchester. Any man would have called them finished, but I saw in them one last fight before nothing more could be expected of them. So did Old Jack.

The hills on the south and southwest of Winchester that Jackson had so fretted about were only weakly held by Banks' skirmishers, and they were quickly routed. Banks' army awoke to find the Stonewall Brigade and its artillery looking down on them from the opposite ridge. The Federals opened with their artillery, sending accurate fire into the Stonewall Brigade's ranks, pinning them down on the heights on our left flank. The enemy position was a strong one and anchored the Federal right flank. The Stonewall Brigade's commander, General Charles Winder, sent word to Jackson that he was in need of help. Jackson replied, "I shall send you Taylor."

Once more the Tigers were called forward into the thick of the fight to solve a problem. It was becoming obvious that anytime Jackson needed a hard job done, he called upon Taylor's Louisiana Tigers to do it. The brigade moved forward from our positions in the rear as reserve, and Jackson pointed to the hill that anchored the Federal right flank and said simply to Taylor, "You must carry it."

We moved to the left down into a ravine, skirting the hill, his intention to flank it. Jackson was with us as we came under artillery fire from the Federals on the ridge. Some of the Tigers flinched and ducked as would be expected under the circumstances. Taylor flew into a rage. "What the hell are you ducking for?" he shouted. "If there is any more of that, you shall be halted under this fire for an hour!"

Jackson reached over and touched Taylor on the shoulder, and by way of reproach, said softly, "I am afraid you are a wicked fellow." He then turned and rode back toward the Pike.

We continued our march to flank the Federals, and when Taylor was satisfied we were in the best location for the attack, he formed us into line-of-battle. With the dawn breaking bright and the fog lifting, Taylor ordered his brigade forward at a steady marching gait across a field of clover and lush spring grasses. We moved forward in perfect formation, rifle barrels and bayonets glistening in the early morning light, our blue pelican battle flags flapping in the light breeze. Our stern faces were set upon our task as we stepped smartly across the fields of clover with Taylor riding out front, his sword held over his head. A more magnificent sight to stir the hearts of veterans cannot be imagined. Some who were witness to it said this was the most perfectly executed charge of the entire war.

The Federal gunners directed their fire toward the threat marching steadily forward, and their shots cut through our ranks, but not a man flinched. Federal cavalry charged down on our left, but Taylor simply ordered Lieutenant Colonel Frances T. Nicholls and the 8th Louisiana to delay and wheel to meet the charge. A single volley from the 8th emptied dozens of Federal saddles. Wheat held back and turned, sweeping even further to the left, posing a more serious threat to their flank.

To the beat of the drums, the rest of us continued our cadenced sweep toward the Federals. Balls whistled around our heads and some of our fellows fell, clutching at the wound that struck them down. Halfway across the field, Taylor bellowed loud enough that I am sure the Yankees heard him over the rattle of muskets and booming cannons, "CHARGE!"

The Louisiana Tigers surged forward with deafening Rebel yells. Our mad charge into the guns must have un-nerved our foe. As we gained momentum in our headlong screaming charge up the hill, they began to falter. From his position Jackson saw that victory had been handed to him by the Tigers and immediately turned to an aide. "Order the whole line forward! The battle is won!" Ewell had also seized the initiative on the right, and all Federal resistance began to crumble.

Jackson was suddenly taken by his success. He had defeated Banks! He took his kepi off and shouted uncharacteristically, "Very good! Now, let's holler!" And he charged forward, his face alight with victory. On every side our boys surged forward, and the Federals vacated their positions and ran from the gray onslaught of screaming and cheering Confederates.

The Louisiana Brigade continued its charge in spite of the Yankees pouring volley after volley into our ranks, and we flushed them from their positions and chased after them. The whole line swept magnificently forward against their strongest position and pushed them from it as if it were of no matter. It seemed that nothing could stand before us.

The Yankees fell back through Winchester in disarray. The citizens of the town did all they could to impede the retreat of the despised occupiers. Men and women shot at them from windows and threw hot water and missiles of every description at them. Banks joined his own men in their pell-mell rush to get away from the charging Rebels.

Hundreds of Winchester's citizens clogged the streets to greet their liberators. We moved through the vacant Federal positions and into the town in pursuit of the foe. One young and pretty woman rushed up to a Tiger from the 8th Louisiana and yelled frantically, "Oh, you are too late—too late!" He took her in his arms and planted a kiss on the surprised woman's lips then declared with a French accent, "I'm never too late!" and then continued on after the enemy, leaving the girl standing there with a surprised expression on her face.

Banks had set fire to his abandoned supplies, but Rebels and Winchester citizens alike formed bucket brigades to save the precious and much needed spoils of war.

"Push on to the Potomac!" yelled Jackson, and he turned to look for his cavalry to have them pounce upon Banks's retreating disorganized army. But once more the cavalry had let us down. Though brave and daring in battle, they were an undisciplined lot and often failed to live up to what was needed of them. This was not the first time they were not where they should have been, and it would not be the last.

Artillery was brought forward, and the gunners unhitched the artillery horses and mount them as makeshift cavalry. After the punishing fire they had received earlier in the morning, the artillerymen eagerly shot down retreating Yankees, giving no quarter in their pursuit of the frightened and demoralized Federals.

Banks's army quit the field in total disarray and fell back across the Potomac River. He left behind nearly 500 killed and some 3,000 prisoners. Jackson had used the Tigers to strike fear into the enemy, and they had unquestionably carried the day at both Winchester and

Front Royal. Surprisingly, we had suffered just twenty-one killed and 109 wounded in the Louisiana Brigade in those three days of fighting.

The most gracious Banks left us so many spoils of war we were scarcely able to carry them away. Jackson, not one to leave anything to the enemy, was beside himself. Considering the shear amount of supplies we had captured, we did not have enough wagons to carry off the booty and were forced to procure more from the surrounding farms and towns. The Valley Army rested and gorged on captured meats, sweets and delicacies we did not have in our army or had even imagined they had in theirs. We tossed away our tattered clothing for new Federal trousers and shoes and traded our old smooth bore muskets for newer rifled ones. Jackson issued a proclamation by way of apology to his men, thanking them for their suffering and bravery. We forgave him.

Because of our victories at Front Royal and Winchester, Lincoln was convinced that Jackson was in command of an army many times our true size and thus threatened the security of Washington. He called off the siege of Richmond and called his armies back to protect his own capitol. "Jackson's Foot Cavalry," as we were now calling ourselves, only some 16,000 strong, had saved the Confederate capitol and turned the tide of the war— prolonging it for three more bloody years.

Blue managed to collect his share of the booty, and we ate like kings. He prepared meals, the likes of which we had never even thought of. Even Taylor joined our mess for some of Blue's cooking. "This man is a gem! I think I shall commandeer him as my personal chef!"

"You may have a fight on your hands if you pursue that aim, sir," I replied. "But you are welcome to join our mess anytime you wish."

Taylor nodded with a smile.

5 June 1862

Jackson is rampaging wild in the Valley! He fought his way North all the way to Winchester, defeated and routed the Federal armies and forced most of them to leave the Valley. The northern papers say he is commanding a huge army and is a threat to Washington.

Doctor J's friend in Richmond sent him some Richmond papers with accounts of the battles. Once more the Louisiana Tigers, as Taylor's Louisiana

Brigade is now called, acted as the tip of the southern spear that pierced the northern heart.

No doubt Ethan is with them, and I pray he is safe.

Chapter 10 – Fighting Withdrawal

The north was in a panic as rumors spread that a great Rebel host was about to march into Maryland and take Washington. Secretary of War Stanton sent a frantic telegram to the governors of thirteen states of the Union demanding state militias answer the emergency. Mr. Lincoln believed that Jackson's thrust was more than just a raid. He immediately began devising a plan to trap Stonewall and crush his army with overwhelming numbers of Federal troops. The elements of his avenging force were already in the field and very nearly in position. If only the generals would do as he tells them, he could trap Jackson and destroy his army. But they had thus far shown a tendency to ignore him.

General John C. Frémont was in command of an army presently awaiting orders in the Alleghenies not thirty miles from Harrisonburg, which sits astride the Valley Turnpike eighty miles to Jackson's rear. With Frémont at Harrisonburg, Lincoln could block Jackson's escape route and cut his supply line, thus Frémont was ordered to march immediately to Harrisonburg. Old Abe planned to cut off Jackson's escape route and use Shields and Banks to hammer him against the anvil, Frémont. He then ordered Shields to return to the Valley and take Front Royal. Banks was ordered to turn around and re-cross the Potomac. The battered Banks, of course, protested that his army was demoralized and shattered, and it would take time to regroup before he could take the field again.

John Frémont, the Pathfinder as he was called for his early expeditions out west, had already had run-ins with Jackson when Stonewall defeated Malory, who was under Frémont's command, at

McDowell. The Pathfinder was something of a timid campaigner and a peacock that surrounded himself with other peacocks. Early in the war, he was appointed a major general and placed in charge of the Western Department, but his freewheeling ways forced Lincoln to remove him and place him in command of the Alleghenies, where it was assumed he would not get into trouble.

Frémont received his orders to march on Harrisonburg and promptly marched in the opposite direction for Moorefield instead. Lincoln demanded an explanation, and Frémont replied that he thought he was at liberty to interpret his orders as he saw fit, but if Lincoln demanded *literal* obedience to his orders, he should, by all means, say so. Thus, Frémont was already out of position when the campaign began. With Frémont too far from Harrisonburg, Lincoln adjusted his plan accordingly and ordered Frémont to march on Strasburg, *literally*. Thus, the original anvil and double hammer plan was changed to a more difficult pincers movement.

On the night of Wednesday, 28 May, we got word that Shields was on the move and headed for the Manassas Gap and Front Royal. Jackson was undisturbed by the news and, on 30 May, took the Stonewall Brigade to Charles Town and demonstrated against Harpers Ferry. Ashby brought word that same day that Shields was less than a day's march from Front Royal. That night Jackson departed Charles Town for Winchester by train, and as Stonewall slumbered, Shields took Front Royal. Meanwhile, Frémont was timidly advancing on Strasburg. The trap was slamming slowly shut behind us, and Jackson appeared not the least disturbed by it.

On the other side of the Blue Ridge, Joe Johnston had taken full advantage of McDowell's absence and attacked McClellan east of Richmond in a battle we called Seven Pines and the Yankees called Fair Oaks. It lasted two days and resulted in a draw, but General Johnston was seriously wounded, and command of the Army of Northern Virginia passed to Bobby Lee.

Old Jack finally began pulling his army south, and by the afternoon of 31 May, all of Jackson's Foot Cavalry were south of Winchester and headed for Strasburg except the Stonewall Brigade. The supply train of captured Union goods, which some said was over eight miles long, was leading the column. We also carried with us over 2,300 Federal prisoners under guard. Ewell's Division brought up the rear, with Ashby's cavalry stretched out between the Stonewall

Brigade back on the Potomac and us. The column head arrived at Strasburg at dusk, but Jackson found no sign of Shields or Frémont. Ewell's division was ordered forward and sent west to meet Frémont with orders to hold the door open until the Stonewall Brigade could escape through.

General Ewell was as excited as a dog about to be cut loose on the hogs. He was spoiling for a fight and looked forward to mixing it up with the Pathfinder. We pushed our skirmishers forward and encountered some artillery fire from advance units of Frémont's army about four miles from Strasburg. Our brigade moved on Freemont's flank and sent the Federals running. In Taylor's words, it was a "walk-over."

With all of Jackson's army safely through the Strasburg trap, we continued our march south on the Valley Turnpike. Frémont was behind us, and Shields was marching south on the Luray Road on the other side of Massanutten Mountain, threatening to cut across the mountain and slam into our flank or beat us to Port Republic and cut us off. With two Federal armies threatening our very existence, our exhausted army was driven hard by Jackson. And once more, we slogged down the Pike at a killing pace, this time pelted by driving rains with Frémont nipping at our heels.

On the night of 1 June, Jackson ordered the Louisiana Brigade off the road to cover the retreating column. We made camp and bedded down cold and wet after a meal of cold rations. Soon after most of us were asleep, we heard gunfire, and Taylor summoned us to fall in. He had learned from some stragglers that Federal cavalry had just forced Colonel Thomas T. Munford's Virginia Cavalry from Strasburg in a running fight. Munford's cavalry and our brigade were all that stood between Jackson's retreating army and the Federals. We marched south in the pitch-black night at a rapid pace. It was so dark we were guided only by the road and only if we stayed right on it.

Soon after we started, a group of cavalrymen suddenly charged through us, cutting and slashing with their sabers and shooting at each other! The swirling mass proved to be a mixture of both Confederate and Union cavalry engaged in a running fight, and we were caught in the middle of it! The Federals soon realized their predicament of being in the midst of a Rebel brigade and retreated in haste. They soon brought up artillery but, in the darkness, their aim was high with most rounds going over our heads. We continued our march in spite of them. We were relieved at dawn by Winder's Stonewall Brigade, but we remained close to lend a hand if needed.

Stragglers were becoming a problem for us. Many of our fellows could not endure the march and fell out to be captured or simply deserted and went home. Many of the Virginians were residents of the Valley. Jackson's Foot Cavalry was down to only 13,000 muskets by then.

We camped near Mount Jackson on 3 June and burned the bridge across the North Fork of the Shenandoah. Frémont would soon build a pontoon bridge, so we slowed his advance only a little by it, but it bought us thirty-six hours rest. The rain was still falling, and the rivers were swollen with the heavy runoff. The roads were transformed into quagmires of mud that clutched at the gun carriages and wagons and clung to the feet of the infantry, making progress agonizingly slow and tortuous.

On 6 June, Federal cavalry and infantry attacked our rear elements in force. The threat was met and repulsed by Ashby and the Marylanders, but Ashby was killed in the fight. He was the driving force that kept our disorganized cavalry functional, and without his noble services, our cavalry was reduced to almost useless. His loss would have a telling effect in another two days.

Shields was bogged down on the inferior Luray Road, and we beat him to Port Republic. He was reported to be but six miles down the Valley when we arrived. As at Winchester, the Valley Army stumbled into town exhausted and near spent.

Port Republic sits at the confluence of the North River and the South River where they form the South Fork of the Shenandoah River. The little town is nestled right against the two smaller rivers in the apex formed by their joining. A bridge at one end of town was the only nearby crossing of the North River. Two fords, the Lower Ford, near the mouth of the South River, and the Upper Ford, a bit upstream at the other end of town, were the only crossings of the South River. High water from the rains had made the fords dangerous to cross but not impassable. Main Street ran through the middle of town, turned right at the end of town and passed the Kemper Estate. There it turned left and led off to Brown's Gap in the Blue Ridge a few miles away.

Jackson sent Ewell across the North River to Cross Keys, about seven miles away, to keep Frémont occupied, then deployed the rest of his army on the far side of North River from Port Republic, simply called "Port" by the locals. The supply train was sent off on the road toward Brown's Gap, which was to serve as Jackson's escape route.

The high water in the rivers made the bridges and fords at Port Republic critical to the operations of both armies, and Jackson intended to use the swollen rivers as a means to keep Shields and Frémont from joining forces to attack him. With Shields on one side of the South Fork and Frémont on the other with no bridge for their use, he could deal with them one at a time. He intended to fight Frémont first then withdraw across the North River and burn the only bridge before attacking Shields.

We settled into camp that night wet and exhausted, expecting to get a day of rest before we had to engage either army. And we needed it. I do believe Jackson was himself exhausted, because he had made what I thought was a serious tactical mistake when he deployed his army that night. All of his army was across the North River, and all of his supplies were on the Port side. Only several small units stood guard on the Port side of the North River, an infantry company guarding the bridge and the fords along with an artillery battery fresh in the field and so new they were not fully outfitted. Only a few other troops guarded the supply wagons and prisoners on the Brown's Gap Road. Jackson made his headquarters at the Kemper Estate at the south end of town and retired for the night. With Turner Ashby dead and his cavalry out of control, the stage was set for a disaster.

Taylor summoned me early the next morning, Sunday, 8 June, and I was given some dispatches to deliver to Jackson in Port Republic. I saddled Pepper and rode out of camp and headed for Port. The dawn was breaking clear and promised a day without rain for a change. I soon arrived at Port, crossed the North River bridge, and made my way down Main Street to Jackson's headquarters at the Kemper Estate at the far end of town.

I was not more than two squares down Main Street, when I heard the unmistakable scream of an artillery round overhead. I looked up and, to my utter shock, saw the shot falling directly toward me! There was no time to do anything but close my eyes in preparation for meeting my Maker. It crashed into the street right between Pepper's legs and exploded with a deafening roar, knocking both Pepper and me to the ground.

I rolled clear and could do little more than lay there stunned by the blast with my ears ringing. Pepper struggled to his feet, screaming to wake the dead. From the sounds he was making, I was sure I would find his gut torn open, and I would be forced to end my noble steed's agony with a shot from my Colt. My terror-stricken warhorse found his footing and bolted like a cannon shot in the direction from which we had just come. I rolled over and looked up the street to see my cowardly mount deserting under fire. He slowed just long enough to decide he wanted nothing to do with that bridge and turned left and headed up the road following the North River. I whistled for him to come to me, but he did not stop and only whinnied back in answer, which if it could have been translated into English, I am sure he was saying something to the effect that I could go straight to the Devil. I figured, if he could move that fast, he couldn't be hurt all that bad, and I turned my attention to my own wounds.

To my immense relief, I found only a minor scratch on my left forearm. Except for that and ringing ears, I was unhurt. Meanwhile, I heard another round coming in and turned over onto my belly, covering my head with my arms. It exploded down the street, and I scrambled to my feet to get away from my exposed position. The second round was followed by two more, one of which slammed into the steeple of a church we were using as a hospital.

As I stood, I saw Federal cavalry crossing the Upper Ford and cursed Pepper for leaving me there like he had. Our own cavalry were in retreat and scampered through town in their haste to get away from the advancing Federals and very nearly ran me over in the process. I ran up Main Street as more artillery shells careened into the town. I took cover near the church, and Jackson came riding by. Doctor McGuire was busy loading wounded into wagons and swearing at the slow moving orderlies, as was his usual manner. Stonewall reined in his mount and admonished the doctor, "Sir, don't you think you can manage these men without swearing?" McGuire nodded and promised to try. Satisfied, Jackson spurred his mount into action and headed for the bridge at a gallop. Most of his party barely escaped capture and crossed the bridge just as Federal cavalry entered Main Street at that end of town. Colonel Crutchfield, Jackson's artillery chief, was not so quick and was taken prisoner only to escape later.

I drew my revolver and prepared for a fight as Union cavalry thronged the bridge end of town. Soon two cannons were brought up and unlimbered at the entrance to the covered bridge, their muzzles pointing across the river. I figured we were in a real fix then. Jackson and his army were across the river, cut off from their escape route by Union artillery and cavalry sitting on the only bridge. I knew I couldn't storm their position alone and wasn't doing any good staying where I was. I figured the Federals would surely go for the supply train sitting conspicuously out on the road at the other end of town and made my way toward the Kemper Estate as fast as my legs would carry me. My hope was I could find others with whom I could make a stand.

In Kemper's yard, I found Captain Sam Moore of the 2nd Virginia and his small company of only twenty muskets, which had been assigned to guard the fords. He was preparing to make a stand at the Kemper house and had already placed his company along a plank fence that surrounded it. I attached myself to this small band, and we set ourselves for the charge that was sure to come. We had not long to wait. Blue Coat cavalry came up Main Street at a walk and turned the corner headed straight for Kemper's house and our ambush. We crouched behind the fence and allowed them to get closer before Moore stood and yelled, "Fire!" And twenty muskets barked. I stood and fired with them. The startled Yankees never knew what hit them, and we emptied numerous saddles. They retreated in haste back up Main Street but began regrouping for another go at us.

Captain Joseph Carrington and his Charlottesville Light Artillery with a battery of two guns joined our little group. Carrington ordered both guns unlimbered and moved them closer to the fence. He loaded with double canister as the Federals came up Main Street toward us. Carrington hadn't the time to take down the boards on the fence in front of his guns. He aimed them as best he could, point blank, and moved to rip down the boards. "Leave them," I yelled. "Just shoot through them!" He nodded and stood by his pieces, as the Yankees came at us again, at a gallop this time. With a jerk of the lanyards the two guns roared, blowing big holes in the fence boards, and we fired with pistol and musket, emptying more Yankee saddles. Once more they retired in disarray, leaving more dead and wounded on the street.

Major Dabney of Jackson's staff arrived from the Kemper house and did little but encourage us. Carrington limbered up his guns and moved them closer to the river for a shot directly down Main Street. Moore and the rest of the infantry moved to support the guns. The Yankees charged again, and once more we let them have a taste of canister and Minié. The canister swept the street and sent the survivors running for cover at the far end of town.

Across the river, the 37th Virginia Regiment, under Jackson's instructions, was preparing to assault the covered bridge, while the Rockbridge Artillery pounded the Federal positions from the far shore. Meanwhile, Taylor had been ordered to bring his brigade on the double quick. At least a regiment of Federal infantry was moving for the fords, but artillery fire personally directed by Jackson from the far side of the river forced the Federals to quit their positions at the covered bridge, abandoning their guns just as the Virginians charged. To my astonishment, the retreating Federals failed to burn the bridge. Had they done so, the events of that afternoon and the next day might have turned out very differently.

We pushed them back across the fords, and our artillery pounded their retreating ranks. We had won the day. That surprise attack could have been a disaster for us had they burned that bridge and separated Jackson and his army from his supplies.

The brief little fight over, I was standing near the Kemper's house fence reloading my Colt, when I heard a familiar whinny and looked up to see my wayward steed standing there, looking for all the world to be as contrite as the most repentant sinner on a Sunday morning. "So, you came back! Skedaddled and left me to face a Yankee horde alone!" I fairly yelled at Pepper. He whinnied and shook his head as if he understood what I was saying and was making his defense.

I didn't know it at the time, but Jackson had returned and was witnessing my outlandish verbal attack on my horse. "Cowardice under fire! Ran from the enemy you did! I cannot believe that you would do such a thing to me after all I have done for you!"

Pepper snorted forcefully, and I heard laughter coming from behind me. I turned and saw Jackson and his staff watching the show and realized what a spectacle I was making of myself by talking to a dumb horse in such a manner.

Jackson's expression was as stern as ever. "Would you have me court martial him, Captain Joubert?" asked Old Jack without cracking a smile.

I grinned sheepishly, and I know I was red in the face. "No, sir," I replied. "It's the first time he ever did that. With your permission, I'll give him a chance to redeem himself."

"Very well. As you wish, Captain." Jackson nodded and rode on up to Kemper's house, his staff following, some still laughing. To this day, I believe Jackson was serious about the court martial.

I turned my attention to Pepper and examined him for wounds but found only some minor scratches on his belly and two of his legs, nothing of any consequence. "Scared you, didn't it?" I grunted at him.

"Sure did!" he replied in a high-pitched whinny. It at first startled me, but I heard snickers coming from the other side of Pepper and looked under his belly to see one of Carrington's gunners about to split a gut laughing. Others who had been in on the joke burst out laughing then, and we all had a good belly-grabber at my expense. Lord knows we needed it.

Chapter 11 – "I must have those guns!"

I thought we were going to get a chance to rest, but the sound of cannon fire coming from the northeast signaled a major engagement. Frémont had found his courage and was colliding with Ewell who was sitting on well-chosen ground near Cross Keys. After delivering my dispatches, I mounted Pepper and started on my trip to rejoin Taylor. His services no longer needed at Port, he had been ordered to reverse his march to rejoin Ewell. I caught up with them as they arrived on the field of battle and found the fight mostly over. Our brigade was held in reserve and only lightly engaged, while Ewell fought Frémont to a standstill even though heavily outnumbered by the Pathfinder. Night found the lines basically unchanged, and both sides settled into an uneasy truce.

Jackson made his plan for the morrow, and it was a daring one. He intended to engage and defeat two armies on the same day. He would secretly withdraw Ewell's force during the night, leaving only Trimble and Patton's regiments to hold the line against the timid Frémont. He planned to move his army across the North River then the South River and attack Shields, expecting to dispense with him by 10 a.m. and then return to give Frémont his share of the drubbing.

The Louisiana Brigade, being closest to the Port, moved out first and marched for Port Republic. Behind us the rest of Ewell's division slipped from their positions under the cover of darkness and followed our lead. Trimble and Patton redeployed to face the Pathfinder should he find his courage again. At the Port, our Pioneer Corps was busy building a makeshift bridge of wagons placed end to end across the South River at the Upper Ford. Boards were placed in the wagon beds to form a surface for us to walk on. Jackson planned to have the bulk of his army across before dawn. But that makeshift bridge would prevent that from happening. As we crossed, it began to give out, and we could cross only in single file and slowly at that. The schedule fell hopelessly behind, and units backed up at the bridge waiting to cross. No amount of urging could get the infantry to plunge into the swollen river and use the ford. The bridge was our only means of getting across.

The Stonewall Brigade had crossed long before we arrived at the Port and were already moving down river with Jackson. Federal pickets were encountered only a mile and a half out, and by 7 a.m., Jackson was heavily engaged. Advance units of Shields's army under Brigadier General Erastus B. Tyler held solid positions that stretched along Lewiston Lane, a road leading from Lewis Mill on the South Fork of the Shenandoah to the Coaling, a little more than a half mile from the river.

The Coaling was used to make charcoal from trees felled in the foothills of the Blue Ridge and sat on a finger ridge of the Blue Ridge with a commanding view of the wheat fields between it and the river. The Yankee line was solidly anchored by the river on their right flank and the Blue Ridge on their left. We would be forced to cross open wheat fields while under galling musket fire from their Lewiston Lane positions and artillery fire from both the center of the line and the heights of the Coaling. The artillery positions on the Coaling were, by far, the most dangerous. From their elevated position, the six guns there were able to sweep the entire battlefield. The enemy had chosen the ground well.

Uncharacteristically, Jackson plunged into the fight with only a part of his army available for action. He had only the 5th Virginia, 27th Virginia, 4th Virginia and the 2nd Virginia regiments plus Poague's battery of smoothbores and Carpenter's Parrott guns.

The Louisiana Brigade had just crossed the bridge and stopped for breakfast when the battle started. The rest of the army was on the other side of South River and moving across only slowly. Jackson began throwing his units into the fight piecemeal instead of waiting until he had massed enough of his army to give him numerical superiority, something he usually avoided doing. The 5th and 27th Virginia waded into the wheat field and came under heavy musket fire from the Lewiston Lane line. Accurate artillery fire from the guns on the Coaling cut gaping holes in the ranks of the Virginians. Jackson sent the 2nd and the 4th Virginia around through the woods along the base of the Blue Ridge in an attempt to flank the guns on the Coaling. The artillery and the infantry supporting the guns quickly ran them off.

Our available artillery was smoothbore guns and lacked the range to duel with the Federals, but Carpenter brought his rifled Parrott guns into action near the center of our line and shelled the Federals on the Coaling on an attempt to silence them. Since the Coaling was elevated, most of his shots went high and did little damage.

Meanwhile, the Virginians caught out in that wheat field were being slaughtered. Their advance stalled, they soon began to fall back under heavy pressure from the Federals. Dead and wounded were left on the field, and the trampled and shot wheat dripped blood.

The first Louisiana unit to arrive on the field was Kelly's 8th. Jackson immediately sent them after the Union guns on the Coaling. Taylor arrived at the front soon after and reported to Jackson. As I waited nearby, I had a chance to scan the battlefield, and in spite of Pepper's nervousness, I was able to get a good clear look at the problem. I could see our Virginians pinned down in the wheat field to our front and left and being cut to pieces by the guns on the Coaling. I immediately saw what others already had: Those guns on the Coaling had to be taken, or this fight was likely lost before it got good and started. I also saw that Old Jack thought it a job made for the Tigers.

"Delightful excitement," he said dryly to Taylor in an attempt at sarcasm. He then turned to Lieutenant Robert M. English and said simply, "Take General Taylor around and take those batteries."

Shields' boys knew what they were about, and I knew then we were in for a real fight this time. We had finally met our match, and I figured they weren't very likely to give up those guns without a full-fledged kicking and spitting catfight to the finish. One of Jackson's staff leaned over to me and whispered, "Good luck, Captain. Two Virginia regiments just tried to take that position and got run off right handily." That only served to confirm my suspicions, and my stomach knotted. I almost wished Pepper would turn tail and run, taking me with him this time.

English led us off to our right flank and into the woods at the base of the Blue Ridge, and we soon found our movement impeded by the dense understory. I was forced to dismount and use my sword to hack my way through the brush and mountain laurel. Jackson detached the 7th Louisiana and sent them to aid the battered Virginians in the wheat field, and the Tigers were added to that meat grinder. The Virginians and the 7th Louisiana charged back into the wheat field only to falter at a fence crossing the field about half way and roughly parallel to the Lewiston Lane. Only a few dared cross that fence, and they soon regretted it. Hunkered down behind the fence, the Confederates tried to make a stand of it, but the Yankees poured musket fire into their ranks, cutting them down. And the Coaling's guns poured shot and shell into them from above.

We were still hacking our way through the woods and making slow progress. The Coaling was out of sight, so we had to move to the sound of the guns, our only guide to their location. Taylor intended to move us past the Coaling to attack it from the rear if possible, or at least on their flank. We took a higher route through the woods than did Kelly who was somewhat below us and also having a rough go of it. In some places the understory was so thick, we had to get down on our hands and knees to crawl through. Out on the plain, our boys were taking a terrible beating as they waited anxiously for us to bring them some relief by taking those cursed guns.

We broke out of the woods onto a narrow logging trail and followed it in the direction we thought would take us around the Coaling. Soon the sound of the cannons was to our left. Thinking we were on the flank or even behind the Coaling, we turned and marched directly for the sound of the guns. Our skirmishers found the edge of the woods at the same time Kelly and the 8th did. We had both come out at about the same place, almost directly in front of the guns and only slightly on their left flank. A steep ravine stood between the Coaling and us, but the Yankees were not yet aware we were there in the woods opposite them.

On the plain below, the Federals came out of their positions on the Lewiston Lane and charged our boys in the wheat field. They had little choice but to break and run. The Yankees shot them down as they ran, bayoneting those who stood and fought or were too hurt to escape. Across the field they swept, pushing the Virginians and

Louisianans back. Ewell had arrived on the field with some of his division and moved to the right between the Coaling and the wheat field in an attempt at flanking them and putting himself in a position to support us if possible.

We were still in the woods, attempting to form into line for the charge when a cheer went up from the Federal line. With that, we knew they were winning. There was no more time to waste. Ready or not, Taylor ordered a charge immediately. The Tigers surged out of the woods with a yell and into the ravine and up the other side. The gunners on the Coaling turned in shock to see us scrambled up the side of the ridge screaming at the top of our voices. Wheat had his horse shot out from under him by the infantry supporting the guns. He calmly stepped off his dead mount and continued on foot waving his sword over his head. I was already on foot as I had left Pepper in the woods with some of the other mounts.

Down on the plain, they heard our wild yells, and all eyes turned to the Coaling as the Tigers from Louisiana once more took center stage and charged headlong into the most formidable obstacle on the battlefield. Surprise was in our favor, and the gunners did not have time to turn the guns on us. We were upon them before they could, shooting, slashing, bayoneting and busting skulls with clubbed muskets. They soon abandoned their guns and skedaddled. We could hardly believe our good fortune! The six guns on the Coaling were ours!

At the same time, Ewell slammed into the Yankee infantry's left flank in the wheat field and sent some of their number running. On the Coaling, we were cheering, slapping each other on the back and laughing in celebration of our success, but it was short lived. Artillery fire from the guns on the Lewiston Lane cut through our ranks, and we looked and saw their infantry massing for an attack. They wanted those guns back and were coming to take them.

Someone yelled, "Kill the artillery horses!" Without them they could not retrieve the guns, even if we were evicted from the Coaling. Wheat drew out his Bowie and immediately began slashing the throats of the artillery horses nearest him. The rest of us joined in, shooting them in the head or slashing their throats. The frightened and wounded horses screamed as we moved among them killing them with no mercy. Soon the Coaling looked like a slaughterhouse with dead and dying horses mixed among the dead Union and

Confederate soldiers. Blood flowed in little rivers down the road and sides of the Coaling. It was impossible to take a step with out getting your feet covered with bloody red mud.

The Yankees were soon upon us in force, and we were pushed off the Coaling and down into the ravine and into the woods again. The gunners then turned their attention back to the wheat fields to continue the slaughter. Taylor attempted to regroup his mixed and confused regiments for another go at the Coaling but had little luck at organizing us into units again. We went back anyway. Some of Tyler's sharpshooters behind the Coaling were making our lives miserable, so Taylor sent two companies after them.

Once more, the Louisiana Brigade poured out of the woods with a yell and into the ravine. All eyes on the fields below again turned to the Coaling as we surged forward, yelling like demons and charging up the steep side of the ravine. The Yankees tried to remove the guns by hand, but we put a stop to that. We were soon upon them in fierce hand to hand fighting. These were the most determined foemen we had yet met. They fought until we pried the guns away from them once more and sent the gunners and the infantry running. We did not have time to cheer and celebrate this time as Federal brigades were veering out on the field and coming to save the guns. Their fire was galling, and we were forced from the Coaling once more and back into the woods.

As we regrouped in the woods once more, a courier arrived with a message from Jackson that said simply, "I must have those guns!" A wounded and exhausted Tiger said sarcastically, "If he wants them so bad, why don't we all just take up a collection and buy him some damn guns!"

Federal infantry appeared to have control of the Coaling in numbers greater than our shattered brigade could stand against. Taylor looked around at his blown and demoralized brigade and considered his options. More Federals were arriving on the Coaling and forming to charge the pesky Rebels to be rid of them once and for all. Taylor looked at the swelling ranks of Blue Coats on the coaling and said, "Well, boys, there's nothing left for us to do but set our backs to the mountain and die hard!"

That wasn't exactly what I had in mind, but like Taylor, I saw few other options with a solid wall of Blue Coats advancing toward us. We had given it our best against a determined foe and had been beaten in a stand-up fight. Our exhausted brigade staggered into line to make a stand and began loading muskets. To our left we heard loud thrashing in the bushes and feared we were also about to be flanked. Who should appear but Ewell riding up and swinging his saber at the entangling vines and bushes like it was a machete? We gave a wild yell for our lone reinforcement, but on his heels were the 44th and 48th Virginia Regiments. With the Virginians in support, we had a chance of making another go at the guns a success.

With wild abandon and screaming Rebel yells, the Tigers immediately hurled themselves at the Coaling one more time. A shell exploded under Ewell's horse and instantly killed it, but Ewell, focused on those guns, simply stepped off and continued on foot, waving his saber and kepi over his baldhead. Over the top our line of screaming Tigers surged, and the Yankees were forced once more to abandon the guns. So sudden was our charge that Ewell's Virginians were little able to catch up with us, and by the time they did, the Coaling belonged to the Tigers from Louisiana.

In the wheat field, the Virginians and the 7th Louisiana were surging across the field as the Yankees fell back. Our batteries put shot into the infantry facing us near the Coaling. They stiffened, fired off a hasty volley and skedaddled.

Ewell formed a scratch gun crew from some of his Virginians, and they manhandled one of the guns around and turned it on the enemy. I gathered some Tigers, and we did the same with one of the other guns. I quickly directed them how to fight the gun then took command. "Swab the bore!" A Tiger ran the swab down the bore to extinguish any sparks remaining. "Canister, double load! Cut the charge from the second load." Two Tigers shoved two loads of canister into the bore, the second with the powder charge removed, and then the rammer rammed it home.

I sighted the gun, adjusted the elevation, and pierced the powder bag through the priming hole with the prick. "Stand clear!" I took a quick look around to ensure none of our men were in danger of the shot or the recoiling gun, then inserted the friction primer and stepped away the full length of the lanyard. Turning my back to the gun, I yanked the lanyard. The gun roared, and I quickly turned to see where my shot went. It cut a swath through the Yankee ranks.

"Reload! Swab the bore!" And we repeated the steps, this time faster because of our experience. I called for an exploding round this time, "Shell! Three second fuse!" I sighted the gun and pierced the powder bag. "Stand clear!" After a quick check I inserted the friction primer and once more turned my back and yanked the lanyard. This shot upset a gun carriage on their line, disabling the gun. We continued the fight in this manner until there were no more Federals to shoot at. They had all skedaddled with our men in pursuit. By then most of Jackson's army was on the field, and we enjoyed numerical superiority.

I stood beside my gun and looked around the Coaling for the first time and was shocked at the sight of so many dead men and horses. In some places, they were stacked more than two deep. We must have killed fifty or sixty horses. One was still standing, having fallen against a tree after being shot in the head and looked almost alive. I was told that many came and marveled at it for days after the battle. We lost 19 officers and 269 men at Port Republic, the highest casualty rate of any of Jackson's brigades in that fight.

When I turned back toward the wheat field, I saw Jackson come riding up to Ewell and said, "Was that you fighting that gun, General?"

"Yes, sir. Captain Joubert was in command of the other gun, and he did a fine job. Some of my shots went high, but his were dead on the target."

Jackson nodded. "I would expect no less from the captain. I personally trained him at VMI." With that, he saluted, turned and left.

With the destruction of Shields having taken longer than anticipated and no time left to turn on the Pathfinder, Jackson had given up on his plan to engage Frémont and recalled Patton and Trimble. He had them burn the North River bridge once their troops were all safely across. The Pathfinder arrived to find the bridge destroyed and deployed his cannon along the river on the far side and contented himself with shelling the parties giving aide to the wounded on the Port Republic battlefield, hurting and killing his own fellows as well as Rebels. We were forced to abandon the wounded as long as Frémont persisted with his misguided efforts to inflict harm upon the Confederates.

The Valley Campaign ended on this note. Stonewall Jackson, with an army of some 16,000, had out-generaled three Union generals and handily defeated them and their armies that totaled 90,000. By maneuver and deception, he had kept the Federals guessing as to his exact strength and whereabouts, and in so doing, had kept the initiative. Major General Thomas J. "Stonewall" Jackson was the hero of the south, and his army of Foot Cavalry was adored and praised in song and poem. Our deeds were heralded across the south as a great victory for the cause. Even some papers in the north reported the campaign as it actually happened instead of as a northern victory, which it most assuredly was not.

As for the Tigers, we had proven our mettle. In General Ewell's official report after the battle, he said, "To General Taylor and his brigade belongs the honor of deciding two battles—that of Winchester and Port Republic." Taylor had made good on his promise to have his boys remembered for something other than our disreputable behavior. The Louisiana Tigers emerged from the Valley Campaign with a reputation as an elite brigade of fierce fighters to be feared in battle and who lived up to their colorful nickname.

19 June 1862

Jackson has had his way with the Union armies in the Valley, handily defeating them and sending some from the Valley in full retreat.

Even the "Richmond Wig," which seems to favor the exploits of the Virginia units to the exclusion of all other volunteers, heaped praise upon the Tigers. The Wig stated that the Louisiana Brigade virtually won the battle, and that the world produces no better fighters than the Louisianans. They even suggested there was a little touch of the very devil in the Tigers.

CHAPTER 12 – AN OLD FRIEND

As Jackson's Army departed the Shenandoah Valley, his weary Foot Cavalry trudged up the Brown's Gap Road that would take us across the Blue Ridge Mountains, effectively ending the Valley Campaign of 1862. Blue and I rode side-by-side, the both of us exhausted from the last few days of marching and heavy fighting. At the foot of the Blue Ridge, we passed a farmer's field where thousands of Federal prisoners were being held in preparation to be moved east. The number of guards seemed insufficient for the number of charges they were responsible for.

I felt sorry for the prisoners. They had been thrust into an unknown situation as captives of their enemy and were unsure of what their fate might be. Most of them were mere boys very new to army life and death. I, on the other hand, was seasoned by my experience with the Brave Rifles before the war, then the war's first major bloodletting the previous summer at Manassas, followed by a month of hard campaigning with Jackson in the Shenandoah Valley. As a result, I had become hardened to the sight of mutilated bodies, the smell of death, and all the uncertainties that are a part of the killing fields. Most of these boys were not yet inoculated against the horrors of war, and fear of the unknown showed in their faces as we rode past that field.

At first I did not hear my name being called out, but Blue brought it to my attention. "Someone calling to you, Cap'n Ethan?"

I halted Pepper and turned in the saddle. Then I heard it! "Ethan! ETHAN!" coming from the field of prisoners.

I turned to the long line of prisoners along the split-rail fence watching us pass and saw a prisoner waving his arms at me. "Ethan!" And there was the familiar, grinning face of Miles Herndon, my old roommate from VMI.

"Miles?"

I dismounted and led Pepper over to the fence. "Miles, what are you doing here?" It was a silly question, but the first to come to mind. I motioned to a guard to allow Miles to cross the fence to come to me.

He threw his arms about me in a bear hug of an embrace. "I figured you would be with Fool Tom when I realized Taylor's Brigade was part of the Valley Army." He stepped back. "Captain Davis, eh?"

"Captain Herndon?"

"Yes, I'm with the Quartermaster Corps posted in Washington."

"Then, what are you doing in the Valley?"

"Banks was peeved about how some of the supplies he was requesting were reaching him, and I was dispatched from Washington to determine the nature of the problem. I was in Winchester when your boys arrived somewhat sooner than we expected and bagged a bunch of us before we could get out of town. So, I'm your prisoner." His smiling expression changed to one of concern. "What do you think they will do with us?"

"You'll be paroled. We have no facilities for housing large numbers of prisoners. I expect you'll be back in Washington, enjoying a fine meal and a soft bed inside of two weeks, a month at the most."

"That's a relief!" He said. "What of your family, Ethan?"

I really did not care to discuss some of what had transpired concerning my family, considering how my friendship with Miles had been damaged when he left my sister standing at the alter, so-to-speak. But such would not be my choice to make.

"Captain Joubert!" I turned and saw Captain Daniel Wilson of the 7th Louisiana gesturing to me from the road. "I wish to personally convey my thanks to you. I understand you were commanding one of the captured guns on the coaling. Fine shooting, sir! Fine shooting, indeed! The 7th was being slaughtered in that wheat field. You helped turn the battle. My compliments, sir!" I nodded and thanked him before he touched the bill of his kepi and marched on.

Miles looked at me questioningly. "Captain Joubert?"

I ignored that question. "You asked about my family? Analee is fine, or was last I received a letter from her a month ago. Peyton is dead, died of pneumonia last winter. And Sarah died nearly two years ago."

"That would have been right after we broke up?"

"Yes, after we arrived home."

His expression grew grave. "How did she die?"

"She hung herself."

"Oh no! Ethan, I'm sorry."

"My mother called it a broken heart, but there was a lot more to it than you breaking the engagement."

"She broke the engagement," he reminded me.

"While that may be true it isn't completely accurate, and you know it."

"I never thought she would—"

"Nor did the rest of us. Let's just let it go, Miles."

He changed the subject. "Your father?"

"Morgan died a year ago in April."

"How did he die?"

"That answer is complicated. Let's leave that one alone, also."

"My word, Ethan! What of Rachel? You did marry her?"

"I did not."

His mouth fell open. "I'm thinking there's a story here?"

"And you would be correct. Morgan was her father."

"She's your sister?"

"She is not."

"Now, I'm confused."

I shrugged. "That's why my name is Joubert and not Davis. So, now you know."

He nodded as that sank in. "I will assume your real father is named Joubert and leave it alone."

"Pernell Joubert, and yes, best to leave it alone."

"Where is Rachel now?"

"I don't know. When she found out Morgan was her father, she ran away."

"Still thinking she was your sister?

I nodded

"And you don't know where she went?"

"I've gotten two letters from her, but she gave no clue where she was. Says it would hurt too much to be near me now. She may have sought help from her old roommate from that school in England, Miriam Hupmann. I think she is from up north somewhere. When Rachel and I were corresponding through your father's business and Miriam, do you recall anything of where she might be from?"

He slowly shook his head. "Nothing comes to mind, Ethan."

"I can think of no other place for her to go and was hoping you might remember something."

A lieutenant excused himself for intruding. "Captain, we have to begin moving the prisoners now."

"I understand," I replied then turned to Miles. "I must go. My compliments to your family when you see them."

He nodded. "One more thing, Ethan. Aimee has been very worried about you. She reads every paper she can get her hands on to look for your name in the casualty lists. I'll tell her she was looking for the wrong name."

"And give my compliments to Mademoiselle de Beauchamp when you get back to Washington. But tell her not to worry about me."

I had not seen Aimee in almost two years and was glad of it. While I did feel affection for her as an old friend, I was convinced she was potentially dangerous for me to be around. On that night Rachel and I spent together, she suggested as much herself, and I detected a bit of jealousy on her comments, which was understandable. While Rachel and I were being kept apart by Morgan, Aimee and I were socializing, and she even pretended, quite happily, to be my fiancé in my attempt to convince Morgan I had forgotten all about Rachel.

Aimee was a beautiful woman, but she was indeed dangerous.

29 June 1862

The Hupmanns again received bad news. Miriam just told me her other brother, Gregor, was killed at Port Republic. Herr Hupmann flew into another of his rages and struck Miriam. He seems to somehow blame her for being alive while her two brothers are dead.

130

Doctor J tried to reason with him, but he would not hear of it. He called Doctor J some awful names for having me living with him.

Miriam fears for her father's sanity.

1 July 1862

I was having one of my moods yesterday. Of course, the always-astute Doctor J noticed and questioned me about it. "I should imagine what has happened to you is once more weighing on your mind?"

"How can it not? So many dreadful things have happened to me: the loss of my home, my baby, the man I love. Ethan and I were—are—deeply in love, and I knew it almost from the moment I met him, though I did not understand what I was feeling then. What Morgan did to separate us only seemed to deepen our love and devotion to each other. Ethan used to tell me there is a future written for us in heaven, and I believed it. God had brought us together, so how could we not be made for each other? He let us taste what we were sure was our future then He ripped us apart in a most violent manner. I was devastated when I learned Ethan was my brother, and we could never be together as husband and wife. I am sure he is just as pained as I am. That was the first blow, then came the pregnancy followed by the spontaneous abortion, and I was sure God was punishing me for something terrible I had done—or we had done. How can God allow two people to love each other so and yet tear them apart?"

Doctor J made his usual huffing noises when he disagrees with you. "So, you think God is in this?"

"He must be," I replied.

"There was a time when I might have believed that. Like you, I had the love of my life, and from that union came my precious daughter. Like you, I have neither today. I could not understand how God, if He even existed, could be so cruel? We are whatever we are. Our circumstances are self-made."

"Circumstances are self-made? But that does not explain how or why Ethan and I are separated now. Did we self-make that?"

"No. You are merely the victim of circumstances. There is no God moving providentially in our lives," he insisted.

"If that's true, then what do we have to live for?"

"Each other and only each other!"

I sighed as I thought about that. "No! I cannot accept that. There is a God, and He did act in our lives. He did bring Ethan and me together, and He did it for a reason. There is something good that must come of all this." I looked at him. "You have read the Bible. What does Romans 8:28 say?"

"And we know that all things work together for good to them that love God, to them who are the called according to his purpose." He pursed his lips. "I used to believe that."

"You used to be alone and unhappy. What are you now?"

He smiled. "I am no longer alone, and your presence in this house makes me happy."

"Then perhaps all that has happened to you had a purpose?"

He became angry and leaned forward in his chair. "God killed my wife and daughter to bring you here?"

"That is not quite what I meant, and you know it! God took your wife and daughter to build you up, not take you down. Which way you go depends on how you respond to the circumstances."

He seemed stunned. "If that applies to me, it also applies to you, does it not?"

"Indeed, it does. I am compelled to believe that God has a purpose in what happened to Ethan and me. Thank you for helping me to see that again! And I submit to you my presence here is for the benefit of both of us. God is doing something through both you and me, whether we believe that or not."

Miles was paroled and back in Washington before the month of June was out, and he went straight to Aimee de Beauchamp's apartment.

Aimee heard him announce himself to the maid. "Miles? We heard you were taken prisoner," she said as she came out to greet him with a hug and pecks on the cheeks. "I was worried about you."

"I am very much alive. They paroled me."

She turned to the servant. "Brandy, please."

"Come, Miles, tell me all about your adventure."

The brandy was served, and Miles took a seat on the settee. "I was captured in Winchester. The Rebs were upon us before we even knew it. We didn't think they could move as fast as they did. They call them 'Jackson's Foot Cavalry' because they march so fast."

Miles belted down his brandy and poured himself more. "And you will never guess who I ran into."

"Ethan?"

"Yes, Ethan. He is a captain on Dick Taylor's staff. Evidently, he has made quite a name for himself. I heard an officer with the 7th Louisiana congratulate him on his heroic actions in the Battle of Port Republic."

"How is he? Is he well?"

"Appears to be fine."

"Rachel? Did he mention Rachel?"

Miles smiled. "Indeed he did. And you are going to love this." Miles told Aimee everything I had conveyed to him.

"So, he isn't married?"

"Not married and doesn't even know where she is. It would appear that as long as she does not discover Ethan's real father is this Pernell Joubert, she will not reveal her hiding place to him. He has received letters from her and tells me she is so distraught over all this she feels as if she cannot ever be around him again."

Aimee let out with a laugh. "This is incredible! I have never heard such a tale of lost honor and deceit in all my life." For a long moment, she thought about what Miles had told her. "Where is he?"

Miles shrugged. "Somewhere in Virginia. Jackson has joined Lee. Wherever the Army of Northern Virginia is, there you can expect to find Ethan."

She lifted her head confidently and smiled a very broad smile. "Then I shall go to him; now, while Rachel is out of his life and he is in need of consoling."

Miles looked at her with an expression of complete unbelief. "Are you crazy? There is a war going on. You can't just go traipsing around battlefields as if it were Pennsylvania Avenue."

"Why not?"

"They won't allow it; besides, it is too dangerous!" he exclaimed as he poured himself another brandy.

"Miles, look at me. Can you think of anyone else who could do this?"

He shook his head. "You are going to use diplomatic credentials, aren't you?"

She smiled again. "Indeed!"

"And your father will approve of this?"

"He will sign them."

5 July 1862

I am beginning to think Doctor J is a Copperhead. He frequently receives southern newspapers from his friend in Richmond and seems favorably disposed to the southern states rights position, although he remains much opposed to slavery and secession. His getting these newspapers does allow me to keep up with the

Louisiana volunteers and Ethan. The reporting in northern papers is obviously slanted and rarely mentions southern units. I can also read the casualty reports to see if Ethan is listed. So far, he has not shown up in any, although I did get a scare when a Davis was listed as killed, but it was not Ethan, thankfully.

I questioned him about this, and his answer was a bit vague, but I did learn more about his history. "I was born in Virginia and went to school there."

"So, you are a southerner at heart?"

"If you wish to see me that way, then so be it," he replied in an attempt to end the discussion.

But I pressed him. "And your friend in Richmond?"

He huffed. "We went to school together in Paris and remain in touch. That's all!"

I let the conversation drop there. He needs to have some privacy.

I have completed the three new commissions and collected my payments, which went immediately into the bank. Doctor J is still acting as my agent and has brought in two more commissions for portraits, and a third for a painting of a local home. While portraits are my specialty, I can do a passable job on architectural subjects. The money will be helpful in replenishing my reduced financial resources. My mother left me some money, and Morgan managed it well enough for me, but sending me to two expensive schools to keep me away from Ethan reduced the total considerably. I need the commissions to live on or find myself a husband, and I do not feel inclined to find one just now.

15 July 1862

Miriam is gone.

With the loss of his second son, her father sank into a stupor and refuses even to eat. I know the feeling well and sought to speak to him in the hope I could express to him that I knew how he felt. It was to no avail, He threw me out of the house and forbad Miriam to ever speak to me, someone of such low moral character, as he put it.

She packed him up and took him to Baltimore, where they have relatives and put the house up for sale.

I shall miss her. We were such good friends in school, and she tried to stand by me when her father kicked me out of his house.

Chapter 13 – Aimee and the Mechanic

After being summoned to General Taylor's tent just before dawn, I made my way across camp with the morning dew heavy on the ground. "You sent for me, Sir?"

He pointed to his left. "He did."

A young man I had not noticed before stepped from the shadows beside the tent. He looked fresh out of school, clean-shaven and almost baby-faced. He was medium height with dark hair and eyes. He was a handsome man but something struck me about his appearance: he seemed very restrained and deadly serious, and his face showed no emotion. I figured he was someone's aide. "Captain Riddle, at your service, sir."

I acknowledged his introduction. "I am Joubert. How may I help you?"

He opened his dispatch case and handed me a document. "Your orders, sir. I'm to escort you back to Richmond."

"It says I am to report to the Secretary of State. Am I in some kind of trouble?"

"I would not be at liberty to say even if I knew, sir."

"When do we leave?"

"Immediately, I need to get you there this day."

I turned to Taylor, who had watched the whole proceeding. "It seems, sir, that I must leave."

"Hopefully, your services will not be needed for an extended period. I need you here."

I alerted Blue that we were leaving for Richmond and gathered up my kit, saddled Pepper, and we were off. Captain Riddle was silent the whole trip and mostly ignored my questions and attempts to make small talk. I did learn he had traveled all night to come for me. We arrived later that evening, and I was billeted at the Spotswood Hotel, owned by Louis D. Crenshaw, who also owned the "White House of the Confederacy," which was not actually white but a shade of gray.

Bright and early the next morning, Captain Riddle arrived and took me to the Virginia State Capitol Building, which was being used by the Confederate government. As we climbed the stairs to the second floor, I marveled at all the activity even at this early hour. Gray uniforms were everywhere in evidence. At the top of the stairs I was led to a small office where Captain Riddle announced me to the secretary, "Captain Joubert to see the Secretary of State."

The man looked up from his work, nodded and went to announce us. He came out a moment later and bade us enter. "He will see you now."

We entered the office of the Secretary of State of the Confederate States of America, the Honorable Judah P. Benjamin, and Captain Riddle receded into the shadows of the office like someone who wished not to be noticed.

Mr. Benjamin was a rather stout man, barely over five feet tall, with soft features, a round face, dark wavy hair and beard sans moustache, a rather handsome fellow. He was sometimes known as the "Hebrew" or the "Israelite," and at other times, the "brains of the Confederacy." He was, by all reports, very intelligent, an attorney from New Orleans. Before the war, he had twice been offered nomination to the United States Supreme Court and refused the offer both times. Though a Jew, he married a New Orleans Catholic, Natalie Bauché de St. Martin, and they had one daughter. Both mother and daughter resided in Paris during the war. He stood and came from behind his desk, a warm smile on his face and his hand extended. "Captain Joubert, thank you for coming on such short notice."

"At your service, sir," I replied.

"Please forgive me for the urgency, but your presence was required immediately." He seemed nervous. "Please accompany me down the hall, and we shall tell you how you may be of service." Benjamin led the way, I followed, and Riddle silently fell in several paces behind me.

At the end of the great hall, we entered another office and again went through the announcing of visitors. "I will tell the President you are here."

The President?

After the secretary came back out and indicated the President was ready to receive us, Benjamin bade us enter. Once inside the President's office, Benjamin approached Davis, and Riddle once more stayed in the background and blended into his surroundings like some two-legged chameleon.

President Jefferson Davis, a very distant relation to my deceased stepfather, was a slender man with angular facial features. With only a tuft of a beard under his chin, he reminded me of a clean-shaven Abe Lincoln.

Benjamin began. "Sir, this is the officer of whom I spoke, Captain Joubert."

Davis stood behind his great desk. "Good day to you, Captain. Thank you for your haste."

"I am honored. How may I be of service, sir?"

Before he could answer, we were interrupted when another gentleman, an aging brigadier, entered the office. "My apologies for being tardy, gentlemen."

Davis did the introductions. "General Winder, this Captain Joubert, the officer we spoke of earlier."

Winder nodded. "Captain Joubert."

"General Winder," I replied with a nod. I was somewhat familiar with the general and his responsibilities to rid the capitol of its many Yankee spies. He was a heavy man with tight lips on a jowly face and a full head of gray hair. His uniform was impeccable, which some said was one of the many bribes he was accused of taking.

"General Winder," said Davis by way of explanation, "is the provost martial of Richmond and the man responsible for catching that Pinkerton spy, Timothy Webster."

"I heard about that. You are to be congratulated, sir."

"Thank you, Captain. It was nothing at all. Simply a day's work."

Davis turned to Benjamin. "Will you please answer the good captain's earlier question about why he is here?"

Benjamin looked slightly perplexed as if unsure how to begin. "Sir, are you acquainted with Mademoiselle Aimee de Beauchamp?"

I groaned inwardly. "Yes, sir. We are friends. We met five years ago."

"What do you know about her?" asked Benjamin.

I did not like where this was going. "Not a lot, lovely girl, bright, intelligent. She has a twin, Annette. Her father is a diplomat posted in Washington."

"When is the last time you communicated with her?"

"She wrote several letters to me when I was in New Mexico with the Brave Rifles before the war. I replied only once, and it was short, only to assure her I was fine. Why, sir, are you asking about her?"

Benjamin ignored my question. "No communications since then?"

I shook my head. "No. I lost contact with her after that. Haven't spoken to her since before the war. Did she do something I should be aware of?"

"She is here in Richmond," replied Davis flatly.

That surprised me. "For what purpose?"

"We were hoping you might know that."

"Why would I know?"

"Because she showed up three days ago, presented diplomatic credentials to me and asked to see you," Benjamin replied. "We are very concerned about the reason she's here. The fact that she presented diplomatic credentials suggests it is official business, but she did not indicate that. Your thoughts?"

"Her father indulges her. The twins are his very life. He would do anything for them."

"I presume you are not aware that Monsieur de Beauchamp does not seem to have any diplomatic responsibilities at the embassy. If that is true, what does he do for France? Our sources tell us Lincoln suspects him and his daughters of spying. Annette is currently in Britain, and the British also suspect her of being a French spy. Do you see why we are concerned?"

I nodded slowly. "I'm unaware of suspicious activities by any of them."

"It's even more complex than that. As you are probably aware, we desperately need either Great Britain or France to recognize the Confederate States as a free and independent nation. If one of them will do so, the other almost certainly will follow. Such recognition would present many opportunities for the Confederate States that are currently denied us. Lincoln claims we are merely a breakaway warring faction, and France and Great Britain should stay out of American internal affairs. We consider it a possibility that she is here under the cover of visiting you but acting as a spy to determine, for France, our true viability as a nation. If this is her mission, it is absolutely essential that we convince her that we are a free and independent nation capable of standing up to the aggression of the United States, or any other nation, for that matter."

"I see your point."

"Good! But there is yet another possibility: She has been turned and is a spy for the United States working for Lincoln." Benjamin paused, took a breath, and continued, "As if that were not enough to consider, our sources tell us they have detected a plot to kill her while she is here."

I had to think about that for a moment. "If she is killed while under our care, this could damage our relations with France, and we may never get them to recognize us?"

"Precisely," added Davis. "The situation is very complex and very dangerous."

"A plot to kill her would suggest the Yankees are involved," I replied.

Benjamin rubbed his chin. "It would seem so. Regardless, we cannot allow even one strand of hair on that woman's head to be harmed. But we are still perplexed as to why she specifically asked to see you?"

I thought about how I would answer that, and there was no way I could think of that was both honest and not embarrassing for me. "There is something else you should know. She is in love with me—or thinks she is. She also knows I am pledged to another, but that person is currently lost to me. I suspect she was told this by a mutual friend, Miles Herndon, my old roommate at VMI, who is serving with the Union Army. He was captured at Winchester, and I spoke with him before he was paroled. I'm betting he went straight to Aimee and told her everything I told him about my current plight concerning the woman I previously mentioned. She now sees a chance to win me."

Benjamin looked at me with a confused expression on his face. "You mean she's here because she's love-sick over you?"

"No, she's here because she's crazy."

"Indeed!" exclaimed Winder. "I suspected as much. She is not a spy but merely some love-struck, silly female. We are wasting our time with her."

Davis glanced briefly at Winder before leaned back in his chair and looked first to Benjamin and then me. "That may be true, Captain, but it does not change the intelligence we have that she may be the target of an assassination attempt. And it still leaves open the door that if we can convince her we are a nation deserving of recognition and admittance into the family of nations of this world, she will carry that message back to her father and ultimately to Napoleon."

Benjamin picked up the conversation after a brief pause to think about what the President had said. "If this is about her being in love with you, it can actually help. She will listen to what you have to say to her. But until she leaves, we must protect her at all costs."

"Indeed," added Davis, "she must be protected!"

Benjamin nodded toward me. "Captain, you will have the responsibility of guarding her and seeing that she learns whatever she needs to learn to convince her that France should recognize the Confederate States. She knows you, wants to see you, so you will be the one to escort her during her stay with us."

My first thought was *there goes any hope of a field command.* First, I was Wheat's gofer, then Taylor's, and now the Secretary of State and President of the Confederate States of America. I suppose that could be considered advancement.

Benjamin continued, "I have read your war records and several field reports by Taylor and Jackson, and both speak highly of your abilities. Good head on your shoulders, a reliable man for a sensitive job. You will need help, of course, and that will be Captain Riddle and his associates. I think you'll find Captain Riddle very capable in spite of his boyish looks. His men are presently guarding Mademoiselle de Beauchamp."

I turned to Riddle, still in the back of the room leaning against a bookcase. He nodded to me. To Benjamin I asked, "Where is she?"

"Room 208 of the Spotswood Hotel. She has been told to expect you today."

"What am I supposed to do with her?"

Davis smiled. "Whatever makes her happy, Captain, whatever makes her happy. We will prepare a list of places for you to show her and things we want you to stress to her."

Benjamin stood, indicating the interview was closing. "Meanwhile, you need a new uniform. Yours looks like you have been fighting a war, if you get my jest? Captain Riddle will see to that before you go meet Mademoiselle de Beauchamp. We will expect daily reports. Good luck to you, Captain."

As Riddle and I made our way down the stairs, I stopped him and asked, "You work for Winder?"

He shook his head and made a disapproving face. "He's a bumbling old fool. He knows no more of espionage than does my horse. Benjamin understands that even if Davis doesn't."

"Then for whom do you work, and just what is it you do?"

He looked at me for a long moment as if he were determining how much he should tell me. Slowly a faint smile crossed his lips before he replied. "I work for whomever needs my services. Right now, that's Benjamin. What do I do?" The smile disappeared and his eyes narrowed. "You might say I'm a mechanic. If something needs fixing, I fix it, but if something needs breaking—I break it."

I decided I had very likely underestimated Captain Riddle.

It was past noon. In my new uniform custom tailored in a matter of only two hours, I stood staring at the number 208 on the hotel room door with my hand poised to knock. Riddle had already sent his "associate" to stand watch at the end of the hall, and he stood about twenty feet away expressionlessly watching me. I rapped lightly on the door twice.

And that melodious voice of the ever-lovely Aimee de Beauchamp answered from the other side. "Who is it?"

"Your knight in shining armor," I replied.

"Ethan!" And the door swung open! She looked up and down the hallway, saw Riddle, and fairly dragged me inside, slamming the door behind me. Her arms wrapped tightly about my neck, and her mouth was upon mine. I immediately had a mental vision of her and that Christmas past under the mistletoe at the Herndon Estate, and her offer came back to torment me—the offer she made for me to marry Rachel, and she would be my mistress, no questions asked and no demands.

"Aimee! Please stop!"

"No! I will not stop!" And her lips locked on mine again.

I pushed her away. "Aimee, please."

She acted hurt then. "I forgot. You do not like to kiss me."

"That is not true, and you know it."

Suddenly her tone changed as if what had just transpired had not. "Miles told me how you lost Rachel. Ethan, I am sorry, truly I am."

I did not believe that for a second. She was glad I lost Rachel, and that was why she was here. I tried to change the subject. "So, Miles was paroled?"

She ignored my question. "My, but you are handsome in that uniform."

"Yes, a recent acquisition," I spit out, somewhat annoyed at being her chaperone and having to deal with her feminine wiles. "Aimee, I was serving on Taylor's staff in the field when I got called to Richmond to find you were here and asking for me. My dear, you do realize there is a war going on?"

"Of course I do. Can you imagine what I had to do to get through the lines?" she fairly barked in her French-accented English. Then her demeanor changed again, and she smiled. "But it was worth it to see you again and find you well."

I told Davis and Benjamin I thought she was crazy. When I said that I meant it only as a half-truth exaggeration, but in these few moments with her, I was not so sure it was only half true.

"I must get out of here. They have kept me cooped up in this room since I arrived. Let's go for a walk. Maybe have some coffee?"

That sounded like a good idea. I wanted to get away from that bed in the next room. I wasn't sure how Riddle would feel about that, but I decided he would have to live with it. As soon as we opened the door, he was there. "We're going for a walk and coffee." He nodded and fell in behind us about thirty paces.

Her arm in mine she leaned against me. "Who is that?" referring to Riddle.

"Just a mechanic."

She nodded and seemed satisfied by my answer.

We made our way down the stairs and out to the banquette in front of the hotel. A four-gun battery of rifled Parrott guns and their crews passed the hotel as we came out the door. The gunner's uniforms were as new as mine, and I knew they were just arrived to

142

the fighting. The streets of Richmond were crowded with military and civilian pedestrian traffic, and with so many uniforms in evidence, it had the appearance of an occupied city. I had earlier seen a coffee shop a few blocks away and headed for it.

As if on some holiday, Aimee frequently stopped to window shop along the way. Riddle stayed about thirty paces back. "The styles are so out of date here," she said commenting on some dresses in a window.

"Lincoln's Anaconda blockade prevents much by way of consumer goods from coming in from Europe. War material gets priority."

As she was examining the goods in yet another shop, I glanced in the glass of the window near the recessed entrance and noticed the reflection of a man about fifteen paces back who seemed very interested in Aimee. I turned to get a better look at him and he turned away, pretending interest in something down the street. Riddle was some fifteen paces behind him and seemed unconcerned, so I brushed it off as my imagination playing tricks on me.

We moved further up the street, and she found yet another window to examine in great detail. "Oh, Ethan. It may be dated, but this bonnet is lovely, don't you think?"

I wasn't paying attention, because I had picked up the reflection of the same man I had seen before. I was sure of it. He was wearing a brown suit with satin trim on the collars and a dark brown bowler pulled low to hide his eyes. Riddle was nowhere to be seen, lost in the crowded street. So as not to alarm Aimee, I quietly released the flap on my holster and suggested we enter the store. She hesitated. I insisted and pushed her inside. "Go to the back of the store and wait for me there!"

"What is this all about?" she asked in a huff.

"Just do as I say, and do it now!"

My tone must have frightened her, and she immediately moved to the back of the store. I positioned myself at the door where the man could not see me unless he tried to enter, and that's what he did. I stepped up to the door as he opened it. My very serious expression and my hand on the butt of my pistol must have startled him, for he turned and started to leave as his hand went into his pocket.

When he turned, he found Riddle blocking his way. Riddle quickly grabbed his hand and twisted it behind his back and pinned him against the window glass. "Steady there, fellow!" he said as he put even more upward pressure on his twisted arm. Riddle whistled and two more of his "associates" suddenly appeared out of nowhere.

"I didn't do anything!" the man in the bowler bellowed as Riddle's men forcefully dragged him down the street.

Riddle turned to me. "Good catch, Captain! I saw him following you and suspected he was up to no good. Moving her into the store and ambushing the suspicious gentleman was a nice move. However, I would prefer you stay with her and let me handle the other—shall we say—problems. How is the lady?"

I turned and saw Aimee standing nearby with a questioning expression on her pretty face. "What is this all about?"

Riddle nodded. "I will leave that question to you, Captain." He turned and left the store.

The coffee shop was only three doors away. We found a table near the back where I could watch the front entrance and detect trouble in time to get her out the rear or take other defensive actions.

The coffee served, she asked again with concern in her expression and voice. "Ethan, what happened back there?"

"Perhaps nothing. We were just being cautious."

"Why? And who is that mechanic, as you call him, and the other two who suddenly appeared?"

"They're here to protect you."

"From whom?" she asked indignantly.

"Aimee, we have information that someone may want to harm you."

She gasped. "Why? No—don't answer that. The idea is absurd!"

"It isn't as absurd as you think. We believe someone may try to kill you while you are here."

Her defiant tone faded. "You are serious, aren't you?"

"Very!"

"Why?"

"Think about it. You are here on diplomatic credentials. For you to be killed or hurt while under our care could be very damaging to relations between France and the Confederacy, and at a time when good relations are critical to this country." I glanced at the front door as a new patron entered, a woman and her soldier companion. They looked innocent enough.

144

Aimee was thinking about what I said. "All I wanted was to see you again. Maybe I should go back to Washington?"

"Even if you go back, we would have to escort you to be sure you arrived safely."

"Then I shall stay. There, no more discussion. I will be safe with you and your mechanic friend watching over me."

That was not what I wanted, but I had a feeling the President and the Secretary of State would not want her leaving so soon, since none of their efforts to convince her of our sovereignty had even been initiated.

That night we had dinner in the hotel dining room with Riddle hovering protectively nearby. I saw her to her room and managed to escape her clutches once more before Riddle and I reported to Secretary Benjamin.

Benjamin began. "What happened?"

"Captain Joubert detected a suspicious person following them, and he took actions to protect our charge. When I saw what he was doing, I moved to assist. We arrested the suspicious person."

"The man you arrested—and roughed up—was the son of a judge. He claims he was merely smitten by Mademoiselle de Beauchamp's beauty and wanted to get a closer look at her. The fellow is known as a bit of a rounder, so his story fits his history."

"He put his hand in his pocket. I thought he was armed!" I protested.

"All he had in his pocket was a handkerchief. We apologized to him and his father. They seem to accept that. On one hand, this error is disturbing, but you should know that I understand the complexity of your assignment. It is better to ere on the side of caution than for your charge to be harmed. We will handle any complications that may arise. But, please, do try not to kill anyone unless you're sure they are a real threat."

Benjamin withdrew a paper from a folder on his desk. "Captain Joubert, here is your agenda for the next few weeks. At the bottom of the page is a list of points we want you to stress to Mademoiselle de Beauchamp. But first we want to test her and determine what she is up to. I suspect she is a spy. If she is, I want to confirm that, because we may be able to use that against the North."

Chapter 14 – To Trap a Spy

Benjamin proposed a simple test to determine if Aimee was indeed a spy: We would feed her certain information and see if that same information showed up on the other side in the form of briefings, telegrams, orders, etc. How he would know if it did was something he did not see a need to explain to me. The first test was I would casually drop into a conversation that Lee was very sick, and it was being kept quiet for obvious reasons. I did slip that tidbit into a conversation over dinner the very next night.

Not four days later, Riddle and I were summoned to the Secretary of State's office. We were no sooner seated, and Benjamin announced, "We just received information that McClellan got a telegram stating that Lee is believed to be very ill."

"Who was it from?" asked Riddle.

"Not sure, but it is thought to be from Pinkerton. McClellan has been using Pinkerton's Agency for intelligence purposes."

"That would suggest that Aimee is working for Pinkerton?" I added. "But that makes no sense; Pinkerton was McClellan's spy, and Lincoln fired Little Mac. Pope leads the Grand Army of the Potomac now. Why would Pinkerton be involved in this?"

"McClellan is using Pinkerton and Mademoiselle de Beauchamp to get back in Lincoln's good graces?" offered Riddle.

"Pinkerton must have figured out she was spying for France and turned her, and when they found out about her feelings for me, he figured to use that to get her into our confidence."

"Quite likely," muttered Benjamin with a nod.

"That would suggest that the rumor of the threat to her life may have been started by Pinkerton to throw us off his scheme?"

Benjamin nodded again. "Yes. If we think the Yankees want her dead, we would not be inclined to suspect she is working for them."

Riddle became very pensive before asking, "Very well, but how is she getting the information to Pinkerton? She is watched twenty-four hours a day. She has no contact with anyone but Captain Joubert and those few we introduce her to."

"Good question," replied Benjamin. "That is something we must determine, and quickly so we can manage it." He thought for a moment. "I propose another bit of false intelligence be leaked to her. This time we tell her that Lee has made a remarkable recovery and has resumed active command."

I dropped that bit of information into a conversation the very next morning at breakfast. A short while later, Aimee suddenly felt ill and asked to be taken back to her room to lie down for a while. This raised my suspicions. As I was leaving her room, I found Riddle waiting down the hall and immediately told him what happened.

"You may be right, Captain. Something seems to be afoot here."

"Why her room? Does she have some communication device there?"

"Possibly. I'll station a man across the street to watch for any strange behavior around her window. Keep watch here while I see to it."

I nodded, and Riddle hurried off to post someone on the building across the street to watch her window. It seemed he was gone a very long time as the room linen service had come and gone before he returned.

"It's set," he said, "Any strange activity here?"

"None."

A few hours after she returned to her room, Aimee felt better and peeked out to see if I was still there. She asked to be taken for a walk and maybe a light lunch.

I spent the next three days escorting her around Richmond showing her munitions factories and stocks of military supplies. All the while, she acted as if I was her betrothed and we were deeply in love. I went along with this to the extent I felt comfortable with, but I was worried I might be giving her the wrong impression of my feelings for her. But Davis said do anything that makes her happy. I had long concluded there would be a limit to how far that would go.

Three days later, during our debriefing, Benjamin reported to us that McClellan had received a telegram, this time Pinkerton was identified as the sender, and it informed McClellan that Lee was fully recovered.

Riddle shook his head. "How did she get it out? We were watching her every minute! There was no suspicious activity associated with her window."

As I sat there, I considered the last three days in detail. I ruled out the third day and possibly the second day, because that would not have allowed enough time for the intelligence to get up north and be disseminated to McClellan unless they used telegraph to get it out of Richmond, which was unlikely. I reasoned it had to have been sent the first day. If so, how?

Riddle was also considering the problem. Suddenly, his face lit up. "Wait! Captain, you said the hotel linen service came into her room while I was setting up the observation site across the street?"

I smiled. "Yes, and I believe you have just discovered how she did it."

Benjamin added, "We have long suspected spies associated with that hotel. Many people important to the Confederacy and the war stay there while in Richmond. It would be a perfect place to collect intelligence."

Riddle's mind was still on the linen service. "The same Negro girl works that floor every day, but sometimes Mademoiselle de Beauchamp is not in the room when she comes."

"And maybe she doesn't even have to be there to pass the information?" I added. "Maybe she leaves a message hidden somewhere in her room for the girl to find?"

Riddle nodded affirmatively. "That's it! Very well, we must plant more information for her to send north, and we'll search her room to find where she is hiding it."

Benjamin devised yet another lie to pass to Aimee. This time I told her the army was running dangerously short of gunpowder. The plan was that I would tell her late in the evening when I brought her back to the hotel for the day and get her out early the next morning to give Riddle enough time to search the room before the linen service came, which was usually after nine in the morning and before ten.

That evening over dinner, I mentioned the gunpowder "crisis" in the Army of Northern Virginia. After dinner we took our leisure along the streets of Richmond before returning to the hotel. We walked in the moonlight, her arm in mine, her head resting on my shoulder, just like old times when I was a cadet at VMI, and Aimee and I had met first at the Herndon party and later spent time together in Washington. Had I not known I was "romancing" a spy, I might have even enjoyed my time with her that night just as I had years before. While she had nothing of Rachel's personality, Aimee's being more conniving with her affection for me mainly on the physical level, she did remind me of Rachel in build, hair, blue eyes and beauty. And at times she could be very charming. By comparison, Rachel's feelings for me were deep and genuine, not that the physical attraction wasn't there, but it was more a means of expressing the love she had for me, and I for her. Aimee's was more lust and the filling of the need to be wanted and to control her partner. She was manipulative and loved seeing men grovel at her bedside.

I represented a real challenge to her. I had not realized it at first, but because of my fidelity to Rachel, even after Aimee's multiple hints and one outright offering of herself to me, I had become for her a "prize," in a manner of speaking, and she felt compelled to win me at any cost. That knowledge meant I must be ever watchful around her, lest she break down my defenses. As enticing as it was, I did not want to fall into that trap. To do so might mean she would gain control over me. For Rachel, wherever she was, I refused to allow that to happen, but Aimee was persistent.

When I dropped her off that night, she playfully pulled me into the room and, with a mischievous grin on her pretty face, she threw her arms around my neck and pressed herself against me. For a long moment she just smiled up at me then rimmed her lips with the tip of her tongue. I knew what was coming. And it did! She drew herself even closer, and with parted lips, kissed me hard. It had been a long time since I had been kissed so, and that had been with Rachel over a year before at Catahoula when we spent the night together—the night before we were to be married—the night she showed me just how much she loved me—the night before we were torn apart and I lost her.

I imagined it was Rachel in my arms—Rachel's lips on mine—my hands tracing the curves of her body—and I so dearly wanted it to be her—so much so I very nearly gave in to Aimee's advances. "NO!" I pushed her away.

"What is wrong? Don't you want me?" She smiled that coy smile of hers. "I know you do. Rachel will never know. You will never see her again, and you know in your heart that is true. Over a year! And the war prevents you from even searching for her, and you don't even know where to look. She will have married another and moved on by the time you find her, if you ever do."

She was right. Rachel would never know—but I would. And it was true I was prevented from looking for her with her trail already over a year old. It would be even colder before the war was over, and I could resume my search. And it was true the longer it took me the more likely Rachel will have found another and moved on as Aimee charged. But I was not going to give up yet. I was still convinced God had paired Rachel and me, and that had to stand for something. But there were times I would forget that and turn to strong drink to numb my fears and doubts, and I was sinking into that state of doubt at that very moment. Then something Blue once said came to mind, "Adversity makes you better or bitter, but you choose which."

"I will pick you up at eight in the morning." And I turned and left. Aimee slammed the door behind me.

Riddle was waiting just down the hall and smiled. "I think you pissed her off."

I did pick her up at eight, and we had breakfast at a restaurant near the hotel, while Captain Riddle searched her room for her means of communicating with her handler.

Later that evening after touring more sites designed to convince her the Confederate States should be recognized by Napoleon and I had dropped Aimee at her hotel, we met with Secretary Benjamin. I arrived late after Riddle had already briefed Benjamin. "What did you find?"

Riddle smiled. "She is indeed leaving notes for the linen girl."

"Where?"

"It was too easy. I found it in less than five minutes. She writes the note on hotel stationary and leaves it as the last sheet in the stack. The linen girl must sneak it out in the dirty linen."

Benjamin added, "There was more there than just the false information we planted. Riddle says there were other details of military importance in the note."

"What now? We send her home, and I can get back to my job with Taylor?"

Benjamin shook his head. "Not yet."

I groaned inwardly.

"We understand little Mac is back in command after the recent whipping they took at 2nd Manassas. We use this and feed the Yankees a lot of false information. I have even arranged to get General Lee involved. Tomorrow you will take her to Lee's headquarters. He is preparing to launch an important new action, and we want to make Little Mac think Lee is headed somewhere other than where he will be going, and he is anxious to get moving before the North recovers."

Riddle and I walked out together. "Something else you should know, Captain. I found a bottle of laudanum in her belongings. Know any reason she would be using that?"

I thought about that for a moment before I answered. "I've never known her to use opiates before. Maybe she has some physical issue that is causing her pain, and she takes it for that?"

It was the second of September when we arrived at Lee's headquarters by carriage. Riddle and one other associate rode along as our bodyguards with Blue driving the carriage. We arrived in camp and, as fate would have it, passed through the bivouac area of the 1st Louisiana. Many of my old friends still alive stood gawking at the beautiful belle passing through their camp. Many reverently took their hats off. Eventually, the few who could take their eyes off her recognized me sitting beside her.

"Look! It's Captain Joubert in the carriage with her!" one yelled as he trotted along beside the carriage. "Where'd ya find such a pretty lady, Captain?"

Aimee smiled, enjoying every minute of it. "Friends of yours?"

"Best friends!"

By the time we reached Lee's headquarters, we had a large entourage trotting along beside the carriage shouting greetings out to Aimee. She waved and smiled at them. They stopped suddenly as we neared Lee's tents and held back but stood around to get another glimpse of the ever-so-lovely Mademoiselle Aimee de Beauchamp.

An officer directed Blue to bring the carriage up to the ring of tents where we were to dismount. Lee had come out to see what the commotion was about and was soon joined by Generals Longstreet, Jackson, Stuart, Pickett and several others.

The ever-gallant cavalryman, J.E.B. Stuart stepped up to the carriage and offered to help Aimee down, which she graciously accepted. She had them in the palm of her hand. Even Bobby Lee was beaming at the sight of her. I hastened to introduce her to Stuart and then stepped aside and allowed Aimee to spread her charm.

Stuart immediately introduced her to Lee, who bowed and kissed her offered hand. "Enchanted, Mademoiselle!" he said. And I do believe he was.

"General Lee, I have heard so much about you and your exploits since assuming command of the Army of Northern Virginia. Up north, your name is on everyone's lips."

"And I suspect preceded by more than a few words unspeakable in polite company?"

She smiled broadly. "And you suspect right, mon général. But much of it is indeed with high regard for your leadership. You are much feared and respected."

While these pleasantries were being exchanged, I looked around, and it occurred to me that the camp had likely been cleaned up and uniforms and bodies ordered washed, because the troops looked better than I expected they would. Their uniforms were badly worn and patched from months of hard fighting, most of which I missed caring for Aimee, but they were clean and as neat as could be expected under the circumstances, although many of the men were shoeless.

Aimee was introduced to the rest of the party before they retired to tables covered with white tablecloths for a light meal and refreshments. I hung back and was soon joined by Riddle. "My word, Captain, but she is a charmer!"

I looked to Riddle. "That she is, at least when she wants to be, but I suspect there is also a bit of a show being put on by Lee and his generals to impress her. She will be shown things she would never have expected to be shown as they feed her all manner of mostly useless information. My guess is she'll need a whole ream of hotel stationary to make this report."

Riddle smiled and then let out a small chuckle.

"Riddle! At one time, I thought you completely humorless. What has gotten into you?"

"A man has to let down the facade once in a while. Besides, I have nothing to break just now."

That night we had a grand soiree at a nearby plantation home. Several of the officers had their wives in attendance, and the matron of the plantation and her daughters acted as hostesses. The band from one of the divisions played lively tunes for singing and dancing. Aimee was the center of attention. Even the other women were attracted to her. And the generals very nearly fought duels to dance with her.

I waited outside and was joined by Jean and Sean. "Well, I was wondering when you would show up? I was hoping you two were still above ground."

Jean laughed. "Came close during the 2nd Manassas scrap. The ball holed my jacket and bruised my ribs. Luckily, it was near spent when it hit me. You missed a good one there, Ethan—er—I mean Captain Joubert."

"And since he was made a lieutenant," snorted Sean, "The lad has gotten right cocky."

"I see that, and well deserved, in spite of what the little Irishman here thinks."

After a long pause and in a solemn tone, Jean said, "I guess you heard Wheat was killed at Gaines Mill?"

"Yes. A sad day," I replied. "After he survived his wounds last summer, I could not imagine a ball that could strike that giant down. Many changes. Wheat's Battalion was disbanded, and Taylor was promoted to Major General and sent to Louisiana?"

"Aye, we'll miss him, but not his attitude when his 'tiz is acting up. He can be downright nasty when sick," said Sean.

"The brigade wanted to go with him, but David refused. We also heard he wanted to take you with him," added Jean, "but that got slapped down right quick. And seeing as what you have been doing the last couple of months, I would be very thankful he didn't get his way." He glanced toward the dancers inside. "Now, I'm assuming that is not Rachel?"

"Not Rachel! Not even close. Pretty like her, but definitely not her."

"Any word of the fair Rachel," asked Jean in a more serious tone.

"None."

"What's the story on *this* lovely lady ya brung with ya?" asked Sean.

"That is Mademoiselle Aimee de Beauchamp, and old friend come to visit me, and I have just about had my fill of her. Been escorting her around for over two months now and getting right tired of being out of the real action."

Jean turned and glanced inside to see Aimee dance by the window in the arms of Stuart. "And why the special treatment?"

"Long story and one I am not at liberty to speak about. Someday I'll tell you, but not now."

We departed the next day, but not before Lee had filled her pretty head with nonsense. Several Richmond newspaper reporters were allowed to interview her, and a photographer took pictures of her with Lee and several other general officers. At Aimee's insistence, I was dragged into that one.

Upon arrival back at the hotel in Richmond, Aimee claimed she was exhausted and wanted to retire early. I suspected it was to write her report. I took her to breakfast early the next morning, and Riddle searched her room while she was gone. Just as we expected, he found a written report that filled eleven pages of hotel stationary, which the linen girl faithfully retrieved when she serviced the room.

After that, things got a bit complicated.

It all started three days later after Lee had already crossed the Potomac in his invasion of Maryland, I was walking Aimee back to her hotel late in the evening. As usual Riddle was tagging along about thirty paces back. By then he had assigned his other associates to other duties, so only Riddle and I were guarding Aimee. We believed there was no real threat to her life, considering she was working for Mr. Lincoln and company. We were wrong.

It was late, and the streets were nearly empty of pedestrian traffic, when I noticed three men with determined expressions on their faces walking toward us. Riddle and I had previously established a series of signals to communicate certain situations to each other. For danger in front, I was to look back at Riddle and then point to the threat. But when I looked back, I saw three more gentlemen behind Riddle also looking very determined and advancing up behind him rapidly. Riddle saw the surprised expression on my face and immediately knew there was a problem, but from which direction? I yelled, "Behind you!"

He spun and the three were but a dozen paces from him. I don't think I have ever seen a man move as fast as he did. He reached into his coat and withdrew a Colt from its shoulder holster. As he did so, the three also came out with pistols.

I immediately spun and saw the three in front of me were closing the distance at a brisk pace and drawing their weapons. I slipped the flap on my holster and drew my Colt as I grabbed the totally unaware Aimee and dragged her toward a nearby alley.

I think Riddle got off the first shot and dropped one of the three to our rear. The other two likely got off the next shots, and one nicked Riddle in the shoulder.

All three in front of me fired off shots, and all three missed, because I was moving and dragging a screaming Aimee along with me. Moving targets are hard to hit. I finally got off a shot and hit one just as we reached the safety of the alley.

Riddle was blazing away at the two behind him as he moved toward our alley and put another one down. One pistol empty, he drew a second from another shoulder holster as he reached our alley. "Anyone hurt?"

"Not yet, and I want to keep it that way!"

"Take her up the alley and find a way out! I'll cover you from here!"

Aimee had stopped screaming but was obviously shaken. I grabbed her arm and moved her deeper into the dark alley. It made a turn and went behind a building. Empty, discarded crates and other trash made moving down the alley difficult. Behind us, I heard Riddle get off a few more shots in answer to those directed at him. Shortly, he rounded the corner and joined us. "I am empty! Hold them while I reload!"

I didn't have much of a choice. The alley was a dead end illuminated only by the light from two windows above. We were trapped! "Aimee, get down behind those crates and stay there until I call you!"

She nodded and did as I said. Riddle took up a position behind some empty crates across the alley from me and continued the arduous process of reloading his revolvers. I was down the three chambers still charged. One of our assailants stuck his head around the corner, and I let fly a round that chipped the bricks near his head. That encouraged him to stay back. I was down to two rounds, and Riddle was still reloading, but he was putting caps on the nipples, so I knew he was near finished.

One of them showed himself and made a dash across the end of the alley to the cover of empty crates on the other side. As he dived for the cover, I got off a shot but missed. Behind the crate, he felt safe. But I figured it must be empty, so I estimated about where he might be in relation to the other side of the crate and put my last round through it. I heard a moan and saw his hand and arm appear at the base of the crate and not move. I had obviously hit him.

By then Riddle was reloaded. "I've had enough of this! Get reloaded so we can end it!"

I worked the rammer as fast as I could. As I was capping the nipples, one of our adversaries stuck his pistol around the corner and let fly an un-aimed round intended to get us to duck. I knew they would be rounding the corner next. And they did. Both Riddle and I stood and worked the hammers of our Colts as fast as we could. We each put at least three rounds into both of them.

The gunsmoke slowly drifted away as we stood there looking at three dead men at the end of the alley. "You hurt?" asked Riddle out of the side of his mouth.

"Not touched, but looks like you might have been hit." I pointed at his shoulder.

"Oh that? Didn't even know it was there."

We moved cautiously down the alley to be sure there were no more assassins and found none. Riddle turned to me. "Stay with her. I'll check the street."

We had taken out all six in a short but intense gunfight, but the need to reload had convinced me I needed to get a second Colt, or at least a second cylinder for faster reloads.

I retrieved a very shaken Aimee as the police arrived alerted by the gunfire. Riddle handled them, while I tended to Aimee. "Are you hurt?"

She shook her head. "No, just shaken. Robbers?"

"I think not. Assassins. Your friends up north may have decided you are of no more use to them. Killing you in Richmond would have seriously damaged what relations we have with France."

"Then, I can't go back up north."

"That may be the only place you're safe. Up there, they wouldn't dare allow any harm to come to you after we protected your life. It wouldn't look good for them."

Her hand went to her lips. "You know?"

I nodded.

She gasped. "What will you do with me now? Am I to be hanged?"

"No. You'll be sent home."

"Ethan, they made me do it. They told me I would be hanged as a spy, and they would also arrest my father and hang him, too. I'm sorry."

"It doesn't matter now. You did what they wanted, and they got certain information, which they wanted. You are of no more value to them, which is why they tried to kill you. They wanted to use that against us. In another month or so, we'll let them know we knew all along, which will make you even less useful to them. I suspect your dealings with Pinkerton are over."

"It wasn't Pinkerton but someone who said they worked for him."

"Makes sense. It isn't Pinkerton's style to kill his informants."

Our little gunfight made the news in Richmond. Benjamin made sure to stress that the assailants were from up north to discourage any more attempts on her life. Aimee's protection detail was increased considerably, and Benjamin quickly made arrangements for her to sent north before anything else could happen to her. Riddle and I, along with a detail of cavalry, escorted her to the agreed meeting point on the Potomac River upstream from Washington.

A boat crossed the river to retrieve her with her father as one of its passengers. He embraced his daughter as soon as his feet hit dry land. After their emotional greeting, he scolded her, "I told you this was a bad idea!"

"I know, Papa. You were right, as usual. But there is more you need to know. I'll explain later."

I suspected her father didn't know she had been turned. He then said to me. "Captain Joubert—or Davis—whatever your name is, I wish to thank you for protecting my precious Aimee. She will not be a problem for you any longer. I'm being recalled to France, and she will be coming with me."

"Monsieur de Beauchamp, you should know that your daughter and I are very close. I would never allow anything to happen to her if it were in my power to prevent it. Take her home and please keep her there."

He nodded. "Merci!"

Aimee stepped over to me with that mischievous grin on her face again, and I knew I was in for trouble. She slipped her arms around my neck and stood on tiptoes, her lips almost touching mine. "So, Captain Joubert, you do care for me? You just told Papa so." With that she kissed me with a passion that should be reserved for the boudoir. Monsieur de Beauchamp turned away and pretended interest in their rowboat.

I disengaged from her grasp and helped her into the boat. As they began the crossing back to the other side of the Potomac, Aimee waved and threw me a kiss. Once again, Mademoiselle Aimee de Beauchamp was out of my hair, hopefully, for good this time.

As I watched them cross back over the Potomac, I though about how close I was to Rachel at that moment. She was on the other side of that river somewhere. "Riddle, may I ask you a question?"

"Of course," he replied in his usual soft, even tone.

"If I were to go look for someone over there, what would be the best way to go about doing that?"

His twisted little smile returned. "You mean go find Rachel?"

I turned and looked at him questioningly. "What do you know of her?"

"Depends on which of the many stories circulating is true. I do know you lost her, and she's over there somewhere." He nodded toward the north.

"By 'many stories,' what do you mean?"

"The story of you and Rachel is well known in the Army of Northern Virginia. I first heard it about six months ago and several more versions since. You two are legendary. Sometimes the names are not exactly right, and the details can, at times, be a bit fuzzy or even expanded upon. The men who tell it and those who hear it are deeply moved by it, a tale of love, honor, and fidelity in the face of extreme adversity—with hope for a brighter future. And that's what they need right now—hope."

I was astonished. "I didn't know this."

"You need to write a book about it after you find her, and based on my experience with you these last couple of months, I am quite sure you *will* find her. You have any clues to work with?"

"I think she went to the home of her friend from school, Miriam Hupmann, but I don't know where Miriam lives."

"The campfire legend says she came north on a ship and landed in New York. Is that true?"

"Yes."

"Then I would start there and find that ship's captain. Hopefully, she said something to him or someone else on that ship that might give you a clue. Otherwise, you are doomed to searching city directories for Hupmann. If it comes to that, I would start in states with large German and Dutch immigrant populations: New York, Maryland and Pennsylvania. Start with the larger cities and you might find this Miriam or a relative who knows where she lives. But that'll be the hard way."

"I can't do much until this war is over."

"I have associates up north and will make some inquiries for you. Maybe we'll get lucky."

"I would appreciate that."

"No problem."

"You know, I don't even know your first name."

He frowned. "It's Silas."

"Why don't we dispense with the rank and you just call me Ethan."

He nodded. "Very well, and you can call me Riddle."

I guess he didn't like his first name.

Riddle and I spent a three more days in Richmond with Benjamin getting our reports straight before we parted ways, and I was released to rejoin my brigade. Because of the danger we had shared, we had formed a bond. He was still mostly an enigma to me, but he liked it that way. It was his protection, because the little "mechanic" often operated under the threat of exposure and even death, especially when he needed to break something. The fewer people who knew any details about him the better.

5 September 1862

Lee has crossed the Potomac into Maryland and taken Frederick, Maryland!

10 September 1862

We are now hearing that some Confederate units have moved as far north as Middletown and Hagerstown just across the border from Pennsylvania! This puts them as close as 30 miles from Gettysburg. Some of our friends in Gettysburg are in a panic over this, and I questioned Doctor J about it.

"No need to fret," was his answer. "They'll not come as far north as Gettysburg. Lee is not capable of sustaining such an invasion. I suspect he's taking advantage of his recent victory and the fact the Army of the Potomac is in such disarray. He may also be in need of food for his army. Surely, Northern Virginia has been picked clean by now, but McClellan will eventually drive him back across the Potomac."

"Ethan will be with them!" I blurted out.

"Does that worry you?"

"Yes. He might find me!"

"Even if they came to Gettysburg, it is unlikely he could discover you are here. I should think he would be more concerned with fighting than searching for you. In the confusion of war, he would have to find you quite by accident. Highly unlikely."

13 September 1862

Doctor J just returned from his walk with a copy of a Richmond paper he received from his friend and offered it to me to read while he made tea. When I opened it, my eyes fell upon a familiar name, Aimee de Beauchamp! The article had an engraving of her with Lee and some of his generals from a photograph taken 2 September.

Doctor J came in with the tea and noticed the shock on my face. "Is something wrong?"

"This picture of Lee and Miss de Beauchamp…"

He set the service down, sat beside me and leaned in to view the paper. "You know her?"

"In a manner of speaking, yes. Ethan knows her well, and that's him on the extreme left in the picture."

"He put his spectacles on to see better. "How can you tell? It is a hand engraving from a photograph."

"I know Ethan when I see him."

"The caption says 'Captain E. Joubert.'"

I stabbed the paper with my finger. "I assure you, that is Ethan!"

"Then why is the name Joubert?"

"An error? I don't know, but that is Ethan, and it says he is the escort for Mademoiselle Aimee de Beauchamp. She lives in Washington! Why is she there? Why is he escorting her?"

Doctor J looked at me with a smile on his face. "Do I detect a twinge of jealousy?"

I glared at him for a moment, but he only continued smiling. "Ethan met her when I was in Britain, and they became close friends. She pretended to be his fiancé at his graduation to convince his father that Ethan and I had lost interest in each other. In letters I received from Morgan, it certainly sounded like she played the part well."

"You are indeed jealous!"

"What do you expect?" I snapped. "I do still love him, you know?"

"How well I do know. Perhaps you should write him again and ask about the name? And perhaps explain this de Beauchamp woman?"

"I shall not do so!" I shut my eyes tightly, for I hated what I was about to say. "Since we cannot be together, I have no right to interfere in his relationships with other women."

Chapter 15 – The Bloodiest Day

After Lee's stunning victory at Second Manassas, which the North called Second Bull Run, the Union army was demoralized, while the morale of Lee's army was soaring. Unfortunately, the army was also exhausted from the fight, and its supplies were depleted. Resources to feed the Confederates in war-ravaged Virginia were also near exhausted, but a rich fall harvest awaited us in Maryland and Pennsylvania. So, Lee decided to take the war to the North to allow Virginia's farmers to harvest what little remained of their crops. Such a move would also end any thoughts Lincoln might have of attacking Richmond and might even initiate enough discontent with the war in the North that Lincoln would be forced to sue for peace.

In spite of the weakened condition of his army, Lee decided to act quickly. Even while we were visiting his headquarters with Aimee de Beauchamp, Lee was setting his plan in motion. While he had asked Davis for permission to take the war north, he did not wait for an answer but crossed the Potomac into Maryland only four days after Second Manassas.

The Union army was once more under George McClellan. In spite of his cautious nature that often allowed opportunities to slip by, he was a consummate organizer, exactly what Lincoln needed for his shattered army.

Lee's movement into Maryland was virtually unopposed, and he easily took Frederick, Maryland. This put the Army of Northern Virginia well north of Washington and in a position to threaten the capitol. Lincoln had to react, and he sent McClellan to engage Lee and defend the capitol.

On 10 September, Lee daringly split his army into four parts. Longstreet and Hill went north and threatened Hagerstown not far from the Pennsylvania border. This aroused the concern that Lee intended to move into Pennsylvania, and he would have, but later circumstances prevented such a move.

Lee needed to secure his supply lines, and that meant eliminating the Union garrison at Harpers Ferry. Once that barrier was gone, he could move supplies up the Shenandoah Valley into Maryland safe from any threat from the Federals. The task of removing that threat fell mainly to Jackson's Corps along with two divisions from Longstreet's Corp, those of John Walker and Lafayette McLaws.

Meanwhile, Lee sought the safety of the western side of the South Mountain, which was really a long ridge rather than a single peak, and used it as a buffer against the approach of McClellan's army from out of Washington to the southeast. That protection lasted but a few days before McClellan eventually flanked the South Mountain passes. But Lee's fighting blood was up, and he withdrew west to the little town of Sharpsburg and chose the high ground on the western side of Antietam Creek to make a stand.

With the collapse of Lee's defenses around South Mountain and withdrawal to Sharpsburg, Little Mac cautiously moved to occupy the void. One of his advance parties stumbled upon a bundle of cigars wrapped in paper that had been dropped by the retreating Confederates. The paper wrapping proved to be Lee's Special Order 191, which spelled out, in detail, the disposition of his disbursed army. Little Mac was ecstatic and told his staff he had what he needed to whip Bobby Lee, or he would go home. Fortunately, he was also convinced that Lee was commanding an army of 120,000, three times its actual size, and that fed his cautious nature. On that same night, Lee received word from a southern sympathizer that McClellen was in possession of Special Order 191, and Lee accelerated the massing of his army around Sharpsburg, thus the intelligence McClellen possessed became useless.

Jackson once said he would rather take Harpers Ferry fifty times than defend it even once, and for good reason. It was in a valley closely hemmed in by high ground. It was impossible to hold Harpers Ferry for any length of time if the attackers held the heights, and Jackson did.

I caught up with the 1st Louisiana and was informed I had been transferred to Jackson's staff and should report to him. After the Harper's Ferry garrison surrendered, he was force-marching his corps to join Lee at Sharpsburg only 12 miles from Harpers Ferry. With the anticipation of a decisive fight at Sharpsburg, Jackson's fighting blood was also up. I found Old Jack near the head of the column.

"Welcome back, Captain. We missed you," he said as I eased Pepper up beside him astride his favorite mount, Little Sorrel.

"It is good to be back, sir. I'm sorry I missed a few fights, but the Secretary of State had me occupied for a spell."

"I understand, and you are forgiven." I was never really sure when he was serious or joking. "We are headed for Sharpsburg, where Lee plans to make a stand. You'll get your fill of fighting very shortly, I'm sure."

We arrived late in the day of 16 September, and Lee deployed us on his left flank facing Meade and Doubleday of Hooker's Corps. Some minor skirmishing ensued as the two sides made final dispositions of their forces.

Blue and I reconnected with our messmates, Sean and Jean, and both were glad to see us again. I think they missed Blue's cooking more than they missed me.

"Well, Captain, what became of that comely French lady you were courting?" asked Jean right off.

"She went back where she belongs, and I am glad to be shed of her."

"Now, if that were me," chimed in Sean, "I would rather be back in Richmond in her arms than here."

"You do not know what you would be in for, sir," I replied sharply.

Jean raised his eyebrows in mock anticipation of some titillating revelation, "Indeed, perhaps you would care to share the details of your conquest with your friends? We lead such boring lives, you know."

"That isn't what I meant," I snapped. "She goes by another name, which is 'Trouble,' and I've had enough of that from her."

Blue handed me a plate of food. "All these boys talk about is women they left behind. That gets kinda old after a spell."

"Never gets old for me," replied Jean.

17 September 1862

The Confederates have withdrawn from the Hagerstown area to Sharpsburg, bringing a great sigh of relief from the residents of Gettysburg. But we hear a battle there has started this very morning.

Doctor J received a two-week old newspaper from his friend in Richmond today, and in it is an article about an attempt on the life of Mademoiselle Aimee de Beauchamp. The article says she was "...facing certain death at the hands of nefarious assassins sent by northern interests to embarrass the southern cause, she was saved only by the quick and brave actions of her bodyguard, Captain Ethan Joubert." The article mentions an unnamed associate who aided in spoiling the attack. The two men "heroically withstood murderous pistol volleys from the six assassins and dispatched all of them." It then adds, "The shaken Mademoiselle de Beauchamp was helped from the scene of this heinous crime by her bodyguard with his arm protectively about her shoulders."

I think I am going to be sick!

It rained that night and into the predawn of 17 September, chilling everyone, but it stopped before sunup, leaving an eerie ground fog hanging low over the battlefield. The day's festivities soon kicked off at 5:30 a.m. when Hooker launched his attack. The early focus of the battle was what would become known as the Cornfield, an infamous twenty acre field of ripe corn standing as tall as a man's head, and a little white building called Dunker's Church beside Hagerstown Pike. The church was so named because its congregation was Baptist and believed in baptism by complete emersion. The brigades of Douglass and Tremble occupied the Cornfield with Hays' 1st Louisiana Brigade in support about 300 yards to their rear. Hays had replaced Taylor after his departure. These brigades were all part of Lawton's Division of Jackson's Corps.

The morning began with heavy cannonading as the two sides exchanged fire across the Cornfield and the pastureland around it. The shelling was so intense that it soon became one continuous roar like one very long roll of thunder, and individual shots became indiscernible. The casualties soon started mounting.

The first assaults came from the north and were quickly repulsed, but Hooker noticed the Cornfield glistening with the polished bayonets of the men of the brigades of Douglass and Tremble and brought up four batteries of artillery to deal with them. The canister shot cut the corn down as neatly as if it had been harvested with a knife, and the Confederates hiding there fell in rows as if in formation.

The Federal line pushed forward, and some of Hookers men entered the Cornfield, stepping over the dead and wounded. But as they emerged on the other side they came under the blistering fire of a Walker's Brigade from Georgia. With but 200 yards separating them, the two sides cut each other down in a bloody exchange of musketry. So many fell that both sides required reinforcement by fresh brigades, and the slaughter simply continued unabated.

By 6:30 Walker's Brigade began withdrawing having lost over one third of its 700 men. Douglass' Georgians had even heavier loses with half of the brigade killed or wounded. Douglass died on the field, and five of his six regimental commanders were also lost.

Jackson saw the urgency of the situation and called to me. "Captain Joubert, report to Hays and tell him to move forward immediately."

"Yes, sir!" I replied, and not wanting to be merely a messenger in this fight, I asked, "Sir, may I remain with Hays?"

Jackson glared briefly at me and reluctantly agreed, "As you wish. Now get to it, man!"

I rode forward and found Hays. "Sir, General Jackson's compliments. He urges you to move forward in support of Walker immediately!"

He nodded and turned to his staff. "We are in it now, gentlemen!" And we pushed off. I stayed close to Hays in the event he needed me to communicate with Jackson.

The 550 screaming Tigers of the 1st Louisiana crossed those 300 yards under murderous artillery fire that cut our fellows down. In spite our losses, we plunged headlong into the Cornfield and collided with the Federals in a bloody melee of musketry, bayonets and clubbed muskets that eventually drove the Yankees back. The 12th Massachusetts received most of the attack.

I caught a glimpse of Jean leading his company and Sean right behind him as they ran, fired, reloaded and fired again. The Yankees were resisting stubbornly and falling back slowly.

We advanced to within 250 yards of the Federal line in the East Woods and faltered against stiffened resistance. Trapped out in the open fields, we were hammered by artillery and musket fire. The dead and wounded fell in staggering numbers.

That is when I saw Sean go down and rode over to assist him. I jumped off Pepper and knelt down and lifted his head, but blood ran from his nose, and he coughed up frothy-red spittle. He was lung-shot and died within a few moments. That is when I felt the impact of a ball striking my body followed closely by a deafening explosion of a shell nearby that knocked me over. I fell across Sean's body, stunned and with my ears ringing. That was all Pepper needed, and he decamped like he had at Port Republic.

For a long moment, I lay there confused. My world was completely silent without even the sound of yelling, musket fire or cannonading. No sound at all! I was thinking I must be dead. If so, I should be face-to-face with the Lord, but where was He? Slowly, the noise of battle came back to me, and reality again took control of my senses. I was not dead! I rolled off Sean and felt for my wounds. I had a sensation of wetness on my left hip and leg, but upon cautiously probing with my hand, I found no wound I could identify as such. I twisted around and saw my canteen had been holed, but I was otherwise unhurt.

Still a bit dazed, I got back on my wobbly feet to see Henry Richardson of the 6th Louisiana shot from his horse before my eyes. His foot became entangled in the stirrup, and he was dragged helplessly around the field by the frightened animal until someone finally shot it.

We were driven back into the Cornfield. The Federals brought up cannons and unlimbered them on its very edge. At point-blank range, the Tigers received their fire and were shot down by the score. I threw myself on the ground and tried my very best to mingle with the roots of the corn plants, as canister balls whistled over my head and cut down Tigers who remained standing. How I was not hit, I do not know.

Hays called for a withdrawal of what was left of his brigade to Dunker Church. I scrambled to my feet and helped a wounded man stand, draping his arm over my shoulder to support him, and together we joined in the retreat while the gunners reloaded. The Federals advanced into the Cornfield, and Hooker's Texans charged right past us and drove the Yankees back, but they, too, were stopped at its edge.

Near Dunker Church, Hays took stock of his losses. In a mere thirty-minute exchange, he had lost over 60% of his brigade. Every staff officer and regimental commander had been shot. Jean was wounded twice and carried from the field waving his fist and loudly cursing the Yankees in French. I helped Hays rally his shattered brigade in case the Yankees came back. And they did.

The Federals poured more troops into the fight and gained the initiative again. Hooker's exhausted Texans were pushed back from the Cornfield. A Confederate regiment broke and ran from the onslaught, and most of the rest of McRae's brigade folded. The Federals reached the high ground near Dunker Church and, short on ammunition, faltered but held their ground. We were pushed back even more. The attack ran out of steam, and by 9:00 a.m., the fighting on the Confederate left entered a brief lull.

To the west of us and north of Dunker Church, Starke's 2nd Louisiana Brigade had entered the fight about the same time as Hays and encountered stiff resistance from the Yankees. Long, rolling volleys of musketry dropped many of Starke's Tigers. Colonel Williams of the Second Louisiana was shot through the chest, and Starke was mortally wounded when three balls knocked him from his horse. Despite the murderous fire and Starke's death, the Tigers pushed the Yankees back. Gibbon's Iron Brigade attempted to flank the Tigers, but Stafford, taking over from Starke, wheeled the brigade to face the threat, and the two sides exchanged deadly fire across a chest-high rail fence. Federal sharpshooters began picking off the Tigers, and a Union battery unlimbered only 75 yards away and poured canister shot into them. The Tigers withstood the fire for fifteen more minutes before the shattered brigade withdrew, fighting stubbornly all the way back to Dunker Church. In but an hour, both brigades of the Louisiana Tigers had been utterly decimated by the Federals and was *hors de combat*.

At about 9:15 Sedgwick's division of Sumner's Corps crossed Antietam Creek and headed straight for the West Woods in an attempt to turn the Confederate left flank. Lee had sent reinforcements earlier, and they hit the Federals. Within minutes Sedgwick lost almost half of his division killed or wounded. Gordon's Brigade came to Sedgwick's aid, and it too was destroyed by the Confederate reinforcements.

French's Division crossed Antietam Creek and veered south toward Sharpsburg, where it ran right into the brigades of Anderson and Rodes hidden in the well-worn Sunken Road with high sides providing an excellent trench-like position to defend. From the relative protection of Sunken Road, Confederate volley after volley poured into French's Division cutting down the attackers. Soon Richardson's Division arrived on French's left, and they too absorbed the murderous fire from the Confederates. The Yankees faltered at the Sunken Road, but some gained the high ground on the flank looking down the road, and from there, laid deadly enfilade fire upon the Rebels taking cover in the road. The Confederates faltered and gave way, leaving behind dead and wounded stacked three deep in some parts of the Sunken Road.

Little Mac had broken the Confederate center, but he failed to take advantage of the opportunity by not sending in fresh divisions to exploit it. The Federal divisions already engaged were bombarded by artillery and eventually forced to fall back.

The fight moved south to the other side of Sharpsburg when Burnside's Corps was thrown back again and again as they tried to cross the little stone bridge over Antietam Creek, which would become known as Burnside Bridge. A Federal unit flanked the position by crossing at Snavely Ford further south and attempted to cut Lee's line of retreat. That was stopped by the fresh arrival of A.P. Hill's Division just up from paroling Yankees captured at Harpers Ferry. Hill turned the Federal left and pushed them back across Antietam.

By 5:30 the Battle of Sharpsburg was over, and though both sides claimed victory, it was, at best, a draw. It could have been a decisive victory for Little Mac had he committed the two corps he so cautiously held in reserve. Total losses for both sides were over 22,000 dead, wounded, and missing in one single day of vicious fighting! One out of every four men committed to the fight became a casualty. The battlefield was littered with dead and wounded. The Sunken Road had become a trench of dead men in such numbers that the bodies had to be dragged to either side of the road and draped over the rail fences to allow wagons to pass through. The sight was sickening to even the hardest veteran on the field. Nothing we had experienced before compared to the horror of that September day, absolutely nothing! The fight left a lasting impression on me, adding to the many things that I already found troubling—and my nightmares returned.

Too weak to continue the invasion, Lee's decimated army limped back to Virginia to lick its wounds and to prepare to fight another day. The ever-cautions McClellan failed to aggressively pursue us.

I rejoined Jackson after being relieved by Hays and found Jean in an ambulance wagon. "How bad is it?"

"Leg and side." He winked then let out a stream of curses in French. "They think they finished me, but I'll show them!" Then he moaned and became pensive. "What about Sean?"

"Gone. I was with him when he died."

The ambulances began moving south, and I went in search of Blue. I found him caring for the survivors, giving them aid and comfort with water and food, or brandy or rum when he could locate some. When he saw me he jumped up. "Cap'n Ethan! When I saw Pepper come trotting up to me, I thought you wuz dead."

"I'm alive but barely."

"I kin see that," he said as he started counting the bullet holes in my uniform. He found four that I was not even aware of. "The Lord was watching over you this day!"

I glared at Pepper standing nearby. "Should have let Jackson court martial you at Port Republic like he suggested! You do that one more time and I'll kill you myself!" He snorted as if he understood, but I doubt he did.

20 September 1862

We are beginning to get more details of the great battle that took place three days ago south of us in Sharpsburg, Maryland. Some of the wounded are returning to their families here in Gettysburg to convalesce. From them and a few scant newspaper accounts, we are hearing the battle was brutal in its violence, and the dead and wounded number over twenty thousand!

I was concerned the Confederates might come all the way to Gettysburg and Ethan might find me, but all I can do now is worry about his safety. Did he survive; was he wounded. Does his lifeless body lie on some field near Sharpsburg, and I shall never look upon his face again?

Doctor J tries to allay my fears, but it isn't helping.

This is just like before the war when Morgan was trying to keep us apart. One day I am happy, well, perhaps not happy but comfortable with my relationship (or non-relationship) with Ethan, but other times it is pure misery, and I worry about him. There are times I wish I did not love him at all and could push him and his memory from my mind, and other times I want him so much it hurts, and the thought of never seeing him again depresses me. My eating habits reflect my emotional state, and Doctor J is worried about me.

23 September 1862

Yesterday, 22 September, the complexion of the war changed when Lincoln issued the Emancipation Proclamation, freeing all the slaves in the south. It will change little for the slaves, because it is not enforceable except in those areas of the south occupied by the Union, and it did not include the Union states. But it will impact the South in other ways. Doctor J believes it will prevent Britain or France from entering the conflict in support of the Confederacy in any form, because the war is no longer about saving the Union. It is now unquestionably about ending slavery, and they will not be seen as supporting that institution.

CHAPTER 16 – THE AWAKENING

The long line of caissons and cannons, ambulances, supply wagons, and weary men crossed the Potomac and slowly plodding south away from the killing fields of Sharpsburg, Maryland. The army was both physically and mentally spent, incapable of taking the field again anytime soon. It needed to rest, to recover, rebuild and re-equip before it would again be an army.

In that September of 1862, the giddy victories of the year before had given way to the soul-numbing realities of a brutal and bloody war. Beginning with the Valley Campaign in the early spring and continuing all summer through to Sharpsburg, what had seemed glorious the year before became for all a dreaded experience that promised only more pain, suffering, and death. Those who believed this war would be over quickly came face-to-face with the sobering realization that it would likely go on for a long while and cost many more lives.

Thomas Paine once said of another war, "These are the times that try men's souls." When a man's soul is tested by the worst of what life can throw at him, especially when he looks death in the face, he becomes contemplative of his mortality. Unnoticed by all but a very few, a change was taking place; an "awakening" was slowly spreading over the army. It would begin in the Army of Northern Virginia and eventually spread to all of the armies of the Confederacy. It would profoundly impact the lives of the many soldiers touched by it, and it would eventually be felt elsewhere in the nation long after the war ended.

I first became aware of its presence during our withdrawal from Maryland. I was dismounted and walking along with Blue as we led our weary mounts south. One of the Tigers from the 1st Louisiana, his face still blackened with gunpowder from biting off the ends of the paper cartridges to reload his musket, a bloody bandage around his head, shoeless, and his uniform in tatters, stepped out of the formation and approached us. "Beggin' yer pardon, Captain, may I have a word with you?"

"Of course," I replied. "How may I be of service?"

That is when I noticed he was weeping, though he tried to hide it. "Sir, I understand you are a good man, a godly man who knows the Scriptures, an' I need to ask ya something."

"What is it?"

"I ain't much for church-goin'. Preachers just seem to preach, but I've seen the Lord in you. I seen you in that bloody-awful Cornfield, how you helped the wounded, protected them, and gave comfort to the survivors when we were driven back to Dunker Church. You weren't 'fraid a nuthin'. They was balls flying all around you, but you weren't scart at all. But I was scart, plumb scart of dying and especially knowing I'm going to hell. An' I don't want to go there. I been through enough hell right here, and I reckon the one in the Bible has be a whole lot worse." He paused to collect his thoughts. "Something happened to me in that Cornfield, and some of the boys said you were the man I need to speak to about it."

I knew exactly where this conversation was going and was a bit taken aback by his comment about seeing the Lord in me. I hardly thought of myself as a pillar of courage and faith, much less the one to show him the light of redemption, considering how I had fallen from grace so many times myself, especially into the use of strong drink in excess and bouts of depression when I had lost faith in the Lord's provisions for me. As long as I was occupied with the war, I was indeed a rock of faith, but when my heart ached for Rachel, I was a complete failure as a Christian. I fully understood that, but I reminded myself that I was only human, a fallen man like everyone on the road that day, and even such a weak vessel as I was could be called to help a man find Jesus. "What's your name?"

"Jacob Watkins, sir."

"Jacob is a biblical name."

"That's what my mother told me. Said I was named after ole Israel hisself."

"Yes, Jacob was the father of the twelve tribes of Israel. It's a good name, a strong name."

He nodded. "Can you help me, Captain? I don't know if I can go on, being as I am such a sinful man. I carouse with women, I steal, I tell lies, and I get drunk, blind stinking drunk! Can the Lord forgive a man like that?"

I pulled him off to the side of the road to the edge of the little creek running along side. Blue, sensing what was coming, took Pepper's reins from me and stood nearby watching silently.

To Jacob I said, "It's true. God cannot overlook our sins. His righteousness demands that they be judged and the punishment, death, be administered, but fortunately for you—and me—someone else was judged for our sins and took the punishment for us."

"Jesus!" His eyes watered even more and a tear broke free washing a clean path through black gunpowder on his face.

"Yes. Do you believe Jesus was the Son of God? Born of a virgin? Went to the Cross and was judged in our place? Died, was buried, resurrected on the third day, and sits on the right hand of the Father today?"

He was making no attempt to hold back the tears. "Yes, sir! Show me where I can read that in the Good Book! My momma taught me how to read!" He reached around and pulled a bloodstained Bible from his haversack and handed it to me.

"This yours?"

"No, sir. I found it in the Cornfield. It was justa-laying there on the ground between a Reb and a Yank, two poor momma's darlin's. It was in a pool of blood, their blood all mingled together. I couldn't take my eyes off it. Something told me to pick it up, and I did. Then I walked out that Cornfield standing straight upright just as pretty as you please with canister shot and Minié balls whistling all around me. It was like I didn't even know they were there, and none of them could touch me, nohow. I knew right then I had to speak to someone about this, and folks said it was you."

I opened the Bible to the Book of Ephesians and handed it to Jacob. Pointing to Chapter 2, I told him, "Read verses 8 and 9."

He took the Bible and studied the words for a moment, then with halting speech began reading, "For by gr—grace are ye saved thro—I mean, through—faith; and that not of yourselves: it is the gift of God: not of works, lest any man should boast." He looked up at me. "This says I can't do nothing to be saved!"

"That's right. Salvation is a gift from God because of your faith."

I took the Bible back and turned to the Gospel of John and opened it to chapter 3 and found bloodstains there. "Now read verse 16 of chapter 3."

Jacob took the Bible, found the passage and began reading as he traced it with a dirty finger, "For God so loved the world, that he gave his only be—begotten Son, that whosoever believe—believeth in him should not perish, but have everlasting life."

"Now read verse 18."

He looked back at the pages of the Bible and moved his finger to verse 18. "He that believeth on him is not con—condemned: but he that believeth not is condemned already, because he hath—hath not believed in the name of the only begotten Son of God."

"Do you see it?"

He looked up at me, the tears flowing freely. He took out a dirty rag and wiped his eyes. "It says I must believe—not work! If I believe in…" he looked back at the passage, "…the only begotten Son, I will not be condemned and I will have everlasting life!"

"Yes, Jacob. If you believe all that I have showed you, you will not go to hell."

"I do! I do!"

He dropped to his knees and began weeping all the more as he clutched my hand and that bloodstained Bible. I touched his shoulder then helped him stand. Through his tears he exclaimed, "My momma was baptized. I want to be baptized like her! Can you do it? Right now, right here in that creek?"

"Absolutely!" We stripped down to our unmentionables and stepped carefully off the bank and out into waist deep water. Others began dropping out of the passing line of soldiers to watch what we were doing. General Thomas J. "Stonewall" Jackson was among those in the little audience on the creek bank.

I had Jacob put his arms across his chest and pinch his nose. I put one hand behind his neck and the other on his forehead. "On the basis of your profession of faith in the Lord Jesus Christ as your personal Savior, I baptize you in the name of the Father, the Son, and the Holy Ghost." I leaned him back and pushed him under the water, full emersion, just like the congregation of Dunker Church would have done.

Jacob came up grinning the biggest grin I have ever seen on any man, and we hugged each other out there in the middle of that creek. Those on shore who understood what had just transpired began applauding. As Jacob climbed out onto the bank, they met him with helping hands and slaps on his back, calling him "brother."

I noticed Old Jack sitting astride Little Sorrel up near the road. We made eye contact and looked at each other for a long moment. I felt amazingly renewed! He smiled at me then nodded as he touched the bill of his well-worn kepi with two fingers before rejoining the march south.

That was just the beginning! Jacob attached himself to me and wanted me to explain every verse of the Bible he could remember his mother ever teaching him when he was a boy, and she had taught him a lot of verses! Several others who had witnessed his baptism joined us as we walked along with the column, and they had just as many questions as Jacob. Some of them were believers and had been baptized themselves but wanted to know more, while others had not yet accepted Christ as their personal Savior and were searching for answers like Jacob.

Soon after we went into winter camp at Port Republic and before Fredericksburg, Jacob approached me with several men in tow. "Captain, tell these men what you told me. They don't believe that you can't earn your way to heaven."

Like most who have recently found Christ, Jacob had become an enthusiastic Christian, spreading the Good News every chance he had and was totally unafraid of what anyone would think.

"What about it, Captain?" asked one of them, a raggedly dressed corporal I knew to be from Baton Rouge.

"He's right. It is a gift, and you can't earn it."

The corporal scoffed. "No offense, sir, but that's just a license to sin! A man has to keep the Law."

"No sir, it is not a license to sin; it's a license to serve. You believe the Bible?"

He nodded. "Yes, sir! I do. It's God's Word!"

"Then let me show you something in God's Word." I opened my Bible to the Book of Galatians, chapter 2. "Read verse 16 for us."

He took my Bible and began reading. "Knowing that a man is not justified by the works of the law, but by the faith of Jesus Christ, even we have believed in Jesus Christ, that we might be justified by the faith of Christ, and not by the works of the law: for by the works of the law shall no flesh be justified."

"There, can keeping the Law save you?" He didn't respond. "What does Paul say in verse 21?"

He looked back down at the Bible. "I do not frustrate the grace of God: for if righteousness come by the law, then Christ is dead in vain."

"If you can be saved by keeping the Law, then the Cross served no purpose; it would be unnecessary. So, you can't be declared righteous before God by keeping the Law, can you? Then how can you be declared righteous before God?"

He was confused then. "I don't know."

"Let the Word of God answer that. Turn to Romans chapter four and verse five."

He shuffled the pages and found the passage. "But to him that worketh not, but believeth on him that justifieth the ungodly, his faith is counted for righteousness."

"Working will not gain one bit of righteousness for you, but faith will. Look now at the Epistle to the Philippians, the third chapter and the ninth verse."

He turned the pages and the others with him drew even closer to look over his shoulder. "And be found in him, not having mine own righteousness, which is of the law, but that which is through the faith of Christ, the righteousness which is of God by faith."

"Whose righteousness?"

He looked up at me. "The righteousness, which is from God."

"How is it appropriated?"

He looked back down at the passage. "Through faith."

"So, is salvation by keeping the Law or by faith?"

"But, what about keeping the Law? You never answered that."

"The Law was given to Israel, and Romans chapter five and verses fourteen and sixteen say we are not under the Law but under Grace. Israel was given the Law to set them apart from other nations and demonstrate the perfect righteousness demanded by God, and to point to the failure of man to be able to keep every point of the Law. James says if you fail even one point, you are guilty of the whole Law.

It was demonstrating man's inability to keep the Law. It was also pointing to the need for a redeemer, someone who could keep the whole Law, Jesus Christ, the Lamb without spot or blemish."

"But what about where Jesus said if we love Him we will keep his commandments?"

"The keeping part is a result of our love of God and gratitude to Him, not to gain the love of God. And the only way you can ever keep His commandments is by the Grace provisions of God. You are saved by faith and the power of God. You also live the Christian life by faith and through the power of the indwelling Holy Ghost. It is a supernatural lifestyle."

"How do you know all this?" He retorted almost angrily.

"By reading the Bible and not listening to preachers who don't."

One of the others added, "Captain, can you show us more in the Bible? I mean, can you teach us more about what's in the Bible?"

I wasn't prepared for that.

Jacob jumped right on it. "Good idea! How about it Captain, can you show us more?"

And so it began with only six men. Within a month we had over twenty, including General Jackson. By Christmas, we had nearly fifty attending the class. And the Great Awakening continued to spread throughout the Army of Northern Virginia, and many more came to a saving knowledge of Christ and wanted to be baptized—and learn more about their newfound faith. For these men, it wasn't enough to simply repeat rituals week in and week out; they wanted to know what the Bible had to say to them and soaked it up like dry sponges.

Normally, when we were having inactive periods, I would dwell on my own problems, but I was no longer doing that. It isn't that I never thought of Rachel, but rather the confidence I once had in God's providence was renewed. I knew she was out there somewhere, and someday, someway I would indeed find her. But that winter of '62 and '63, I had the feeling I was doing what I was being called of God to do, and that brought a sense of peace I had not experienced in a very long while.

Chapter 17 – A Day of Mourning

In December, Fredericksburg, a little town along the Rappahannock River, was the scene of the final scrap of 1862 for the Army of Northern Virginia. Lincoln sacked Little Mac in November, and in his seemingly never-ending search for a "general who would fight," put Ambrose Burnside in charge. Burnside fought all right and was promptly defeated by making some of the most basic tactical mistakes possible. First, he underestimated his enemy, then he dawdled, claiming high water in the Rappahannock River, before crossing and attacking, allowing Lee to mass his army to meet the new threat at Fredericksburg. And lastly, Burnside fought from the weaker position when he allowed the Confederates to control the high ground. He followed that with a frontal attack from that much inferior position against the much superior one. After five days of fighting and at the urging of his generals, Burnside withdrew with a loss of over 12,000 dead and wounded. Lee lost less than half that. The two Louisiana brigades were held in reserve at Fredericksburg, but the 1st Louisiana lost fifty-four men and the 2nd Louisiana lost thirty-three from the heavy Yankee shelling.

20 December 1862
  The Army of the Potomac has endured yet another defeat at the hands of Lee, this time at Fredericksburg, Virginia. The President replaced McClellan, placing Ambrose Burnside in command, and he seems to have failed just as the several generals before him. Doctor J says Burnside made several tactical mistakes, and those were the cause of his defeat.

I cannot tell if the Louisiana brigades were involved, but surely they were in some capacity. They seem to be always in the van of any action. They seem always to be actively used by Lee.

This was an unusual campaign for so late in the year. The armies are normally in winter camp by December. I expect with this defeat, there will be no more activity by the Army of the Potomac or the Army of Northern Virginia until spring.

Many men had been absent without leave, and some began to return to their units after Sharpsburg. The ranks were further filled out with conscripts, but these were generally disliked and distrusted by the veterans. The regiments had originally been made up of men from the same regions, even the same towns, but that was changing with the addition of conscripts. The two brigades from Louisiana began to fill in their depleted ranks, but they would never be back to full strength, nor would any other brigade in the army, for that matter.

We eventually settled into a winter camp routine, but the fall of 1862 and winter of '63 were nothing like the previous fall and winter. The army was destitute of supplies. Many of the men were shoeless and without even the most basic clothing needs to provide protection from the cold winds and snow of the Virginia winters. We wrote our congressman from Louisiana, and he managed to secure some shoes for our brigades. Blue set up his Blue Bidness and purchased shoes in Richmond, which he sold. We had very few tents for shelter and many lived outside shivering around weak fires as their only source of warmth. Some built huts or even burrowed into the ground and used a scrap of canvas or gum blanket to close the hole to the elements. Rations were also very short and hunger was common. Our men looked like scarecrows with their ragged and dirty uniforms draped over their emaciated frames. Winter was a long miserable affair, and we were anxious for spring, even if it meant another summer of hard campaigning. The first fight of 1863 would be one long remembered, and its impact on the army would be profoundly felt for the remainder of the war.

In late January of '63, several of us from my old mess were sitting around a fire in an attempt to find some relief from a biting wind out of the north. Blue had scraped together a meal from the last of our meager rations and was spooning it into our pans when Jean, recovered from his wounds, approached waving a newspaper at us, "We best be afraid, boys. This here paper says Lincoln has gone and fired Burnside and has himself a new general to lead his army."

"Who might that be?" I asked.

"General Joe Hooker and his nickname is 'Fighting Joe.' Aren't y'all scared now? That name must have given Lincoln some confidence he has at last found his fighting general!"

"I've heard of him," I replied. "Hooker is indeed a scrapper, but he is also arrogant and ambitious and reportedly a heavy drinker."

Blue passed a plate of hot food to Jean, which he cradled in his hands to warm them. "But I hear he is good at building organizations."

"So was McClellan and look how that went for Lincoln."

Blue took his plate and joined our circle around the fire. "You boys think we will be fighting right here at Fredericksburg come spring?"

"Probably," I replied. "But if I was Mr. F. J. Hooker, I sure wouldn't attempt a frontal attack against these heights again."

"What would you do, Ethan?" asked Jean before shoveling in a mouthful of Blue stew.

"Only choice for them is to flank us, and that would likely be upstream. FJ needs to get his army across the river without us bombarding it with cannon and draw us out into the open where he has some room to maneuver. Yep, that's what I would do if I was Fighting Joe."

With the coming of spring the two sides were facing each other across the Rappahannock at Fredericksburg. As I predicted, another crossing and frontal attack did not seem prudent to Mr. F. J. Hooker. He had another solution that he was sure would end in defeat for Lee.

Lee sent Longstreet's Corps south to forage for provisions and protect the Virginia and North Carolina coasts from any possible Yankee incursions, which left only 40,000 to hold at Fredericksburg. Even though Hooker had a much larger force on the other side of the river that would have been sufficient to hold our superior positions in the heights overlooking the town.

Since re-crossing the Rappahannock and making another frontal attack at Fredericksburg was not an option for Hooker, in Late April 1863 he deployed 70,000 of his men to the west and moved them quickly across the river upstream in an attempt to flank Fredericksburg.

Lee parried the move but left Early with the 1st Louisiana to hold Fredericksburg. Some skirmishes between Lee and Hooker resulted, but Fighting Joe suddenly drew back to defensive positions around Chancellorsville on the south side of the Rappahannock and sat there.

I was present when Jackson was studying a map with his staff, and one man quietly mused to himself, "What's Hooker doing?"

Though deep in thought, Jackson must have heard him and looked up. He jabbed his finger at the map. "He wants to draw us out. He wants to choose the ground and have us come to him, so he can fight from a strong defensive position; thinks he can beat Lee that way."

Jackson looked around at his staff to observe their reaction to what he had just said and stopped when he got to me. "Captain Joubert, I have seen that expression on your face before back at the Institute. Something on your mind?"

I was somewhat startled but tried to quickly recover. "Yes, sir. I would have thought Hooker would understand that wars are not won fighting from the defensive. One must go on the offensive to completely defeat the enemy."

Old Jack smiled. "As I recall, you were one of the few who remained awake during my lectures. You're right. It is possible that Hooker could win the battle but only if he inflicts unsustainable casualties on us. But he'll not win the war this way, and why will he not, Captain?"

I shook my head in the negative and replied softly. "Lee won't fall into that trap."

"And you would be correct. Lee is no fool. If you were Lee what would you do?"

I looked closer at the map and the dispositions of the two forces. "Well, sir, if a frontal attack is out of the question, then the alternative is a flanking maneuver." I looked to Hooker's left flank, the preferred choice to flank him, since it would sever his avenues of supply and retreat. "Hooker's left flank is anchored on the Rappahannock, so we can't get around that way; we would have to punch through it, which is almost the same as a frontal attack against the center." My focus shifted to the western end of Hooker's line.

"His right flank appears to be in the air. If so, and he hasn't reinforced it in anticipation of a flanking move, we might be able to move a large force undetected through the Wilderness and get around him that way."

Old Jack nodded. "You did pay attention in class. See any problems with that maneuver?"

I felt like I was back at VMI and being tested by Jackson. All eyes were on me to see how well I would do in this exam. "Yes, I do. Longstreet's Corps is still detached, and Early is holding at Fredericksburg, so the Army of Northern Virginia has already been divided into thirds." I pointed to Chancellorsville on the map. "To take this largest third here before Hooker's much superior force—and divide it again—is something any text on military strategy would advise against." Several nodded in agreement. I looked to Jackson and smiled. "But that's precisely what you have in mind to do."

Jackson did not smile often, but he did that day. "Dividing an already weaker force in the face of a vastly superior one will be very risky, but such is what Hooker would never expect us to do. This discussion must remain with this group. No decision has been made yet. We must wait and see how the situation develops."

Jackson's strategy was always to "mystify, confuse and deceive." Before this fight would be over Hooker would be all of that—and out-flanked.

The battlefield was centered at Chancellorsville, which was little more than one house at a crossroads where several major roads converged, mainly Plank Road and the Old Orange Turnpike. Chancellor House was the home of Fannie Pound Chancellor, the widow of George Chancellor. They had nine children; seven of them were present at the house—one young son and six unmarried daughters, and all six were quite comely. Hooker took over the house as his headquarters.

His left flank was to the northeast about two and a half miles from Chancellorsville and was anchored on the Rappahannock. His right flank was about two miles west of Chancellor House, but because of the terrain, it was indeed "in the air," meaning it was not anchored on any terrain feature that offered any natural protection from flanking movements by the enemy.

The terrain was low hills and mostly wooded with the majority of the cleared fields around Chancellorsville. The surrounding area was called the Wilderness, which was very heavily wooded. Most of the first growth trees had been harvested to make charcoal. The new growth that came up was a tangle of trees and underbrush virtually impenetrable in many places, just like we had encountered at Port Republic when we flanked the Coaling. The woods on either side of many of the roads and trails so closed in on them that they were almost like verdant tunnels through the forests. This presented a problem for Hooker as it made anchoring his right flank difficult. He compounded the problem by placing Howard's XI Corps there with his weakest and most untried units; many had never seen combat, and some were nearing the end of their enlistment contracts. Hooker obviously did not expect an attack to come on his right flank.

Elsewhere, Hooker had chosen very strong positions from which to fight and was quickly fortifying them. He probed and withdrew, trying to draw Lee into a major engagement. Lee came to fight and had already reconnoitered Hooker's left flank with the hope he might flank him and cut him off from his supplies across the Rappahannock but found that way unacceptable, because of the dense Wilderness and Hooker's strong positions.

Lee made a decision that went against every established doctrine taught at West Point or any other military academy, for that matter. In the face of a superior force, Lee was going to do the unthinkable: divide his small force yet again. Lee and Jackson had a war conference, and it was decided that Jackson would be sent around Hooker's right flank and even get behind him if possible.

The problem then became to find the best route through the Wilderness that would shield Jackson from observation by Hooker. If Hooker discovered Jackson's flanking movement, he would understand that Lee was weak before him and attack with overwhelming force.

Beverly Tucker Lacy, Jackson's chaplain general, was from the area and knew it well. He was summoned and asked the best route for such a flanking movement. He had a ready answer and mapped out a route that would keep the flanking force from being seen by the Yankees, except for one portion where they would be within 1000 yards of Hooker's lines and visible. That would not do, so they needed another route. The owner of Catherine's Furnace, Charles Welford, was told of the problem, and he was aware of a new road cut recently through the Wilderness that would take them well away from any possible detection by Hooker's forces. His son agreed to guide the army to be certain they took the right roads.

That evening, sitting on hardtack crates, Lee and Jackson reviewed the map with Welford's hidden route drawn on it, and it was agreed to proceed with the plan and move around Hooker's right flank and get behind him. Jackson would take the bulk of the army Lee had at Chancellorsville, 26,000 men, leaving Lee with only a small holding force of two divisions, a total of 14,000, to face Hooker's 70,000 and keep him occupied on the center.

May 2 dawned with a chill in the air, but soon the rising sun warmed us. It was close to seven o'clock before we stepped off, an uncharacteristically late start for Jackson, who was delayed by some Federal cannonading. Lee watched his corps pass, and Jackson soon joined him for a brief conversation.

Our route took Furnace Road southwest until it came to Brock Road, but instead of turning right at Brock Road, the column moved further south until it came upon the road Welford had identified as the route that would take us away from detection. Welford Road would take us northwest until it intersected Brock Road, which we would follow to Orange Plank Road. It was believed Hooker's right flank was somewhere in the vicinity of Wilderness Church on the Orange Turnpike near where Orange Plank Road intersected it.

One section of Furnace Road was visible to Yankee observers in tall trees. About 8 o'clock they began reporting that a steady flow of Rebels were moving across that open space and toward the right. Dan Sickles got permission to bring up some of his rifled guns and shell the troops still passing, but the shelling caused no real damage.

Because of a misunderstanding of a dispatch from Lee, Early began withdrawing much of his corps from Fredericksburg to join Lee, leaving only Harry Hays and the 1st Louisiana Brigade and some artillery to hold that position. The Federals across the Rappahannock detected this withdrawal and reported it to Hooker. Early's movement and the report of Confederate units moving past the Furnace combined to convince Hooker that Lee was retreating.

The roads Jackson's Corps traveled were narrow, leaving little room to maneuver and forcing the column to move only four abreast. Thus, his train was very long with the last elements departing around one o'clock in the afternoon. It took Hooker from eight in the morning to one in the afternoon to respond. Dan Sickles sent

David Birney's division and Berdan's Sharpshooters to attack what Hooker thought were the retreating Confederates on the Furnace Road. They were disappointed, because by the time they got there, Jackson's Corps was gone, but he had left Colonel Emory Best's 23rd Georgia to handle any such demonstrations against his rear. A scrap resulted, eventually drawing other units from both sides into it.

Meanwhile, the head of the flanking column was already looking for Hooker's right flank. Jackson used cavalry to seal off all the roads between the column and the Federals to prevent early detection. When the head of the column reached Orange Plank Road, Tom Munford's 2nd Virginia Cavalry turned up the road to reconnoiter and encountered a Yankee cavalry picket. As soon as they saw Munford, they turned and ran. Munford pursued briefly but halted, because his orders were to shield the flanking force from detection and not engage the enemy any more than absolutely necessary.

Munford put out his own pickets and climbed a nearby knoll. From the top he had a commanding view of the Federal lines and immediately sent for his commanding officer, Fitz Lee. Fitz Lee took one look and immediately went for Jackson. I had just been speaking to Jackson about the number of VMI's former cadets who were leading the army that morning. To which Jackson's reply was, "The Institute will be heard from today!"

Fitz Lee approached and reported, "Sir, a moment please!" The urgency of his request for an audience was obvious from his excited tone.

Jackson nodded.

"General, if you will ride with me, halting your column here, out of sight, I will show you the enemy's right."

I accompanied Jackson to act as a courier should he need one, and the three of us hurried to the knoll from which Munford had first observed Hooker's lines. We climbed to the top, and I gasped at the sight. There before us spread all along Orange Turnpike was Howard's XI Corps, Hooker's right flank, and they had no idea such a force as ours was nearby or that we were observing them.

They appeared to be completely at ease. Their arms were stacked behind their fortifications along the road. Behind the line the men were gathered in small groups, some reclining on the ground relaxing, some playing card games, and no doubt engaged in light conversation—and unaware of our presence. Further back the cooks were butchering beeves for a meal. We could see the positions to about a half a mile to the east of where Plank Road intersected Orange Turnpike. To the west we could see the Talley homestead, home of Melzi Chancellor, the son of the founder of Chancellorsville, and Dowdall's Tavern, but the forest obscured further view of how far the line extended to the west.

Old Jack studied the enemy through his binoculars for several minutes, while Fitz Lee pointed out their positions. Finally, Jackson turned to me and said smartly, "Captain, tell General Rodes to move across the Plank Road, halt when he gets to the Old Turnpike, and I'll join him there."

"Yes, sir!" I quickly made my way down to Pepper, mounted and was off at a gallop to find General Rodes at the head of the column.

Jackson returned to the column with his face aglow with anticipation of what he was about to accomplish. Rodes moved the mile and a half to the Turnpike and about half a mile east on the Pike before halting at John Luckett's farm. He encountered no Yankee pickets. The extreme of Hooker's right flank was just up the road and completely unaware of the host about to fall upon them.

As more trailing units arrived, Jackson arranged for their deployment on the road and on either side. The clearing at Luckett's was barely 400 yards wide, not enough room to get the units properly into line-of-battle. Some had to be deployed in the woods on either side of the clearing and road. This had to be done in complete silence, no bugle calls, no shouted commands, no cheering, lest the enemy just up the road discover our presence.

Our line extended for about three quarters of a mile on either side of the Pike. It was two ranks deep and about 8,000 men. Skirmishers were pushed out about four hundred paces in front. Jackson formed a second line two hundred yards to the rear of the first and dispatched several brigades to the Plank Road to secure that from being an avenue of attack by the enemy. Cavalry were pushed out on either side of the formation to guard its flanks.

Jackson's planning was meticulous in its detail, and he had ample time to deploy his forces to exert the maximum surprise and effect. This would be a battle that would be studied at West Point for decades, and appropriately so—it was magnificent in its planning and execution.

By late afternoon Jackson had around 21,000 men primed for the attack. He instructed his commanders, "Once we start, be aggressive and do not stop for anything! Push on! I am granting authority to those of you commanding the forward units to directly call for help from the reserves behind you if you needed it. Don't wait for me to approve it. Artillery will advance with the infantry and unlimber to reduce any strong points encountered, then limber-up and continue with the advance. Nothing must be allowed to stop us, not even the approaching darkness."

J.E.B. Stuart sent two of his cavalrymen ahead to reconnoiter. They encountered three of the enemy who neither challenged them nor shot at them and, evidently, never reported the sighting to their superiors. Soon we heard cannonading to the east. That was Dan Sickles engaging Lee under the assumption that Lee was retreating. He was so convinced he had a chance at trapping Lee that he called for Howard's help, and Howard sent his only reserves to Sickles, leaving Hooker's right flank even more vulnerable.

It was near sunset, about 5:45 in the evening, when the Federals on Hooker's right began to sense the pending disaster about to befall them. At first they heard a commotion in the woods, distant bugle calls, shouted commands, and yelling that was the signal to advance. Suddenly, coveys of quail noisily fluttered forth from the woods. They were soon followed by frightened rabbits scampering frantically about, then came the deer and even a bear, all being pushed before our lines advancing on the enemy's positions.

George Dole's Georgia Brigade sitting astride the Pike encountered units from New York, who were aligned facing south instead west from which the Georgians came. The New Yorkers turned and skedaddled without even firing a shot. Some of the Federal units managed to make token stands but were eventually forced to abandon their positions in the face of overwhelming enemy forces on their right flank and rear.

Like a terrible hurricane, Jackson's force fell upon the enemy and crushed them, driving them back to the east toward Chancellorsville. One Federal unit kept running until it eventually encountered Lee's forces on the left side of Hooker's line. Though some units attempted an organized resistance, their lines were pushed back to within a mile of Chancellor House. Jackson intended to stay on the offensive. Even though the sun had set, and twilight was rapidly fading, it was just one day short of a full moon, which could offer sufficient light to maintain the attack. An army off balance must be kept off balance, and he urged his commanders, "Press on! Press on!"

General Rodes' Division was the lead element in the attack down the Plank Road, and during the rapid advance, his units lost cohesion and were low on ammunition. He requested of Jackson that A.P. Hill's division, directly behind his, advance to replace his to allow him to reorganize. Jackson agreed, and Hill began the process of replacing Rodes' Division.

Around 8 o'clock, with the last light of twilight almost gone, Jackson and a dozen or so of his staff were at the very vanguard of our line on Plank Road. We rode through Hill's division, and Jackson asked Hill how long before he could resume the attack. "In a few minutes," he replied as he had almost completed replacing Rodes' division. Our party continued up Plank Road through Jim Lane's North Carolina brigade, part of Hill's division, deployed on either side of the road.

We were about 100 yards out ahead of Lane's Brigade with Hill and a small party of his staff about fifty yards behind us. Only Lane's skirmishers were between the enemy and us.

This was Old Jack's style. He wanted to see the battlefield for himself. Some of Jackson's staff became concerned about the danger, and Sandie Pendleton finally asked, "General, don't you think this is the wrong place for you?"

Old Jack replied, "The danger is over. The enemy is routed. Go back and tell Hill to press on."

I did not think the danger was yet over, and though the enemy was routed, some were putting up an occasional spirited resistance when well led by their officers. And we did not know exactly where the enemy was. Had they stopped and prepared to make a stand, and we were about to blunder into them? Like Pendleton and others in our party, I had a most uncomfortable feeling about this scout.

We reached a clearing with an unfinished church about 150 yards out from Lane's lines. I was riding behind Jackson when a single shot rang out to our right. It sounded to me as if it came from our rear where two of Lane's North Carolina regiments were deployed. Others though it might have come from our right front. That shot was soon followed by several others, and that swelled into almost continuous firing like a string of firecrackers going off. I had no doubt then. The firing was coming from Lane's North Carolina Brigade to our right rear.

Blazing fire suddenly tore though our party and Hill's! Several of Jackson's staff were wounded or killed immediately! Two horses were shot from under their riders, and others wounded and frantic tore off in every direction. More shots rang out, screaming horses and screaming men, and those still in the saddle headed for the nearby woods.

Jackson took cover in the woods to our left away from the firing only to be met by more musketry on that side. Lane's North Carolina Brigade had mistaken us for Federal cavalry! Lieutenant Morrison jumped from his wounded horse and ran toward the North Carolina lines screaming for them to stop firing. One of the Carolina officers yelled it was a lie and to keep firing!

While blundering through the dark woods, Jackson was hit in the right hand and left upper arm, shattering the bone near the shoulder. Little Sorrel was also wounded, and the frightened animal ran back out on the road and away from the firing toward the Federal lines! Jackson managed to get control of his mount with his wounded hand and the help of Captain Wilbourn and signalman Wynn who brought him to relative safety on side of the road.

I somehow remained unwounded, but Pepper was decidedly unhappy about all the shooting and managing him was difficult. I joined Wilbourn and Wynn with Jackson, who they had laid down under a tree. "How bad are you hurt, sir?"

Grasping his left arm, he looked up at me. "I fear my arm is broken," he replied almost calmly.

Wilbourn turned to Wynn. "Quickly now, go fetch Doctor McGuire and an ambulance!" He then bound the wound to stop the bleeding and said, "General, it is remarkable that any of us escaped."

Jackson agreed, "Yes, it is providential."

Hill showed up and helped Wilbourn fashion a sling for Jackson's arm and sent for the closest brigade surgeon.

I heard someone approaching from the east, and fearing it might be the enemy, drew my pistol as I went to investigate. I found two Yankees who had been flushed from the woods by all the excitement. "Don't shoot!"

"Advance! Hands in the air!" They came forward, but we found no weapons on them, and they were taken away.

Lieutenant Morrison and I went forward to a low crest in the road to see if there were any other threats and discovered the Yankees were unlimbering a battery to fire directly down the road. We took one quick glance at each other before we ran back to the party tending to Jackson.

"We have to get away from here. The Yankees have unlimbered a battery just up the road!" Morrison announced.

With that, Hill immediately departed to take command of his division. We tried to get Jackson up to walk, but he was too weak from shock and blood loss. Fortunately, a litter soon arrived we could use to carry him from danger.

With a deafening roar, that Federal battery we had seen unlimbering opened fire with canister shot. The balls skipped down the road throwing up sparks when they hit anything hard. The road was no longer safe with the Federal guns completely covering it, so we attempted to move Jackson along the side of the road and away from danger. Another round of canister tore down the road, and one of the litter bearers was hit. Jackson was placed on the ground and the remaining litter bearers attempted to shield him with their own bodies.

We got Jackson on his feet and, careful to avoid further hurt, moved deeper into the woods where we were able to get him back on the litter. The litter bearers hefted the litter to their shoulders and continued moving away from danger, but one of them tripped, and Old Jack spilled out to land on his broken arm! He had not previously acknowledged his pain, but he groaned piteously then.

We got Jackson back on the litter and again made our way to the Confederate lines. We tried to keep his identity a secret, but one soldier got a good look in the moonlight and exclaimed, "Great God, that's old General Jackson!"

General William Dorsey Pender of Hill's division arrived and reported the situation was very confused, and we might have to fall back. Jackson retorted, "You must hold your ground, General Pender! You must hold your ground, sir!"

The litter party continued on and soon met Doctor McGuire with an ambulance. The doctor administered whiskey and morphine and helped get Jackson into the ambulance. Jackson said to his old friend, "I'm badly wounded, Doctor. I fear I'm dying."

Using torchlight, the ambulance was slowly and carefully moved down the rough road to the 2nd Corps field hospital at Wilderness tavern. I followed on Pepper, who had calmed down now that the shooting was well behind us.

At the field hospital, McGuire allowed Jackson to rest and recover before he subjected him to a thorough examination. McGuire administered more whiskey and covered Jackson to rest. A few hours later, he determined Old Jack was strong enough to undergo an examination and treatment. He and three other surgeons agreed the arm needed to come off, and Old Jack was awakened to tell him.

"Do for me whatever you think right," he told McGuire.

They administered chloroform, and the damaged arm was amputated just below the shoulder. A half hour after the surgery, they woke Jackson up and give him some coffee, to which he said, "Very good; refreshing."

On 3 May with General J.E.B. Stuart commanding Jackson's Corps, the Confederate advance on Hooker's right flank resumed. Though it lacked the element of surprise and some of its vigor it had enjoyed the day before, Hooker's lines were eventually pushed all the way to Chancellor House, where he was having a war conference with his generals in an attempt save what was left of his army. The withdrawal of the thoroughly defeated and devastated army was completed on 6 May. Mr. F. J. Hooker would soon be dismissed, and Lincoln would once more look for a general who could fight.

Lieutenant General Thomas J. Jackson lingered on for a week after his wounding. At first he seemed to rally and recovery seemed likely, but then he took a turn for the worse and eventually succumbed to pneumonia on Sunday, 10 May.

When told by his wife the doctors thought he would not live through the day, his reply was "It will be an infinite gain to be translated to heaven."

About mid-afternoon, he suddenly and calmly said, "Let us cross over the river and rest under the shade of the trees." He passed shortly after, and the Army of Northern Virginia went into deep mourning.

12 May 1863

The Grand Army of the Potomac has suffered another disastrous defeat at the hands of Bobby Lee. This time it was at Chancellorsville. Fighting Joe Hooker turned out to be not much of a fighter.

We are hearing that the famous Stonewall Jackson was wounded during the battle and later died.

Chapter 18 – He's Here!

Lee fully understood that a war couldn't be won with only a defensive strategy. Other than the South's brief foray into Maryland the previous September, Lee had mostly been on the defensive and reacting to northern moves. While the South was winning the battles, it was sustaining unacceptable losses of men and equipment and losing the war. With its smaller population, those losses could not be replaced, but those of the North could. The longer the war dragged on, the Confederate Army would only grow smaller, while the northern army grew larger. The only solution was to take the war to the North again, threaten major northern cities and even Washington to convince the population up North that it was in their best interest to sue for peace. With the latest series of northern defeats, Lee saw a chance to make that strategy work, and he was smart enough to know this was probably his last chance to do so. With his army rested and in good spirits, Bobby Lee planned to shift to the offensive and take the war to the North.

With Jackson's death, General Ewell took over 2nd Corps. After the big cavalry scrap at Brandy Station on June 9, Ewell put us on the road the very next day, crossing the Blue Ridge Mountains and entering our old haunt from the spring of '62, the Shenandoah Valley. We began the process of pushing the Yankees out of the Valley, and by the 13th, we were engaging the enemy just south of Winchester. Two Federal forts stood in our way, but Ewell soon realized, if we could take the western most fort, we could easily dominate the other. In what some later described as the most magnificent charge of the war, Harry Hays' Tigers took the fort, and soon after, Winchester fell. The next day, we began crossing the Potomac into Maryland and headed for Pennsylvania. The rest of the army was soon following our lead.

15 June 1863

The Confederates are on the march again! They crossed the Potomac and entered Maryland. Doctor J says there are no northern forces in place to stop them. He thinks they are likely coming to capture some northern city like Baltimore or Philadelphia or even Washington.

With only orders to advance on a broad front, Lee gave Ewell considerable discretion to act according to how he saw fit. He sent Rodes' division up the Cumberland Valley toward Chambersburg. On 24 June, Rodes entered Chambersburg with Early moving north on a parallel route to the east. The Yankees were not prepared for this and offered little resistance.

25 June 1863

Elements of Ewell's Corps, of which the Louisiana Brigades are a part, have now been reported to be north of Gettysburg and threatening Carlyle and Harrisburg. Doctor J thinks Harrisburg may be their objective.

Gettysburg is in a panic and some are leaving.

We have a defense, though a weak one. A Pennsylvania militia regiment has taken up positions to defend the town. I asked Doctor J what he thought.

"My dear, if you put your trust in these fresh Pennsylvania boys, it would be folly. They are too few in number and mustered into service only yesterday. I'm of the opinion they are not up to the task against the more experienced Army of Northern Virginia."

"Should we leave?"

"Where would we go? They are all around us now. There is little we can do but watch and wait."

"What if Ethan is with them?"

He shook his head as if to make light of my concern. "Jenny, I wouldn't worry about that. He probably is with them, but even so, the chances of you two having any kind of an encounter are too small to calculate."

That gave me but small relief. This is so sudden, and though it has been over two years since I left Catahoula, I am not yet emotionally prepared to see Ethan. Frankly, I thought I would be stronger about such a meeting by now, but I was wrong. Even seeing him with Aimee in the newspaper and his apparently moving on from our relationship had not dulled the ache in my heart for him like I thought it would—like I tried to use it to do. In my heart, I know I cannot yet face him and, now, with that possibility, however small, doubt I will ever be able to. How does one stop loving another?

On the 25th, Ewell drove northeast through Carlyle and Harrisburg, and Early's division moved on York and Wrightsville, marching through the area of Gettysburg. On the 26th, Early approached Gettysburg and routed a regiment of Pennsylvania militia defending the town.

26 June 1863

They are here!

Early's Division easily brushed aside the raw Pennsylvania militia regiment protecting us and sent it into full retreat. Confederate soldiers roamed freely through the town right down East Middle where we live. Many of us hid in our cellars, but I peeked out a window to see if I could see any of the blue Louisiana flags emblazoned with a nesting pelican. Thank goodness, I saw none. Ethan is not likely with this group.

The Confederates looked like they had not eaten in months, thin as fence rails, gaunt, dirty, and often barefoot. They were mostly polite and did not molest the civilians of Gettysburg, but there was some stealing of chickens for food. The citizens of Gettysburg treated them kindly, I think mostly out of fear.

Doctor J approached some and asked their unit and where they were going. They did not seem to know where they were headed next, and all soon moved on, much to our relief. Perhaps we are done with them and they will not be back. I feel like my crisis of meeting Ethan may be over.

The next day, York surrendered, and Carlyle fell into our hands. Still, the Yankees offered little resistance. Jenkins and Early were threatening Harrisburg and could easily have taken it, but Lee got word through a spy that Lincoln had replaced "Fighting Joe" Hooker with Major General George Gordon Meade, and Meade had the sleeping Army of the Potomac on the move to put an end to Lee's freewheeling frolic through Pennsylvania. Some northern units had been seen not many miles east and moving to engage our forces.

Our cavalry, "Lee's eyes," should have warned us of that, but J.E.B. Stuart's merry band of mounted rogues had taken a "glorious" ride around the rear of the whole of the Union army and been completely out of contact with Lee since 25 June and would remain absent until the coming battle was almost over. Stuart would be of little use in the pending battle.

Cavalry or none, Lee had enough information to smell a fight coming and immediately ordered his much-disbursed army to concentrate near Gettysburg.

On June 30, General Pettigrew of Hill's division proceeded to enter Gettysburg from the west in search of much needed shoes that had been previously reported to be there and saw John Buford's cavalry division entering the town. Rather than engage, he withdrew and reported this to his superior.

30 June 1863

Federal cavalry moved through Gettysburg this noon and took up positions to the west of town. Doctor J inquired of one of their officers and was told they had seen Confederates west of town as they were entering from the east, but the Confederates retreated. He also told Doctor J he thought the fight was likely to be somewhere around the Gettysburg area, as he understood that Lee was concentrating his forces near here.

I though the threat was over, but now it is beginning to look like we will be in the midst of the fight!

Hill did not believe Pettigrew and moved to Gettysburg the next day on the Chambersburg Pike. Heath's division of Hill's Corps encountered Buford at Seminary Ridge on the west side of town, and the fight was on!

1 July 1863

Today began dark and gloomy with heavy clouds and a light drizzle to dampen the sound of muskets along Seminary Ridge where Buford's cavalry are engaged with Confederate units. We do not yet know whose brigades they are; not likely Louisianans, as Ewell is still north of Gettysburg.

Soon, artillery batteries rolled noisily through town, and the booming of cannonading, enough to cause the earth to tremble, joined the ebb and flow of the rattle of muskets.

Since the fighting was west of us, Doctor J and I did not seek the shelter of the cellar and remained in the house.

Union infantry moved through the town and joined in the battle. We could hear distant shouting of excited men, bugle calls, and rolling drums when the muskets fell silent for brief spells.

I sat on the sofa sipping a cup of tea and silently considered the possibilities. I knew, in my heart, Ethan would soon be here—here in the very town to which I had escaped to get away from the horror of learning that we had a common father. I thought I would be safe here—that he could never find me. I was certain of that after the first year, and Ethan had not come for me. That assured me I had not revealed that Miriam was from Gettysburg in any of my many letters I had written to him from England. I was sure, if I had, he would have showed up at my doorstep within the first year, if not in the first few months. I convinced myself I was safe, but now I was not so sure in spite of Doctor J's assurances that the chances of seeing him here and now were too small to calculate.

Doctor J interrupted my thoughts. "You are thinking about Ethan, aren't you?"

I could only nod as I tried to hold back my tears.

"I think you want to see him. And I think you should. Furthermore, I think you should speak to him. You have many unanswered questions, like this Aimee de Beauchamp and his name change?"

More Union troops moved through town heading north. I jumped to my feet and paced at the first sound of them. North was the direction from which we thought Ewell and the Louisiana brigades would likely approach Gettysburg.

"You didn't answer me," Doctor J chided.

I glared at him. "Yes, I do want to see him, and no, I cannot possibly speak to him. Please do not ask me to do so again!"

"As you wish, but I do believe you would be happier if you did speak to him. Both of you would. This separation is tearing you apart inside—and likely him as well. You need to end it."

"NO!" I shouted and then broke down weeping.

Doctor J moved to console me, but I pushed him away. "Please!"

"I am sorry, Jenny. I should not have been so forward."

By 11 a.m. the fighting subsided, and a two-hour lull ensued as each side brought more units into position. Ewell's 2nd Corps approached Gettysburg from the north and encountered Federal units of Howard's XI Corps.

It has been quiet for a while. All we heard was the distant rattle of muskets and occasional boom of the cannons from the west and now the north, which sounded like it was coming from the Harrisburg Road. Eventually, the sounds of battle grew louder, and Union soldiers, both as units and single stragglers, began moving south through town toward Cemetery Hill. We saw many wounded being helped by their fellows. From our window vantage point, we watched the trickle of Blue Coats grow into a flood.

"It's a retreat," said Doctor J softly. "They are falling back, probably to take positions on Cemetery Hill, which would be a strong place from which to fight."

Suddenly, the glass in the window to my left was shattered by a loud buzz and a hole appeared in the wall opposite.

"Down!" Doctor J yelled, and we dropped to the floor as several more balls pierced the clapboard walls of the house. "Time to move to the basement! Stay low. Come along now!"

We crawled to the stairs and made our way down to the basement. The musket fire grew louder and closer as Doctor J slammed the door at the top of the stairs behind us. Only after we had made it to the bottom of the stairs did we dare to fully stand. Doctor J pulled a crate over to one of the basement windows and cautiously peeked out.

"They're running now. The Confederates must be close on their tails." Just as he said that, we heard another ball strike the side of the house somewhere above his head. He ducked and dropped down to the floor. "That is too dangerous," he said as he pulled up some boxes for us to sit on. Seated, we were well below where we could be hit by a stray ball.

"Are you all right?" he asked.

I was shaken by the experience of being shot at, but I felt strangely unafraid. "I'm fine."

"We'll stay here until things settle down. We have enough food and water to last for a while. We'll be fine down here."

A sharp fight commenced, and the Yankees withdrew south under heavy pressure. We pushed them back through town all the way to Cemetery Hill, where they rallied to offer stiff resistance.

We entered the town in the late afternoon to find the streets littered with the debris of war along with dead and wounded and frightened stragglers hiding in homes and cellars to be routed out with musket and bayonet.

We spent the next several hours hiding in the cellar. Much of the shooting had stopped with only periodic bursts of musketry.

I was alone in my thoughts when I heard a sound upstairs that startled me. "You hear that?" I whispered.

Doctor J was almost dozing off when I heard the sound, but he was wide-awake then. "Yes! Someone is upstairs!"

The cellar door was violently thrown open and a blue clad figure appeared in the opening. He stood there for a moment and then collapsed and fell down the stairs all the way to the bottom.

Doctor J rushed to his side. "He's wounded! I need my bag!"

"I'll get it!" And before he could argue with me, I was halfway up the stairs. At the top, I dropped to my hands and knees and crawled through the wounded soldier's blood to where Doctor J kept his medical instruments. Since I had to stand to retrieve his bag from the shelf of his closet, I took the opportunity to glance through the shattered window and saw out in the street a Confederate waving the blue pelican flag of Louisiana. I froze. He's here!

"Jenny, I need you!"

Doctor J's call broke the spell, and I ran to the cellar not even bothering to crawl. When I reached the bottom of the stairs, Doctor J had the man laid out on a blanket on the floor and his coat and shirt open. He had a hole in his chest under his right arm, and each time he breathed it gurgled foamy blood, and when he took a breath, the wound sucked air. "Chest wound! He is in danger of his lung collapsing. I need to prevent that!"

I handed him his bag. "No, you! Open it. There are cotton bandages inside. Give me one."

I searched the very large bag. "This?" I asked holding it up.

"Yes. Tear off about a foot and roll a roll up."

I did as he asked and handed it to him. He took the wad, rolled it in the man's blood to soak it then said to the soldier, "Breath out as much as you can!"

A frantic expression on his face, he attempted to expel the air in his lungs. When it looked like he got out all the air he could, Doctor J shoved the bloody bandage into the hole in his chest. It stopped the bleeding and the sucking sound.

"Will he live?"

"Not likely," he replied softly. "I may have prevented his lung from collapsing, but it is probably filling with blood now. I do not see an exit wound, so the ball is still in him.

As he was saying that, another Blue Coat appeared at the top of the stairs. "Hide me! The Rebs are just outside!"

Then we heard a loud yell. "Don't move!" The Blue Coat turned to the sound of the voice and dropped to his knees with his hands raised. "Please, spare me! I have a family!"

A barefoot Confederate appeared at the top of the stairs and placed a pistol to the man's head.

"NO!" I screamed.

That startled the Confederate, and he looked down the stairs, peering into the feeble light of our single candle. "Who's there?"

"We're civilians! Please! Don't shoot!" I yelled back.

The Reb grabbed his prisoner by the collar and pushed him down the stairs ahead of him. At the bottom, he saw the wounded man. "I have me two Yankees now."

"I think not," said Doctor J. "This one is dead."

The Reb looked at the two of us. "I'll take what I kin get. Now, you two get upstairs with me. You're my prisoners now." He marched us up the stairs. "Outside!"

Once outside in the daylight, I saw the streets littered with military equipment, mostly abandoned muskets and a few dead and wounded men, both blue and gray. "I'll need my bag," said Doctor J.

"Whut bag?"

"I am a doctor. I can help these people," he replied sharply, pointing to the street.

"I'll get it," I said.

"You're my prisoner!"

"We're civilians!" I countered.

He grunted. "Well, maybe..."

"Well maybe nothing!" I had had enough of this bumpkin. "You can't take us prisoner!"

Two more soldiers joined the argument. "What's the problem, Ezra?"

"I got me three prisoners and one's a doctor and wants his bag."

"Well, let him get it. Besides, two of them are civilians."

Our captor nodded. "Very well. You get it, Miss. Kin I trust you to come back?"

"Just where would I go?" I replied with a shrug. Without waiting for an answer, I turned and went down to the cellar for the bag.

As I was ascending the stairs, I heard a commotion outside, and when I passed the window on the way to the door, I saw our captor manhandling Doctor J. I then broke into a run, but just as I arrived at the door, I saw a Confederate officer on a big gray horse ride right through the altercation between Doctor J and the soldiers. ETHAN! I stopped and ducked back inside.

"What are you doing?" Ethan yelled as he dismounted.

"I got me three prisoners!" replied our captor.

"*I see only two, and one is a civilian that looks old enough to be of little danger to you. Why were you handling him so roughly?*"

"*He was harboring blue-bellies and then was arguing with me.*"

Doctor J stepped up. "*I am a doctor, sir. I was only aiding a wounded man who came to me for help.*"

"*He's a lying damn Yankee,*" retorted one of the three Rebs.

"*He's a civilian, and you are under orders not to molest any of the civilians.*" Ethan turned and called out to a passing sergeant. "*Sergeant! Over here!*"

"*Yes sir!*"

"*These three stragglers are from the 9th Louisiana. See that they rejoin their unit.*"

"*Yes, sir!*"

Ethan turned to the three Rebs. "*Gentlemen, and I use the title loosely, the war is that way.*" And he pointed toward Cemetery Hill.

"*Yes, sir,*" replied our captor.

"*First, apologize to the doctor.*"

All three reluctantly turned to Doctor J, and one spoke for the others. "*We are sorry if we have offended you, sir.*"

"*Good!*" snapped Ethan. "*Now return to your regiment.*"

After they left under the supervision of the sergeant, and the Union prisoner had been led away, Ethan turned to Doctor J. "*He said there were three prisoners. Where is the third?*"

Doctor J looked over his shoulder at the house. "*My daughter, Jenny, is the third. She went to retrieve my bag.*"

"*Sir, you have my apologies for the behavior of these men. It will not happen again. We mean the civilians no harm. If you have any problems, I'm on General Ewell's staff. Please let me know, and I'll see that the problem is taken care of. Here is my calling card.*" Ethan reached into his jacket pocket and handed a calling card to Doctor J. "*I'm Captain Ethan Joubert.*"

Even from my hiding place peeking through the cracked door I could see the shock on Doctor J's face. "*Captain Joubert?*" He fairly stuttered as he turned and looked back at the house.

"*Everyone knows me. Any of these men can find me.*"

"*I'm Doctor Johnson. I may be able to be of service with your wounded.*"

"*Our surgeons may indeed need help.*"

"*I see two wounded men out on the street. Have your men bring them into the house and I'll treat them.*"

I panicked. Ethan called out two the soldiers tending to the wounded and ordered they be brought to Doctor J's house for treatment.

A very large Negro on a mule rode up to join Ethan and Doctor J. "Cap'n Ethan, sir, General Hays is asking for you. He is just up this street near the square."

"Thank you. Blue, this is Doctor Johnson. Will you please help the good doctor with the wounded?" he asked as he tied Pepper's bridle to a post then gesturing to Pepper said, "And would you feed him when you get a chance."

The big Negro nodded and touched his slouch hat. "Yes, sir."

Doctor J asked Ethan, "Your servant, sir?"

"My friend. He's a freedman and can be trusted." With that Ethan tipped his kepi to Doctor J and headed up East Middle to see Hays.

I was much relieved.

I found Hays near the square in the middle of Gettysburg. "You wanted to see me, sir."

Hays looked up at me from the map he was studying. "Yes, Captain. You've seen the Federal positions on Cemetery Hill?"

"I got a look at them from a distance."

"Your thoughts?"

"We take them now or not at all."

"That's what I thought you would say. I agree. We cannot allow them to harden their positions. It must be now. Then I will count you as a vote to keep pushing?"

"You may. Is there a problem?"

Hays nodded and sighed. "Ewell wants to hold where we are. Says Lee ordered him not to bring on a general engagement because Longstreet is not up, and even if we broke through, he has no reserves to support us."

"That's very unfortunate. If we try to take that position tomorrow or the next day, it will be a slaughter."

"I agree. Most of the brigade commanders want to continue the push on to Cemetery Hill and dislodge the discouraged enemy before they have a chance to reinforce and fortify their positions, but Ewell is under orders." There was much grumbling that Ewell was not Jackson, and Old Jack would have pushed on to exploit the advantage we clearly had at that moment.

I helped Doctor J with the two wounded men. He taught me how to clean wounds and bandage them to keep out foreign matter and flies so the wounds could heal without festering. When our work was done and the two wounded men were resting, I made some soup for them and took some out to Ethan's man, Blue. By then it was nearly dark.

"Some soup?"

He turned from brushing down Pepper and sniffed the air. "Yes, mam! That sure smells good! Thank you, kindly. My name is Blue, and how might I refer to you?"

I was not expecting that, and it took a moment to form a story. "My name is—Jenny," I replied as I handed him the bowl of soup and a fresh biscuit.

"Doctor Johnson's daughter?"

"Yes," I stuttered.

"Pleased to make your acquaintance, Miss Jenny."

Blue sat on the edge of the street and shoveled in a huge spoonful of the soup. And Pepper snorted. He obviously remembered my scent, as he was looking right at me, nodding his head making those peculiar noises he often makes when he wants something. I took a biscuit from my apron pocket as I went over to him. I stroked his neck and fed it to him.

Blue jumped to his feet. "Miss Jenny! Please be careful around that horse. He don't much take to strangers."

I smiled and replied, "Don't worry, Pepper won't hurt me." Then I realized what I said, but Blue appeared to take no notice of me calling Pepper by name, and I relaxed and tried to change the subject. "Are you Captain Joubert's servant?"

Blue looked up from his soup. "I'm his keeper, so-to-speak. Captain Joubert won me in a duel…"

"A duel?"

"Yes, ma'am. It was in New Orleans just as the war started. He saved my life and then he set me free after he got out of jail."

"Jail? What was he in jail for?" I asked.

"They say it was murder, but Cap'n Ethan was only defending hisself."

"What do you mean by 'keeper?'"

"I try to keep him out of trouble. Sometimes I can and sometimes I can't?"

I frowned. "Trouble? What sort of trouble?"

Blue shrugged. "Sometimes he gets melancholy over losing his Rachel, and he takes to drinking."

My eyes began to water, and I did not want to pursue that line any longer. "Joubert? That's French, isn't it?"

"Yes, Missy."

"His father is French?" It was a silly question but all I could come up with.
Blue looked beyond me. "Why don't you ask him. Here he comes."

I stole a quick glance over my shoulder and saw Ethan rounding the corner of the street. "Maybe later," I said to Blue as I fairly snatched the empty bowl from his hand and went inside as fast as I could without actually running.

In the fading light, I noticed Blue talking to the woman, but she went inside before I reached them. Something about the way she moved seemed familiar, but I shook it off. "New friend, Blue?"

"Yes, sir. That was Miss Jenny."

I glanced at the house and replied, "Doctor Johnson's daughter?"

"Yes, sir."

"Couldn't tell much in this light, but she looked like she might be quite pretty. Was she?"

Blue nodded. "Oh, yes, sir. She had beautiful blue eyes that just pierced you all the way to your heart."

"Sorry I missed her. Maybe I will get a chance to meet her before we leave this place."

"She makes good biscuits, too," he said as he handed me the remaining half of his.

As I had not eaten since the night before and was starving, I popped it into my mouth. "This is good. Reminds me of the ones Mammy used to make."

Later that evening, as we listened to the sounds of the enemy frantically working to fortify Cemetery Hill, Lee, Early, Rodes, and Ewell held a council of war to plan the actions of 2 July. It was agreed that Ewell would attack Cemetery Hill in the morning as a diversion for Longstreet's attack on the Round Tops on the Federal left south of us. Early thought any attack on Cemetery Hill would now be risky at best and likely unsuccessful with a frightful loss of life, since the enemy had the chance to harden their positions and bring up more troops.

Culp's Hill, just to the east of Cemetery Hill, was to be part of the diversion attack. It was thought to be unoccupied by the enemy, but it was discovered later that evening such was no longer the case. They occupied positions on the Culp's Hill that would preclude a flanking movement on Cemetery Hill.

With our wounded cared for and either returned to duty or carried away to be attended to by the Confederate surgeons, Doctor J and I finally got to sit down and rest over a cup of tea. Both of us were exhausted from all the excitement but still too excited to sleep.

Even though I could barely see his face in the flickering light of the one candle we dared burn, I could see Doctor J smiling at me. "Well, I suppose the odds were a mite better than I calculated. Now you have seen him, what do you plan to do?"

I did not know how to answer that and paused a long while as I thought about it. "Seeing him was worse than I imagined it might be. Every emotion I have ever felt when I was around him came rushing back like a wave that crashes down and overwhelms my heart. Nothing has changed for me. I still love him with all the intensity I felt for him before… I don't imagine that will ever change."

"Have you changed your mind about speaking to him?"

"No. That would be quite impossible for me to endure."

Chapter 19 – Close Enough to Touch

In the pre-dawn darkness of 2 July, we began positioning our forces for the attack on Cemetery Hill. The 5th, 6th, 7th, 8th, and 9th Louisiana Regiments of Hays' Brigade and the 6th, 21st, and 57th North Carolina Regiments moved into positions in Winebrenner's Run, a shallow creek bed under Cemetery Hill. Moving into the run in daylight would have exposed them to sharpshooters on Cemetery Hill. Once the sun came up, the run's banks offered some protection, but only as long as you remained low and exposed nothing to the enemy.

Later that morning, Lee visited Ewell, and the two stood off alone and had a conversation. I saw Ewell shake his head, and knew that was not good. After Lee left, Ewell called his staff together and told us the attack was being pushed back to 4 p.m. "Captain Joubert, will you please notify Hays of the change?"

"Yes, sir."

I left Pepper in the care of Blue at the Johnson home and made my way down South Stratton Street to find Hays. Aware of the threat of the sharpshooters, the closer I got to Winebrenner's Run, I moved more cautiously from cover to cover to present as small a target as possible for them to take any interest in. At the end of South Stratton, I asked some Rebs taking potshots at Cemetery Hill from an abandoned building where I could find Hays.

"He's in Winebrenner's Run, sir. You ain't planning on going down there are ya?"

"Yep."

"You sure you need to do that, Captain? They'll be takin' shots at ya with them Whitworth rifles with the telescopic sights all the way down to the run. You'll be a big fat target from here on." He gestured toward the back corner of the building, and I saw a dead Confederate slumped against the wall with the top of his head shot away. "Ask him; he'll tell you. He stuck his head out to just have a little peek, and splat! Them Whitworths are deadly. You'll know when you've been shot at by one, 'cause the bullet makes a shrill whistling sound on account of its hexagon rifling."

That was sobering.

I nodded, and he shook his head. "It's your funeral."

I took several deep breaths to steel myself to run the "Whitworth gauntlet." *No use waiting any longer,* I thought and pushed off. I had at least sixty paces of open ground exposed to observation from Cemetery Hill before I had any more cover, a small shed sitting forlornly out in the open. I was not even halfway there, when a ball kicked up dirt not two paces past me. Before I was to the little shed, a shot went past near my head, making the shrill whistling sound just described to me. Any slower, and I would have been hit. I reached the shed just as another round chipped wood splinters from its edge.

Some of the boys down in the run saw me coming under fire and began to cheer. I sunk down behind the shed to catch my breath. For good measure, one of the Yanks put a round through the flimsy little building to remind me of the difference between cover and concealment. The ball whistled through the wooden structure right over my head. Had I been standing instead of crouching down as I was, I would be dead.

I peeked around the building to see my next objective, and they put a ball into the edge of my little shed just as I withdrew my head. I was most impressed with both their rifles and their shooting skills. I did see enough to know this next leg was going to be a long one. There was a sizable oak tree about ninety paces away. I took two deep breaths and then stuck my head around the left side of the shed to draw their attention but quickly withdrew it and ran around the other side and headed for my oak tree.

The ruse worked. They put three balls into the edge of the building where I had stuck my head out, but they were not prepared for me to show myself at the other side. I ran like I was headed for the Baltimore Pike then cut back in the other direction. They fired two more shots at me just as I changed directions. I made it to the tree as another ball chipped bark off its side. The stout oak was more than concealment; it was cover. The cheering from Winebrenner's Run grew louder as others joined in, but I was getting tired.

One last dash left to go. This one was only about forty paces and then the relative safety of the run's high sides. Even though I was getting winded, I could not afford to wait and allow the Yankee sharpshooters time to reload, so I took one quick breath and broke from behind my tree and headed for the run. I ran left then zigzagged right, then left again with balls hitting all around me. As I neared Winebrenner's Run and leaped into the air to clear some brush on its bank, I felt a ball tear through my shell jacket. I landed in a heap against the far side of the run and pulled myself up against its protection as close as I could get. Cheers went up and down the line. I even heard a cheer from the Yankees on Cemetery Hill.

I examined myself to make sure I had not been perforated and only found entry and exit holes in my shell jacket but none in me.

"They ventilated your jacket, Joubert?" asked a familiar voice. I looked up and realized I had landed almost in Hays' lap.

"My apologies, sir. With the compliments of General Ewell..."

He smiled. "Must be important to send you all the way out here to get shot at. What is it?"

"The attack has been pushed back to four this afternoon. You are to wait for the sounds of Johnson's attack on Culp's Hill to start."

Hays was not happy with that news, and it plainly showed in his expression. "That means these men will have to lie under the hot July sun all day or risk being picked off if they try to move!"

I nodded. "Yes, sir. Any message you need me to take back?"

"Yes. You can tell Ewell we should have finished this last night like I wanted to!" I had hoped he would not send me back through the gauntlet, then he said, "But I will not ask you to risk your life for that. You had better stay here with us."

I was much relieved, but without food and extra water it would be a long miserable day for those trapped in Winebrenner's Run. I took a sip from my canteen and hoped I had enough to last until four. I drew my Colt and checked to be sure it was fully loaded. I did not have my sword and was glad of that. It would only have gotten in the way while running the Whitworth gauntlet.

Then I heard another familiar voice say, "Welcome to the party, Captain."

I looked to my right and saw my old messmate, Jean Dubassey, pressed against the side of the bank.

"Fancy meeting you here, Captain Dubassey. And congratulations on the promotion."

Jean lifted his slouch hat to greet me, and a Yankee, with one of those Whitworth rifles, put a ball through it. "My word!" he exclaimed as he examined his newly ventilated headwear. "A man can't even acknowledge a friends compliments without becoming a target. And that was my favorite hat," he said as he wiggled a finger through the new hole.

At a low crouch, I moved down the run and flopped down beside Jean. "There's no accounting for manners with this bunch," I said as I gestured with my thumb toward Cemetery Hill. "Nice hat— I mean *was* a nice hat."

"I paid a two whole dollars for it just last week. Figured to splurge and celebrate my promotion and such." He became serious. "I saw you talking to Hays. Any news you can share?"

I glanced back at Hays. He was busy explaining to some of his regimental commanders what I had just told him. "You'll find out soon enough, but looks like we are stuck in this ditch until four."

In disgust he tossed his head back against the run's bank. "This is going to be a long day," replied Jean with resignation in his voice. "We should have finished this last night when we had the chance."

"That's pretty much what Hays said. Most of the officers and men feel the same."

"Ewell is a good general but he ain't Old Jack, is he?"

I could only nod in the affirmative. "To be fair, Ewell was under orders from Lee not to bring on a general engagement until Longstreet came up."

Jean looked at me from the corner of his eyes. "That wouldn't have stopped Stonewall if he had smelled even a chance of success."

2 July 1863

The day dawned bright and with it came the sound of skirmishing to our south. This went on all morning and into the afternoon, punctuated with periodic cannon duels, the sound coming from the east and the south as the two sides exchanged shots. Since we were not far from Cemetery Hill, the noise was very loud at times. The windows of the house rattled.

I took some coffee and biscuits to Blue and a biscuit for Pepper.

"Where is Captain Joubert this morning?"

Blue gestured with the thumb of his free hand as he took a sip of coffee. "Heard all that shooting a little while ago? That was likely him. He was delivering a message to General Hays down in Winebrenner's Run."

I looked south as if I might catch a glimpse of him, but of course that was quite impossible. "Do you think he was hurt?"

"Don't reckon so. I heard cheering from both the Rebel lines and from the Yankees on Cemetery Hill. I expect he made it just fine."

I looked back in the direction of Cemetery Hill. "He can run plenty fast when he needs to," I replied softly, remembering the time he was chased by that big hog, Old Bull, when he took me hog hunting at Catahoula so many years ago.

"You say something, Missy?"

I realized I had slipped again. "Nothing," I replied, grateful Blue had not heard me.

I went back inside to help Doctor J finish preparing the house to receive the wounded. All the carpets were rolled up and stored, and the furniture was moved out of the main parlor or pushed to the side to allow more room for the wounded. We cleared off the dining room table and covered it with an old canvas tarp. Doctor J set up his instruments on the server and began the process of explaining to me how to be his assistant. While we were finishing, we heard skirmishing over in the direction of the Baltimore Pike, and not thirty minutes later, the wounded started arriving.

And they did not stop coming. By mid-afternoon we had treated over two-dozen men with all manner of wounds, some so grotesque and disfiguring, I could scarcely look at them and hold back my stomach contents. I vowed not to eat again until this was over.

Doctor J was unfazed. Though arthritic, his hands moved with practiced skill to cut off bleeders, dig out balls, and saw off horribly damaged limbs. The screams of the wounded undergoing an amputation without any anesthesia beyond a few snorts of whiskey after he ran out of chloroform are so etched in my mind that I shall never be able to forget it.

I looked into the faces of every wounded man that came in to be sure it was not Ethan we were about to treat.

Orderlies dispatched from the 2nd Corps surgeons showed up and assisted when needed and began removing some of the wounded to the rear in ambulances. But the broken boys just kept coming.

All afternoon we tried our best to keep our heads below the rim of the run, lest a sharpshooter take it off. I tried to make my water last and drank the last of it about four. Others had run out before. The muddy trickle in the run became our only source, and we were grateful for even that.

I checked my watch every ten minutes or so as we neared four in the afternoon, and no sounds of battle came from Culp's Hill to the east to signal that the attack had begun. Four-twenty, four-thirty, five, and no sounds of battle yet came from Johnson. And we waited.

It was near dusk when we finally heard the sound of battle coming from Culp's Hill, followed by a bugle call signaling the attack to begin. Our artillery began to pound Cemetery Hill in earnest, and we stood and formed into line-of-battle to begin the assault.

As the sun was setting, the sounds of battle south of us around Culp's Hill and Cemetery Hill suddenly increased in tempo. The cannons boomed almost ceaselessly and the rattle of muskets merging with the yelling of men going into battle. I heard the famous Rebel Yell for the first time, and it was indeed the same yell I had heard from Ethan on that hog hunt. And I prayed for him. With darkness full upon us, it did not cease, rather the battle raged on into the night.

We stepped off smartly and began our assault, which broke into a running charge. I stayed close to Jean when we began the assault on the hill but lost him in the confusion of the fight. The Yankees stood behind their earthworks and poured volley after volley into our ranks, but we did not falter. It was full dark when some of us finally reached their lines and pushed them back. They rallied and fought with bayonet and clubbed muskets, and we did likewise. They brought up more reserves, but we repulsed them and assaulted their gun line, capturing some of their cannons. It was all hand-to-hand at that point. My Colt was empty, and I picked up a dropped musket and used its bayonet or its butt as needed. Illuminated only by the flash of the cannons and muskets, men of both sides engaged in a desperate struggle to gain control of that hill and, in the darkness, we warriors fell together in death's embrace, one upon the other.

We had broken their line and pushed them back in confusion, but we had no reserves to throw into battle sufficient to sustain our gains. Rodes was to attack with his division from Seminary Ridge, but

216

his attack faltered, and he turned back. Gordon's brigade was left in reserve back in the run but he never got the word to advance. We were all alone on that hill, and in spite of our gains we were compelled to withdraw.

As I moved back through the gun line again, a hand grabbed my ankle. "Ethan!" I looked down, and in the flash of an exploding shell, I saw the face of Jean. He was clutching his stomach. "Help me!"

I knelt. "You hit? How bad?"

"I'm afraid they've kilt me, Ethan," he got out in a horse whisper.

"Not if I can help it," I replied as I looked inside his jacket and saw blood everywhere. I lifted him up in my arms and was grateful for his small stature, making him lighter than most. I carried him down Cemetery Hill, through Winebrenner's Run and up the other side. I was headed for Doctor Johnson as fast as my exhausted and wobbly legs would carry me.

Blue saw me coming and moved ahead to open the door for me and my charge. He got a look at his blackened face. "Captain Jean?"

"Doctor Johnson!"

I immediately recognized his voice and turned to see Ethan brush right past me with his friend in his arms. At first I froze then quickly turned my back to him as Doctor J came to investigate.

"Put him on the table!" said Doctor J, pointing. Ethan gently set him down, and Doctor J held a lamp over the wounded man to examine him. "Get his clothes off!"

Ethan stripped open his jacket and then ripped his shirt completely down the front. Then he tore his unmentionables in a likewise manner, revealing several wounds. Doctor J leaned over and looked closer and wiped blood away to reveal the extent of the damage.

"How bad is it?"

Doctor J looked up at Ethan then over to me standing off in the shadows and watching with a panicked expression on my face. Ethan started to turn to see what Doctor J was looking at, but Doctor J finally answered, "Very bad!" That redirected Ethan's attention back to his friend.

Blue burst into the room. "Cap'n Ethan! General Ewell is asking for you!"

Ethan leaned over his friend. "Jean, can you hear me?"

He opened his eyes, and that is when I realized this was the same Jean that had challenged Ethan to a duel back at Catahoula.

"Ethan?" he replied in a hoarse whisper.

"Yes. You're in good hands..."

"Cap'n Ethan, General Ewell said come quickly," Blue insisted.

Ethan snapped, "I heard you, Blue!" Then he turned back to Jean. "You'll be fine. Doctor Johnson will take care of you. I have to go now, but I'll be back."

With that he turned and rushed from the house passing not five feet from me, but he gave no indication he recognized me or even realized I was standing there. After his passing, I stood fixated on the empty doorway through which he had departed.

Doctor J's stern reprimand snapped me out of my stupor. "Rachel, I need you here. Now. And focused on this problem."

I went to Jean's side and saw three wounds in his stomach and chest. At least one looked like a bayonet puncture. All three were bleeding. I looked up at Doctor J for reassurance that it was not as bad as it looked to my untrained eye. He slowly shook his head in the negative. "How long?"

"Hard to tell. Minutes, hours, maybe another day. I'll do what I can, but his bowels have been perforated and likely an artery from the extent of the bleeding."

That's when I noticed the smell for the first time. I took his hand and leaned over him. Jean opened his eyes and looked at me. A confused expression crossed his face as he stared into my eyes. He continued to focus on my face for a long moment, and then he smiled.

I smiled back. "You know who I am, don't you?"

He nodded weakly. "Rachel?" he barely got out, his voice even weaker than before.

"Yes." I replied as I lightly squeezed his hand and brushed his hair back from his face with my other.

He struggled to speak. "I'm Jean—re-re-remember me?"

"Of course, I do. The duel on a sandbar in the Red River in five feet of water with ten-pound mauls. How could I ever forget?"

A weak smile crossed his lips as he remembered the occasion. It soon disappeared and his eyes slowly closed. I looked up at Doctor J, who felt for a pulse and found one. "Not yet but soon."

"Jean, can you hear me?"

He slowly opened his eyes again and looked into mine. "Ra-rachel, I have to tell you—some—thing."

"No, don't speak, rest, and I will stay here with you and hold your hand."

He tried to speak again, but as he struggled to breathe, foamy blood issued forth from his nose and mouth. "Ha-have to! E-e-than—looking—for you. Tell you—Morgan is dead..."

That was the first I heard that my father was deceased. Jean tried to continue. He reached over and grabbed at my arm with a burst of energy such that I could not imagine from whence it came, and pulled me to him. "Ray—Rachel..." He coughed and more blood came forth from both his wounds and his mouth and nose. "Please! Go to Ethan—he—will tell—you. I can't—I can't..." With that, he partially closed his eyes and stopped breathing.

Doctor J felt for a pulse and found none. He looked at me and shook his head in the negative. "He's gone."

After giving Ewell my report on the assault on Cemetery Hill, I returned to Doctor Johnson's home to see about Jean. I found the doctor hard at work tending to the wounded. He was being assisted by two of our medical orderlies. I was told his exhausted daughter rested in her room.

The good doctor saw me enter and bade me to come to his side as he worked. I stepped over a wounded man and stood beside him as he amputated another man's leg. Fortunately, the man was unconscious. "Your friend passed away soon after you brought him in. We did what we could, but his wounds were mortal. I am deeply sorry for your loss, Captain."

My shoulders slumped. Jean was one of the last of my friends from New Orleans. Only Blue was left, and thankfully, Blue always remained in the rear and well clear of any fighting. Hopefully, I would not also lose him. "This war has been one loss after another for me. First, I lost the woman I love and now most of my friends."

Doctor Johnson motioned to the orderly to finish applying the bandage on the man's stump and bade me to follow him to the kitchen where he offered me a cup of coffee. "This is a terrible war. So many killed..." His voice trailed off before he took a sip of coffee. "Tell me about the woman you lost? Was she killed?"

I thought about that for a moment then bolted down the last of my coffee and replied, "That one is too personal—and too painful for me to discuss. Thank you for what you did for my friend. Good night, sir."

He stopped me as I started to leave. "Will we see you again?"

"Probably not. I understand we are being repositioned to the east. I'm not sure how far or when."

"In that case, Captain, let me say that I'm glad we met, and I sincerely hope you find what you are looking for."

I shook his offered hand and departed. I was not exactly sure what he meant by his statement. I assumed he was alluding to me finding happiness again.

On 3 July, Lee, believing our efforts on the Federal right flank at Culp's Hill and Cemetery Hill and Longstreet's on the Federal left flank at the round tops had weakened the center, launched a frontal attack following a bombardment. Lee was wrong, and the attack failed with an enormous loss of life.

The following day, 4 July, with the sky heavy and a thick mist shrouding the fields of death, we deployed to positions on Seminary Ridge west of town. Union troops cautiously entered Gettysburg following our withdrawal and captured a few stragglers. Lee began evacuating our wounded in preparation of a general withdrawal back to Virginia.

On the morning of 5 July, we began withdrawing from our positions on Seminary Ridge down Fairfield Road toward Hagerstown with Early's division acting as a rear guard for the retreating Army of Northern Virginia. Meade did not pursue vigorously, much to Mr. Lincoln's chagrin.

By 6 July, both armies had decamped from Gettysburg, leaving behind only Federal burial details to bury the dead and medical teams to tend to the wounded. The citizens of Gettysburg were left with all the destruction and horror associated with an abandoned battlefield.

I am sure what happened on 2 July of 1863 will be long debated by the historians. Some will say the Confederate advance ran out of steam after taking the Federal gun line to be pushed back by more northern brigades thrown into the fight.

Others will say the outcome would have been far different if only Rodes and Gordon had thrown everything they had into the battle to exploit what we had accomplished.

Still others will say it would not have mattered even if they had, because the Union forces would have been just too strong for the Confederates to push much beyond where we had.

But I believe the answer is more complicated than that. Looking at pure numbers does not tell the whole story. After the war, some who were there on the other side that night of 2 July told me the South almost won the whole thing. Had we exploited our gains and pushed even a little further, enough to at least appear as if we were threatening to cut the Baltimore Pike south of Cemetery Hill, whether actually able to or not, all Federal resistance might have collapsed for fear we were about to cut off their only supply and escape route.

It is claimed the high tide of the Confederacy was on 3 July with Pickett's charge in the Federal center. I contend it was the night before at Cemetery Hill on the Federal right flank. Either way, the end of the war was sealed at Gettysburg, but it would drag on for nearly two more bloody years.

I do know this much: The Tigers from Louisiana complained that once again they had gained for the South the potential for a great victory, only for that opportunity to be lost for want of forces to exploit what we had won with our precious blood.

5 July 1863

Ethan is gone, and I am trying to understand what I am feeling now. It has been over two years since I last saw him, and we spent such a wonderful night together in his cabin completely immersed in our love for each other with the rest of the world and all its cares out of our thoughts. It will be impossible for me to ever forget that night, and yet I must try to do so. I thought I had made some progress in putting Ethan and our love behind me, but seeing him again, hearing his voice and feeling his presence close enough I could have reached out and touched him, proved the folly of that thought.

What am I to do? How can I forget what we mean to each other? How can I not love him? I am becoming reconciled to the thought that I will never find romance again; I will never find someone who will love me like Ethan did; and I can never find someone I can love as I do so love Ethan, even now.

Author's Note: Before the attack, General Ewell and engineer Captain H. B. Richardson rode forward near Hays' position and were warned about the Whitworth sharpshooters. Ewell scoffed at the danger as they were over a half-mile away. Soon after, Ewell took a ball from the sharpshooters in his wooden leg and Richardson was shot through the body.

An Eternity of Four Years

Chapter 20 – Face to Face

As the Army of Northern Virginia moved south to lick its wounds, General Ewell sent me back to look for stragglers and guide them if I found any. I had gone about five miles back and found none but the dead and some cast off equipment littering the road. Here and there I found broken supply wagons or artillery caissons and a few dead horses and mules. The few stragglers I encountered I encouraged along, lest they become prizes for the Yankee cavalry likely shadowing our tail.

Satisfied that most our people were all up with the retreating army, I turned and hurried to catch up. As I rode along at a canter, I noticed movement off to my right on a farm road that intersected the road I was on. At first I believed the horsemen I saw to be Confederate cavalry screening our retreat. With one look through my spyglass, I soon I realized my grave mistake. They were Federal cavalry, a small skirmish party of six men. With but a hundred yards separating us, they saw me about the same time I realized my error. Two shots rang out from their Sharps carbines, and the balls buzzed angrily passed as I touched spurs to Pepper's flanks.

The chase was on!

Pepper and I dashed down the road for about a mile with the Yankees in hot pursuit, and though I was well mounted, their horses were fresher, and they were gaining on me. I knew my chances of outrunning them were slim. Pepper, however, loved to jump, and I hoped the Yankee mounts did not, at least not all of them. Taking to the fields cross-country seemed my best chance. There, Pepper would be in his element, and tired or not, he would have the advantage. With his love of jumping, he would also likely find new vigor.

Ahead, I saw the road turned sharply to the left. I had no intention of making that turn, instead I would let Pepper jump the stone fence bordering the road and head for the woods across the fields beyond. I gave my big gray his lead and hunched down low behind his neck. I could swear Pepper anticipated my wishes, for he increased his speed as we drew closer to the turn and the fence. Two more shots buzzed passed my ears as we sailed over the stone fence pretty-as-you-please. Pepper hit the soft sod of the field and dug in, surging ahead with newfound vigor. I looked back and saw the Yankee troopers approaching the fence. Five sailed over as easily as we had, but the last horse balked at the last second, and rider went over his mount's head and into the stone fence headfirst, which likely broke his neck.

I still had five troopers in pursuit and bent to catch this lone Rebel prize, but Pepper was no longer loosing ground to them, the softer surface working to his advantage. More shots rang out, and the balls buzzed passed. I was thankful they were lousy shots. As we crossed the field, we came upon another low stone fence, no challenge for Pepper or our pursuers, for that matter. Over we went into a pasture, and I drew the Colt, deciding it was time to make the Federals a bit more cautious. I turned in the saddle and hung from Pepper's side, leveling the big pistol at my pursuers and let fly two .44 caliber balls. One trooper rolled off his horse onto the ground, and the other four split apart to offer a more difficult shot for me.

Over another fence and down into the woods we went. Being used to this sort of a ride chasing dogs and hogs back home, Pepper and I had the advantage. With me down low behind his neck, Pepper avoided the trees, low branches and rocks with practiced ease, while the Federals behind us had difficulty and lost ground to us. We went over a shallow creek and up a ridge. As we topped it, I looked back and saw the Yankees just jumping the creek, a good seventy yards behind. I went down the other side of the ridge, Pepper slipping and sliding on the forest bed of dead leaves and barely avoided hitting a tree. Down in the bottom, he picked up speed, and we turned to our left and up another ridge. Behind us, the Federals had trouble negotiating the steep and slippery slope, and one slammed into the tree we had barely avoided. The trooper hit a low branch, taking the blow right in his neck. That was the last we saw of him that day.

Only three remained now, the odds had narrowed right nicely. We broke out of the woods into another field, a wide and rolling pasture with woods on the other side some two hundred yards distant. I headed Pepper for the woods, hoping another dose of trees might dampen their ardor for this chase. Halfway across the field, I turned in the saddle and saw the remaining troopers had cleared the woods but were still about seventy-five yards or so behind us. More shots rang out, and I hugged Pepper's neck to present a smaller target. One of the troopers was a sergeant, and he let fly a round as I was looking back at them. The ball went by close enough I felt it passing. I picked out a clearing in the trees at the edge of the woods up ahead that seemed like a good place to jump the stone fence separating the field from the woods and touched spurs to Pepper's flanks. Once more, I was gaining on the Yanks and felt I just might avoid capture or death this day.

I gave Pepper his lead as we approached the fence. As we cleared it, I saw that I had made a poor choice of a place to enter the woods. The ground dropped away sharply on the other side. The slope was steep and slippery with forest litter, and two cows were in the bottom and directly in our path! Pepper saw the problem and tried to adjust his landing to no avail. We slid pall-mall down the slope with Pepper down on his haunches as he plowed into the side of one of the cows. The impact threw me from the saddle. I tried to hang onto my mount's neck and failed, slamming into the bony hip of the cow. A sharp stabbing pain in my side nearly caused me to blackout as I flipped over the cow's back and onto the ground. The cow went down with Pepper on top, and I just barely got clear of the two of them.

Both animals struggled to their feet, and I scrambled to get clear of them and get to my own feet in spite of the stabbing pain in my right side. Somehow I had managed to hang onto my Colt. I looked up and saw the first of the Yanks clear the fence and the astonished expression on his face as he realize his mistake of following me. I threw up the Colt and fired, rolling him from the saddle before his mount even hit the ground again. The second was right behind him and just to his right. Like his friend and me before him, he realized his error the moment he cleared the fence. I gave him a ball in the chest, and he slid off the side of his horse as the frightened animal slipped down the slippery slope right for me. I managed to dodge the horse and looked for the third Yank, the sergeant that was surely right behind. He did not come over the fence in the clearing as the rest of us had done, but rather jumped his mount right through the bushes at the field's edge to the right of the opening and directly above me. I looked up to see a horse and rider plunging through the greenery like some specter from a nightmare and headed straight for me with branches and leaves following him. I managed to get off one wild shot that missed as his mount slammed into me and knocked me down, throwing him from the saddle at the same time.

Something struck me in the head. I was knocked to the ground and very nearly lost consciousness as a result of the blow. For a long moment, I lay there with my head in a fog, not knowing where I was. With stinging blood in my eyes, my vision was blurred. I looked up and was barely able to discern the Yank sergeant coming at me with his saber raised over his head to strike a mortal blow. I rolled clear of his saber as he cut the ground where my head had been only a fraction of a second earlier. Somehow, I managed to get to my feet and found my Colt was gone. I drew my own sword just in time to deflect the slash of the Yank's saber, and the sound of cold steel on steel rang through the forest.

My attempts to wipe the blood from my eyes with my hand or my sleeve proved fruitless. In spite of seeing only shapes and few details, I managed to awkwardly deflect another slashing blow from the Yank, but he came right back at me. I was never very good with the sword, and by this man's movements, I could tell that he was. There was no question in my mind that I was outclassed. I could do little more but fend off his blows and retreat, unable to take the offensive.

He drew blood first, as my parry to his thrust was deftly deflected, and he slashed at my face, the tip of his blade catching my nose and left cheek right below the eye. I knew the cut was deep. I felt the blade hit the bone of my cheek. That made me angry. I swung back aggressively, catching him off guard, but he quickly recovered. Once more, steel crashed together, and sparks flew, and I was barely able to deflect the blows. As I backed away from his hammering slashes, I tripped and fell. He saw his chance and slashed downward, the silver blade aimed at my neck. I barely got my saber up to block, his blade slamming heavily into mine near the quillon. I hadn't enough leverage. His stroke followed through, with his blade finding my shoulder and cutting deeply into the muscle. Had I not blocked the slashing blow, it would surely have taken my arm off.

I kicked at his groin and connected. He doubled over, and I scrambled away from him like a crab until I could find my footing again. My left arm was now hanging useless at my side. I also felt the warm wetness of my blood on my neck and chest from my head wounds and could taste its iron saltiness in my mouth. I had three wounds that were bleeding heavily. I was growing weaker by the moment.

I wobbly found my feet and leaned on my sword for support. My antagonist regained his composure and came at me once more, this time screaming as he thrust at my belly. I barely managed to deflect the thrust away. I realized he was also tiring, but I found little solace in this fact, as he had not yet received even a scratch from me. Once more he came at me, slashing savagely. I weakly deflected the blows able to do little more as I backed away.

With one mighty heave he swung at me, and I managed at the last possible moment to get my sword up to block him. So heavy was the blow, it carried my blade with it, wrenching it from my hand. He recovered and thrust at my chest as I backed away and dodged at the last second. His blade entering my left side just under my arm and came out my back at the same level. The power of the thrust very nearly knocked me down. His face, little more than a blood red silhouette, was but inches from mine, but I could see just enough to discern that he sported a wide handlebar mustache. I managed to get my Bowie out, and brought it from behind my back, ramming it forcefully upward under his ribs all the way to the hilt. As the blade tip reached his heart, he looked at me with an astonished expression on his face.

And he said in a thick Irish brogue, "Ya kilt me, lad!"

My heart sank as he collapsed against me. I pushed him away as if that would change what I had done, and he fell facedown at my feet. Using my already bloody sleeve, I wiped my eyes as best I could to get a better look at him. He was tall, bowlegged and had flaming red hair! And I became sick to my stomach.

His saber was still in my side buried all the way to the hilt. I stood there and wobbled back and forth as I tried to stay conscious and stay on my feet, but darkness descended upon me.

Chapter 21 – "Call Me Taylor."

15 July 1863 (From diary entries recording earlier events.)

Both armies are gone, and we are left with the remnants of the great battle. Words cannot begin to describe what awaited us as we ventured out of our homes and hiding places after the armies left. Broken wagons, gun carriages, caissons, abandoned muskets, canteens, sabers, ration boxes, ammunition—all manner of military equipage is everywhere, not to mention all the damaged or destroyed buildings.

The entire town is permeated with the stench of corruption. It is especially bad when the wind is blowing from one of the main battlefields. Dead animals and dead men have lain out putrefying in the hot July sun! One cannot escape the smell. It seeps into everything, your home, your clothing, your very being, it seems.

The flies have descended upon the town like some Biblical plague. They are everywhere, and you cannot escape them! They are in your face, in your nose, and even your mouth if you open it too wide to speak. Eating a meal, if one can stomach food with the smell of death so strong, is a battle with the flies.

It has been five days since the battle was joined; four days since Cemetery Hill, and three since the great Southern charge against the Union's center that some are calling "Pickett's Charge," so named for the general who led it—and they are still finding wounded men on the many fields and in the woods and buildings all around Gettysburg. Poor hurt men incapable of escaping the heat of day, dying for want of a sip of cool water to quench their thirst, exhausted from crying out for help, or unconscious from the pain of it all.

We are still tending to the wounded left in the care of Doctor J when the Army of Northern Virginia departed. Union medical orderlies came yesterday and took away the two blue-coated soldiers we were caring for, but they left us with over a dozen Confederates.

Doctor J has also been assisting with the wounded in the church down the street where there are many more needing medical help. The poor man is exhausted as am I. We take turns caring for the men left with us to give the other a chance to get a little rest.

On the sixth, near sunset, I was changing the bandage on the amputated leg of one of the men in our care. With the soiled bandage removed, I put my nose close to his stump to smell for corruption and found none. I bathed his stump with a cloth soaked in brandy. I then carefully wrapped it in freshly washed bandages. As I finished and tied off the end of the bandage, I heard a voice say, "Excellent work! Were you trained by Miss Clara Barton?"

I looked up and a young Union officer, a major, stood in the doorway. He was almost as tall as Ethan but had sandy hair and light blue eyes. With his boyish looks, he appeared to be not much older than I, and I must confess, very pleasing to look upon. His uniform was well tailored and clean. Even his boots were shined. He wore no sword or pistol on his belt, which I thought strange. Obviously, he had quietly observed me as I changed the bandage. I had not realized he was there.

I stood, and in a weak attempt to make my unkempt self a bit more presentable, smoothed out my apron and brushed back the hair that had fallen into my face. "No, sir. I was not trained by Miss Barton."

"Are you Doctor Johnson's assistant?"

"Yes, and it was he who trained me, such training that I do have. My first lesson was but five days ago."

"He taught you well, and you must learn fast. Did he also teach you to bathe the wound in spirits?"

"Yes. He believes it helps prevent corruption, but he's not sure why."

The major moved closer. The first thing I noticed was he smelled clean, and I realized I must have smelled like a pig. I had not had a bath in nearly a week, and my clothing was soiled with my own perspiration and the blood of the wounded. He smiled. It was a warm smile that made me feel at ease with him. "You must be Miss Rachel, and I was not expecting what I found."

"And what exactly were you expecting, sir?"

"I just arrived here from Washington, and all I've seen since has been ugliness wrapped in the smell of death. You, Miss Rachel, are the loveliest sight these poor eyes have beheld in a very long while—if you will forgive me for being so forward?"

I was shocked and flattered by his statement and could only stammer, "Thank you, sir. It must be the fading light of day that deceives your eyes? I am quite a mess just now."

"No, my eyes have not been deceived, I assure you."

I could think of little else to say. "I believe you have the advantage?"

He smiled that warm and inviting smile of his and replied, "Forgive me! My manners… I'm Doctor Taylor Anderson, and I'm most pleased to meet you, Miss Rachel." He seemed to emphasize the "Miss." "I was told of the work you and Doctor Johnson have been doing, and you still had wounded in your care. I came to see for myself and relieve you of some of that burden." He turned and gestured to several men with litters waiting outside. "I believe these wounded men are all Rebels?"

"Yes. Your people came and took the Union wounded in our care away yesterday, but they left the Confederates."

"We'll move them all down to the church. It will be easier to care for them there. They'll be treated same as the men in blue, I assure you. Is Doctor Johnson about?"

"Did I hear my name?" asked Doctor J as he entered the parlor pulling on his coat.

"Doctor Johnson, I'm Doctor Anderson, and we're here to help with your wounded. It was kind of you to take these men in, Rebel or Yank."

"I am a doctor first, an American second."

"I understand, sir. We are still woefully short of medical help. Would it be possible for you and your able assistant to continue to help with the wounded?"

Doctor J looked first at me, and I nodded. "We would be honored. What can we do?"

"I hate to ask this of you, but there are yet wounded men unattended on Cemetery Hill. Can you help us there?"

"Of course."

The sun fully set and darkness upon us, our charges removed to the church, we joined Doctor Anderson in an ambulance for the short ride to Cemetery Hill. As we approached, we saw men with lanterns moving over the north face and the top of the hill. With the weak ethereal light of the lanterns casting ghostly dancing shadows as the men moved about the hill and examined the many bodies there for some flicker of life, it looked like a picture out of some hideous nightmare.

We dismounted near the gate of the cemetery. They had tents set up, and in the light of lanterns, we saw litters of wounded men lying out in the open air for as far as could be seen in the weak light.

And the stench of death! It was even stronger there!

Doctor Anderson brought us inside a large tent set up as an operating theater with several tables for conducting procedures, each held a wounded man with orderlies or surgeons tending to them. I felt sick to my stomach and wanted to fall down and weep for what these poor men had been going through, but I steeled myself and called upon the Lord to give me the strength to endure what I knew I would be facing. And I needed every ounce of help He would give me.

Doctor Anderson assigned Doctor J to one of the tables. An orderly and I assisted. This went on through the night. As soon as one man was attended to, his wound treated, his arm or leg amputated, they carried him off and brought in another, one long stream of broken men, one after another.

With the coming of dawn, Doctor Anderson brought us coffee and suggested we rest for a while. I took my coffee to go outside and get away from the blood and gore to hopefully enjoy the sunrise. Doctor Anderson followed me. "Miss Rachel, I would suggest you remain inside."

I ignored his warning. "I must see the sun!" But when I stepped outside, and my eyes adjusted to the light of the early dawn, I dropped my coffee! What was hidden by darkness during our arrival was now fully visible.

Death! It was everywhere! I looked to the north and saw the bodies of men clad in blue and gray, some stacked upon each other, some sprawled across broken gun carriages, some with their bodies twisted into positions God never intended them to ever assume, and still others only a part of a man with missing arms, legs, heads, and sometimes missing a whole half of his body, his entrails spilled out on the ground.

I fainted! Doctor Anderson caught me as I went down.

I awoke a short while later to the pungent aroma of smelling salts and Doctor Anderson tending to me with Doctor J standing nearby looking concerned. "I tried to warn you," he almost pleaded.

"I should have listened. So, this is a battlefield…" I stated as a matter of fact with resignation in my voice.

"Not very pretty is it?" replied Doctor Anderson.

I tried to rise, but he pushed me back down. "Rest a moment."

"No!" I insisted. "I have too much work to do!"

There was indeed "too much work to do," and we went about it as exhausted as we were, because they were still finding wounded men on the field for us to attempt to repair their broken bodies. I became almost calloused to their cries of pain as we tended to them. I had to. We all had to. Their wounds needed treatment, and that often involved pain, though we did, at least, have chloroform for amputations.

This went on for three more days. We worked for as long as we could keep our eyes open and then rested for an hour, maybe two or three if fortunate enough, grabbed a quick bite of something or a cup of coffee, and went back to our loathsome task.

And the wounded kept coming. They found a barn full of wounded Confederates, some of whom had died for want of care and just a sip of water. One man bribed the landowner to bring them water and send for help.

The burial details went about their gruesome task of collecting the thousands of bodies and burying them as quickly as they could, but it was never quick enough. The smell of death was overpowering, especially when the wind blew from one of the several major battlefields still littered with the dead.

I lost track of the time. Doctor Anderson told me to go home and get some rest. I refused. He insisted.

"What about Doctor J?"

"My dear, he is leaving, also. I am about to forcefully confine him to a cot in the tent next to this one—under guard if necessary."

"He needs to go home to rest," I insisted.

"No, he does not need to go home, because I need to keep an eye on him. I don't like his color."

That disturbed me. "Is he sick?"

"I think he is only tired. He is doing too much for a man his age and needs the rest even more than you do. Now, get out of here. That is an order. Rest assured, I will take good care of Doctor Johnson for you."

He literally took me by the arm and escorted me from the tent and instructed an orderly to take me home. I was too exhausted to resist.

Once back at the house, the mess in which we had left it days before was still there to greet me: dried blood on the floor, the table, and even the walls. Bloody bandages and sodden bedding had been left by the wounded. The house stank nearly as bad as Cemetery Hill. Tired as I was, I set about cleaning it up by first throwing open the windows to air the place out. I then set about scrubbing floors, disposing of the refuse left by the wounded, and changing our bedding.

I don't know how long it took, but I got the house clean enough I could tolerate it (my standards of cleanliness were, by then, greatly reduced from what they had been before the battle). After getting a good fire going in the stove, I fried our last two eggs and very nearly inhaled them. I then boiled water, made a cup of tea and poured a steaming hot bath. With my cup of tea in hand, I slipped into the tub and sank into pure heaven on earth. That bath felt better than any I had ever experienced in my entire life. I soaked until the water was tepid then washed with soap from head to toe—three times to be sure I was completely clean! I put on a clean nightgown, fell into a freshly made bed, and was fast asleep the moment my head hit the pillow. I dreamt a strange dream of Ethan sitting at the foot of my bed watching over me as I slept.

With a start, I was awakened by the sound of the front door opening. I threw on a dressing gown and went to investigate to find Doctor J casting off his coat. He still looked tired but his color was better. "Are you well?"

"Tolerable. They no longer need us on the hill," he replied. "The worst of the wounded have been moved to the church or evacuated to Washington or Baltimore if they can handle the trip. Others able to do so have been sent home to convalesce or returned to duty."

"I missed a lot. How long have I been gone?"

"I reckon about eighteen hours. Doctor Anderson came down to look in on you a few hours ago. He was gone quite a while. What did you two talk about?"

"I never spoke to him—or even saw him."

"He said you were fine, so he must have spoken to you."

"I was asleep until you came in." Then I remembered the dream. Was it Taylor Anderson sitting at the foot of my bed?

Doctor J and I continued our work with the wounded at the church. There were still some surgical procedures to perform, mostly amputations when wounds began to gangrene or to remove balls missed earlier. My duties were mostly changing bandages and helping the wounded to be as comfortable as possible.

I soon discovered I was much in demand as a female voice, who reminded them of a mother or sweetheart back home. These poor hurt boys needed that perhaps more than any other treatment. Healing begins in the mind is what Doctor J once told me. A man who is comfortable and has someone to comfort him heals much faster than one whose mind is conflicted with stressful thoughts. These men had been through much, and many were mere teenagers. One was barely thirteen, a drummer. They should be home tending to chores, fishing, hunting, and courting sweethearts, not killing other men.

Doctor Anderson was ever nearby and often took time to speak an encouraging word to me. "Whatever you are doing, don't stop. I have men all over this church asking about the beautiful nurse with the blue eyes and soft voice. And they smile when they ask. They all want to know when you will be back to visit them?"

"I just talk to them or listen when they want to talk, or write a few letters home for them. I do portrait sketches of them if they want. I make them small enough they can be mailed home to a mother or sweetheart to place in a locket, watch or small frame. They seem to very much appreciate that."

"I heard you are an artist. What you are doing lifts their spirits. Keep it up." He paused for a moment. "And it helps mine also. It is nice to have something lovely to look at in the midst of such ugliness."

That set me to thinking. "Which reminds me. When you sent me home, while I was sleeping, I had a dream that—someone was watching me. Was that you?"

He blushed and looked down as if caught in some mischief. "Guilty." Then he looked into my eyes, his gaze penetrating. "I came to make sure you were well. Not wanting to disturb you if you were sleeping, I entered the house very quietly and found you sound asleep. You were such a lovely sight, I could not stop watching you."

"How long were you there?" I queried with a stern reprimand in my expression and in my voice.

"Just a minute..."

Like I had learned from Analee back at Catahoula, my left eyebrow went up. "How long?"

It worked. He stammered, "Well, maybe it was a little longer..."

"Sir, I am not accustomed to entertaining men in my bedroom."

He sighed with a hangdog expression on his face, which I am sure was for my benefit only. "I apologize. But you looked so captivating..."

"What am I to do with you, Major Anderson?"

"Shall we start by saying you can call me Taylor?"

Chapter 22 – Wounds Physical and Emotional

As my eyes tried to adjust to my hazy surroundings, I became aware I was in some kind of warehouse building. All around me I could hear a thousand voices and men talking or weeping and moaning in pain. As I slowly regained my focus, I saw Blue hovering over me tending to my wounds.

"Where am I?"

Blue looked up from his task and smiled. "Welcome to the world of the living again."

"You didn't answer my question," I replied weakly.

"Richmond."

"How did I get here?"

"I brung you. Found you almost dead and brung you to the surgeons. They didn't think you would live, said you had lost too much blood, but I told 'em I would make sure you lived if they would treat your wounds. They did, and I was right. You're alive, ain't you?"

"I am not so sure about that. My chest hurts!"

"You have two broken ribs on the right side and a nasty wound on the other. Saber?"

"Yes, saber." I barely got out. Speaking was painful.

I don't know how I managed to rejoin our retreating column. Blue told me later he came looking for me when I didn't return soon enough for his liking. He found me on Pepper just two miles from the tail of the column. I had somehow strapped myself into the saddle. I'm sure I didn't have sufficient strength to climb up onto Pepper on my own. I had taught him to lay down before we went west to serve with the Regiment of Mounted Riflemen. I can only assume I made him lie down so I could crawl onto the saddle. There is no other way I could have gotten on his back. I have no recollection of removing the saber from my side, but I did and somehow wrapped myself with a bandage I kept in my saddlebags.

The wound to my head was not bad; it merely bled a lot, and the blood blinded me during the fight. The saber cut to my face was a bit worse, but the surgeons stitched it closed easily enough, which they also did with the more severe wound in my shoulder. Today, I wear scars as a reminder of the event.

The saber wound in my side was far worse but not as bad as it could have been. Twisting at the last moment saved my life. The tip caught my side and glanced off a rib rather than penetrating my chest and lung. The entrance and exit wounds were nasty and bled a lot but were not life threatening. The broken ribs from hitting the cow were another matter. Breathing was painful for me for months after.

I lost consciousness after the fight and did not regain full awareness of my surroundings until I awoke in a hospital in Richmond nearly a week later. I had only some vague memories of being jostled around in an ambulance on the way to Richmond but nothing more of how I got there. Blue told me I had a fever much of the time and spoke nonsense about all manner of things, mostly Rachel and Tom Sullivan.

The fight in that bottom slowly began to come back to me, and I recalled what I had done. In my mind's eye, I could see him lying there on the ground, bleeding out from my knife thrust to his heart, and I again became sick at my stomach and nearly threw up, which would have been exceedingly painful with my broken ribs. Of all the men in the world I could come face-to-face with on a battlefield, why him? As a result, I sank into a melancholy that was deep and long.

I did not want to live. Rachel was still lost to me, Sean and Jean were dead, the Cornfield, Cemetery Hill, and now this? A man can take only so much pain before his mind says "enough!" And my mind was saying it had enough—enough of all of it, enough of Rachel gone, enough death, enough killing, and enough of this damn war. ENOUGH!

"I'm worried about you, Cap'n Ethan. The doc say you ain't getting any better. In fact, he told me you was getting worse. I can tell something is paining you in the head. Maybe you should talk to Old Blue about it?"

He was right. I was getting worse, but I did not care any longer. "Not something I want to talk about, Blue. Just leave me alone."

"You already alone—inside your head, and you need to come out where the rest of us are."

I became angry and replied sharply, "I said, leave me alone!"

He snorted a half laugh. "That ain't goin' to happen, Cap'n Ethan. I told you way back in New Orleans I'm responsible for you now. I'm not going to let you just go crazy. Now, tell Blue what happened out there?"

"It's none of your business."

"I'm making it my bidness."

"Well don't bother!'

"Then let's try this: where is your God, Cap'n Ethan? You should be prayin' and callin' on Him right now"

I snorted a half laugh. "Why? He doesn't care about me."

"Look at you, a sorry mess of a man all soaked with sweat and talkin' crazy. God does care 'bout you! Where'd you get that silly notion? God loves you!"

I turned over and glared at him as hard as I could in my addled state. "He gave me a wonderful woman to love then took her away. He gave me a friend, and I killed him! And I am stuck in the Confederate Army in a war with no end; unable to find that woman He gave me—and killing my friends in the process. Why? Honor? Well. Honor. Be. Damned! This war *was* supposed to be about defending my home and my state, which is now occupied by the enemy—ironic isn't it? But now, the war is about defending this peculiar institution, and I am not even a slave owner. What am I doing here? No! Don't answer that, just leave me alone." And I turned my back to him.

"You need to get him out of here." I heard a surgeon tell Blue. "This place is doing him no good."

"I can see that, but where'll I take him?"

"Some of the local citizens are taking in the wounded to convalesce, perhaps one of them? If he stays here, he'll die—or go insane, if he hasn't already. You need to get him out of this melancholy state he is in. To do that, he needs to be away from the war for a while."

Then I heard a woman's voice join the conversation. "And what have we here?"

"Ma'am, Captain Joubert here is badly hurt," the surgeon replied. "His body is slowly healing, but his mind is not. He's suffering from nostalgia. There's nothing more I can do for him. You know anyone who can take him in until he heals?"

"Oh, dear." She bent over and touched me on the shoulder, expecting I would turn to face her. "Captain?"

"Go away!"

She paused, making no reply as she cocked her head.

"Somethin' wrong, Missy?" asked Blue.

"I thought…" she started to say something then shook her head. "Captain, I'm here to help with the wounded. Won't you let me help you?"

That voice sounded familiar. I turned over to face her, and she gasped, "Ethan?"

"You know this man?" asked the surgeon.

"Yes, I do. Ethan, it's me. Laura."

I squinted at her.

"Ethan, it's Laura. Don't you remember me?"

I tried to focus on her face. She looked familiar. "Laura?"

"You do remember!"

"Go away," I replied as I turned away from her.

She stood tall and placed her hands on her hips. "Not this time, mister! You aren't dealing with the same little, love-sick seventeen year-old you told that to seven years ago." She turned to the surgeon. "Is he well enough to travel?"

"As long as it isn't too far."

She then looked to Blue and snapped, "You his servant?"

Blue took a step back. "I'm his friend and protector, ma'am."

"Then pack him up. You two are coming with me."

27 July 1863

Many of the remaining wounded were moved east a few days ago; only a few are left in our care, and there are ample surgeons and medical orderlies to see to their needs so our work is drawing to a close.

The burial details, however, continue with their ghastly task. Thankfully, the stench of death has abated somewhat, even though most of the dead remain unburied, a task that is overwhelming. The Union dead were buried first, and the

Confederate dead after, and both were buried where they fell. The union dead were usually buried in individual graves, and the Confederates in mass grave trenches with them laid out in a row. When one trench was filled with dead packed shoulder to shoulder, another was dug to extend it and its dirt was used to cover the one just filled with dead. Often they were buried little more than a foot or eighteen inches, sometimes less with a toes or a face still visible above the ground. The graves are marked and their locations are recorded.

Taylor walks me home from the church each night, and we talk of many things, but especially not about the war. His father was also a surgeon, and his mother died when he was but seventeen. He has two sisters back in Baltimore where he is from. One is married with two children. Her husband is in the army with Grant. The other is engaged to a young cavalryman. Taylor went to medical school when he was very young, and once in the army, advanced in rank rapidly due to his surgical and administrative skills. He's is the same age as Ethan.

I enjoy his company, but he expects to get orders sending him somewhere else in this war. I will miss him. His warm smile, his jokes, his many compliments, his soft touch on my arm, all make me feel like a woman again and less like some lost soul. It just might be possible to fall in love, after all.

That said, my mind still brings up images of Ethan to confuse me. In some ways Taylor reminds me of Ethan, but perhaps a quieter more contemplative version.

When Taylor walked me home tonight, he seemed unsure of himself at first. Then he blurted out, "I will be leaving soon, and I'm going to miss you. May I have your permission to write you?"

"Of course. And I shall miss you, as well."

He smiled his mischievous smile and tilted his head. "How much will you miss me? A lot? A little?"

"Major Anderson! We hardly know each other, and you ask such questions?"

"Rachel, in case you've not noticed, there is a war on—"

"Oh, I have noticed, sir!"

"Then you must understand such tends to shorten what normally might take longer."

I smiled at him in a questioning manner. "And what are you suggesting?"

He frowned and looked down as if embarrassed. "I am not good at this. What I'm saying is I've grown very fond of you, and I was hoping your feelings for me might be likewise."

I was not prepared for this discussion. "Taylor, there are things about me you do not know and you should. Perhaps some day I can explain it all to you, but for now, let me just say I may not be ready for a—relationship yet."

He looked stunned. "There is someone else?"

"Yes and no. It did not work out for us, and I have not yet recovered from the experience. I'm flattered by your interest in me, and I hope we can get to know each other better."

"What did he do to you?"

"He did nothing wrong, but someone else did and destroyed what we had."

"You were in love with him?"

"Yes."

"And you still are?"

I had hoped not to face such a question from Taylor just yet, and I hesitated to answer truthfully for fear of offending him.

"I'll take your silence as a yes."

"I'm sorry, Taylor. You must give me some time to adjust to all this."

He nodded, but his expression was one of disappointment. "I understand. I can be patient."

He said that, but I knew he didn't mean it. We bade each other goodnight, and I kissed him on the cheek before I went inside to find Doctor J waiting for me. "Major Anderson seems to be smitten by you."

My Analee eyebrow went up. "You were listening?"

He made some fluttering gestures with his hands as if confused. "I was just passing by the door."

"Sir, the door is a bit out of the way to be just passing by..."

He ignored my challenge. "What are you going to do about him?"

I sighed. "Nothing yet. I don't want to rush into something I'm not ready for."

"And what of Ethan?"

"What has he to do with this?"

He seemed frustrated at my answer. "You are still in love with him. That has a lot to do with this, as you say."

"I'm getting the impression that you think I should not be so quick to cast off Ethan?"

"Quick? You don't do anything having to do with the heart at any speed I would remotely call quick. I am just saying you should speak to Captain Joubert before you —shall we say—move on."

"I am sorry. I cannot do that."

"Well, so am I."

He turned to go to his room and paused then grabbed the back of a chair before clutching his left arm.

"Doctor J? Something wrong?"

He stood upright and continued on his way. "I'm fine. Pulled muscle in my arm," he snapped.

28 July 1863

I awoke the next morning with little to do but prepare some breakfast and continue with my housecleaning. With the stove fired up, I started some biscuits using the same recipe Mammy taught me back at Catahoula. They were Ethan's favorites. Once they were in the oven, I retrieved a side of bacon from the cellar and sliced off enough for the two of us. I so wanted some eggs to go with the bacon and biscuits, but the Confederates had eaten all our chickens.

With the bacon fried and the biscuits fresh out the oven, I called to Doctor J, who was usually up by then.

"You sleeping late?" But I got no answer.

Then I remembered the episode of the previous evening when he grabbed at his arm, and I went to his door and knocked softly. "Doctor J, are you awake?" And I still did not get an answer.

I became alarmed and opened the door to find him in bed with the covers pulled up to his shoulder. "You were tired," I said softly as I crept over to kiss him on his forehead. And my lips touched cold skin! I screamed!

3 August 1863

The last few days were among the worst in my life, as bad as the death of my mother when I was just fourteen and losing Ethan five years later. Taylor was always at my side, and I leaned heavily on his physical and moral support. He stayed with me, usually his arm about me pulling me close to his side.

We buried Doctor J on Cemetery Hill where he had worked so hard to bring relief and medical aid to the wounded, both those in blue and those in gray. As one of Gettysburg's most loved citizens, many in the town attended his funeral. Throughout those three days, I did not shed a tear, just as I had not for my mother when she passed. Once more I was alone in this world. All those I loved had been taken from me; I had no one to turn to—except Taylor, whom I hardly knew. Had he not been there, I could not have endured the times.

After the funeral, we returned to Doctor J's house where some of his friends had gathered to remember him. Taylor was ever by my side. When everyone but Taylor had left for the evening, I sank into the sofa feeling completely spent. There was a weariness that reached all the way to my bones, and I felt as if I would not be able to stand again. Taylor sat beside me and put his arm around me.

"Rachel, I cannot begin to express my feelings for you at this time. I know how much Doctor Johnson meant to you, and I know he thought of you as his own daughter."

I put my head against his chest and with a feeling of security much like when Ethan held me that evening on the "Shreveport Belle." I wept bitter tears for Doctor J. and was incapable of stopping until it was all out of me.

"What shall I do, Taylor?"

"You are a strong woman, Rachel. I was told that you have been through a lot and got through it. You'll get through this, as well."

I looked up into his sad eyes and saw his sympathy for my plight. I also saw his confidence in me. And he kissed me!

I withdrew. "Please, Taylor. I am not ready for this!"

He shook his head. "How utterly stupid of me. I have so wanted to kiss you, but…"

"But not yet."

"I'm sorry for doing that," He said with his hangdog expression on his face.

"And I am sorry I had to refuse you, but I am not ready."

"And when will you be ready?" He asked almost pleadingly.

"I shook my head. "I don't know. Give me time."

"Well, I have more bad news. I didn't want to tell you while you were dealing with the funeral, but I have orders to join the Army of the Potomac. I must leave tomorrow."

"Oh, Taylor, just when I've come to depend on you so!"

She was right! This was not the Laura I knew back at Catahoula when we were kids. She and Blue had me packed in the back of a buckboard within the hour, and we began the trip to Rosedale Plantation just outside Richmond. The ride was miserable. We bounced over rutted roads with me slipping from consciousness into delirium and back again during that nearly hour-long ride. Blue drove, and Laura sat in back with me and tried to comfort me as best she could.

By the time we arrived, I was soaked with sweat. Laura called one of her Negroes to help Blue get me into an upstairs bedroom.

Once she had me down on the bed, she started barking orders. "Strip his clothes off, Blue. All of 'em! Unmentionables, too."

Blue looked at her with a bewildered expression on his face.

"Blue, don't look at me that way. I've seen a naked man before. I've even seen Ethan naked when we were swimming in the Red

River—except we were just kids at the time. Now, get his clothes off. I'm going to clean him up and get a fresh nightgown on him. He stinks!"

I was too weak and dazed to protest the proceedings, but Blue did as he was ordered and got my soiled clothing off. And she washed me good! She started at my head and scrubbed down as far as possible. Then she started at my feet and scrubbed up as far as possible. And then she gave "possible" a good scrubbing, too! I was cleaner than I had been since the war started! And it broke my fever.

"Feeling better?" she asked as she took a seat on the bed beside me after helping me into one of her husband's nightgowns, and I was all tucked in.

"Feeling clean—and hungry."

"Good. I had Mary, my cook, prepare some chicken soup. They say chicken soup will heal any sickness."

"Why did you do this, Laura? I told you to go away."

She smiled. "You didn't think I was going to listen, did you?"

"Actually, I did."

"Like I told you in that miserable hospital, I'm not the teenager you knew back at Catahoula."

"That is quite obvious. Where is your husband?"

She frowned. "Like so many other men in this war—dead. He was killed at Sharpsburg. Were you there?"

"I was, and it was a very bad place to be. I'm sorry."

"No need be. He was a mistake."

That statement set me back. I had not heard anything that cold come out of her mouth in all the years I knew her. "Any word from your father and brother?"

"My brother was killed at Shiloh. Poppa is at Big Cypress, and I am sure, struggling to handle everything. I haven't heard from him since Vicksburg fell and the Yankees gained complete control of the Mississippi."

"When did Vicksburg fall?"

"A month ago."

"That means the western Confederacy is now cut off from the eastern half. Did your father mention Analee or Catahoula in his letters?"

"He did several months ago, but only in passing, and he didn't say much. Ethan, things are pretty bad back there."

I turned away from her, thinking of what my mother must be going through, but there was nothing I could do about her situation. I did write several letters to her in an attempt to let her know I was alive, but I never heard back from her and didn't know if the letters got through or if she was even able to reply. I did not hear any news of her for the rest of the war.

Laura changed the subject. "The doctor told me you were sick in the head."

"You don't mince words these days, do you?"

"I haven't time for that, Ethan. We are in a war for our survival. Are you?"

"Am I what?"

"Sick in the head?" she blurted out as if exasperated with my questioning her.

"Well, I reckon so."

"Over what? Rachel?"

"She's part of it."

"Didn't you marry her?"

"It didn't work out."

Her expression changed to something akin to a combination of a frown and a smile. I thought more smile than frown, though.

"Really?"

"I don't like that grin on your face."

"Get used to it, mister. What happened?"

"Morgan was her father," I finally replied after a long pause.

"You know, I suspected that. Your father had a reputation. I heard my pop and brother talking about that once. So, you and Rachel are brother and sister?" Her smile came back.

"No. Morgan wasn't my father."

The smile disappeared and a surprised expression washed across her face. "Oh! You mean Analee—?"

"Once."

"Ethan, am I going to have to interrogate you all night to get the whole story?"

"Pernell Joubert!" I blurted out. "My mother was in love with him before she entered the marriage of convenience with Morgan. I've taken his name."

"So, you and Rachel aren't siblings? Then, where is she?"

"I have no idea. She ran away, thinking I was her brother, and I can't find her to tell her the truth."

Laura smiled again. "No idea?"

"None."

"There's more, isn't there?"

"Yes, but I don't want to discuss it."

—⚏—

My screaming alerted the whole house I was having a nightmare. Blue was first to help me, being as he was sleeping in my room on a cot at the time. I was sitting straight up in bed and screaming my lungs out.

"Cap'n Ethan! Wake up! You're having a bad dream!"

Still trapped in my nightmare, I did not respond immediately. Blue sounded as if he were far off.

Laura was next to arrive. "What's happening?"

"He's having one of his nightmares."

By then I was coming out of it. The dream was like those I had concerning Cornelius, the slave Morgan killed by beating him to death, only different; I was the one dying—and killing at the same time.

"Ethan! It's me, Laura. Calm down. You're safe!"

I looked at her in the dim light of the lamp she had brought into the room. "Laura?"

"It's all right, Ethan. Calm down." She and Blue helped me to lie back down and tried to calm me.

"Laura?" was all I could get out. I was shaking and sweating profusely. Eventually, my surroundings began to make sense, and I began to relax.

Laura stroked my hair. "It's all right, Ethan. Relax."

My breathing slowed back to normal.

"It was just a dream," she said softly. "You are safe with me now. I won't let anything hurt you." I felt exhausted and tried to go back to sleep. She looked to Blue. "How long has this been going on?"

"Since Gettysburg. This is the third time it happened."

"I've seen this in other men at the hospital. Nightmares are one of the symptoms of nostalgia. The mind can only take so much horror before it rebels against it. He never did this before Gettysburg?"

"No, Ma'am. He has had some bouts with melancholy and sometimes takes to the bottle to drown his sorrows with whiskey, but nothing like this."

"Those are also symptoms of nostalgia. Looks like this has been going on for a while."

I listened to them talk about me as she stroked my hair and exhaustion crept over me. I knew something was wrong with me, but I didn't know how I could get well again. For a while, I thought finding Rachel would repair what was broken inside, but I was slowly coming to the realization the solution might be a bit more complicated than that. Rachel could have helped. No one knew me like she did, and she would know what to do. With that thought, I fell back to sleep.

—⚅—

"Wake up, Ethan! And get out of bed!" she ordered with the rays of the bright morning sun no longer obstructed by the heavy drapes she had thrown back.

"What time is it?"

"Daytime, and time for you to get out of bed."

"Laura, I have two broken ribs and ..."

"And I don't care what you have. Get out of bed." And with that she threw the covers back. She then unbuttoned my gown and examined the saber wounds. "I see that episode you had last night has that wound in your side bleeding again. I need to change the bandage. Get up."

Blue stood nearby shaking his head.

"Get him up, Blue."

He helped her get me into a sitting position, and she set about removing the bandage around my chest. With a fresh bandage applied, she sat beside of me and put my arm over her shoulder. "Blue, get on the other side like this."

The two of them lifted me painfully to my feet. "Can you stand?"

I was a bit wobbly after they let go of me with every wound paining me. "I think so."

"Walk for me."

I took a few hesitant steps.

"Good. Use this." She handed me a cane to help me maintain my balance. "Get some clothes on. You'll find some of my late husband's in that armoire. He won't mind you wearing them, seeing as how he's deceased. Then come downstairs. Blue will help you. Be there in fifteen minutes." She turned and left the room with a flourish.

Blue looked at me, and I looked at him. "She wasn't always this bossy," I assured him.

Once downstairs, Laura fed me breakfast then made me go outside. "You need some sun. Your color is awful. You look dead."

"That was very flattering. Thank you," I replied sarcastically.

She got me seated out in the morning sunshine and put a sheet around my neck and over me leaving my head exposed. She then commenced to lather my face. "I'll let you keep the moustache and mouche, but the rest is history."

"I have no say in this?"

"No," she replied calmly and went to shaving me. That was followed by a haircut. She stood back and admired her handiwork. "There, you look half-human again."

Mary came out with a pot of coffee and a bottle of brandy. Laura poured a cup for me and added a dollop of brandy.

"Better enjoy this. It is the last of the real coffee I have."

"I didn't know there was any left in the South. Laura, why are you doing this?"

"You really need to ask that question? I'm doing this because I love you, and yes, I understand you won't ever love me back, least ways not the same way. And I can't stand to look at the whimpering and depressed little man you've become. I want the real Ethan back, the one I fell in love with years ago."

"I don't think you can just shave him into existence."

"Maybe, maybe not, but that won't stop me from trying."

"You weren't like this back in Louisiana."

"Like what?"

I hesitated. "You know? Pushy."

She grinned at me. "Oh yes I was, I just kept the real me subdued and played the dutiful southern belle role you men expected. I haven't time for that anymore. I'm seven years older and a whole lot wiser, and not terribly inclined to put up with bullshit, especially yours."

"Laura!"

She put her hands on her hips and cocked her head. "Did that shock you? Good! That was my intention. I don't usually use such language, but in your case, it was used for effect."

"Effect?"

"To get you to understand that I am not going to put up with any foolishness from you." She paused before continuing, "Ethan, I can help you, but you need to tell me what happened after Gettysburg. What got you so upset last night?"

"I told you, I don't want to talk about it."

She took a seat beside me and poured herself a cup of coffee but without the brandy. "Then you get to sit out here until you change your mind."

I looked at her as if she was crazy, and for a moment, considered the possibility that she just might be. "You would do that?"

"Rain or shine." She glanced at the few clouds in the sky. "And it looks like it just might rain. Try me!"

I turned to Blue, sitting off to the side watching this. "You gonna help me?"

He shook his head. "No, sir. I'm thinking Miss Laura might be right. You need to talk about this."

"But what if I don't want to talk about it?"

Laura shrugged. "This isn't about what you don't want; this is about helping you recover from whatever gremlin has a hold of your mind. I've seen men with these same symptoms before. They call it nostalgia, and it is very common with those who have seen a lot of war like you have. I understand it helps to talk about what you've experienced. You need to face it and come to terms with it."

I looked at Blue and then Laura as I considered my options. The surgeon said I was going crazy, might already have arrived, and maybe Laura was right. Maybe, I did need to talk about it?

Resigned to my fate, I hung my head as I began the story. "I was chased by a detachment of Yankee cavalry." I shuddered as the scene began to play out in my head, almost like I was reliving it as I told it. "I managed to lose or kill three of them, but the other three caught me in a bottom after Pepper ran into a cow, and I was unhorsed. That's when I broke my ribs. I killed two of the remaining three with my pistol. The third trooper, a sergeant, and I engaged in a fight with sabers. I had blood all over my face and in my eyes and was barely able to see, much less defend myself effectively. He stuck me through the side with his saber..."

The rest was painful for me to even think about. I resumed my story, speaking barely above a whisper. "When I was with the Brave Rifles in New Mexico, there was a sergeant who took me under his wing. He taught me everything I needed to know about soldering, Indian fighting, and how to stay alive. We became friends, *very* good friends. When I resigned my commission to come home, he made a statement to me in parting. Since he was remaining in the US Army and knew I would likely end up in the Confederate Army, he said he hoped we would never meet in a battle." I paused again as tears welled up in my eyes.

"He was the sergeant who sabered you?" asked Laura.

I nodded. "Then I stabbed him with my knife and killed him. It was when he said to me 'you kilt me, lad' in that Irish brogue of his, that I realized I had just killed my friend Tom Sullivan."

I broke down sobbing then, and Laura put her arm around me. "Ethan, you didn't know."

"That changes nothing, Laura."

Chapter 23 – Lincoln's Address

9 August 1863

I have not had a commission since before the battle and was in need of cash, so I walked into town to the bank. The banker, Mr. Carter, saw me at the teller's window. "Miss Rachel, could I see you in my office, please."

"Of course, sir," I replied, dreading what I was sure the conversation would be about.

Mr. Carter softly closed the door behind me and bade me have a seat before his desk. "I know it has only been a few days…" He paused as if embarrassed. "Forgive me, but…"

I decided to help him get to the point. "How long do I have before I have to vacate the house?"

He looked confused. "I-I don't understand?"

"Doctor J's house. How much time do I have to find another place to live?"

"Why would you do that?"

"It isn't my house."

His expression relaxed. "Oh, you thought…? You don't have to get out of the house. It's yours now. Maxwell left it to you. I'm the executor of his will. I just need you to sign some papers, so the house can be deeded over to you."

"He left the house to me?"

"Yes. He also left his bank account to you, and it's a tidy sum, if I may say so myself." He pulled some papers from the top drawer of his desk. "Maxwell had no living relatives, and he considered you as his adopted daughter. Miss Rachel, Maxwell loved you dearly, and I have no doubt you feel as strongly toward his memory. He wanted you to have what you need to get on with your life after he was gone."

He paused again as if to think through what he was about to say. "You didn't know this, and he forbade me to tell you, but he had a heart condition and knew he would likely die soon. And you should understand he died doing what he loved most, helping hurt people, and doing it with the one he loved most at his side, you. He died a happy man!"

By then I was weeping. "I miss him so. He was the best friend I ever had."

"We will all miss him, Miss Rachel. He was a fine gentleman, and I'm proud to have called him my friend." He leaned back in his chair and laced his fingers together over his ample belly. "And I owe you an apology."

"For what?"

"Gettysburg is a small town, and when you came here, there was a lot of talk. Hupmann was the source of much of it. And to our shame, some of us became a part of it. When Maxwell asked you to move in with him, and Hupmann began telling everyone you were with child—and without a husband, the talk got worse. Maxwell called us all down on it, but it didn't change our minds, especially of some of the wives. You living with him was—shall we say— perceived as unseemly. But it soon became obvious that your presence in the house had done wonders for Maxwell's emotional health. He was a miserable soul after the loss of his wife and daughter. Suddenly, he was happy once again. There were some old biddies who could never understand that, but many of Maxwell's friends eventually realized the relationship was much to the benefit of Maxwell's general welfare."

He looked upward as if unable to face me, and I noticed his eyes were watering. "It was Maxwell who convinced us to buy your portraits, as I am sure you know. But do you know he paid for mine to start you on your road to success?"

I nodded. "I suspected as much."

"But that was the first and last one he paid for. Once everyone saw how talented you are, they were willing to pay for their own. And by the way, I've taken the liberty of returning the cost of my portrait to his account." Mr. Carter sighed. "Miss Rachel, you are a remarkable woman, and I am quite certain you will go far in this world."

"Thank you, sir. And your apology is accepted."

Laura did as she threatened: She had me out of the bed no matter how much I complained. And she put me to work, too.

"If I am going to take care of you and feed you two, you are going to earn your keep."

She started easy on me by having me balance the plantation books. Blue went to work in the kitchen with Mary, and the two seemed to get along well.

Laura had a white overseer to manage the field hands, and like many overseers in my experience, he was of a dubious quality. I met Mr. Larson about a week after I arrived. Laura had me propped up in her little office, working on the books when she and the gentleman entered.

"Ethan, this is Mr. Larson, my overseer. Mr. Larson, this is Captain Joubert, and old friend who will be staying with us while he recovers from his wounds."

Larson nodded with what resembled a frown on his face, which I eventually learned was just his usual expression. I tried to stand and gave that foolishness up. "Forgive me, sir. It seems I haven't the strength to stand just yet."

Larson nodded. "Captain Joubert."

He was in his late thirties, I judged. Of medium build and height and wearing a beard, he was a bit rough looking. His clothing was soiled but in good condition. His face seemed hard and his glare unforgiving. My first thought was why is he not in the army?

"Captain Joubert is going over my books. I expect he may have a few questions before he is finished."

Larson nodded and said, "Anything you need, sir?"

"Nothing at the moment. Thank you."

Once he was gone, Laura returned to the office. "Not a man of many words," I commented.

"Go easy on him, Ethan. It is hard to find a good overseer with so many men in the army."

"And why isn't he in the army?"

"Bad back I was told."

I grunted my acknowledgement as I searched for a paper among those I had spread out on the desk. "Ah, here it is. Laura, this is a list of runaway slaves?"

"Yes, many of the plantations have lost their Negros."

"This looks to be nearly half of your able bodied men? How much land do you have under cultivation?"

"Only about 800 acres. When I arrived here in '60, I found the place in horrible condition. My late husband had not managed it well after the passing of his father. The land was spent and the cotton often stunted, yielding an insufficient harvest to pay for any more than the cost of the overhead. As a result, he was deep in debt. I learned enough from my paw to know the land needed to lie fallow to replenish itself. Even the Bible calls for Israel to allow the land to lie fallow every seven years, does it not? He protested, but we began rotating the fields. Last year was the first harvest from a rested field and yields were better. But we weren't profitable yet, so I put every penny I had in the place to save it until I could get it profitable again."

"That is a common story in the South. With labor so cheap, it was more profitable to keep burning out the land and growing the size of the plantations rather than manage land usage. What do you have planted—not cotton, I hope."

She smiled and took a seat across the desk from me, carefully spreading out her skirt. "As soon as I understood Mr. Lincoln's Anaconda plan to blockade our ports, I knew cotton would be near worthless if you can't get it to the markets in England. I planted corn and beans in the fields under cultivation, and I graze cattle in the fields lying fallow. I can sell both to feed the army. I can also get by with fewer Negroes."

"Smart girl!"

"But so far, my Negros don't seem to be very good at managing cattle."

"Larson any help there?"

"Some, but he is a planter's overseer. My husband hired him before he left for the army."

"Maybe I can help when I get better. I've watched the wranglers work with our beeves."

"So, you now intend to get better?"

"Do I have a choice?"

"Not really." She stood and smiled at me before she left the office. As I think back on that smile, it was more like a grin of triumph.

As I watched her walk through the door and down the hall, I was reminded of how lovely she was. Some say she was not very comely as a young girl, but she was the sort that only got prettier with age, and she had indeed matured into a beautiful woman. Had Rachel not come along back in '56, I would almost certainly have married

Miss Laura, and I suspect she would make a fine, loving wife. I shook off those thoughts and got back to my books.

18 November1863

I received a surprise today! Taylor showed up for the dedication of the new cemetery, which promises to be a grand affair. Even Mr. Lincoln is here.

I was pleased to see Taylor again. He had written an almost continuous stream of letters in his absence, so many I struggled to keep up with replies. The man can be verbose when he is motivated, and I seem to have very much motivated him!

There was a knock at the door. I answered and found him standing there resplendent in a fresh uniform and smelling clean. I love the way this man smells! He swept me up in his arms and spun me around!

He had me in bear's hug with my feet dangling above the ground. "Doctor Anderson!" I was barely able to get out. "This is most improper!"

"I don't care! I am just glad to see you again!"

"Please put me down, sir!"

He finally obeyed, and I attempted to straighten my dress. "What are you doing here?"

"The dedication of the new cemetery, of course. I had hoped you would be glad to see me."

I blushed. "I am, Taylor, but this is so unexpected. You never mentioned a visit in your last letter."

"I thought I would surprise you."

"Well, I am indeed surprised—and glad you are here. I did miss you."

"That's better. I was beginning to think you didn't like me."

"That isn't so, and you should know that by now."

"Well then. Would I be so bold as to expect a kiss?"

"Of course, sir." I stood on tiptoes and pecked him on the cheek.

"That is not the sort of kiss I was hoping for, but I will take what I can get," he said with disappointment in his voice.

I did my best to ignore the comment. "Coffee or tea?"

"Some of your marvelous tea would be fine."

I set about boiling some water in the kitchen, and Taylor followed to lean against the wall to watch me.

"I love to watch you work, even just making tea. I bet you didn't know I was watching you when you were working with the wounded."

I glanced in his direction before answering. "I saw you doing that more than once."

"And what were your thoughts?"

"I was flattered you should show such interest in me."

He smiled in a way it appeared he knew something I did not. The man has such a lovely smile.

"I have someone I want you to meet, an old friend from Baltimore. We were best friends until I lost touch with him when I went off to school. I ran into him on the train coming here from Washington, and he'll be at the ceremony tomorrow. I'm sure you'll like him, but be careful, because he is quite the ladies man."

20 November 1863

The dedication of the Soldier's National Cemetery was yesterday, 19 November. It was such an intense day that I am just now getting to record what happened. I will begin with some history first.

As I wrote earlier, there was much haste to inter the dead to avoid the spread of disease and to give rest to those poor souls. Graves were hastily marked or not marked at all and so shallow the weather eroded the soil covering some of the poor souls.

It was proposed that the Union dead be disinterred and reburied in a cemetery dedicated to them. Land near where General Pickett penetrated the Union lines on 3 July only to be repulsed was appropriated. This was adjacent to Evergreen Cemetery where Ethan fought on 2 July. The process of moving the Union remains began in October and was not yet complete at the dedication on 19 November.

The statesman and orator Edward Everett of Massachusetts was chosen to deliver the main speech, and President Abraham Lincoln was asked to deliver a few appropriate remarks. After Mr. Everett's two-hour oration on the causes of war and the events that led to the Battle of Gettysburg, President Lincoln rose and spoke for but two minutes. It was the most profoundly moving two minutes of oration I have ever had the pleasure of hearing. I was able to get a copy and record it here below.

—◆—

Four score and seven years ago our fathers brought forth on this continent a new nation, conceived in liberty, and dedicated to the proposition that all men are created equal.

Now we are engaged in a great civil war, testing whether that nation, or any nation so conceived and so dedicated, can long endure. We are met on a great battlefield of that war. We have come to dedicate a portion of that field, as a final resting place for those who here gave their lives that that nation might live. It is altogether fitting and proper that we should do this.

But, in a larger sense, we cannot dedicate, we cannot consecrate, we cannot hallow this ground. The brave men, living and dead, who struggled here, have consecrated it, far above our poor power to add or detract. The world will little note, nor long remember what we say here, but it can never forget what they did here. It is for us the living, rather, to be dedicated here to the unfinished work, which they who fought here have thus far so nobly advanced. It is rather for us to be here dedicated to the great task remaining before us—that from these honored dead we take increased devotion to that cause for which they gave the last full measure of devotion—that we here highly resolve that these dead shall not have died in vain—that this nation, under God, shall have a new birth of freedom— and that government of the people, by the people, for the people, shall not perish from the earth.

Taylor escorted me to the cemetery for the dedication. The crowd was large with people pressed close together, but Taylor was able to get me close to where the speeches would be given. I stood barely twenty feet from Mr. Lincoln as he spoke.

Taylor seemed preoccupied much of the time as he searched faces in the crowd for his friend. After the speech and as the crowds were disbursing, a suddenly flash of recognition swept over his face. "There he is!" I looked in the direction he was pointing and saw a handsome young officer with a broad smile on his face coming toward us.

Taylor grabbed him by the arm. "This, sir, is the lovely young lady I have been telling you about who has stolen my heart." He turned to me. "Rachel, this is my good friend, Miles Herndon. Miles this is Miss Rachel Whitcomb."

Miles and I stood there staring at each other, neither able to speak. Taylor looked first at the expression of shock on my face and then the one on Miles' face. "You two know each other?"

Miles remained speechless. I was the first to reply. "Hello, Miles, it is so nice to finally meet you," I said as I offered my hand.

Miles slowly reached out and took my hand, and then broke out in laughter. "I have heard so many stories of strange coincidences in this war, but I never expected this. Rachel, the pleasure is mine." He turned to Taylor who was standing there with a confused expression on his face. "Yes, Taylor, we know each other, in a manner of speaking."

Miles turned back to me. "May I ask where is Ethan?"

"Ethan? Who is Ethan?" asked Taylor.

"You have not told him of Ethan?"

"Some, but not all."

"Well, where is Ethan?"

"Will someone please tell me what this is about?"

I placed my hand on Taylor's arm. "I am sorry all this is coming out this way. I would have preferred to explain myself—when I was ready. Shall we retire to my home to discuss this in private?"

Once back at the house, I prepared tea for Taylor and Miles. After serving it, I took my seat on the sofa next to Taylor, anxiously seated on its edge. I did not know where to begin, and since Miles obviously did not know about what had happened, I began there.

"Miles, you asked about Ethan. We did not marry." Miles seemed strangely unsurprised by that.

I looked to Taylor, afraid of what I would see in his face. "Ethan is the man I was to marry. His father, Morgan Davis, was an old friend of my mother, and after she passed when I was fourteen, I was brought to his plantation in Louisiana. There I met Ethan..." Taylor's face was fixed in a blank stare. "And we fell in love. I told you someone did something to destroy our relationship. That person was Ethan's father. On the very day we were to be married, Morgan confessed that—" I hated to even think of the rest much less speak of it. "Morgan confessed that he was also my father."

Taylor relaxed and set back in the sofa. "My word! No wonder you didn't want to tell me about it."

"As you might imagine, I was devastated and knew I could not remain at Catahoula Plantation with Ethan there, so I ran away without telling anyone where I was going."

"Is there more, Rachel?" Asked Miles, and I thought the question strange at the time.

"Not really. I came to Gettysburg and found shelter with an old friend where I could hide from Ethan. I was sure he would be searching for me."

"Where is this Ethan now?" asked Taylor.

"With the Confederate Army."

"A Rebel!" snorted Taylor.

I ignored the intended insult. "He was here at Gettysburg in July. I saw him."

Miles leaned forward in his chair. "Did you speak to him?"

"No, I couldn't bear to."

"You still love him, don't you?" asked Taylor.

260

Unable to face his piercing gaze, I looked away. "Yes."

Miles picked up the story. "I was Ethan's roommate and friend at VMI, which is how I know him—and Rachel."

"I have a question for you, Miles, one that has been troubling me. Do you have any idea why Ethan would change his name from Davis to Joubert?"

Miles leaned back in the chair and first crossed his legs and then his arms. "Why no. Has he changed his name? And how would you know that?"

"I have his calling card with that name on it."

Miles appeared to be deep in thought before answering. "I can think of no reason he would change his name. Perhaps he was in some trouble?" he offered.

I recalled that Blue had mentioned a murder charge for dueling. "So you've had no contact with him since the war started?"

"None. Why would he contact me?"

"You two were friends in school, and I thought perhaps he might approach you to see if you knew where I might be."

Miles stood, obviously uncomfortable. "Perhaps it is time for me to leave. You two seem to have some things to discuss. I'll see you back at the hotel, Taylor. We have an early train to catch."

I saw Miles out, while Taylor waited in the parlor. When I returned, he was looking as if he was a bit uncomfortable. "Well, now you know." I said.

"How long, Rachel?"

"How long for what?" I replied, confused.

"How long will you pine for this man, your brother, who you cannot ever be with?"

"Perhaps you can tell me how long it takes to stop loving someone?"

He shook his head then stood erect, his chin held high. "However long it takes, I'll wait for you." He retrieved his kepi and moved to the door.

I stopped him. "I am sorry, Taylor."

He nodded. "I'll write," and he turned and left.

I picked up the tea service and cleaned the kitchen before going to my bedroom in my empty and lonely house. With no Doctor J, no commissions, and no future in Gettysburg, I decided it was time for a change in my life.

Winter came and I had recovered from my physical wounds nicely, but the pain in my mind had barely abated. I struggled with my usual demons: losing Rachel and not being able to find her, killing Tom, and of course, the war which was occupying much of the time I spent inside my head. My involvement in it was making less and less sense. I was coming to view it as a lost cause, and so were many others. If it was about the South defending slavery, as Mr. Lincoln had made it out to be with his emancipation proclamation, then for me, someone who did not support that peculiar institution, I was on the wrong side of history. But I had taken an oath.

An incident that occurred not long after I arrived impacted my thinking concerning my place in history. Laura got me dressed in her deceased husband's finest one Sunday morning to attend church even though I was barely able to walk without assistance. Blue drove the carriage. We arrived just before the service began, and Blue helped me down from the carriage and up the steps of the church. At the doors, with the pastor there greeting people, Blue turned to return to the carriage to wait for us. "Where are you going?"

"I'll wait in the carriage."

"No, you will come in with us."

Blue glanced at the pastor then me. "I don't think that'll be acceptable."

The pastor, an elderly man much overweight and balding, said. "There is a Negro church just down the road."

"But this is where we are coming to worship our Lord, and this man is redeemed same as I am. He comes in with me."

"I am sorry, sir, but that is not possible," replied the pastor assertively.

Two men stepped up to the conversation. One said, "No niggers allowed in a white church, sir."

I looked at Laura and then at them. "Is that so? Then I reckon I won't be worshiping with these whitewashed tombs, either," I replied, in a reference to Jesus' comment to the Pharisees in Matthew 23:27. "Let's go, Laura."

"Ethan?"

"I'm not staying here."

Back at the carriage, I instructed Blue, "Find that Negro church he mentioned." And soon enough we did. It was little more than a slave cabin but there was music and singing coming from inside, a joyful sound.

We entered as quietly as possible, since the services had already begun, but that didn't prevent our disrupting them. The singing slowly came to a halt after we entered, and the pastor came down the aisle to greet us with the entire congregation anxiously watching.

"Massa, I believe the church you are looking for is down the road?"

"You mean we are not welcome here?"

"Oh no, sir. I thought you may have gotten confused about the churches."

"We can stay?"

He looked confused then. "If that is your wish, sir."

"Well, it is my wish, pastor."

"Certainly. There are some seats down front," he offered.

"No, sir. I don't wish for us to be any more of a disruption that we already are. The lady will sit in this empty chair here in the back, and Blue and I will stand. Please proceed with your service."

He nodded and turned and went to the front, but the eyes of the congregation remained suspiciously on us until he announced another hymn. His sermon was on Jesus and the two thieves at the crucifixion and how one was repentant and the other was not, and that Jesus promised the repentant thief he would be with him in Paradise that very day. It was a bit more emotional that I was accustomed to, but the content was excellent.

Like other churches I had attended, the pastor was at the door to say his goodbyes to the congregation. We were among the last to leave and found much of the congregation waiting outside for us, curious about the two white folks attending a black church.

"Pastor, I believe I have not heard that passage taught so well in all my years. Very good, sir." And I extended my hand.

He looked perplexed. "Thank you, sir. My name is Jethro Smith."

"And I'm Ethan Joubert, visiting from Louisiana. And this is Miss Laura of Rosedale Plantation. This giant of a man is my friend and companion, Blue."

He acknowledged each. "May I ask, Massa Joubert, why you attended my church today?"

"It's really quite simple. They wouldn't let Blue in at the white church down the road, so I decided to come where the truth was taught—and practiced."

That moved Pastor Smith almost to tears. "I thank you, sir. And you are welcome to come back anytime you wish."

I smiled and replied, "We'll be back."

As I grew stronger, I ventured more and more away from the big house to observe the operations of the plantation and help Laura find profitability. The corn was sold as soon as it was harvested, and it made good money for her. She sold off some of the cattle, being careful to keep breeding stock for the future of the herd. That brought in even more money, and Rosedale was profitable for a change, at least for that year, but there were still old debts to settle.

Blue and Mary seemed to be getting along famously, and she joined us for services at the Negro church. Their budding relationship did not surprise me. Blue could be a very pleasant fellow to be around. My relationship with Mr. Larson remained somewhat less than friendly. I believe he resented me taking a hand in running the plantation.

As for Laura, I was unsure of what to make of our relationship. She was always nearby, asking me to explain what I was doing and why, that is when she wasn't fussing at me for complaining about some ache or when I had slipped into one of my melancholy moods. Even with her fussing at me, I came to enjoy her company much like when we were kids back in Louisiana—before Rachel came along. Only we were no longer children but two adults, both of whom had been hurt by life, and such shared experience can draw two people closer together.

Chapter 24 – Painful Parting

The cold of December and January confined us to the house much of the time seeking warmth. My physical wounds were healed with Laura's continuing efforts, and she tried not to allow my mental wounds to fester either. Talking about it had helped. The nightmares had not stopped, but they were far less frequent. By late fall, I had been able to do more physical work and did so to build my strength back from my long bouts with the fever and depression of the summer before. I tended to the animals and repaired the house and barn as weather and my strength permitted. Mr. Larson slowly warmed to my interference in his domain. While we never became fast friends, he came to realize if he worked with me, he could keep his job, which is a point I tried to make abundantly clear to him.

Laura and I spent many cold evenings together before the big fireplace in the main parlor and talked mostly about the old times we had together back in Louisiana. These fireplace discussions often went on late into the evening over cups of hot toddy before a roaring fire. Laura could remember things I had long forgotten, and she was skillful at making me laugh at some of the silly things we did together as kids.

She reminded me of the time we swam in the Red River completely nude. We had been down by the river fishing for catfish on a hot August day, and I wanted to cool off in the water. She dared me to strip down; and if I would, she would. She was close to twelve at the time.

"You were afraid to take your pants off, as if I had never seen a naked man before, being around my brother and my paw all my life."

"I was not! I couldn't get my fly buttons undone," I retorted in my own defense.

"So you say, but you sure looked embarrassed."

"Not as embarrassed as you were when I did get my pants off. You should have seen the expression on your face. Then I thought you had tricked me, because you were still dressed."

"I started out that way, but I did eventually strip down to my birthday suit, and we did it again several more times before the summer was over. But that was the last summer we did that, as I commenced to mature into a woman over the winter."

I nodded. "Actually, I figured the game would be much more interesting the next summer, but you were having no part of that."

As usual, I drank more than I should have during those discussions. It was my way of escaping everything that was weighing so heavily on my mind. But by the spring of '64, something else was bothering me, and that was the war itself. It had begun for most as a glorious adventure bound to be over in less than a year. Then, nearly three years later, the folly of that thought was abundantly obvious to all of us. It was also becoming obvious that Gettysburg was the high point for the Confederacy. The defeats that followed and the loss of so many irreplaceable men meant we were on the losing side of the war. Still, the Richmond government held out hope for some kind of battlefield or political miracle that would end it in the favor of the South. I had long since given up of any hope of that ever happening. Moreover, I was wondering if I even wanted the South to win at all.

I had somewhat reluctantly entered into service in '61 because of my circumstances, being charged with murder and facing the hangman, that is. My service was reluctant because it interrupted my search for Rachel. Had that not been a problem for me, I would have voluntarily joined up, but for reasons I found rather weak in my retrospection in '64. I had felt a need to come to the defense of my state, my family, and my friends from what many, including me, considered as northern aggression. In fact, we often called the war we were then waging the War of Northern Aggression.

The issue that concerned many in the South was states rights and the Federal government's usurping authority that was reserved to the states. We were a union of individual sovereign states joined together for our common defense. I stress the use of the term "sovereign states." That was the original intention of the founding fathers. While slavery may have been the trigger, the Constitution was what the war was about, or so we told ourselves. In reality, it was about money. The north could not afford to lose the tax revenue from the southern states, and the economy of southern states was based on slavery. Lose the "free" labor of the slaves and the financial investment they represented, and the southern economy would collapse. In the institution of slavery, we had ourselves a tiger by the tail. We could not hold on forever, but neither could we let it go, lest the tiger consume us.

With Mr. Lincoln's Emancipation Proclamation, he changed the whole complexion and purpose of the war. It was no longer about the Constitution or preserving the Union, rather it was openly about freeing the black man. Ironically, most of the southern soldiers, including me, did not even own slaves, and few had any hope of ever becoming a slave owner. Yet they fought on. Why? Not so they could own slaves. They fought because they still believed it the original southern concept of the purpose of the war—it was a War of Northern Aggression. As the popular song went, "Hurrah, hurrah, for southern rights, hurrah. Hurrah for the bonny blue flag that bears a single star..."

I was struggling with that, and I imagine many other non-slave owning southerners were, also. I had long held that slavery was wrong in spite of what some preachers were saying in churches all over the South. I had not realized it at the time, but the incident of Morgan killing Cornelius when I was only three was the beginning of my somewhat un-southern views on the peculiar institution. Befriending several slaves at Catahoula, such as Old Zeke and his son Little Zeke and Mammy, who was like a mother to me, had further complicated matters. Then there was Brandy, the daughter of Mammy and, as it turned out, my stepfather. She had an eighth or less colored blood in her and was as pale as any white woman, yet she was carried on our plantation books as a Negro. We grew up together, and she was like a sister to me. Perhaps, it was Brandy's plight that really brought the problem into focus for me.

That made my decision to free the slaves at Catahoula before I went to search for Rachel a lot easier. I felt like I had accomplished something for people I loved by giving them the most precious gift I knew, freedom. As a result, I was conflicted over the war. I did not want to return as a combatant, but I knew I must eventually do so, because I had taken an oath.

Then there was Laura. She had brought me back from the brink of insanity and given me another chance, though I was then still uncertain I even wanted one. I tried to hide my bouts of melancholy from her, lest she give me one of her stern lectures and resume barking at me as she had when we first arrived.

Laura gave me something else. She gave me the love of a woman, something I had been without since the loss of Rachel. I had not experienced that feeling in a long while. And I am compelled to confess, at that point in my life, I was beginning to give up on ever finding Rachel. I knew the longer I waited to search for her, the longer my chances of finding her became. I did not allow myself to outwardly admit this doubt, but looking back on that period after the war, I can see how it was there all along, just not acknowledged.

25 February 1864

I sold my house in Gettysburg to Mr. Carter and moved to Washington. I had previously contacted Miles and asked for his help in locating a suitable place to live with a room I could use for a studio. He found such on N Street not far from his own house on L Street.

My new home is a lovely brick row house of three stories, with plenty of room on the top floor for my studio, and it even has a northern exposure. It took me almost two weeks to get everything moved from Gettysburg and set up housekeeping in my new home.

I love it! I feel like this is a fresh start for me.

Miles assured me there would be plenty of commissions simply for the asking with all the high-ranking officers and politicians in town, wanting their portraits to hang in their homes and offices. I have been here less than a week, and Miles has already found two commissions for me. I think Washington is going to work out very well.

15 March 1864

Miles and I have become fast friends. He has been so helpful, getting me settled and gaining portrait commissions. I now have a waiting list two generals and three politicians long! I can barely keep up with the work.

Two days ago he invited me to be his guest at a gala ball, which he assured me would be attended by all of Washington's wealthiest and most politically connected. With so many potential customers, I could not refuse. I even had a new gown made for the occasion, which was a bit of a trick on such short notice.

Miles called for me at seven, just as I was attending to final adjustments of my gown in the hall mirror. He arrived in his finest uniform complete with sash. Miles is indeed a handsome man with curly hair and a slender build, and the uniform made him look all the more the dashing gentleman warrior. He took one look at me and stepped back, making a circular motion with his finger, indicating I should turn, which I did.

"Rachel, I will be the envy of the ball with you on my arm. Ethan certainly has good taste in women." He saw my expression droop. "I'm sorry. I should not have said it that way. I was only trying to express how lovely you are."

I recovered and smiled for him. "Thank you, Miles."

The ball was in one of the hotels near the capitol. Its ballroom was elaborately decorated with gas crystal chandeliers, gilded moldings, and fine draperies. The room was a sea of soldiers in dress blue uniforms, politicians in formal wear and white ties, and lovely women in fancy ball gowns. Miles took me around the room and introduced me to so many generals and politicians that I lost track of their names. Several asked me to dance and questioned me about my portraits.

"Captain Herndon tells me you are the finest portraitist in Washington. I must see your work. My wife wants a portrait of me now that I have been promoted to brigadier. Do you think you can fit me into your schedule?"

"I do have a waiting list, sir, but we can work something out." After the dance I gave him my calling card.

"I shall be calling upon you, Miss Rachel."

"And I shall look forward to it, sir."

Miles intervened and took my arm. "Don't I get to dance with the girl I brought?"

"Of course, Miles." And he swept me out onto the floor and spun me around until I was dizzy. I was having a marvelous time. Washington is nothing like Gettysburg!

We retired to the punchbowl for refreshments. As Miles was reminding me of the names of those I had met and needed to remember, a woman called out in French-accented English, "Miles, is that you? It is you!"

Miles turned to the voice, and a shocked expression swept over his face. "Aimee?"

"Aimee?" I said softly to myself as my Analee eyebrow went up. I turned to see a beautiful young woman making her way to us, a broad smile on her face.

Aimee swept into the conversation with a flourish worthy of the finest stage actor. Miles was speechless. "Aren't you going to introduce me to your lovely, new lady-friend?" she asked, nodding to me.

Miles looked to me anxiously before beginning the introductions. "Mademoiselle Aimee de Beauchamp, may I present Mademoiselle Rachel Whitcomb. Rachel, Miss Aimee de Beauchamp."

That broad smile of hers fell from her face such that I would almost swear I heard a thud when it hit the floor. She glared at me for a moment and seemed unable to speak, but she soon recovered. "You are Rachel? And may I call you Rachel? I feel as if I already know you..."

"Of course..." but she did not allow me to finish, and frankly, I am glad she did not, for what I was thinking of saying was not flattering.

"And you must call me Aimee. We are almost old friends, aren't we?" Getting no immediate response from me, she turned to Miles. "Miles, aren't we like old friends?"

Miles could barely get in a nod before she continued, "I must say, Rachel, you are as lovely as Ethan said you were. That's a beautiful gown; it shows off your trim figure so nicely."

I did not have a chance to respond before Miles attempted to regain control of the conversation. "Aimee, I thought you were in France?"

"I was. I went home with Papa right after I visited Ethan in Richmond two years ago." She glanced at me to see my reaction to that. "As you know Papa was called home for a spell, but now he is posted in Mexico, and I have come back to America to be with Ethan again. I have not seen dear Ethan in almost two years, and I am so anxious to see him."

I wondered how she intended to do that, considering the current state of the war in Virginia. She paused and took a deep breath. "Oh, I'm sorry, Rachel. You may not be aware that I spent nearly three months with Ethan in Richmond back in the summer of '62. He is well, or at least he was then."

I was getting a little sick of the way she was dropping Ethan's name into the conversation in what was certainly an attempt to stake her claim to him. I did not bother to give her the satisfaction of knowing I was indeed aware she had spent time with Ethan or cared—or that I had seen him only nine months ago.

She then put on her pity-face. "Rachel, I am so very sorry about how things worked out for you and Ethan. He told me all about it when I was with him."

She emphasized the "with him" in what, I must assume, was her petty attempt to tell me she had slept with him while in Richmond. I tried not to let that bother me, but it did. I wanted to punch her. And though she said she was sorry about what happened, I knew there was not even an ounce of truth in that sentiment. She wasn't sorry in the least; she was giddy with happiness that I no longer stood in the way of her having Ethan.

And I wonder just what Ethan sees in this shallow ~~bitch~~. (Goodness! Did I really write that? I meant to write "ditch" with a "d.")

April became May, and the two armies stirred from their winter slumber and clashed in the Wilderness near where they had the previous year. From the reports I saw, it was not the rout that the previous engagement had been. Both sides had heavy casualties, especially the Louisiana Brigades. But the Army of the Potomac suffered even more under Mr. Lincoln's new "fighting general," U. S. Grant, fresh from his victory at Vicksburg.

The Wilderness was soon followed by Spotsylvania in mid-May with more dead and wounded, over ten thousand on each side. Grant seemed unafraid to take casualties, and why not, his could be replaced. Our losses could not. Then Spotsylvania eventually became Cold Harbor, and it seemed the war would never end.

I was becoming more and more restless, knowing my place was with the army. The conflict in my soul grew ever deeper, both the conflict concerning my place in the war and the conflict of my relationship with Laura.

Laura was no longer the naïve somewhat silly little woman I knew back at Catahoula when we were kids. She was more pragmatic, her head less filled with a young woman's dreams and illusions about life. Reality had taken their place, and she was tougher for it. Yes, the Laura of 1864 was very different from the Laura of 1856. She had been hardened by the war and the circumstances she found herself in. It had matured her. The desperation she had demonstrated in '56, when she sensed she was losing me to Rachel, was no longer there. Perhaps, she had long ago reconciled herself to losing me, or perhaps, the "new" Laura simply did not allow herself to reveal her own vulnerability. Either way, it was as if Rachel no longer stood between us. We were friends again, and she seemed comfortable with that relationship. We worked together, went to church together, took long walks together, and just conversed during lazy evenings we spent together. I was becoming comfortable being around Laura.

Then everything changed for both of us one night in late May. We were having one of our sessions around a small fire in the main parlor. I had been drinking heavily because of so many things tormenting my thoughts, having no ready answers and avoiding making any decisions because of that. She was sitting on the large sofa, her shoes off and her feet tucked up under her. I was tending the fire and turned to see her smiling at me over the glass of brandy she held almost to her lips.

"What are you smiling at?" I asked, thinking she was remembering one of her stories about our childhood.

"You. You look so domestic tending the fire, and I am reminded of how much I enjoy having a man around, especially you."

I resumed my seat in stuffed chair next to the sofa and took up my own glass of brandy but said nothing by way of a response.

"You'll be leaving soon, won't you?"

I nodded. "I took an oath. My wounds are healed. I have to return."

"To whom do you owe your word, a country on the edge of destruction? Or would you rather stand for what you believe is right?"

"You referring to my dislike of slavery."

"Yes," she replied softly.

"How do you feel about it?"

"Negroes are incapable of managing their lives; they need someone to tell them what to do. What would they do if given their freedom? Most would only run away and starve to death."

"I freed our slaves at Catahoula before the war. Some did run away, but others stayed to help my mother run the plantation. They were doing just fine last I heard from Analee."

"They stayed because you offered them land. They are still working your own land just like they did before you emancipated them."

"True, but with one big difference: They are doing it with the expectation of a reward for their efforts—as freedmen."

"You freed them, you reject slavery, yet you still feel compelled to return to the war?"

"Ironic, isn't it?"

"You don't have to go back, Ethan. No one will think less of you. I certainly won't." She became pensive for a long moment. "Tell you what. I'll consider freeing the slaves at Rosedale, if you will stay and help me. I don't want you to go."

"Do it now or do it later when the North wins this. And they will win this." My head already buzzing, I downed the last of the brandy in my glass and said, "But I can't stay." Not wanting to pursue that conversation any further, I rose and announced it was time for me to retire.

I went to my room and stripped off my coat, vest, and boots, then added two logs to the fire to take the slight chill off the room. That done, I removed the rest of my clothing and slipped between the two clean sheets and lay there thinking about what Laura had said. To whom did I owe my oath? Then I thought about her request for me to stay, and that was tempting. I had grown comfortable being there—between clean sheets instead of huddled in the cold under a sodden blanket, being away from the killing fields, being away from the dirt, away from the blood, from the death, the stench of it all. And being *with* Laura. That was the most troubling part.

I don't know how long I lay there, bathed in the warmth and the flickering light of the fire before she entered my room. Drawn by a soft squeak of the door's hinge, I looked in that direction, and she was standing there in a silken nightgown, her long blond hair down about her shoulders. The expression on her pretty face was one of apprehension. She stood there for a long moment before she softly closed the door and walked over to my bed. There, she paused and looked at me for some sign of rebuff. I imagine she was recalling that night after my eighteenth birthday party back at Big Cypress, when I had indeed rejected her in favor of Rachel. I am sure that must have hurt her deeply, and she was afraid I would do it again. Seeing no indication of a refusal from me, a flirting smile crossed her lips. She reached down and pulled the covers back and sat on the edge of the bed.

I sat up then, took her hand and said, "Laura, this is not a good idea."

Her smile disappeared and she looked away. Her eyes began to water. She sighed, stood, and left my room without a word.

I lay back down and considered what had just happened. Was I a fool for rejecting her? Most men would have said as much. I spent the next few hours sleepless as I considered my place in the war, Laura, slavery, Catahoula, and most of all Rachel. I felt a need to get on my knees and pray about it, and I did. As I did, things started becoming clearer to me, and I began making decisions.

My first decision was it was long past the time I should have left Rosedale Plantation. My staying longer than I should have had encouraging Laura to hope we could be together, and that was not possible. She had helped me find myself again, but it was time to get focused on what I should be focused on. Then something I told Rachel a long time ago came to mind, "There is a future written in Heaven for us." Did I really believe that when I said it? And I decided I did. As impossible as it seemed, that promise became very real to me once more, and I grabbed onto it with both hands like it was some kind of life preserver. It was time to stop thinking about me and start thinking about finding her.

I still had to deal with the war and my place in it, but I figured however that ended for me was in God's hands. Whatever He had in store for me, I was sure of only one thing: My future was out there somewhere, and I needed to go find it.

Near dawn I got up off my knees and dressed in my uniform, strapped on my pistol, and packed my few remaining possessions in my saddlebags and bedroll. I briefly considered leaving a letter for Laura, explaining what I had done and why, but decided against it.

With the eastern sky dimly illuminated by the false dawn, I slipped from my room and softly made my way to hers, opened the door and eased inside. She was asleep, curled into a fetal position. I took a seat on the chair next to the window and watched her sleep. She clutched a handkerchief in her fist, so I knew she had been weeping and had fallen asleep doing so. As the sun slowly rose, I quietly sat there and watched her sleep.

6 June 1864

The armies have risen from their winter's slumber to continue with the bloodletting. Grant has been threatening Richmond, and Lee has countered by sending Early with the Louisiana Brigades into the Shenandoah Valley once again. And as before, the Confederates are pushing the Union armies out of the Valley.

Taylor has resumed his almost ceaseless writing. How does he ever find the time? After the dedication last November when everything came out about Ethan, I, at first, received only a few letters from him, but the frequency has gradually increased. He seems to have gotten over the shock of my history.

He expects to be transferred to Washington and looks forward to spending more time with me. He is a sweet man, and I do not want to hurt him, but I'm struggling with accepting all the attention he showers on me. I like him; I enjoy his company, but I do not love him. Perhaps with time that will change.

Miles, in spite of Taylor's warning about his reputation, has proven to be the perfect gentleman. He has gone out of his way to introduce me to the right people and help me get commissions. I have so much work I barely have time to answer Taylor's endless stream of letters.

And Aimee; she has become my new best friend! (For anyone reading this after I am gone, that statement was intended to be sarcasm!) She lives but two blocks away and visits often, usually in the evening. She asks an endless number of questions about Ethan but talks incessantly, so I don't really get a chance to answer her. I really don't want to talk about Ethan, especially with her. She thinks she is helping me to understand that we can never be together again, but she is only making me recall how much I love him instead.

She tells me she hired a detective in Richmond, but he has thus far been unsuccessful locating Ethan. He did report that he was badly wounded after Gettysburg. I hope the detective can get better information about his condition, even if it means Aimee will rush immediately to his side.

Aimee likes to shop, and she tries to get me to go with her. While I may be earning good money with my paintings and have a healthy bank account, I am not the spendthrift she is. Besides, I haven't the time to shop and jabber with her.

The woman drives me crazy, and I never cease to wonder what Ethan sees in her.

Laura was a lovely woman any man would be a fool to walk away from. And I was about to walk away. I remembered the times we shared as children back in Louisiana and smiled at the thought of them. Then I recalled the guilt of what I had just done by rejecting her, hurting her in the process, and I felt sick.

She needed me, a man in her life, much like thousands of other women who were widowed by the war. As strong as she had become, she needed to know there was more to life than just the pain she had experienced. But more than anything else, she needed me to need her. And that is where I had failed her.

I did indeed need her, but not the way she wanted me to. There was a hole in my heart that needed filling, and she was—convenient. Unlike Aimee, Laura was genuine and someone I actually had deep feelings for. And I did not want to hurt Laura, because I did love her, perhaps not the same way I loved Rachel, but I loved her none-the-less. The longer I stayed with her, the harder it would be for me to leave—and the more hurt my leaving would cause.

She opened her eyes and saw me sitting in the chair watching her. She smiled before she realized I was dressed in my uniform, and her smile slowly disappeared. She sat up in bed. "You are leaving." It was a statement and not a question, for she knew the day had been coming.

"Yes. It's time for me to go."

"Because of what I did last night? I'm sorry, Ethan. Please don't leave me."

"I have to. Staying will only make my inevitable leaving harder. It was wrong for me to let you think we could be together. I don't belong here, and I think you know that as well as I do."

"Where do you belong, Ethan?"

"I wish I knew. I only know I cannot remain here with you. If I stay, I'll only end up hurting you even more than I already have, and I don't want to do that. You deserve better. You deserve someone who loves you, not someone…"

"Not someone who doesn't love me?"

"I didn't mean it to come out that way, because I do love you, Laura, just not the way you want me to, and that is precisely why I *must* leave."

She collapsed back into the pillows and drew herself into a fetal position. With resignation in her voice, she said softly, "Then go, Ethan, just go!"

I stood and walked over to the bed and kissed her on the forehead. "Goodbye, Laura. Thank you for being you and for caring about me." She made no reply, and I picked up my saddlebags and bedroll from the blanket chest at the foot of the bed and left Rosedale Plantation.

I found Blue in the kitchen, and he was alone. He saw my saddlebags and bedroll.

"You leaving, Cap'n Ethan?"

I nodded. "Time for me to go back, but you can stay here."

He shook his head. "No, sir. I'm not finished with you yet. I'll get my things."

I knew it was no use arguing with him, so I nodded and went out to the barn to saddle Pepper. Blue joined me before I was finished and silently went about saddling his mule.

"How did she take it?" I asked referring to Mary.

He looked over. "Not good, but she understands I'll come back for her."

"You really don't need…"

"Don't try to change my mind. I'm coming with you, and that's the end of it."

Chapter 25 – Fort Delaware

The North began conducting a scorched earth policy in the Valley, burning the farms that fed the Confederate Army. Lee was compelled to dispatch Jubal Early, now in command of Hays' Corps, to rid the Valley of its tormentors. (Hays had been sent home to recruit.)

Bearded and cantankerous, Early often had a hard time finding reasons to compliment his subordinates. He was an unforgiving taskmaster who often clashed with the Tigers, but he knew which of his brigades he could depend on in a fight. Early's Corps numbered only around 8,000 men, but most them were from the days when Jackson had been in command, and we had run rampant through the Valley in the spring of '62. Though much smaller and its members much worn out and beat up, the dog still had a lot of fight in it. Early soon pushed the Federals back to Winchester.

I reported to Early as soon as Blue and I arrived in camp outside of Winchester. The army was preparing to move into Maryland and threaten Washington now that the Federals had abandoned their positions, and the road was open. Early was not about to let such an opportunity slip through his fingers.

I found the ranks of the Tigers much depleted. Many of the officers had been killed in the spring and early summer campaigns. As a result, the two Louisiana Brigades were merged under Colonel Zebulon York, yet the merged brigade was still smaller than a regiment. Early arranged for me to take command of one of the regiments in York's brigade. I was the only officer in the regiment with but two non-commissioned officers to assist me. My first sergeant was Daniel Rivers, an able man I knew from my earliest days with the Tigers back in '61.

Rivers and I tried our best to get our tiny forty-two-man regiment back into some kind of shape for the march on Washington. Most of the men were without shoes, and their uniforms were a mixture of gray, butternut, and all manner of civilian attire, almost all of which was in poor condition. We acquired as much as we could from the retreating Yankees and any civilians who would make a donation to the cause, but the pickings were slim with so many men in need of almost everything.

29 June 1864

Aimee's detective has managed to locate Ethan. He was indeed wounded and had been convalescing at a plantation outside of Richmond. He has since rejoined the army and is with Early, but we know nothing more other than Early is in the Valley.

7 July 1864

Not again! The Confederates have once more broken free of the Shenandoah Valley. Early's Corps is near Frederick, Maryland and threatening Baltimore and Washington. Union forces are attempting to stop his thrust at Frederick.

We met the Federals at the Monocracy Creek, with us on one side and them on the other. A frontal attack across the bridge would have been slaughter, so Early demonstrated against the Yankees there while sending Gordon's division downstream. The Tigers were told to remove all equipment likely to make any noise. That meant we had to abandon what few precious possessions we had, knowing we would never see them again. Below the bridge, we discovered a ford shallow enough to cross and flank the Yankees.

York's Brigade formed up along the creek with Evan's brigade to our right and Terry's brigade following, and we slammed into the Federal left flank. After exchanges of musketry, they soon gave it up and skedaddled only to regroup, take a stand, and exchange musket fire with us again. It was a brief and bloody affair, and our little brigade lost nearly half its men in the fight. But the enemy was hurt worse with most of their dead on the Tiger's front. Early gave the exhausted Tigers a rare compliment for what we had accomplished.

We then marched on Washington and were met by a weak resistance of skirmishers, but fresh Union reinforcements made further action impossible, and we began our withdrawal back to the Valley. The Yankees pressed us, and we fought several heated rearguard actions. It was in one of these where the entire complexion of the war changed for me.

With Blue Coats closing on us, I formed my little regiment in line-of-battle in an empty field of knee-high grass in an attempt to make them a bit more cautious. They marched straight at us coming out of some woods and across the field where we stood waiting to receive them.

"Hold your fire, men!" I yelled, lest we waste precious ammunition. "We want them close!"

Rivers trooped the line and encouraged them. "Stand tall, my Tigers!"

They were closing, and I realized there were more of them than I had expected. I waited until they were but 75 yards away before I yelled, "Fire!" And we poured a volley into their ranks.

Through the smoke, I saw many go down, but they paused only long enough to fire a volley at us, striking down three of my men. I knew there was a tree line some 100 yards behind us. "Fall back and reform at the trees!"

My regiment withdrew, running and loading at the same time, and I was one of the last to quit the line. I turned to run to catch up with my men and stumbled over one of our fallen. He groaned. He was still alive, and I could not leave him there. With the Yankees closing, I managed to get the man up and over my shoulders and began running as fast as I could to catch up with my retreating regiment.

I heard a Union officer call for a volley, which I was certain would be directed at me, and it was. I heard the string of muskets and felt the impact of the balls, and I went down with my wounded Tiger on top of me.

I pushed him off me and realized I had only been grazed in my left leg. My wounded Tiger was the one who took the balls, but amazingly, he was not yet dead. I started to push him off my legs and scramble to my feet but realized the Yankees were upon me, six of them with bayonet-mounted muskets pointing at us as they ran to capture their Rebel prizes. There was no time to get on my feet and run, so I threw up my hands while lying there in the grass partially under my wounded friend. They were on top of us by then, but he rolled over and produced a Colt pocket revolver.

"NO!" I yelled. It was far too late for fighting our way out of this situation. He got off one shot before six bayonets were plunged into his body.

"I surrender!" I yelled, still on the ground, my hands above my head. One lunged at me with his bayonet, and I twisted to avoid the blade, which cut through my coat sleeve barely missing my upper arm. "I surrender!" I yelled again.

The man who had tried to bayonet me pulled his blade out of the ground and looked at me with pure hate in his eyes. I figured I was good as dead. He spun that musket around and slammed its butt into my head, and I went out like a candle in a hurricane.

20 July 1863

Taylor is back from Virginia. He showed up out of the blue. When I opened the door he swept me off my feet and spun me around until I was almost dizzy.

"Put me down, sir."

"When I'm ready. I'm so happy to see you and hold you in my arms! I want a kiss! Now."

I pecked him on the lips, but that did not satisfy him, and he demanded more. Captured so in his arms, I could do little to resist.

"My word, sir, but you have become affectionate in your absence!"

"I missed you, Rachel. I have been dreaming about that kiss ever since I left."

He finally put me down, and I attempted to straighten my self and my clothing. "When did you get back? And why no letter telling me to expect you?"

"I arrive in Washington only this morning. The transfer was rather sudden. I had a friend pull some strings and get me back here. I just could no longer stand being away from you."

"That is very flattering."

"It was meant to be. I hope, by now, you realize how I feel about you?"

"I do, Taylor."

"And did you miss me?"

"Indeed." I said that but was uncertain to what extent I meant it. Taylor in my life had turned it upside down. He is sweet and caring but becoming so demanding of my affections. I am just not yet prepared to reciprocate. Ethan is

always there in the back of my mind, haunting me, and I feel guilty about that. Will I ever be able to love another? I suspect, as long as Ethan is alive, such will not be possible.

I awoke about an hour later bouncing around in the back of a wagon with other wounded prisoners. I felt my head and found a small cut scabbed over with dried blood on a swelling on my forehead that hurt to merely touch it. I looked around and saw a long line of other prisoners clad in gray and butternut following the wagon.

A Blue Coat guard poked me with his bayonet. "If you're awake, Reb, git off that wagon and walk!"

I obeyed and slid out of the back of the slow-moving wagon and dropped to the ground and immediately collapsed. Two other prisoners rushed to my aid and helped me stand, supporting me as we continued our march.

"Where are we going?"

"They told us we're going to Fort Delaware," said one of my helpers.

"Lovely place. I understand it is a real hell-hole."

We marched back to Washington where we joined more prisoners and were crammed into boxcars on a train and sent first to Baltimore then to Wilmington. There, we marched to the docks and boarded a sternwheeler for the trip downriver to our new home. We had eaten little in the three days the trip took, and by the time we arrived, most of us were weak with hunger and from lack of water.

Fort Delaware was still shrouded in a morning mist when we arrived. A mass of granite and brick sitting on the south end of Pea Patch Island in the middle of the Delaware River, the fort was designed to protect Philadelphia and Wilmington against the approach by an enemy up the Delaware River. Completed just before the war and never actually used as designed, the fort and the low-lying island it was on did make an ideal site to house political prisoners and captured Confederates.

Pea Patch Island was barely an island at all, as much of it was at sea level and protected from flooding by a levee system. Even then, it sometimes still flooded at very high tides or during high river levels in the spring. The fort occupied the south end, and the land to the north was used for Union officer housing on its eastern edge with the rest used for the prisoners. The prisoner officer's compound was nearest the fort and under its guns. The enlisted compound was north of that with two fences and guard towers separating the two.

The riverboat docked, and angry-looking guards immediately ordered us off. "Move along, Johnny Reb! Move along!"

Once on shore, men seated behind two tables were processing us in. "Form lines! Officers to the right, enlisted on the left! Move along!" And if you didn't move along fast enough, you might get encouraged to make haste with a poke by the pointy end of a bayonet.

There were about two-dozen officers in our group, some of whom I knew. We ranged from second lieutenant to major and formed up according to rank, with the major at the head of the line. The rest of us stood back some twenty feet and waited our turn. While we waited, we were searched for any contraband. I expected such and had hidden what little money I had, my watch, Rachel's locket and one pocketknife in my boot in the hope they would not search that thoroughly. And they didn't.

Finally, I was called forward. "Name, last name first, then first name and middle initial if you have one, followed by rank and unit," said the corporal with his pen poised over paper waiting for my reply. Evidently I didn't answer fast enough, because I got a bayonet poke in the back hard enough to draw blood. I turned and glared at my tormentor, a young, clean-shaven boy that didn't look to be over 16. Unlike the others who had encouraged us off the riverboat, he looked scared when I glared at him.

"Name!" demanded the corporal.

"Joubert, Ethan E, captain, 1st Louisiana, and kiss my Rebel ass!" He looked up me to see what sort of a fool he was dealing with then turned to his left.

A lieutenant stepped over to me and got in my face. "Captain Joubert, it appears that you may need to learn some manners." This man looked serious. He was a few inches shorter than me, and his face was lightly pox marked. His moustache and mouche were neatly waxed. From dark close-set eyes under frowning brows, he glared at me. His face close enough I could smell the alcohol on his breath, he said in almost a whisper, "Listen, Reb, you do *not* want to make me angry. That is your first and last warning. Understand?"

I did not answer, and he repeated once more but much louder, "Understand?"

I nodded. "Understood."

He smiled a crooked little smile then said, "I believe we have another prisoner here named Joubert? Any relation?"

"What's his first name?"

"Pernell. Know him?"

"My father."

His smile grew into a sadistic grin. "Excellent. We shall put you in with your father, and you two can be a happy family again." He turned to a private standing nearby with his musket ready for action. "Take Captain Joubert to Number 2."

"Yes, sir!" replied the private.

The lieutenant turned back to me with that grin still on his face. "I hope you enjoy your stay, Captain," he said in a very even tone.

After I was issued a blanket, a tin cup, a plate, and a spoon, the private escorted me into the bowels of the prison. The enlisted and lower ranking officers were held in a series of wooden barracks behind the main fort that had been hastily built to house the rapidly growing influx of prisoners. The parole system used earlier in the war had been abandoned, when the North discovered they were capturing the same men over and over. They decided detaining them instead would help deplete the South's supply of men faster, using the South's refusal to count one northern black prisoner as equal to one southern white as an excuse to shut the program down. This resulted in a sudden need for prison space. With that haste, often came deplorable conditions, because the new prisons were rarely well suited for their intended purpose. At Fort Delaware, senior officer prisoners of war and political prisoners were held inside the fort under generally better conditions. The rest of us had to settle for something a bit less comfortable.

The private pointed at the open door of the barracks with his musket. "Inside."

I nodded and entered its dimly lit interior. I found it furnished with a long row of bunks on either side. At the far end, four prisoners were seated on stools and boxes around a crate playing cards with two others standing and watching. Near the entrance, three other prisoners were seated on stools talking, at least until I walked in. Once they saw me, conversation stopped, and they stared at me as if something was wrong with my appearance.

"I'm looking for Pernell Joubert, where is he?" I asked.

One man pointed to the other end of the building toward the card game.

I made my way down the aisle and stopped about four feet from the man seated with his back to me. He was dealing the hand. The others look up, but none of them looked like me, so I assumed my father must be the dealer. They looked a mite stunned but said not a word by way of greeting and just continued to stare at me, some appearing as if they were confused. They looked at me then at the man dealing the cards, then at me again and back at the dealer. He finished the deal, and noticing their strange behavior, he soon realized they were looking at someone behind him.

Pernell Joubert slowly twisted around on his stool to see what had captured his friends' attention. When he saw me standing there, the expression on his face changed from curious to shock. He slowly stood, looking me up and down, taking my measure. We were about the same height, and my mother was right, I did look a lot like him, so much so, I felt as if I was looking at myself in a mirror, but the "me" in the mirror was a bit older with some gray around the temples and a face showing a few more lines of age and experience but lacking my saber scar. He was clean-shaven; otherwise, the similarity was uncanny.

Pernell Joubert was speechless at first, but his shocked expression soon turned into a smiling one. "I was beginning to think I would never get to meet you," he said as he stepped closer. He put his arm around my shoulder and turned back to face his dumbstruck friends. With a broad smile on his face, he said, "Gentlemen, I would like for you to meet my son, Ethan." He said it as if he was proud of me.

After introductions, Pernell begged out of the game. "Deal me out and excuse us, please. We have much to talk about."

We left the darkness of the barracks and found a table and two chairs in the corner of a larger room. "I suppose," he began, "we need to decide what you shall call me."

"How about Idiot?" I offered sarcastically.

He pursed his lips and looked as if he was considering my suggestion. "Actually, son, I was thinking more along the lines of Father or Pop. Why Idiot?"

"Because you let my mother get away from you."

He nodded, again as if considering what I had said. "First, I was away at school up north and only found out about the arrangement she entered into a month after it was done. How do you think I felt when I got her letter telling me about it? My father did indeed disapprove of her because of—well—because. But I was prepared to go against his will, because I loved your mother enough to defy his wishes, even if it meant he might disinherit me. Analee never gave me the chance to prove that."

I felt bad about being so hard on him. "She never told me the details. I apologize, sir."

"Accepted. And may I also add, if we had married, you would never have met Rachel."

"Point taken. My mother told you about Rachel? And how did you find out about me, for that matter?"

"The you question first. I began to suspect something before the war when several friends who met you reported the uncanny resemblance and that your name was Davis. In early '62 a letter Analee had written to me almost a year before finally caught up with me. She mailed it to an old address in New Orleans. Then it was forwarded to South Carolina, where it promptly got lost. By then I was back in New Orleans recruiting for the cause. They eventually found it in South Carolina and forwarded it there. By the time it arrived, I had rejoined Beauregard when he was transferred to Tennessee. Not long after that, that letter finally found me. By then, it was so marked up by various post offices and postage due stamps, it was hard to read the original address.

"Her letter confirmed my suspicions about you. At first I was angry with Analee for withholding that information from me, but gradually, I accepted the fact that she really had no other choice. I wrote her back, and she eventually replied, telling me about Rachel and all you two had gone through. I had also heard the campfire story by then."

"That story circulated in the Trans Mississippi Department, too?"

He nodded. "I tried to get transferred to Virginia to find you. I didn't want to introduce myself in a letter; I wanted to meet you face-to-face."

"As did I."

"I finally got a transfer and arrived in Virginia right after the Gettysburg scrap. I couldn't find you. Some said you were killed and others said you were wounded. No one seemed to know where you were."

"I was wounded and sent to recover in the care of an old friend outside Richmond. I didn't rejoin the 1st Louisiana until a month ago. When did you get captured?"

"I was captured at Spotsylvania. That ended the war for me, and I began to lose hope I would ever get to meet my son, but I prayed about it." He smiled broadly and reached over and slapped me on the shoulder. "But the good Lord brought him right to me! Fancy that!"

"The Lord moves in mysterious ways."

"Indeed. And what of Rachel? Did you find her?"

"Haven't even been able to look. She's somewhere up north. Her trail is cold now. I have all but given up hope of finding her."

He shook his head. "Don't gave up hope. There is always a chance something will happen that will change everything." He paused and considered his words. "I have never had a chance to do anything for you, and maybe I can now. I'm thinking I can help you find her. I want to see you two have the life together that Analee and I never had the chance to have."

"I assume she told you Morgan is dead. Perhaps there is a chance for you two?"

He smiled. "She did, and that has crossed my mind—and I believe hers as well. Least ways, she seemed to imply such in her letters."

"Have you heard from her of late?"

My father shook his head, his expression a frown. "Not since the Federals took Vicksburg. Now that they control the Mississippi, getting mail across the river is pretty rare. I wrote her several letters, but I haven't heard if she even got them."

"I have had the same experience. Can we try from here? Will they let us send mail south?"

"It can be done, but it's a complicated process."

"Well, well, well, one big happy family again?" said the man coming up behind me. My father's expression changed immediately from one of hope to one of hatred. It was the lieutenant I met on the dock.

"Forgive me, Captain, as I did not properly introduce myself earlier. I am Lieutenant Abraham Wolf, and I will be seeing that you enjoy your stay here." His smile was not genuine. "After you left, I realized I have heard about you, Captain, and you, also, Major Joubert. I had not connected the names before. There is a campfire legend I have heard some of the prisoners telling about a young man and the woman he loved. Her name was Rachel, I believe."

He paused to see my reaction, but I tried to manage the anger welling up inside me. "Never heard it," I replied.

"Then let me tell it to you. It seems this young man, and his name was Davis like your traitor president—any relation? Probably not, Davis is a common name for a common type. Back to my story—this Rachel and her young man fell in love, but it developed that the young man's father was a philanderer, and Rachel was his daughter, thus the two were siblings, or so it seemed."

His hands behind his back, he leaned down to get his face to my level so I could look into his eyes while he told the rest of the story. "The lovely Rachel made haste to run away from all the heartache of discovering she could not be with her lover. But in her absence, it was discovered that the young man was not her brother, after all." He smiled that sneering smile again. "It seems Mrs. Davis had played the harlot with another man many years before and had a bastard son named—let me recall—Ethan, I believe."

I had endured enough. "Never heard that story," I said as I reached up and grabbed the front of his coat near his throat and pulled down as hard as I could, slamming his face into the tabletop. "Oh no! Did you slip and fall?"

Wolf stood, his hand on his pistol, and glared at me and then at my father who was tensed to strike. It was two against one, and discretion was the better part of valor for Lieutenant Wolf. His handkerchief to his bleeding nose, he said in a somewhat nasal tone, "You were given your one warning at the wharf. Now, you belong to me." He turned and left the room.

My father relaxed. "You should not have done that, Ethan. He is going to do everything he can to make your life miserable, and he's very good at doing that."

"Sorry, but I couldn't take it anymore."

"You had better get used to it."

25 August 1864

There have been times in my young life that have left me stunned and in unbearable pain: the death of my mother, Morgan's schemes to separate Ethan and me, losing Ethan, and the death of Doctor J.

I thought losing my baby was as bad as it could get, but I was wrong. Yesterday was yet another such day and the worst of the lot.

Taylor came to visit late in the afternoon as I was cleaning my brushes after a sitting. Since I was on the third floor, I barely heard his persistent knock at my door. When I let him in, I knew from the grave expression on his face that he had something very important to tell me. "What's on your mind, Taylor?"

"Please be seated."

I took a seat on the sofa, and he sat beside me taking my hand in his as he did. This was looking very serious.

"A little over a month ago I came across a casualty report of Confederate loses in Early's Corps during the recent attack on Washington."

I stopped him. "And you are going to tell me Ethan's name was on the report?"

"Yes."

"Missing, wounded—or killed?"

The muscles in his jaw tensed before he spoke. "I am sorry, Rachel, but your brother was killed just outside Washington."

I did not know what to say, and I looked around the room in a daze, trying to absorb the news. Finally, I took a deep breath and looked back at Taylor. "We know those reports are often not reliable. Perhaps there is an error. We thought he might have been killed the summer before, but he was only wounded. And why did you wait so long to tell me?"

"I waited because I wanted to be sure it was true before I told you. I hired Aimee's detective in Richmond to confirm the report if possible, and he did. I just received a letter from him." He retrieved it from his coat and began reading.

My Dear Doctor Anderson,

As per your request, I sought to determine the status of one Captain Ethan E. Joubert of the 1st Louisiana Brigade of Early's Corps, who was reported killed in action in July of this year. I was able to locate and interview two men from his regiment who were eyewitnesses to the event, one was his first sergeant, and herewith is their account of what happened.

They reported that the regiment was fighting a rearguard action and was heavily engaged with Union forces at the time. Captain Joubert ordered a retreat to a more suitable position from which to fight. He was the last to leave the position being abandoned and stopped to pick up a wounded man to carry him to safety.

The attacking Federals fired a volley at Captain Joubert and the man he carried over his shoulders. The two went down with Captain Joubert apparently wounded. Both men remained down in the tall grass of the field of battle. The Federals approached Captain Joubert and his companion with their muskets at the ready. One pistol shot rang out, and the Federals were observed to bayonet the two wounded men.

Because of the necessity of the retreat by the Confederate forces, the remains of Captain Joubert were not recovered.

The sworn statements of the two witnesses are attached to this correspondence.

Please convey my deepest sympathies to Captain Joubert's loved ones.
Respectfully yours,
Edward P. Wilkinson
Proprietor: Wilkinson's Investigative Services
Richmond, Virginia

—◈—

Hearing that read aloud was more than I could stand. I was numb and unable to think clearly. I wanted to deny the evidence, but it was conclusive. "Taylor, thank you for confirming—this—before telling me, but now, I need to be alone."

He put his arm over my shoulder and pulled me close. "Rachel, I can't leave you like this."

"But you must. I need to be alone. Please!"

He kissed me on the forehead. "Words cannot express what I feel for you just now."

"Then, don't even try."

He stood and moved toward the door. "Send for me if you need me. I'll look in on you tomorrow."

Still stunned and without even looking at him, I could only manage a nod.

Chapter 26 – Wolf's Revenge

25 August 1864 (Continued)

Taylor was gone barely ten minutes when someone was pounding on my door. I was in no mood for visitors and went to answer it with that attitude. I opened it, and in the last light of twilight, I saw Aimee with tears streaming down her face.

"Rachel, may I come in?" She didn't wait for a reply and rushed past me. "Oh Rachel, have you heard? I am so sick!"

"Yes, I heard. Who told you?"

"Miles just told me. As soon as he did, I knew I had to rush over and console you over the loss of your brother."

Everyone keeps calling Ethan my brother, but he was far more than that to me.

"Oh Rachel, I scarcely know what to do or even think. My Ethan is gone forever!"

"Your Ethan?"

"You know how I loved him so, and he said he loved me." She withdrew a lace-trimmed handkerchief from her sleeve and blew her nose. It was grossly inadequate to meet the demands she was placing upon the dainty thing. "Oh, I'm sorry. I forgot that you were in love with him, too."

She didn't forget. She then threw her arms around me and began sobbing all the more. This shallow ditch weeping on my shoulder was not what I needed just then! *"Aimee, please. I know you're upset."*

"Upset does not even begin to describe what I am. Rachel, whatever will we do without him?"

I was beginning to feel as if I were in a stage play. Then even more drama. *"I am near death over this! I may as well end my life, for it is over without Ethan!"*

"We'll do whatever we must."

She pushed herself away and grasped me about my shoulders, holding me at arms length and looking mournfully into my eyes. "You are so strong! I wish I had your strength."

I wanted to slap her, and I should have. "Aimee, calm down. We will get through this."

"Yes," she sobbed. "We'll get through this—together. You're like a sister to me."

That wasn't what I had in mind.

General A. Schoepf (pronounced "sheff") was commanding officer at Fort Delaware. He was an immigrant from Hungary, or Germany, or Poland, depending on who was telling the story. His English was heavily accented, thus, he could be difficult to understand. He was more often disposed to be kind and lenient to the prisoners. His adjutants, Captain George W. Ahl, and my new friend, Lieutenant Abraham G. Wolf, on the other hand, were two of the meanest sons of Belial to ever cast a shadow on this earth, neither of whom could ever be described as kind or lenient by any stretch of the definitions. Their actions reflected poorly on General Schoepf, and he took much of the blame they should have taken. Schoepf was almost certainly misled by his subordinates concerning what was going on behind his back. He was also at the mercy of his superiors, including the Secretary of War, and was afraid of them. Many considered the man totally unfit for command. As a result, Fort Delaware was a hellhole and was later often referred to as the "Andersonville of the North," comparing it to that infamous southern prison in Georgia.

Conditions at Fort Delaware were indeed awful with much overcrowding (over 13,000 prisoners at one time during the war) that aided the spread of diseases. We also had bad food, tainted meat, unsanitary drinking water, and miserable winters spent in poorly built barracks. Unlike Andersonville, where the Yankee prisoners slept out in the open or in holes scratched out of the ground with coverings made from whatever could be found, we had a roof over our heads—most of the time. Many prisoners who died at Fort Delaware died from the terrible conditions, but the death rate was lower than if we had been in a battle, such consolation that might have been.

I had to ask, because I had to know. "What are the chances of escaping?"

My father lowered his voice. "Slim and none. Even if you get past the fences and guards, it's a long swim across some cold and treacherous waters. Some have tried, and many didn't make it, only to drown or be recaptured. As for the others we didn't hear about? Who knows? Maybe they got away. This war is nearly over, probably lasting only a few more months. It's better to wait than risk your life for nothing."

As for my new adversary, Lieutenant Abraham G. Wolf was an unrepentant drunk who was boastful and loud with a love for humiliating and even inflicting pain on prisoners, often just for his own amusement. The man was sadistic. Captain George W. Ahl, by comparison, was a genteel and well-mannered son of Belial, but even crueler than his subordinate. My father did his best to shield me from Wolf with only limited success. Wolf sought me out for his special brand of abuses every chance he got.

My father took me around and introduced me to my fellow prisoners, showed me the mess hall and the infamous "sink" we would have otherwise called a latrine. It was a series of holes in boards over a near stagnant canal. Its contents were supposed to be flushed by tidal flows, but that rarely happened.

"The food is from truly awful with rotten meat and mealy bread and barely edible to almost tasty. Almost, but not quite." I wondered why this subject was mentioned as part of the tour of the sink. "As bad as the food is, I would recommend you avoid the fresh catfish some will offer for sale. They say the fattest ones are caught below the sink."

That really helped my appetite.

"We eat twice a day, and the rations are not adequate to sustain life for very long. Until this summer, the rations were more than what we are getting now. That changed when the Secretary of War ordered a reduction because of some unfounded rumors of how Yankee prisoners were fed in southern prisons."

"I heard as much. What he fails to realize is they are fed the same poor rations our soldiers get, no more, no less. The civilian population is also starving. If this war lasts much longer, there will be no one left alive down South."

"That's their intention."

With our plates, cups and spoons, we formed up and marched to the mess hall. I found bread and bowls of meat spread along the long row tables at intervals. The tables were belly high with no chairs or stools. We ate standing up.

As I set my plate of slop down and considered its unappealing appearance, I heard footsteps behind me followed by the voice of Wolf. "Captain Joubert!"

I looked to my father, and he nodded.

With two black eyes from our earlier encounter and still sounding a bit nasal, he said, "Enjoying your meal, sir."

It was difficult to hold back my smile. "I haven't had a bite yet."

He leaned over and pushed my plate onto the floor. "Oh, such a pity. Your dinner has fallen to the floor. I guess you will have to eat it off the floor. We cannot let you have any more. That would deprive someone else of a meal. After you have eaten it all, you must clean the greasy spot. We do not allow untidiness here at Fort Delaware." He smiled before he continued down the row.

I turned back to my father and took a sip of my weak coffee, which tasted of something other than just coffee. I pushed it aside.

My father passed his plate to me. "Eat this, son."

I pushed it back. "No. You need it more than I do."

"He went easy on you this time. Expect the next one to be worse." He took one bite of the meat and spit it out. "Rancid! Not fit for hogs."

Another prisoner with a rags for a uniform and a long beard and quickly claimed it. "I'll eat it. Mine was good!" With a glassy stare, he looked at me. "You gonna eat yours off the floor?"

I shook my head.

"Then I'll eat it, iffin you don't mind."

My father looked at me with his head cocked. "Welcome to Fort Delaware."

The only water suitable for drinking was found in the hogsheads, and that was reserved exclusively for drinking. If you needed a bath, wash your clothes, wash your plates, you did it in one of the shallow brackish water ditches that laced through camp for that purpose. The ebb and flow of the tides was supposed to flush them out, but the "water gaps" in the ditch ends designed to prevent our escape tended to catch everything and hold it to flow back into the camp at high tide. The putrid water was almost certainly the source of the numerous fatal cases of dysentery that often ran through the camp. Once you got the green-apple-quick-step, death was often as close as the nearest sink. And we would sometimes find the dead ones in the sink, either slumped over the hole or fallen into the water below.

After attending to our duty one morning, my father and I were leaving the sink when a guard on the parapet called out to us, "Move along, Rebs."

My father grabbed me by the arm and nearly dragged me away from the place, stopping only after we were out of sight of the guard.

"What was that?" I asked.

He look back to be sure we were not being observed or overheard. "That was saving your life. He would have shot us had we not moved as fast as we did."

"Just for walking away from the latrine?"

"Just for walking away from the latrine! This past July, Colonel Jones, who was lame in one foot the result of a battle wound, was shot when he didn't double-quick as ordered by a guard. The poor man was incapable of moving faster than a slow hobble, and the guard never even gave him a chance to try before he shot him and killed him. They tell you to move; you move!"

"Was the guard disciplined?"

There was coldness in my father's eyes when he answered. "They promoted him. That has only emboldened the other guards to similar reckless behavior. They'll put a ball past your head to encourage you, and I imagine also just for laughs, and some of these kids aren't very good shots. They may hit you as much as miss you. Grant's extravagant expenditure of the lives of his men has created a need for able-bodied soldiers to fill the ranks. The more experienced 5th Maryland that was guarding us was called to the front and replaced by a 100-day militia unit, the 157th Ohio, and they've had but a week or two of training. They are green and trigger happy."

The weak leadership of Schoepf and his poorly worded Special Order #157, which effectively gave the inexperienced Ohioans limitless discretion in how they treated the prisoners, led to the killing of Colonel Jones and their propensity for firing at prisoners for any supposed infraction. More men would die because of this.

My father introduced me to one of the political prisoners held at Fort Delaware, the Reverend, Isaac W. K. Handy, a Presbyterian minister, arrested the previous summer (1863). He was a man of proud bearing with long hair, a beard, and a ready smile.

"Captain, it's a pleasure," said Reverend Handy, his hand extended.

"The honor is mine sir," I replied. "My father has told me some of your story, and it was very interesting. Would you mind filling in the details?"

"Certainly. It seems, Captain, that I have offended the authorities," he said with a mischievous smile on his face.

"So I heard. They arrested you for a comment about the flag?"

"Indeed. I was visiting with relatives near here, and we were at dinner with several invited friends. I said something to the effect that the flag no longer represented its original high and noble principles, meaning the war was being used as an excuse for our freedoms to be eroded. Among other things, I was referring to the President's suspension of habeas corpus. Someone at the table that night reported me to the authorities, and I was soon arrested for uttering language disloyal to the government, as they put it. I found out just what the suspension of habeas corpus meant. I received no trial, as called for in the Constitution, but was tossed into prison here with you fellows and held without any representation by an attorney."

"They consider that remark as bad as taking up arms against the government?"

He nodded. "They do indeed, sir. We have a government drunk with power, and such drunkenness will inevitably result in abuse of the citizen and loss of freedom. History has proven the accuracy of that statement over and over. This is not what our founders intended."

"I freed my slaves before the war and joined the army, not to defend slavery, but to defend my home against invasion. But Lincoln has turned the war into one of freeing the enslaved black man. While, in my opinion, that is a noble enterprise, it's not why I am here. Like you, sir, I fear the government of the United States."

My father looked about nervously. "Ethan, be careful. Such talk can get you in trouble with both the blue and the gray."

Reverend Handy agreed. "Your father is right. I would advise caution regarding your words. I speak from ample experience. It would seem I further inflamed the authorities after my arrival here. I was originally held inside the fort with the other political prisoners, and many of them are also being held unconstitutionally. There, the comforts were demonstrably better than what you experience here outside the fort. Whatever I said, or they think I said, has gotten me cast out of my 'comfortable' imprisonment into your little hell."

"Advice taken, sir. You have no recourse to your condition?"

He shrugged. "They said I could take a loyalty oath, and I would be freed. I refused, as I consider such to be tantamount to approving the war and their illegal and unconstitutional activities. Thus, I have taken to calling myself 'a prisoner for conscience sake.' I will almost gladly stay here as long as they make me, but in the end, I'll expose them for the charlatans, liars, and usurpers they all are. Evil must be exposed wherever you may find it."

That was not an empty threat. I did not know it at the time and only found out after Reverend Handy was released after spending fifteen months imprisoned illegally in Fort Delaware, but he was keeping a secret journal detailing his incarceration and all the injustices visited upon the prisoners there.

After purchasing some stationary from another prisoner, my father and I composed a letter to Analee. We were allowed only one page, so we wrote, shall I say, rather small.

My father squinted at the page. "Think she can read it?"

"She may need spectacles, but I expect she'll manage."

The letter was placed in an addressed cover, which was left unsealed for the censors, with no postage, since we had no Confederate stamps. That was placed in another cover, also unsealed, but with Union postage. The letter would be reviewed by the censors and, if approved, sent to a designated location where it would cross the lines under a "flag of truce." The Confederates would send it on to the addressee with postage due, assuming it could get past the Union gunboats patrolling the Mississippi River, looking to keep the Western Confederacy isolated from the Eastern Confederacy.

"What do we do with it now?" I asked.

My father sighed. "This is the hard part. You have to give it to Wolf."

My heart sank. "No other way?"

He shook his head. I knew we had wasted our time, but I tried anyway and gave the letter to Wolf the next day.

He smiled as he took my letter from me. "Writing home to Momma, are we?"

"I would much appreciate it if you would forward my letter, Lieutenant Wolf."

His smile became a devious grin as he stuck it in his pocket. "I just bet you would." Wolf turned and walked off toward the gate. After he passed through and was standing on the bridge over one of the little stagnant ditches, he turned back to see if we were watching him. He smiled again and took my letter out of his pocket, tore it into pieces, and spread the strips of paper over the stagnant water of the ditch. That ended our letter writing. We had no way to tell Analee either of us was safe or even alive.

When I arrived in early August, there was much talk of a prisoner exchange, the first since the collapse of the Dix-Hill Cartel in 1863. Some fifty prisoners had departed for South Carolina in June, presumably to be exchanged. Six hundred additional Confederate officers were later selected to go to South Carolina. Again the speculation was they would be exchanged. For obvious reasons, there was much excitement among those selected. They eventually became known as the "Immortal 600."

On 20 August, the selected 600 officers boarded the *Crescent City* and sailed for Charleston, South Carolina. When they arrived they were much disappointed, as their real purpose was to be used as human shields by the Yankees in retaliation for Yankee prisoners being used the same way by the Confederates, a charge that was denied. Those who survived arrived back at Fort Delaware the following March.

My little contest with Wolf was indeed getting worse, and he took every opportunity he had to humiliate me or inflict some form of pain.

I came down with a case of the green-apple-quick-step in September and while returning from the sink one night I was set upon by four guards who beat me and left me unconscious. I was found the next morning and taken to the hospital for treatment.

After an examination and with one cut on my head stitched closed, the surgeon questioned me. "You have some bad bruises and several contusions, maybe even a cracked rib. Who did this to you, Captain?"

My ribs aching as I pulled on my shirt. "No one. I fell."

"If you fell, then you must have bounced several times. You have bruises all over your body. Wolf do this? It looks like his handiwork?"

I did not answer.

He helped me to a cot. "I will give you a day here to recover; that's the best I can do. But you should report him to Schoepf."

"It would only get worse if I did report him."

"But someone needs to stop him."

I lay back down in the cot with great effort. "Perhaps, but on my terms."

On 5 August, Mobile fell to the Union followed by Atlanta a month later. In early November we got word that Lincoln was re-elected, and Schoepf called for a salute by the guns of the fort to celebrate. In mid-November, rumors began to circulate among the prisoners that General Sherman was on a march to the sea in an attempt to slice through the heart of the Confederacy. A month later, he took Savannah, Georgia, completing his mission. The days remaining to the Confederacy were numbered, and that number was getting ever smaller.

20 December 1864

Miles came to deliver some distressing news, as I was finishing for the day; he is being called to the front to join Grant in Virginia. There are logistical problems he is being sent south to help solve. I feel like I am losing a friend. I will miss him.

22 December 1864

Time has passed slowly since learning of Ethan's death. Aimee still visits me almost daily, and she remains heartbroken. She has taken to using laudanum to ease her pain, and hardly even tries to hide it anymore. I have begun to feel sorry for her. Mentally, she is a shattered wreck, but I am not sure her professed love of Ethan with his recent passing is the total reason for her condition.

She spent last night here in an opium-induced slumber. I put her down in my bed and tried to get some rest on the sofa, but sleep eluded me. I could not get Ethan off my mind. It is as if he is still alive and calling to me. The man will ever be in my heart. I realized I needed to put my thoughts of him into a letter. Perhaps that would give me some peace?

I retrieved my lap desk, and with a cup of hot tea, set about to write a love letter to Ethan.

My dearest Ethan,
When I was falling, you reached out and caught me.
When I was alone, you came to me and gave me hope.
When I was hurting, you comforted me.
When I was frightened, you held me, and I felt safe.
When I needed to be loved, you touched my heart and gave me more love that I
could ever have hoped for.
When the world was against us, you stood by my side.
When I had no one else, I always had you.
And now you are gone, and I am once more alone, and hurting, and frightened,
and in need of being loved.
Look into my heart; you are still there.
Look into my soul; you are still a part of me.
Vous étiez ma vie! Vous êtes ma vie!*
I shall miss you always. I shall love you forever.

Rachel

*You were my life! You are my life!

Winter was upon us and with it colder weather with winds
blowing out of the north. Little Pea Patch Island, being what it was,
an island exposed to the elements, there was nothing to slow them.
Our drafty barracks incubated even more sickness among the
prisoners. And the taunts by Wolf continued.

It got a lot worse on Christmas Eve when we had finished our
usually substandard dinner and were returning to the barracks. My
father accompanied me. I saw Wolf ahead with three Blue Coats in
tow. He looked like he had something on his mind. As he was about
to pass us going in the other direction, we were forced to step aside
to allow them the right of way. At the last moment, he lunged in my
direction and bumped into me. He turned and with both hands
pushed me away. "Did you see that?" he yelled. "This Johnnie Reb
assaulted me!"

My father stepped up to my defense. "We apologize, Lieutenant
Wolf. It was an accident."

"Like hell it was. He assaulted me!"

I stepped toward him with my hands raised in surrender, and a bayonet was suddenly thrust against my throat. Another was against my ribs. I froze.

"Arrest him for assaulting me," he demanded. He looked at me with coldness in his eyes. I had seen that look before, and the thought of what might be coming chilled me to my soul. "Hang him!"

"Lieutenant Wolf, please," pleaded my father. "It is Christmas Eve."

He looked at my father and smiled. "I said hang him!"

Two of the soldiers took me by the arms, while the third walked behind me with his bayonet inches from my back. They brought me behind the first of the officer's barracks, where a fourth Blue Coat waited with shackles. This was obviously planned like the attack when I was beaten returning from the sink. My father and two others followed, but they were immediately ordered to their barracks.

The shackles were placed on my wrists, and they were tight. One guard tied a rope to the center of the chain connecting the two shackles and tossed the other end over a beam. Then two of them began hauling me up until my arms were fully extended over my head, and my toes barely touched the ground. I could neither hang from the shackles on my wrists comfortably nor support myself on my toes.

Wolf got in my face again, and like every encounter I had with him before, I could smell the alcohol on his breath. His eyes were glassy and he slurred some of his words.

"How long?" I asked.

He shrugged. "As long as I feel like." He left two guards with me. "No one comes near him, understand?"

Christmas Eve and I was hanging from a beam like some ornament on a Christmas tree. My hands were already beginning to hurt, but I dared not show my discomfort to give them any satisfaction. It was to be a cold winter night, and I was not properly dressed to spend it outside. I knew if I hung there very long my hands would eventually swell and turn purple, and I could lose their use.

I looked to the barracks and saw some of my fellow prisoners at the door watching the proceedings. My father was among them.

Chapter 27 – Friends and Lies

25 December 1864

Last night was Christmas Eve, and while there was little joy in my heart, I decided I needed to at least go through the motions.

Taylor asked me to a party at a hotel near the Capitol. I was expecting it to be interesting enough to improve my frame of mind, and perhaps I could be shed of the melancholy mood I was in. He arrived early, splendidly dressed in a finely tailored uniform. I had a new gown made for the occasion in the hope it would help cheer me up.

As I was making my last minute preparations in the hall mirror with Taylor waiting impatiently nearby, grinning as if he knew some secret, he finally blurted out, "Is this going to take all night? You look even more beautiful than I have ever seen you look."

I smiled at him. "Thank you for the lovely compliment." I turned to face him. "Very well. I'm ready. Why are you in such a hurry?"

At first he looked down as if embarrassed then back at me. "Because I have a surprise for you."

"Oh, Taylor, what have you done? There is a war going on."

He stepped closer and dropped to one knee. I gasped. "Would the loveliest lady in Washington do me the honor of becoming my bride?" And he produced an opal and diamond ring.

This was not totally unexpected, and I had considered many times what I would say when he finally asked. When Ethan was alive, I had an excuse to refuse, though I could not articulate the exact nature of that excuse. But with Ethan gone, I had to reconsider my answer. I am now twenty-two, and Taylor was forcing me to think about what I had previously avoided considering in an honest and forthright way. Taylor is handsome, sweet, affectionate, well educated,

305

and a gentleman, a prize any young woman would grab given the chance. I like him—but I do not love him, and though I hope I can eventually come to do so, I know that is unlikely to happen. Even in death, Ethan's love haunts me still, but I tell myself I must somehow move on with my life.

"Yes!" I heard myself say.

He came to his feet and slipped the ring on my finger. "You make me very happy!" Then he took me in his arms and kissed me—in a way he had never kissed me before, because I had not previously allowed it. It lingered, and he wanted more. My thoughts went immediately to Ethan, and I knew that was wrong and unfair to Taylor.

I pulled away. "Whoa there, don't we have a party to attend?"

He did not release me. "I have wanted one of those from you for a very long time."

I tried to distract him by admiring my ring, forcing him to release his hold on me. "It is a lovely ring, Taylor. Did you pick it out?"

"It was my mother's wedding ring."

"Then that makes it even more special."

The night was cold as I hung between heaven and hell. The pain in my hands grew ever worse until they became numb. I looked up, and in the weak light of the lantern, saw they were turning blue. I tried to stay awake in order to provide some relief for the blood to flow to my hands by standing on my toes, but I was tiring, and my calves were cramping badly. It was hard to tell which end of me hurt worse.

With the coming of dawn, the coldest time of the day, I was reduced to violent shivering from the cold and my inadequate clothing. The camp was stirring, and prisoners making their way to the sink had to pass within sight of me, but none dared do any more than glance in my direction, much less stop or approach me, for fear one of my guards might shoot them. My father was one of those passing, and I could see the look on his face was one of fear and worry.

Lieutenant Wolf showed up to make sure I was suffering sufficiently to his satisfaction. My father called out to him. "Lieutenant Wolf, may I have a word with you?"

Wolf turned and gestured for Pernell to approach. "What do you want?"

"I am begging you to release him."

Wolf sneered at him. "Why should I do that?"

"Because it is the birthday of our Lord, and He would show mercy."

"But I am not Jesus Christ."

Hanging there, listening to that conversation, my first thought was Wolf was very right on that point. There was nothing of Christ in him.

My father nodded. "Indeed. Then I shall have to do something rash."

Wolf looked at him questioningly. "Like what?"

"Report this to Schoepf."

"And how will you do that?"

"He will attend services with the prisoners this morning. I'll tell him then."

Wolf laughed. "Then you shall not attend services."

My father smiled. "I anticipated that. Look over to the barracks, Lieutenant. See all those men gathered there. Must be over a hundred."

Seeing such a large gathering, the guards had called out the sergeant of the guard, and he had called for the company at his command to responding to the potential threat they posed.

My father continued, "Everyone of them has agreed to say something to Schoepf if I am unable to do so. You going to keep all of us from Christmas services? Then how will you explain that to Schoepf?"

Their point made, the gathered prisoners immediately began disbursing before the guards began firing on them.

Wolf considered his options, and they were few. It was obvious that Schoepf would not have approved of what he was doing, otherwise, he would not have hesitated. He glared at my father for a long moment then turned to my guards. "Take him down."

The rope loose, I dropped to my knees as Wolf watched with a sadistic smile on his face. As the guard removed the shackles from my wrist, I looked up at Wolf and whispered, "It isn't over."

"I reckon not," he replied before he turned and left the area.

With the shackles removed, I tried to rub my hands in an attempt to get the blood flowing again, but I had no feeling in them and no control over my swollen fingers. My father and another prisoner each grabbed a hand and began messaging it, but it was so painful I wanted to scream out. After a few moments of that, they helped me to my feet and took me to the hospital.

The surgeon took one look at my hands and said, "Wolf! I recognize his work here. Captain, I told you to report him. Now you must!"

"No," I replied. "I will handle this my way."

My hands remained useless for the next three days. Slowly, feeling started coming back to them. By the New Year, I had some very limited use of them, but it was painful to even hold a spoon. The surgeon proscribed laudanum for the pain, but I rejected it, because I knew it was addictive, choosing, instead, to endure the pain.

27 December 1864

Aimee is beside herself with happiness for me. My engagement seems to have snapped her out of her depressed moods. She is gay again.

She even offered to help me plan our wedding. We have set 8 April for the nuptials, assuming Taylor can get a furlough for at least a few days. The wedding will be here in Washington, and Taylor's family will journey here from Baltimore. He is hoping to take me to meet them in a few weeks.

The war seems to be coming to an end. Grant has Lee bottled up near Richmond with the two sides occupying entrenched lines. The brilliant strategist, General Lee, seems unable to affect a victory over Grant's vastly superior forces.

As for me, the end of the war cannot come soon enough. Just as Ethan predicted nearly four years ago, it was a losing endeavor for the South. I wonder how Analee is doing without a husband to help her run Catahoula and her stepson Payton off in the war? Is Payton even still alive?

I wrote to her to tell her of Ethan's passing and asked Taylor if he could get it through the lines for me. He seemed reluctant at first but agreed. The chances of it getting through are quite slim, but I felt I should try to let Aunt Analee know about Ethan.

We heard the Red River area was the scene of a series of battles last spring, and some of the plantations along the river were burned along with their stores of cotton. I do pray that Catahoula was not touched.

On the afternoon of 3 January I received a summons from Lieutenant Wolf to report to the fort. I complied, and my guard took me to the headquarters' building and passed me off to a sergeant unknown to me. We meet few of those in administrative positions or garrisoning the fort itself. He pointed to a door.

"What is this about?" I asked.

"You have two visitors."

"But we are not allowed to have visitors."

"One is a Union officer, and he has some considerable influence, it would seem. You have ten minutes. Make them count."

I turned and opened the door he was pointing to and went inside.

"Ethan!" exclaimed Aimee de Beauchamp.

I was dumbfounded. My understanding, from her father nearly three years before, was he was taking her to France and out of my life.

She threw herself into my arms and kissed me. Then she drew back repelled by my offensive odor. "I smell pretty ripe I imagine. Bathing here is a luxury few of us get, especially in the winter. Forgive me."

"Ethan, you've lost so much weight! Aren't they feeding you?"

"We get beef steak and ice cream every day."

"Don't make fun of me!"

"I'm sorry. This place is awful. We must make jokes in order to keep our sanity."

I recalled that the sergeant had mentioned an officer using his influence to see me, and I looked around to find a major with his arms crossed leaning against the wall behind me. The open door had hidden him from my view when I entered. His expression was deadly serious as he looked me up and down. I sensed distaste in his demeanor.

"And who, sir, might you be?" I asked.

He pulled away from the wall and approached me. He was a nice-looking fellow, a bit shorter than I, and clean-shaven. His uniform was obviously new and well tailored from excellent material. He did not answer my question but reached down and took one of my hands and examined it, pushing my sleeve back to reveal the scabbed scars from the shackle on my wrist. That was followed by a similar examination of my other hand. "What happened?" he asked.

"I was hung by my hands for an imagined infraction by a sadistic bully wearing a blue uniform."

Aimee noticed the bluish color of my hands and the wounds on my wrists. "Oh, Ethan!" She turned to the major. "Will he be all right?"

He nodded. "It will heal with time."

"Who are you?" I demanded.

"I am Major Taylor Anderson, a surgeon."

I looked to Aimee for an explanation. "He's a friend," she offered.

I turned my attention back to the major. There was something about him I did not like, and I got the sense that feeling was mutual. I shook it off and directed my attention to Aimee. "What are you doing here, and how did you find me?"

She glanced at the major before answering. "A friend found your name on a list of prisoners and told me you were here. They said you could not have visitors, so I asked Major Anderson if he could help me get in to see you. He has many friends and was most helpful. We brought you some things: a blanket, wool stockings, gloves, some food, but they only allowed me to keep the blanket. They took the rest away," she said gesturing to the blanket on a nearby table.

"The blanket will be most helpful and is greatly appreciated. The winters here are harsh."

"Ethan, I'm back in Washington. This war will be over soon. Come to me, and I'll help you." She glanced at Anderson again before saying, "You know I'll always love you."

I nodded. "One more thing, by chance, any word of Rachel?"

Her eyes flashed with anger. "None," she snapped. "Give it up, Ethan. She's gone forever!"

Major Anderson frowned.

The sergeant stuck his head in the door. "Time's up!"

Anderson replied, "We're done here, Sergeant." Then he turned to me. "Captain Joubert, take care of those hands. Rub them frequently to recover blood flow. Keep them warm. Weakened so, they are in danger of frostbite. The gloves Miss de Beauchamp brought would have helped. Too bad they confiscated them. Good day, sir."

Aimee kissed me on the lips. "Goodbye, Ethan. I'll come back if I can. Come to me after the war. I'll take care of you." With that she pulled the hood of her cloak up and left with Anderson.

"Back you go," snapped the sergeant.

When I arrived back in my barracks, I found my father and some or our friends huddled around the stove for warmth. Pernell looked much relieved to see me. "What was that all about?"

"I had two visitors." The others looked at me as if I had gone daft on them. "One was an old friend, Aimee de Beauchamp, the daughter of a French diplomat. I met her before the war. The other was a Yankee major, a surgeon she claimed was her friend. Never seen or heard of him before."

"Miss de Beauchamp's father must have considerable influence," commented Pernell.

"Actually, I think it was the major with the influence. It was a strange experience. He acted almost as if he knew me, and I got the feeling he did not like me very much, either. Regardless, I got this warm blanket out of it!"

7 January 1865

Aimee is back in town from a brief trip to visit a sick friend near Wilmington, and she is eager to help me with my wedding gown.

23 January 1865

I met Taylor's father this past weekend when he came to Baltimore for a visit. Dr. Anderson is in his late fifties, overweight, balding, and sports large sideburns. His demeanor is usually very serious, but Taylor assures me he has a good sense of humor once he gets to know you.

He asked many questions about my background, which I expected, as Taylor had warned me. He is a staunch abolitionist and hates the secesh, as he refers to the Rebels. The fact that I am from the south is troubling for him, I am sure. I tried to assure him I was not supportive of slavery and used the fact that I was residing in the North as proof of that.

All his questions and his stern deportment were stressful, but I think I made a favorable impression.

He seems very proud of his son and is happy he is finally marrying.

31 January 1865

The 13th Amendment to the Constitution passed, abolishing slavery in the United States. There is much celebration in the streets of Washington.

10 February 1865

I have not been completely honest with Taylor. I could not decide whether to tell him things about myself he did not know or keep secrets from him. With my conscience bothering me, I finally decided, if we are going to be man and wife, we cannot withhold anything from each other, especially something that if discovered later could be hurtful.

When he came for a short visit yesterday, I decided it was time for him to know about me—and Ethan—all of it. If he was troubled by any of it, there was still time for him to back out of the marriage.

I prepared him as best I could by asking him if he loved me, to which he replied in the affirmative. I then added, "If you love me, then you will understand what I am about to tell you." That seemed to make him nervous.

"You have asked me about Ethan, and I have told you some things but not all. You are aware of how we met, how we fell in love, how we discovered his father was also mine, which explained why he tried so hard to keep us apart."

I paused and took a deep breath followed by a sigh. "What I did not tell you is that Ethan arrived home from New Mexico the day before we found out the truth about Morgan. That night—Ethan and I spent that night together in his cabin."

Taylor's shoulders sank.

"There is more. When I arrived in Gettysburg, I was pregnant with Ethan's child."

He sat there, unmoving, his eyes staring blankly in my general direction, his face expressionless.

I took his ring from my finger. "If you want this back, I'll understand. I should have told you this before."

"What happened to the child?"

"I miscarried."

He nodded knowingly, his face unreadable.

I extended the ring out to him. He pushed it away. "Nothing has changed. I still want to marry you, but I do wish you had been more forthright with me! It was wrong for you to withhold this from me until now."

"You are right, of course."

He stood. His eyes flashed with anger. "Don't you ever lie to me again!"

"I didn't lie..."

"Yes, you did! Withholding that kind of history is lying by omission."

I began to weep. "Taylor, forgive me for offending you."

"I need to leave now," he said as he shoved his kepi on his head and turned to leave.

"Please, don't leave. Not this way!"

He turned and left without so much as a goodbye.

After he was gone, I thought about what had just transpired, and it frightened me. I had never seen the angry side of Taylor before. I knew all men were capable of such anger, and I needed to learn how to deal with it. Withholding that I had been bedded by another man—and had his child—was more than I should have expected him to handle well.

13 February 1865

Taylor called upon me and took me to dinner last night. He acted as if nothing had transpired at all just two days before. He laughed and told jokes, and I think, drank a bit much.

When we arrived back at my home, he kissed me goodnight, but his kiss was more aggressive than I was accustomed to coming from him. I stopped him and reminded him we were not yet married. He grumbled something unintelligible and left.

After he left, I considered what I said to him. I had allowed, even encouraged, Ethan to go much further, yet, timid as they were, I resisted Taylor's advances. And I am beginning to get the feeling I am more experienced than he is.

Chapter 28 – The Truth

20 March 1865

I do not know what to think about Taylor. Since I told him some of the more personal details about Ethan and me, he seems to have changed. And maybe that's only my imagination?

I have made every effort not to ever even utter Ethan's name in front of him, but he often does. It is as if he is obsessed with him. He drank too much at dinner last night, and on the way home, he commented on the fact that he is shorter than Ethan and wondered if I preferred taller men. At first I tried to ignore it, but then I began to wonder how he even knew how tall Ethan was? I could not recall ever having physically described Ethan to him. Perhaps Aimee or Miles did?

He is a man, and men have urges. Lately, he has demonstrated such to me in his shows of affection. His kisses have become more aggressive, and while I try to show my affection for him, I am not prepared to allow him to take it as far as he seems to want to go.

Two nights ago, things got out of hand, or more accurately, Taylor got out of hand, and it frightened me. He was kissing me, and he suddenly pushed me back on the sofa almost into a reclining position with him virtually on top of me. His hand went to my breast, and I pushed it away. But he insisted! I stopped resisting in the hope that would satisfy him for now. It did not.

His hand shifted from my breast to pulling up my shirt, putting his hand between my legs, and he forced my legs apart with his knee. My skirt and petticoats were in my face and I was virtually helpless. I twisted my face to the side and asked him to stop, but he did not. Instead, he became even more physical. This was not comfortable for me, and I regretted allowing him to touch me, which surely encouraged this behavior.

Again, I begged him to stop, but he only muttered something I could not understand and continued touching me. I had enough and brought my knee up into his crotch. He groaned, and his grip on me loosened enough I was able to push him off onto the floor.

I jumped to my feet and straightened my skirt. He came to his feet and slapped me. I stepped away and held my hand to my face. "Why did you do that?"

"Because you deserved it for rejecting me. You didn't reject Ethan!"

"OUT!" I screamed, pointing at the door. "And don't even consider coming back until you can act like the gentleman I know you are."

"Rachel, we are about to be married in less than a month! You didn't wait for a wedding before you and E..." I slapped him as hard as I could.

"Don't you EVER say his name again in my presence! What happened between Ethan and me has nothing to do with what will happen between us. And unless you change your attitude, there will never be an 'us.' Now, OUT!" And I pointed at the door.

He looked remorseful. "I'm sorry, and you are right. My conduct was inappropriate. You are the first woman I've ever been truly interested in, and perhaps my actions have been a bit, shall we say, awkward. I am struggling with living in the shadow of—him. I feel like everything I do is compared to... Don't you understand how that makes me feel?"

I was beginning to feel sorry for him. What he said about me comparing him to Ethan was true, but I had tried not to allow that to ever come out in my words or deeds. I knew he had lunch with Aimee more than once, and in retrospect, I wonder if she might have said things about Ethan that encouraged this feeling of inadequacy he was having. She could be very colorful and descriptive at times.

While I forgave him, the incident left a disturbing impression on me, and I wonder if I really know Taylor as well as I thought I did? And was my decision to marry him a wise one?

31 March 1865

Friday and I have no sittings scheduled. It seems all my generals are busy with the war and have little time to sit for their portraits. I read in the paper Lee has become active again, and that may explain the cancelled sittings.

After tidying up around the house, I was relaxing in the parlor with a book I have been putting off reading for months when I heard a knock at the door. Perhaps my afternoon sitting can make it after all, I was thinking as I opened the door and saw Miles standing there.

"Come in, Miles. General Grant send you home from Virginia?"

"In a manner of speaking, yes. I am back in Washington to help expedite his supplies. Lee is moving, and Grant thinks this is his chance to end the rebellion once and for all. I have only a few minutes before I must return and much to tell you. Please be seated."

"Every time someone tells me to be seated, it means I am about to receive bad news."

"Not this time." He paused. "Well, maybe both good and bad, depending on your perspective."

"Get to the point, Miles."

"Where shall I begin?" he asked rhetorically. "The beginning, of course." He took a deep breath and blurted out, *"Rachel, I know why Ethan changed his name."*

"You do? Why?"

"Because he has taken his father's name."

"You are not making sense, Miles."

"I know. Let me explain. Morgan Davis, your father, is not Ethan's father." He paused for that to sink in.

I had to think about that. *"How do you know this?"*

"Ethan told me."

"When did he tell you?"

"When I was captured in the Shenandoah Valley in '62. I spoke to Ethan at Port Republic. He told me the whole story of what happened that day when you left, and more importantly, what happened after."

Miles was clearly anxious. *"What did he say happened?"*

"That he had a fight with Morgan. You were listening outside, and it came out you were Morgan's daughter. You were upset, and you left—to make this story shorter. What you don't know is Morgan was killed over this."

"I knew he was dead, but killed? By whom?"

"You won't believe it. Mammy shot him. Morgan had raped her, and Brandy was his child, then he killed the man Mammy loved, a slave called Cornelius. As you know, Brandy ran away, and Mammy lost her daughter. Peyton even had a falling out with him when he announced he wanted to marry some landless, young lady in Alexandria. Then what he did to you and Ethan. It was more than she could handle. She shot him; then she killed herself.

"My word!"

"Ethan was left to settle the affairs of Catahoula for his mother before he could leave to search for you. Analee eventually guessed that you were Morgan's

daughter, and she confessed to Ethan that Pernell Joubert was his father, and he needed to go find you and tell you."

I was numb. "Miles, are you sure about this?"

"Yes, Ethan told me, and I have no reason to doubt him."

I looked up at Miles, and he was clearly distraught over this. "Why did you not tell me the truth when I asked you in Gettysburg a year and a half ago?"

He ignored my question. "There is more. Aimee and Taylor also know this."

My mouth fell open. "How long have they known?"

"I told her as soon as I got back to Washington after I was paroled. I'm sure Ethan also mentioned it to her when she was in Richmond. I told Taylor not long after Gettysburg."

"Taylor has known since then?"

He ignored that question, too. "Ethan has been looking for you since you left. He was not going to enter service until he found you. Unfortunately, he got drunk over just missing you in New Orleans and got into that duel. The authorities charged him with murder. He escaped the noose by joining Wheat's Battalion, and he was stuck for the duration, which many thought would be less than a year."

"That's what Jean was trying to tell me! I didn't listen to him or Doctor J, either. I've been a fool." I was sick. I would have gone to him had I known, and we could have had a little time together. "Why are you telling me this now, Miles? Ethan is gone."

"I thought you should know the truth before going through with the wedding.

"I am not sure I can go through with the wedding to Taylor after he withheld this kind of information from me. I can't trust him."

"Hold on. There is more, the good part. Ethan is alive."

"Miles, please! The casualty report and the detective…"

"Both in error, evidently. Ethan wasn't killed that day; he was taken alive. It's true. I know because both Aimee and Taylor spoke to him just two months ago."

"Two months ago Aimee and Taylor knew he was alive and didn't tell me? Where is he?"

"In prison at Fort Delaware. They both visited him there. And his father is also at Fort Delaware with him."

I was glad I was sitting down, for I felt faint. Less than two weeks away from my wedding, and I was about to marry the wrong man.

"You asked why a few moments ago?" His expression became grave. "The best answer I can give is I was jealous of what Ethan had, meaning you and real

love. All I had were affairs—empty, meaningless encounters. I resented him having what I was trying to find, someone to love me like you loved him. Women were throwing themselves at him, and he was thinking only of you. I realized that two things sustained him: your love and the love he had for his Lord. He failed; we all do, but he always seemed to recover, even during the worst of times. Taylor told me that, even in captivity, his thoughts were of you."

I was weeping then. Miles put his arm around me. "I could no longer carry on this deception, especially seeing what it was doing to you and what I am sure it did to Ethan. This has been on my mind since I left, and I couldn't sleep at night, thinking about how I was hurting two people I care about. Rachel, I can't tell you how sorry I am for what I have done to you and Ethan. I hope by telling you these things now, it isn't too late and it might help. You need to go to Fort Delaware and get Ethan and his father out. I would but I can't leave here, and I haven't the authority."

"If you can't, how am I to do that, Miles?"

"Think about it, Rachel. Through your portraits, you have amassed a vast resource of influential people: generals and Congressmen. They like you. They tell me so. Call in your chits. Find one or more who will help you get him released. I can suggest a few to go to first. The war is ending, and it will be easy for them to show mercy at this point, especially as a favor for someone they like. I have to go, but here is a list to start calling on. You can save him."

It was time for Wolf to get what was coming to him. He had made many enemies among the prisoners and even among our guards. While all wanted revenge, the prisoners took it. The plotting had long been in process, and a plan was hatched for the execution of his sentence to be on the night of 31 March, to be discovered on April Fools Day.

On the evening of 31 March, Wolf got drunk, as was his usual practice, and made his rounds after lights-out. As he stumbled along in the darkness, six men wearing hoods to hide their identity came out of the shadows to meet him. He looked stunned at first but quickly realized something terrible was about to befall him. He was struck from behind and rendered unconscious before he could sound an alarm. Bound and gagged they hauled him away.

On the morning of 1 April, my father and I received a summons to appear before General Schoepf, and we were to bring all our possessions, such as they were. I was certain they had found Wolf, and we had been implicated in the crime. Under armed escort, we were marched off to meet Schoepf in his office. We were taken right in as soon as we arrived. Inside, we found General Schoepf seated behind his desk. Another officer with his back to me stood looking out of the window.

Schoepf stood. "Gentlemen, jew are being transferred to another facility." He waved some papers, which I assumed were the authorizations for the transfer. "Major Riddle, here, vill escort jew to your new facility."

Major Riddle? He turned with a stern expression on his face. He was finely dressed and wore a full beard, but it was indeed my old friend from Richmond.

Riddle gestured to someone behind me. "Corporal Blue, shackle the prisoners."

Corporal Blue? I turned and saw Blue in a snug fitting blue uniform advancing toward us with leg and hand irons, and he was grinning, though trying not to.

My father looked to me. "I don't like this, Ethan."

"It will be all right. Do as they say."

Restraints in place, they marched us out to the wharf where a ferryman was waiting for us. Once on board the little steam-driven ferryboat, we were seated forward away from the pilothouse. My father was still apprehensive.

I looked around to be sure no one was in earshot. "Riddle, what are you doing?"

"Getting you two out of prison. Did you like it there? If you did, I can take you back."

My father looked to me as if I were making no sense.

"Father, this major here is Silas Riddle, an old friend."

"Pleased to meet you, Major Joubert. Your boy and I had some adventures together back in '62. Sorry, but the restraints will have to stay on for now—for appearances, if you know what I mean?"

"The corporal is my friend. You've heard me speak of Blue? Well, meet Blue."

"Major Joubert," said Blue. "Pleased to meet you, sir."

I looked to my father. "I told you not to be concerned."

"I'm confused," he replied.

"So am I. Riddle, how did you find us?"

"I was looking for one of my associates gone missing. I figured he might be a political prisoner at Fort Delaware."

"Associates?" asked my father.

"Long story," I replied.

"And I found your name on the prisoner list. Did a little investigating and discovered your father was in there, too. Figured you needed busting out, so here I am."

"And Blue?"

"Oh, I found him when I showed up here two days ago for the purpose of affecting your removal from the clutches of the hated Yankees. He had also trailed you here and was trying to figure a way to get a message to you. I recognized him, and we joined forces, so to speak." He paused as he shook his head. "You have any idea how hard it was to find a uniform big enough to fit him?"

"What now?" I asked.

"You go find Rachel, and Blue, here, says he knows where she is."

I looked at the grinning Blue. "You know where she is?"

"Yes, sir, think I do. Cap'n Ethan, can I see that picture of Miss Rachel?"

I took out my watch and showed him the picture we had taken some six years before.

Blue examined it carefully. "It's her! I seen her."

"You saw her? Where?"

"Gettysburg. Doctor Johnson's daughter was really Miss Rachel. It was after you ran off those fellas trying to arrest Doctor Johnson. You went off to report to General Ewell, and she came out to talk to me. Brought me some food. And big as you please, she walked up to Pepper and stroked his neck. I tried to warn her he didn't take well to strangers, and she said—now listen to what she said—she said, 'Pepper won't hurt me.' An' I ain't never told her that horse was named Pepper. She knew his name! And Pepper acted like they was old friends. It was her, I'm telling ya!"

I remembered returning that evening and finding Blue talking to a woman who quickly ran inside when she saw me down the street. "It was her! She was there when I brought Jean into the doctor. I saw her there in the darkened corner! I could have touched her! I could have ended this right then!"

"You wasn't supposed to find her then, Cap'n Ethan. God had other plans for you and for her. I think He did want her to see you, though, to remind her once more what you mean to her. But I think now, He wants us to go get her and take her home to Catahoula."

"Stop it!" snapped Riddle, "You two are about to get me to weeping."

"Blue is right, Ethan," said my father. "We know where she is. It's time to go get her."

"You boys need to shush now. We're about to land."

Once on shore, Riddle took us to a wagon covered with a tarpaulin. We rode in the back, while Blue drove. Once on the other side of Delaware City, he took us down a single-track road to a farmhouse set well off any main roads.

Upon arriving at our destination, Riddle removed the restraints. "We're safe now. These folks work for us. They'll feed you and get you some new clothes so you won't look so much like the escaped Rebs you are.

"Pepper's in the barn, Cap'n Ethan, and I got rid of that mule. Traded it for a horse, nice one, too. And bought one for your poppa."

"That's it for me, Ethan," said Riddle with his hand extended.

"You leaving?"

"Yep, I have other work to do. You two were a side trip for me. Find that girl and marry her—and make lots of babies."

"Will I ever see you again?"

"I expect so. Bet you didn't know I am originally from New Orleans? I expect I'll get down there to fix something or break something some day, probably soon. If so, I'll drop by."

"Thank you, Silas."

He glared at me as he shook my hand. "It is Riddle, not Silas." He turned to leave then stopped and turned back. "Oh, I almost forgot. Back at Fort Delaware, they were all animated over a Lieutenant Wolf gone missing. Seeing as how I happen to know you had a few nasty encounters with him, you have anything to do with his disappearance?"

My father started chuckling but said nothing. I smiled. "I expect they'll eventually find him."

"You kill him? 'Cause he needed killing."

"Not unless we misjudged the length of the rope, and he drowned. We left him bound and gagged hanging from a rope about waist deep in the, shall we say, 'water' below the officer's sink. He must be pretty ripe by now?"

Riddle grinned and pointed an accusing finger at me. "Well played, Ethan, well played!"

The family Riddle brought us to were Copperheads, southern sympathizers, and part of an organized, reverse, underground railroad to help escaped Confederate prisoners get back down South. They fed us, and we got to take a real bath with hot water and soap. I scrubbed and scrubbed, and I thought I would never get the grime and smell of that prison off.

We departed for Gettysburg at dawn.

4 April 1865

I write this on the train on the way back to Washington from Fort Delaware. I arrived there on 3 April, a Monday, after securing a letter from one of my generals and endorsed by two senators I had done portraits for. The letter authorized the release of Ethan and his father immediately upon a loyalty oath sworn by both. It was the only stipulation my supporters demanded. I am sure they will agree to that, since the Confederacy is all but gone into the pages of history.

Upon arrival about mid-day, I secured a ferryman to take me out to the prison. A sergeant greeted me as soon as I stepped off the boat and demanded to know why I was there, I showed him my letter and asked to be taken to General Schoepf. After he read my letter, he escorted me to the general's office and asked me to wait outside while a clerk took my letter into him. Momentarily, several officers, who seemed very excited, came out of the office.

General Schoepf followed and saw me sitting there quietly. "You mus' be Miss Whitcomb?" His accent was very strong and sounded German.

"Indeed, sir."

He motioned for me to enter his office then offered a chair before a desk stacked high with papers. "Sitzen sie, Miss Whitcomb." After I was comfortably seated, he took his own seat behind his desk. "Es seems Major Joubert und Captain Joubert are very popular zes days."

"Then you can release them?"

"I'm afraid not, Miss Whitcomb."

I came to my feet. "But the letter. You must release them."

"I cannot, because zey are no longer here. Two days ago, a Major Riddle presented a document ordering zier transfer to Washington. I vas compelled to release them to Major Riddle. Zey are gon' from Fort Delavare."

"Where in Washington?"

"Zee order did not specify ver."

I was crestfallen. I did not even know where they were taken. I offered my thanks and made my way back to the ferry. It was near sunset, and we were about to land at Delaware City when the guns on the fort began firing a salute. At first it frightened me until I realized what it was. I turned back and saw the huge fortress bathed in the glow of its guns firing and the smoke billowing around it.

"What is that for?" I asked the ferryman.

"The Dutchman fires off salutes every time there is a northern victory. I expect this one was all 156 guns. Richmond fell this morning."

We arrived in Gettysburg on the afternoon of 4 April. The town was changed little from my previous visit nearly two years before. The damage had been largely repaired, and Gettysburg still had its small town feel. I found Doctor Johnson's house, but I noticed his shingle was not out front as it was in '63. I asked my father and Blue to wait with the horses while I made inquiries about Rachel.

I knocked on the door and tried to look respectable in my hand-me-down suit. An elderly gentleman answered. "May I help you, sir?"

"I hope so. This is Doctor Johnson's house? I am looking for Miss Rachel Whitcomb. Are they about?"

"You a friend of either?" he asked.

I wasn't sure how I should answer that, being as when I was last here it was with an invading army. "Yes. I know Doctor Johnson."

"I am most sorry to inform you, but Doctor Johnson is deceased well over a year now."

"Then what of his—daughter, Rachel?"

"She was not his daughter, although he almost considered her so. She moved away a year ago January."

"Where did she go?"

"Forgive me, sir. What is your relation to Miss Whitcomb again?"

"None really—yet—we were to be married four years ago."

He put his hand to his mouth. "Then you must be Ethan?"

"Indeed, I am Ethan. Where is Rachel?"

"She moved to Washington, like I said."

"But where in Washington? You have an address?"

"Let me see. Come in, please, and forgive my caution, but I'm sure you understand. I'm Carter. Maxwell was my friend, and I bought his house from Miss Rachel," he explained as he shuffled through some mail on a side table. "Ah, here it is. Her address is on this invitation. Oh dear! You must hurry, sir. She is getting married in just a few days. This is an invitation to her wedding."

"Married?"

"Yes, to a nice young surgeon she met here after the battle."

"A Yankee major named Anderson?"

"Yes, that's his name." He saw the anger on my face. "I am sure if you hurry you can prevent the marriage."

"Thank you, sir. I'm sorry I troubled you."

"Oh, no trouble, young man."

My father noticed my dour expression when I rejoined them. "Something wrong?"

"She isn't here. She's in Washington. We go there in the morning after we have rested the horses and ourselves, but we have little time to waste. She's getting married this Saturday."

"Married? To whom?"

"That Yankee major who was with Aimee when she visited me. He was a bit more than just Aimee's friend; he was Rachel's fiancé. Now, I understand why I did not take to him, and why he seemed not to be very fond of me either."

Chapter 29 – The Reckoning

Author's Note: The following events took place on 5 April 1865. Two sources were used: Ethan's manuscript, written after the war, and Rachel's journal entries, which those dated 5 April 1865 were almost certainly made at some later date and recorded from memory.

I arrived back in Washington late in the afternoon of 5 April. I was tired from my trip and the forced overnight stay in Wilmington because of a missed train. I went home just long enough to be rid of my bag, freshen up, and get something to eat before I confronted Miss Aimee de Beauchamp and Major Taylor Anderson. I decided to take on Aimee first, then Taylor. After a quick meal and some tea to try and calm my spirit, I prayed for wisdom in what I was about to do. As the sun was setting, I made my way out to the street.

My neighbor, Mrs. Needles, was outside tending to some plants by her door and called out to me. "Miss Rachel, glad to see you are home again. Your fiancé, Major Anderson, called for you at least twice while you were gone."

"Thank you," I replied and continued on my way. "Forgive me, for I'm in a hurry, Mrs. Needles."

She persisted. "To see Major Anderson?"

"Eventually, but first I'm going to see Miss de Beauchamp."

"That's nice. Tell her hello for me."

"I will," I replied, anxious to be about my business, and made my way to Aimee's home two streets over.

We arrived in Washington and soon found Rachel's house. Again, I asked my father and Blue to wait with the horses while I reintroduced myself to Rachel.

My heart was racing in anticipation of seeing her again, and I was anxious about how she might receive me after nearly four years of separation. I reminded myself that this had to be God's will for us. She loved me, of that I was still certain in spite of the fact she was about to marry another. That had to be because she was still laboring under the mistaken impression we were brother and sister.

I stood at the door, my fist hovering inches away in preparation of knocking. I looked back at Father and Blue, and they were watching me and feeling as anxious as I was, I am sure. I mustered up my nerve and rapped loudly on the door and waited—and waited, but no one came to the door. I knocked again, this time even louder and longer. Still no answer.

Shortly, a woman came out of the house next door. "Yoo-hoo! You looking for Miss Rachel?"

"Yes, ma'am. You know where I might find her?"

"You just missed her. She is going over to Miss de Beauchamp's house."

"Can you tell me where that is?"

She pointed. "Two streets south. She is on the corner. North facing red brick with white trim. Can't miss it."

I tipped my hat. "Thank you, ma'am."

I very nearly ran back to my waiting father and Blue. "Just missed her. She's headed for Aimee's house two streets over."

By the time I reached Aimee's house, I was angry again and knew that was not good. I needed to control my anger and focus it appropriately. Again, I prayed to calm my spirit.

I noticed Taylor's horse tied outside on the street. I went right in without even knocking and found the hallway dark, as they had not yet lit any lamps, but lamplight was coming from the parlor. Aimee and Taylor were arguing, and I seemed to be the subject.

"Since its me you are discussing, may I join you?"

Both looked to me with surprised expressions on their faces.

"Where have you been?" asked Taylor. "Your neighbor told me you left town for a few days, but you never told me anything about the trip or even where you were going."

"I don't report to you," I snapped back.

"Darling, I was worried about you."

With the last of the evening twilight to illuminate our search, we found Aimee's house easy enough. Only one on that corner fit the description. I noticed a "US" branded horse tied at the curb with a McClellan saddle and an army saddle blanket on it.

"Major Anderson," I muttered to myself before I turned to my father and Blue. "This time, come with me. That's Anderson's horse, and this could get ugly. I want witnesses if it does."

"Need this?" said Blue withdrawing a Colt from under his coat.

"No, you hang onto it. I don't want to be tempted to kill him."

We drew closer to the door and found it ajar, I could hear voices inside: three people, Aimee, Anderson, and Rachel. I pushed the door open quietly and slipped into the darkened foyer. I wanted to understand what I was walking into before I announced myself.

The three of us stood in the dark foyer and could easily see into the parlor, which was illuminated by a single lamp. Aimee and Anderson were facing Rachel, and she had her back to me at an oblique angle. None of the three were aware we were in the house and observing them from only thirty feet away. Since it was then fully dark outside, and with no lamps in the foyer or hall, I knew we could remain unseen unless they came into the foyer where we were. I leaned against the wall near the doorway, peeping around the corner and listened to the conversation.

And once more my heart was racing at the sight of Rachel. *My Lord,* I thought, *but You sure know how to pick them.* Yes, I was biased, but I felt I was looking at the most beautiful woman in the world, and I could not help but smile at the sight of her.

"There was no need for you to worry about me, Taylor. I'm perfectly capable of taking care of myself. I have for these last four years, and even before that when Ethan and I were separated by his—by my father." I chose to emphasize Ethan's name, and perhaps that was a bit spiteful of me.

I smiled at the way she paused and referred to Morgan as "her" father. That told me she knew the truth somehow. Miles? This was getting interesting. Rachel seemed to have a full head of steam, and I sensed she was about to have her way with these two. I decided I would just watch and listen for a spell.

"Rachel, really, if we're to be married you must not be going off without asking me."

"Ask you?"

"Of course!"

"You really expect me to get your permission for everything I do?"

"It is only natural, my dear."

Rachel rolled her eyes. I had seen that look before, and it did not bode well for the major. Rachel wasn't the asking type. She needed to be handled with a bit more finesse than that.

"Darling, you seem to be a little upset," said Taylor as he took a step toward me.

I stuck out my hand to stop him. "A little upset? Sir, you have not yet seen me upset, but you are about to. That little tiff we had a few weeks ago when you got pushy was just a warm-up for what's coming. But first, I want to deal with Miss de Beauchamp. You shall wait your turn—Darling—until after I am finished with her."

Properly chastened, he stepped back.

She spit that "darling" out like it left a bad taste in her mouth. Terms of endearment were not helping his case.

My father leaned over and whispered in my ear. "This woman has fire!"

"You haven't seen anything yet," I whispered. The real fireworks were about to begin, because she was about to lay into Aimee.

"Miss de Beauchamp, I have a present for you."

That seemed to stun her. She at first looked at Taylor as if confused then attempted to recover. "Why, Rachel, whatever for? I should be giving you a gift for your wedding, not the other way around."

"After I give you mine, you may want to keep yours."

Aimee didn't see it coming, and neither did I. Rachel hauled back, made a fist, and punched Aimee right in the nose! Aimee went down taking out an end table and its candy dish in the process, which amazingly did not break, but its hard candy sweets were scattered all over the floor.

"Whoa!" I heard my father say behind me almost loud enough for them to hear in the parlor.

Rachel then stood over Aimee shaking her hand, and I loved what she said—

"I have been wanting to do that ever since I first heard your name. My hand hurts, but the rest of me feels really good right now!"

Aimee's nose was bleeding. She started to rise, but Rachel stopped her.

"Get up and I will give more of that. You stay down there where you belong, you shallow ditch!"

My father leaned over and whispered, "Did she say 'ditch' or something else?"

I wasn't rightly sure. "I think she said 'ditch,' but intended the something else?"

Though he seemed intimidated by me, Taylor felt the need to intervene. "Rachel, really! Was that called for?"

I spun and pointed my slender finger at him. "Back off! It isn't your turn yet! I will get to you!"

Once more he backed down, and Aimee made no attempt to rise after I threatened her.

"Rachel, what is this all about? Why did you hit me?"

"It is about you and your lies. You see, I found out why Ethan changed his name, but you knew long before I did and chose not to share that information with me. Instead, you chose to deceive me, because you wanted Ethan for yourself and figured you could lie and cheat your way into his heart. He isn't that stupid!"

I had to think about what she said. Should I take offense at her use of "that" with "stupid?"

Then the major mustered up some courage. "Rachel, perhaps she was well intended," he said in an attempt to sound innocent.

"Shut up, Taylor, because you knew, also—and chose not to tell me! Yes, you knew, and then you told me he was dead!"

I turned to my father and whispered, "I was dead?"

He shook his head. "Not that I was aware of."

I turned my attention back to Aimee but addressed Taylor. "For goodness sakes, Taylor, can't you give the woman your handkerchief for her nose?" He retrieved it from his pocket and passed it to Aimee.

"I think you broke my nose."

"Better hope that's all I'll break."

I stooped down closer to Aimee for what I was going to say next. "You see, Aimee, I also know Ethan isn't dead, and you—"

She pointed first at Aimee, then that accusing finger swung like a compass needle over to Anderson, followed by her glare.

"—And you—YOU kept that from me. AND, you let me write that letter to Ethan's mother telling her he's dead! My word, what kind of utterly despicable people are you to let Analee and me experience that kind of loss, and for your own selfish desires? Are you so naive to think I would never find out he was alive or that we are not related? And even if Ethan married you, Aimee, how do you think he would feel about you once he discovered how you lied to me— and to him? This conspiracy of yours makes no sense. Either you two are stupid or insane—or both."

Aimee came to her own defense. "Ethan didn't really love you, Rachel. He was in love with me all along; he said as much in Richmond."

I was only able to stare at her incredulously and shake my head. "My word, but you are indeed insane!"

Aimee shifted tactics then. "You say he's alive? But you saw the reports?"

"Wrong! Wrong! And Wrong! He's alive!"

"Then where is he?"

"He was at Fort Delaware, wasting away in that horrible place. And you two could have gotten him out, but you chose to leave him there, because that suited your selfish plans. That, Aimee, isn't love. If you really loved Ethan you would have done all you could to get him out—like I tried to do."

"I wanted to, but Taylor wouldn't let me!"

I turned on Taylor. "That true?"

"Of course not!"

"Know what? Since I can't trust either of you, I won't believe either of you."

The major started a defense of himself, but Rachel was having none of it.

"Shut up, Taylor. You can't say anything to me just now that will change how I feel about you, which isn't good! Meanwhile, when I found out Ethan was alive and in that place, I got some of my friends, my real friends, to help me get him and his father freed, but when I arrived there, he was already gone. They moved him, but I don't know where—yet! But I will find him if it is the last thing I do. He spent the last four years looking for me. I can do no less for him."

I decided this had gone far enough and came out of the shadows. "You don't have to look for me, Rachel. I am right here."

She spun around and threw her hands up to her mouth and just stared at me as if she was beholding a ghost returned from the grave. I went over to her and took her into my arms. She started weeping then.

I could not believe my eyes! He was there, a bit thinner than the last time I saw him in Gettysburg, but there! And alive!

Aimee came to her feet and went to embrace Ethan, but he put his hand out to stop her. "No, Aimee. We are done."

Taylor stood to the side, a dour expression in his face. "I guess this means the wedding is off?" he asked, I think trying to make a joke out of a very bad situation.

"Actually, Major, I think the wedding is on, but you won't be in it."

I turned to Rachel. "You were really going to marry him?"

Her eyebrows went up as if surprised. "I plead temporary insanity?"

She tugged the ring off her finger. "Taylor, here's your ring back." And she tossed it at him. It bounced off his chest.

She looked up into my face and smiled as she slipped her arm around my waist and pulled herself against my side just like she used to do back at Catahoula that summer we first met. "Come along, Ethan. Let's go home."

My father and Blue stood in the doorway of the parlor waiting for us. Rachel saw my father, and even in the weak light, the resemblance was obvious. "Major Joubert?"

He bowed deeply. "My dear, I must say I am most impressed with the lady my son has fallen in love with. And you have a lovely right hook! You didn't hurt your hand, did you?"

She smiled. "A bit. It'll probably be bruised tomorrow."

Blue stepped up. "Miss Rachel, I am so pleased to see you again."

"You knew didn't you?"

"Not until I remembered you called Pepper by hiz name."

"I wish you had picked up on my slip then."

"Miss Rachel, I've been kicking myself for the last few days, thinking the same thing. I should have seen it then."

"Maybe you were meant to miss it? A lot of good happened that might not have if Ethan had discovered me that day."

Rachel got to wear her new wedding dress. We were married the next day with Blue as my best man. My father gave Rachel away. Miles was in attendance, but we did not know that at the time. He slipped in, stayed in the back of the church, and left just as the ceremony ended.

As we walked out, about halfway down the aisle sat Riddle, legs crossed and cocked back in the pew with his arms spread out on its back, a broad smile on his face. He was clean-shaven and wore the uniform of a Navy captain this time.

"So you found her?" he said.

"Thanks to you and Blue."

He stood. "Aren't you going to introduce me to your new bride?"

Rachel looked at me for an explanation. "Rachel, meet Si..." I caught myself. "Meet Riddle, the mechanic. If it needs fixing, he can fix it, and if it needs breaking, he will break it. He is the one who got us out of Fort Delaware."

"Would have done it sooner if I had known..."

Rachel curtsied. "I am pleased to meet you, Captain, Admiral, whatever you are..."

"Doesn't matter, ma'am. Just Riddle will do, and I'm whatever you need me to be."

"I would have invited you, but I didn't know how to find you. How did you know to come and where?"

"Ethan, don't you know by now, it's my business to know things?"

He bowed to Rachel "And the legend of Rachel and Ethan finally has a happy ending. Good day, Madam Joubert. And Ethan, you take good care of her, now."

He tucked his hat under his arm and started down the aisle but stopped near the door and turned back. "Oh, I hear they found Wolf. Took 'em nearly two days to clean him up. Well played, Ethan, well played!" He spun and was out the door to disappear into the bright sunlight like some ghost.

Rachel looked to me. "The legend of Rachel and Ethan?"

"Long story. I'll tell you later."

"And who is Wolf?"

I pursed my lips and frowned making a sour expression. "Euweee! That one, you don't want the details on."

The first light of dawn was breaking through our bedroom window when it hit.

"Ethan! Ethan! Wake up!" She was shaking me. "Ethan! Wake up! You're having a bad dream!"

I came out of my stupor, and Rachel was sitting up and leaning over me. I came to a sitting position as the nightmare abated in my mind and reality once again took control.

"You were dreaming. You started shaking and groaning. Then you got violent. Ethan, what is wrong?"

My breathing slowed as I pulled her to me for comfort. "Right now, I really need you."

"You have me. I am right here. How can I help?"

"Just hold me and let me hold you. I'm scared."

"You scared? Of what? What happened to you?"

I slid back down and pulled her against me like she was some sort of covering that could shield me from the specter in my mind.

"I think we need to talk about this," she said as she drew even closer to me. "Something terrible is bothering my husband. If you will tell me what it is, maybe I can help you."

I looked at her and saw the worried expression on her face. "Rachel, I have seen the elephant, and it is an exceedingly ugly beast."

"What are you talking about?"

"I thought it was over, but it isn't. I thought finding you would make it all go away, but it didn't. Yes, I do need to talk to you about it, and you need to know what happened."

"The war changed you. I saw that soon after you found me. Being wounded, the prison, had to have affected you."

"That's part of it, but it's more than that. Rachel, I have seen things. I've done things—awful things that haunt me, that won't leave me alone, especially in my sleep."

"Something terrible happened to you, something you have not told me about. What is it, Ethan?"

"A lot of things happened, some worse than others but all bad. First, it was losing you and the ever-growing fear I would not be able to find you—not ever. Then it was the war. Killing people was hard at first, then it got easier—too easy. I told myself I was doing this to defend my home and family. Many of us actually believed that in the beginning, but as the war went on, we began to realize it was more than that, or more accurately, less than that. I was fighting for something I did not believe in."

"Slavery?"

"Yes."

"When did all this start affecting you? You seemed normal at Gettysburg when I saw you."

"I think that was the beginning of the realization I was on the wrong side of history." I sighed, because I did not want to face it again, but I knew I had to. "It all started way back in April of '61 when I lost you, got drunk, and killed a man in a duel. Then it was round after round of sober then drunk then sober and drunk again, and one-by-one, I began losing friends: first Sean, followed by Jackson, then Jean. By Gettysburg, everything had built up into a problem I found overwhelming, and I had no solution for any of it—unless you count the alcohol. Then something happened right after Gettysburg that truly brought me to my knees, and I just gave up after that. Walked away from life, walked away from the hope of ever finding you, walked away from God. That is when I was badly wounded, and Laura found me in a hospital in Richmond. She knew

I was hurting inside and said I needed to talk about it if I wanted to get rid of the demons in my head."

"Laura? Laura from Big Cypress?"

I nodded. "The same. She saved my sanity, at least temporarily."

"I know about Aimee and you in Richmond, but this is the first I am hearing about Laura."

"Aimee?"

"Yes, the one you said would never be a threat to us. Remember?"

"What did she tell you?"

"A lot, and there was an article in the paper about it."

"Up north? What are you talking about?"

"Doctor J had a friend in Richmond sending him newspapers. I read all about you being her escort and saving her life. And, of course, after I met her, she bragged about being with you."

I laughed, but that didn't go over too well. Her expression was unchanged. "She was a spy for the North, and I was working for Secretary of State Benjamin to expose her. That's how I met Riddle."

She was still not smiling.

I tried to reassure her. "Really, there was nothing to it."

"That isn't what Aimee suggested."

"Well, she lied. Nothing happened between us."

"Then, let's move on to Laura, your other old girlfriend. So, she found you in a hospital and did what?"

"She took me to her plantation to convalesce. Rachel, nothing happened with Laura either if that is what you are thinking. She helped me deal with my nightmares and gave me a reason to want to live again."

Rachel suddenly began to look contrite. "You're right. I should not have doubted you, and I'm sorry. Let's move on. What happened after Gettysburg to get you into such a state of mind?"

I was unable to reply at first. I tried to form the words, but they would not come. Finally I just blurted it out. "I killed Tom Sullivan."

Her expression changed to one of confusion. "Your friend from New Mexico?"

I could only nod weakly.

"Oh, Ethan, are you sure it was him? How did this happen?"

"Its a long story," and I told her all the important details, leaving out the most painful parts. "When Laura found me, I felt like I had nothing to live for. I had lost you, the war was wrong for me, and I had killed one of the best friends I ever had. I was sick about it all. The surgeon told Laura he thought I might be insane. He called it 'nostalgia.' She said she had seen it before, men like me who had seen—and done terrible things, and were having trouble dealing with it. She helped me come to terms with what I had done, made me get my mind off my problems and onto something else. And I'm not talking about her, although she wanted that. She wanted me to stay, but I knew it would be wrong for me to do so, and I left and reluctantly returned to the Army. I was given command of a beat-up shadow of a regiment and got myself captured outside of Washington. Frankly, I was glad I was out of the war. By then, I really wanted no part of it. And that's how I ended up in prison and finally met my father."

"It must have been awful for you. I saw only the aftermath of the battle after the armies left Gettysburg. But that was enough to sicken me. I assisted Doctor J in an endless number of probing for balls and amputations, all the while smelling death with every breath I took. I thought about you often then. Each boy I helped, I looked into his face, and I wondered if you were safe. So, I know a little of how you must feel. Sometimes I see the faces of those boys in my dreams, and I have difficulty sleeping, too."

"I suppose we could say you have also seen the elephant."

"And it is indeed an exceedingly ugly beast."

"We'll get through this. With your love and patience, I might be able to find a way to forgive myself for things I did. I know God already has, but it is now my job to find a way to do so. Together, we can put this behind us?"

She smiled and kissed me. "Together, we can do anything."

I nodded. "Now that my past is settled, what is your story on Major Anderson?"

She bit her lower lip before she began, "He came along right after I saw you at Gettysburg. I had concluded by then there would never be another you. I was lonely, I missed you, I wanted you, but I could not have you, and he came along and treated me like I was someone special—like you did."

"Did you fall in love with him?"

She shook her head. "I wanted to, but could not."

"But you consented to marry him?"

"Only after he brought me proof you had been killed. As long as you were alive, I knew I could never love another. With you gone, I had to consider other possibilities. I hoped I would eventually come to love him, but in my heart, I knew that would never happen. I was thinking of breaking the engagement even before Miles came to me and told me everything."

"Rachel, all that is behind us now. Somehow we have to move on and help each other find peace with what we did or almost did. We make mistakes, but thankfully, mistakes can be forgiven." I kissed her. "I told you once we had a future written in Heaven. I still believe that."

"And so do I."

She snuggled in closer and kissed me tenderly. That was followed by another one of those kisses she wanted when she said, "You know which ones I mean."

Later as we lay there in each other's arms, she said softly, "I was teasing about Aimee. Once I met her, I knew there could never be anything between you two."

That reminded me of something. "By the way, did you really mean to say 'ditch' like it came out?"

She smiled. "What do *you* think?"

—ww—

On 9 April, Lee surrendered after a vain attempt to break free from Grant's encirclement, and the Army of Northern Virginia stacked arms and surrendered their battle flags. I wasn't there but spoke to many who were, and it was reported to be the saddest day in their lives.

On 14 April, while Washington celebrated the beginning of the end of the war, a man I had briefly met at the hanging of John Brown, John Wilkes Booth, shot President Lincoln while he watched a play at Ford's Theater. The president died the next day.

On 26 April, Johnson surrendered, and on 10 May, Jeff Davis was captured.

On 26 May, General Kirby-Smith was offered terms in New Orleans and surrendered on 2 June, ending "Kirby-Smithdom," that last part of the Confederacy west of the Mississippi that had been cut off from the East since the Union took complete control of the Mississippi River after the fall of Vicksburg.

While the war was all but over with Lee's surrender in April, it stumbled on for another month and a half before the formal hostilities finally ceased when Kirby-Smith surrendered. What I did not realize at the time was the war was not truly over, and some of what followed in the period called Reconstruction was, in some ways, worse than the war itself.

Author's Note: The following events took place on 5 April 1865. Two sources were used: Ethan's manuscript, written after the war, and Rachel's journal entries, which those dated 5 April 1865 were almost certainly made at some later date and recorded from memory.

I arrived back in Washington late in the afternoon of 5 April. I was tired from my trip and the forced overnight stay in Wilmington because of a missed train. I went home just long enough to be rid of my bag, freshen up, and get something to eat before I confronted Miss Aimee de Beauchamp and Major Taylor Anderson. I decided to take on Aimee first, then Taylor. After a quick meal and some tea to try and calm my spirit, I prayed for wisdom in what I was about to do. As the sun was setting, I made my way out to the street.

My neighbor, Mrs. Needles, was outside tending to some plants by her door and called out to me. "Miss Rachel, glad to see you are home again. Your fiancé, Major Anderson, called for you at least twice while you were gone."

"Thank you," I replied and continued on my way. "Forgive me, for I'm in a hurry, Mrs. Needles."

She persisted. "To see Major Anderson?"

"Eventually, but first I'm going to see Miss de Beauchamp."

"That's nice. Tell her hello for me."

"I will," I replied, anxious to be about my business, and made my way to Aimee's home two streets over.

We arrived in Washington and soon found Rachel's house. Again, I asked my father and Blue to wait with the horses while I reintroduced myself to Rachel.

My heart was racing in anticipation of seeing her again, and I was anxious about how she might receive me after nearly four years of separation. I reminded myself that this had to be God's will for us. She loved me, of that I was still certain in spite of the fact she was about to marry another. That had to be because she was still laboring under the mistaken impression we were brother and sister.

I stood at the door, my fist hovering inches away in preparation of knocking. I looked back at Father and Blue, and they were watching me and feeling as anxious as I was, I am sure. I mustered up my nerve and rapped loudly on the door and waited—and waited, but no one came to the door. I knocked again, this time even louder and longer. Still no answer.

Shortly, a woman came out of the house next door. "Yoo-hoo! You looking for Miss Rachel?"

"Yes, ma'am. You know where I might find her?"

"You just missed her. She is going over to Miss de Beauchamp's house."

"Can you tell me where that is?"

She pointed. "Two streets south. She is on the corner. North facing red brick with white trim. Can't miss it."

I tipped my hat. "Thank you, ma'am."

I very nearly ran back to my waiting father and Blue. "Just missed her. She's headed for Aimee's house two streets over."

By the time I reached Aimee's house, I was angry again and knew that was not good. I needed to control my anger and focus it appropriately. Again, I prayed to calm my spirit.

I noticed Taylor's horse tied outside on the street. I went right in without even knocking and found the hallway dark, as they had not yet lit any lamps, but lamplight was coming from the parlor. Aimee and Taylor were arguing, and I seemed to be the subject.

"Since its me you are discussing, may I join you?"

Both looked to me with surprised expressions on their faces.

"Where have you been?" asked Taylor. "Your neighbor told me you left town for a few days, but you never told me anything about the trip or even where you were going."

"I don't report to you," I snapped back.

"Darling, I was worried about you."

With the last of the evening twilight to illuminate our search, we found Aimee's house easy enough. Only one on that corner fit the description. I noticed a "US" branded horse tied at the curb with a McClellan saddle and an army saddle blanket on it.

"Major Anderson," I muttered to myself before I turned to my father and Blue. "This time, come with me. That's Anderson's horse, and this could get ugly. I want witnesses if it does."

"Need this?" said Blue withdrawing a Colt from under his coat.

"No, you hang onto it. I don't want to be tempted to kill him."

We drew closer to the door and found it ajar, I could hear voices inside: three people, Aimee, Anderson, and Rachel. I pushed the door open quietly and slipped into the darkened foyer. I wanted to understand what I was walking into before I announced myself.

The three of us stood in the dark foyer and could easily see into the parlor, which was illuminated by a single lamp. Aimee and Anderson were facing Rachel, and she had her back to me at an oblique angle. None of the three were aware we were in the house and observing them from only thirty feet away. Since it was then fully dark outside, and with no lamps in the foyer or hall, I knew we could remain unseen unless they came into the foyer where we were. I leaned against the wall near the doorway, peeping around the corner and listened to the conversation.

And once more my heart was racing at the sight of Rachel. *My Lord,* I thought, *but You sure know how to pick them.* Yes, I was biased, but I felt I was looking at the most beautiful woman in the world, and I could not help but smile at the sight of her.

"There was no need for you to worry about me, Taylor. I'm perfectly capable of taking care of myself. I have for these last four years, and even before that when Ethan and I were separated by his—by my father." I chose to emphasize Ethan's name, and perhaps that was a bit spiteful of me.

I smiled at the way she paused and referred to Morgan as "her" father. That told me she knew the truth somehow. Miles? This was getting interesting. Rachel seemed to have a full head of steam, and I sensed she was about to have her way with these two. I decided I would just watch and listen for a spell.

"Rachel, really, if we're to be married you must not be going off without asking me."

"Ask you?"

"Of course!"

"You really expect me to get your permission for everything I do?"

"It is only natural, my dear."

Rachel rolled her eyes. I had seen that look before, and it did not bode well for the major. Rachel wasn't the asking type. She needed to be handled with a bit more finesse than that.

"Darling, you seem to be a little upset," said Taylor as he took a step toward me.

I stuck out my hand to stop him. "A little upset? Sir, you have not yet seen me upset, but you are about to. That little tiff we had a few weeks ago when you got pushy was just a warm-up for what's coming. But first, I want to deal with Miss de Beauchamp. You shall wait your turn—Darling—until after I am finished with her."

Properly chastened, he stepped back.

She spit that "darling" out like it left a bad taste in her mouth. Terms of endearment were not helping his case.

My father leaned over and whispered in my ear. "This woman has fire!"

"You haven't seen anything yet," I whispered. The real fireworks were about to begin, because she was about to lay into Aimee.

"Miss de Beauchamp, I have a present for you."

That seemed to stun her. She at first looked at Taylor as if confused then attempted to recover. "Why, Rachel, whatever for? I should be giving you a gift for your wedding, not the other way around."

"After I give you mine, you may want to keep yours."

Aimee didn't see it coming, and neither did I. Rachel hauled back, made a fist, and punched Aimee right in the nose! Aimee went down taking out an end table and its candy dish in the process, which amazingly did not break, but its hard candy sweets were scattered all over the floor.

"Whoa!" I heard my father say behind me almost loud enough for them to hear in the parlor.

Rachel then stood over Aimee shaking her hand, and I loved what she said—

"I have been wanting to do that ever since I first heard your name. My hand hurts, but the rest of me feels really good right now!"

Aimee's nose was bleeding. She started to rise, but Rachel stopped her.

"Get up and I will give more of that. You stay down there where you belong, you shallow ditch!"

My father leaned over and whispered, "Did she say 'ditch' or something else?"

I wasn't rightly sure. "I think she said 'ditch,' but intended the something else?"

Though he seemed intimidated by me, Taylor felt the need to intervene. "Rachel, really! Was that called for?"

I spun and pointed my slender finger at him. "Back off! It isn't your turn yet! I will get to you!"

Once more he backed down, and Aimee made no attempt to rise after I threatened her.

"Rachel, what is this all about? Why did you hit me?"

"It is about you and your lies. You see, I found out why Ethan changed his name, but you knew long before I did and chose not to share that information with me. Instead, you chose to deceive me, because you wanted Ethan for yourself and figured you could lie and cheat your way into his heart. He isn't that stupid!"

I had to think about what she said. Should I take offense at her use of "that" with "stupid?"

Then the major mustered up some courage. "Rachel, perhaps she was well intended," he said in an attempt to sound innocent.

"Shut up, Taylor, because you knew, also—and chose not to tell me! Yes, you knew, and then you told me he was dead!"

I turned to my father and whispered, "I was dead?"
He shook his head. "Not that I was aware of."

I turned my attention back to Aimee but addressed Taylor. "For goodness sakes, Taylor, can't you give the woman your handkerchief for her nose?" He retrieved it from his pocket and passed it to Aimee.

"I think you broke my nose."

"Better hope that's all I'll break."

I stooped down closer to Aimee for what I was going to say next. "You see, Aimee, I also know Ethan isn't dead, and you—"

She pointed first at Aimee, then that accusing finger swung like a compass needle over to Anderson, followed by her glare.

"—And you—YOU kept that from me. AND, you let me write that letter to Ethan's mother telling her he's dead! My word, what kind of utterly despicable people are you to let Analee and me experience that kind of loss, and for your own selfish desires? Are you so naive to think I would never find out he was alive or that we are not related? And even if Ethan married you, Aimee, how do you think he would feel about you once he discovered how you lied to me— and to him? This conspiracy of yours makes no sense. Either you two are stupid or insane—or both."

Aimee came to her own defense. "Ethan didn't really love you, Rachel. He was in love with me all along; he said as much in Richmond."

I was only able to stare at her incredulously and shake my head. "My word, but you are indeed insane!"

Aimee shifted tactics then. "You say he's alive? But you saw the reports?"

"Wrong! Wrong! And Wrong! He's alive!"

"Then where is he?"

"He was at Fort Delaware, wasting away in that horrible place. And you two could have gotten him out, but you chose to leave him there, because that suited your selfish plans. That, Aimee, isn't love. If you really loved Ethan you would have done all you could to get him out—like I tried to do."

"I wanted to, but Taylor wouldn't let me!"

I turned on Taylor. "That true?"

"Of course not!"

"Know what? Since I can't trust either of you, I won't believe either of you."

The major started a defense of himself, but Rachel was having none of it.

"Shut up, Taylor. You can't say anything to me just now that will change how I feel about you, which isn't good! Meanwhile, when I found out Ethan was alive and in that place, I got some of my friends, my real friends, to help me get him and his father freed, but when I arrived there, he was already gone. They

moved him, but I don't know where—yet! But I will find him if it is the last thing I do. He spent the last four years looking for me. I can do no less for him."

I decided this had gone far enough and came out of the shadows. "You don't have to look for me, Rachel. I am right here."

She spun around and threw her hands up to her mouth and just stared at me as if she was beholding a ghost returned from the grave. I went over to her and took her into my arms. She started weeping then.

I could not believe my eyes! He was there, a bit thinner than the last time I saw him in Gettysburg, but there! And alive!

Aimee came to her feet and went to embrace Ethan, but he put his hand out to stop her. "No, Aimee. We are done."

Taylor stood to the side, a dour expression in his face. "I guess this means the wedding is off?" he asked, I think trying to make a joke out of a very bad situation.

"Actually, Major, I think the wedding is on, but you won't be in it."

I turned to Rachel. "You were really going to marry him?"

Her eyebrows went up as if surprised. "I plead temporary insanity?"

She tugged the ring off her finger. "Taylor, here's your ring back." And she tossed it at him. It bounced off his chest.

She looked up into my face and smiled as she slipped her arm around my waist and pulled herself against my side just like she used to do back at Catahoula that summer we first met. "Come along, Ethan. Let's go home."

My father and Blue stood in the doorway of the parlor waiting for us. Rachel saw my father, and even in the weak light, the resemblance was obvious. "Major Joubert?"

He bowed deeply. "My dear, I must say I am most impressed with the lady my son has fallen in love with. And you have a lovely right hook! You didn't hurt your hand, did you?"

She smiled. "A bit. It'll probably be bruised tomorrow."

Blue stepped up. "Miss Rachel, I am so pleased to see you again."

"You knew didn't you?"

"Not until I remembered you called Pepper by hiz name."

"I wish you had picked up on my slip then."

"Miss Rachel, I've been kicking myself for the last few days, thinking the same thing. I should have seen it then."

"Maybe you were meant to miss it? A lot of good happened that might not have if Ethan had discovered me that day."

———m———

Rachel got to wear her new wedding dress. We were married the next day with Blue as my best man. My father gave Rachel away. Miles was in attendance, but we did not know that at the time. He slipped in, stayed in the back of the church, and left just as the ceremony ended.

As we walked out, about halfway down the aisle sat Riddle, legs crossed and cocked back in the pew with his arms spread out on its back, a broad smile on his face. He was clean-shaven and wore the uniform of a Navy captain this time.

"So you found her?" he said.

"Thanks to you and Blue."

He stood. "Aren't you going to introduce me to your new bride?"

Rachel looked at me for an explanation. "Rachel, meet Si..." I caught myself. "Meet Riddle, the mechanic. If it needs fixing, he can fix it, and if it needs breaking, he will break it. He is the one who got us out of Fort Delaware."

"Would have done it sooner if I had known..."

Rachel curtsied. "I am pleased to meet you, Captain, Admiral, whatever you are..."

"Doesn't matter, ma'am. Just Riddle will do, and I'm whatever you need me to be."

"I would have invited you, but I didn't know how to find you. How did you know to come and where?"

"Ethan, don't you know by now, it's my business to know things?"

He bowed to Rachel "And the legend of Rachel and Ethan finally has a happy ending. Good day, Madam Joubert. And Ethan, you take good care of her, now."

He tucked his hat under his arm and started down the aisle but stopped near the door and turned back. "Oh, I hear they found Wolf. Took 'em nearly two days to clean him up. Well played, Ethan, well played!" He spun and was out the door to disappear into the bright sunlight like some ghost.

Rachel looked to me. "The legend of Rachel and Ethan?"

"Long story. I'll tell you later."

"And who is Wolf?"

I pursed my lips and frowned making a sour expression. "Euweee! That one, you don't want the details on."

———

The first light of dawn was breaking through our bedroom window when it hit.

"Ethan! Ethan! Wake up!" She was shaking me. "Ethan! Wake up! You're having a bad dream!"

I came out of my stupor, and Rachel was sitting up and leaning over me. I came to a sitting position as the nightmare abated in my mind and reality once again took control.

"You were dreaming. You started shaking and groaning. Then you got violent. Ethan, what is wrong?"

My breathing slowed as I pulled her to me for comfort. "Right now, I really need you."

"You have me. I am right here. How can I help?"

"Just hold me and let me hold you. I'm scared."

"You scared? Of what? What happened to you?"

I slid back down and pulled her against me like she was some sort of covering that could shield me from the specter in my mind.

"I think we need to talk about this," she said as she drew even closer to me. "Something terrible is bothering my husband. If you will tell me what it is, maybe I can help you."

I looked at her and saw the worried expression on her face. "Rachel, I have seen the elephant, and it is an exceedingly ugly beast."

"What are you talking about?"

"I thought it was over, but it isn't. I thought finding you would make it all go away, but it didn't. Yes, I do need to talk to you about it, and you need to know what happened."

"The war changed you. I saw that soon after you found me. Being wounded, the prison, had to have affected you."

"That's part of it, but it's more than that. Rachel, I have seen things. I've done things—awful things that haunt me, that won't leave me alone, especially in my sleep."

"Something terrible happened to you, something you have not told me about. What is it, Ethan?"

"A lot of things happened, some worse than others but all bad. First, it was losing you and the ever-growing fear I would not be able to find you—not ever. Then it was the war. Killing people was hard at first, then it got easier—too easy. I told myself I was doing this to defend my home and family. Many of us actually believed that in the beginning, but as the war went on, we began to realize it was more than that, or more accurately, less than that. I was fighting for something I did not believe in."

"Slavery?"

"Yes."

"When did all this start affecting you? You seemed normal at Gettysburg when I saw you."

"I think that was the beginning of the realization I was on the wrong side of history." I sighed, because I did not want to face it again, but I knew I had to. "It all started way back in April of '61 when I lost you, got drunk, and killed a man in a duel. Then it was round after round of sober then drunk then sober and drunk again, and one-by-one, I began losing friends: first Sean, followed by Jackson, then Jean. By Gettysburg, everything had built up into a problem I found overwhelming, and I had no solution for any of it— unless you count the alcohol. Then something happened right after Gettysburg that truly brought me to my knees, and I just gave up after that. Walked away from life, walked away from the hope of ever finding you, walked away from God. That is when I was badly wounded, and Laura found me in a hospital in Richmond. She knew I was hurting inside and said I needed to talk about it if I wanted to get rid of the demons in my head."

"Laura? Laura from Big Cypress?"

I nodded. "The same. She saved my sanity, at least temporarily."

"I know about Aimee and you in Richmond, but this is the first I am hearing about Laura."

"Aimee?"

"Yes, the one you said would never be a threat to us. Remember?"

"What did she tell you?"

"A lot, and there was an article in the paper about it."

"Up north? What are you talking about?"

"Doctor J had a friend in Richmond sending him newspapers. I read all about you being her escort and saving her life. And, of course, after I met her, she bragged about being with you."

I laughed, but that didn't go over too well. Her expression was unchanged. "She was a spy for the North, and I was working for Secretary of State Benjamin to expose her. That's how I met Riddle."

She was still not smiling.

I tried to reassure her. "Really, there was nothing to it."

"That isn't what Aimee suggested."

"Well, she lied. Nothing happened between us."

"Then, let's move on to Laura, your other old girlfriend. So, she found you in a hospital and did what?"

"She took me to her plantation to convalesce. Rachel, nothing happened with Laura either if that is what you are thinking. She helped me deal with my nightmares and gave me a reason to want to live again."

Rachel suddenly began to look contrite. "You're right. I should not have doubted you, and I'm sorry. Let's move on. What happened after Gettysburg to get you into such a state of mind?"

I was unable to reply at first. I tried to form the words, but they would not come. Finally I just blurted it out. "I killed Tom Sullivan."

Her expression changed to one of confusion. "Your friend from New Mexico?"

I could only nod weakly.

"Oh, Ethan, are you sure it was him? How did this happen?"

"Its a long story," and I told her all the important details, leaving out the most painful parts. "When Laura found me, I felt like I had nothing to live for. I had lost you, the war was wrong for me, and I had killed one of the best friends I ever had. I was sick about it all. The surgeon told Laura he thought I might be insane. He called it 'nostalgia.' She said she had seen it before, men like me who had seen—and done terrible things, and were having trouble dealing with it. She helped me come to terms with what I had done, made me get my mind off my problems and onto something else. And I'm not talking about her, although she wanted that. She wanted me to stay, but I knew it would be wrong for me to do so, and I left and reluctantly returned to the Army. I was given command of a beat-up shadow of a regiment and got myself captured outside of Washington. Frankly, I was glad I was out of the war. By then, I really wanted no part of it. And that's how I ended up in prison and finally met my father."

"It must have been awful for you. I saw only the aftermath of the battle after the armies left Gettysburg. But that was enough to sicken me. I assisted Doctor J in an endless number of probing for balls and amputations, all the while smelling death with every breath I took. I thought about you often then. Each boy I helped, I looked into his face, and I wondered if you were safe. So, I know a little of how you must feel. Sometimes I see the faces of those boys in my dreams, and I have difficulty sleeping, too."

"I suppose we could say you have also seen the elephant."

"And it is indeed an exceedingly ugly beast."

"We'll get through this. With your love and patience, I might be able to find a way to forgive myself for things I did. I know God already has, but it is now my job to find a way to do so. Together, we can put this behind us?"

She smiled and kissed me. "Together, we can do anything."

I nodded. "Now that my past is settled, what is your story on Major Anderson?"

She bit her lower lip before she began, "He came along right after I saw you at Gettysburg. I had concluded by then there would never be another you. I was lonely, I missed you, I wanted you, but I could not have you, and he came along and treated me like I was someone special—like you did."

"Did you fall in love with him?"

She shook her head. "I wanted to, but could not."

"But you consented to marry him?"

"Only after he brought me proof you had been killed. As long as you were alive, I knew I could never love another. With you gone, I had to consider other possibilities. I hoped I would eventually come to love him, but in my heart, I knew that would never happen. I was thinking of breaking the engagement even before Miles came to me and told me everything."

"Rachel, all that is behind us now. Somehow we have to move on and help each other find peace with what we did or almost did. We make mistakes, but thankfully, mistakes can be forgiven." I kissed her. "I told you once we had a future written in Heaven. I still believe that."

"And so do I."

She snuggled in closer and kissed me tenderly. That was followed by another one of those kisses she wanted when she said, "You know which ones I mean."

Later as we lay there in each other's arms, she said softly, "I was teasing about Aimee. Once I met her, I knew there could never be anything between you two."

That reminded me of something. "By the way, did you really mean to say 'ditch' like it came out?"

She smiled. "What do *you* think?"

On 9 April, Lee surrendered after a vain attempt to break free from Grant's encirclement, and the Army of Northern Virginia stacked arms and surrendered their battle flags. I wasn't there but spoke to many who were, and it was reported to be the saddest day in their lives.

On 14 April, while Washington celebrated the beginning of the end of the war, a man I had briefly met at the hanging of John Brown, John Wilkes Booth, shot President Lincoln while he watched a play at Ford's Theater. The president died the next day.

On 26 April, Johnson surrendered, and on 10 May, Jeff Davis was captured.

On 26 May, General Kirby-Smith was offered terms in New Orleans and surrendered on 2 June, ending "Kirby-Smithdom," that last part of the Confederacy west of the Mississippi that had been cut off from the East since the Union took complete control of the Mississippi River after the fall of Vicksburg.

While the war was all but over with Lee's surrender in April, it stumbled on for another month and a half before the formal hostilities finally ceased when Kirby-Smith surrendered. What I did not realize at the time was the war was not truly over, and some of what followed in the period called Reconstruction was, in some ways, worse than the war itself.

Chapter 30 – Catahoula

We lingered in Washington to settle Rachel's affairs. She had contracts for portraits to fulfill and home furnishings to sell off. Soon after Lee surrendered, Blue said his goodbyes and returned to Rosedale. Seems he left a piece of his heart there and wanted to go back and fetch her. I told him he was always welcome to stay at Catahoula for as long as he wanted. We embraced, and both of us wept, for I was sure I would not see my faithful friend again. I was wrong on that count.

With Kirby-Smith about to give up the fight and hostilities around Louisiana ending, Father and I were both anxious to go see about Analee and Catahoula. Neither of us had heard a word from my mother in well over a year and a half, and she had had no word from either of us. She likely labored under the impression we were both dead.

We began our journey home in late May arriving at Natchez on 29 May. Rachel and I waited on the dock at Natchez beside Pepper and a pile of mostly her luggage, while Father went in search of someone to ferry us across the river to Vidalia.

Off to my right and behind me, I heard a voice that sounded disturbingly familiar. "Well, lad, as I live and breathe!" called out the voice in an Irish brogue. The sound of it shook me to the core, and I was suddenly carried back to that day in those woods after Gettysburg. My mind started spinning. It must have shown in my expression, because Rachel noticed my discomfort.

"Ethan? Something wrong?"

I heard the voice again, and this time it was closer. It said, "Let me tell you a tale, lad, about a time when the Brave Rifles were keepin' the peace out in New Mexico Territory. This was back in '60, and this young shavetail lieutenant joined us."

The voice was drawing nearer. "And he wanted to learn to be an Injun fighter. I'm telling ya, he had a lot to learn, but he listened, and I taught him, and we defeated old Dos Cuchillos in one of the prettiest running scraps I've ever had the honor of being part of."

The voice drew even nearer, and I started trembling. Rachel became concerned and grabbed my arm. "Ethan, talk to me. What's wrong?"

"And he was in love with this little lady by the name a' Rachel." And the voice was right beside me. "And you, pretty lady, must be her?"

Rachel looked at him and smiled, but tears were running down my face, and I could not look in the direction of the voice. Shaking and an expression of fear on my face, I finally mustered the nerve to look at him as she replied, "I am indeed, sir."

"And my name is Sullivan, ma'am, Tom Sullivan, and I am so very pleased to finally make yer acquaintance."

I stared at him, that red hair, that big red handlebar moustache. My breathing was heavy.

"Why, Ethan, you look like you've seen a ghost," he said.

For a long moment, all I could do was just stare at him. Finally, I blurted out, "Tom?"

He smiled. "In the flesh."

"But—but I killed you at Gettysburg in '63!" I fairly exclaimed.

"Ethan, I ain't never even been near Gettysburg. Been with the Brave Rifles, mostly around Tennessee, since you went south. We didn't tangle with Bobby Lee none. Lad, you well?"

I started laughing then, laughing and weeping at the same time, and I couldn't stop. I grabbed Tom with both arms and pulled him against me in a bear hug. "You're alive!"

"Last I looked I was, but you need to let me breathe, or I will be dead. What's this all about?"

I held him at arms length not willing to let him go lest this all be some dream. "It's a long story, Tom, a long story. You cannot possibly imagine how happy I am to see you—alive."

"Well, Lad, I'm glad to see you made it through the war yourself. I've been wondering if ya did. And I was sure hoping you had found Rachel, which I see you have. I heard that story about you two almost three years ago, and I knew right off who they was talkin' about: my old Brave Rifle friend and his sweetheart Rachel."

"Sergeant Sullivan, Ethan spoke of you often in his letters and how much respect he has for you. I'm honored I finally got to meet you."

"The pleasure is all mine, ma'am," he replied with a tip of his kepi.

"Tom, what are you doing here?"

"Been in Baton Rouge and on my way to Memphis. I'm mustering out now that the war is over. Never expected to run into you here, but I did intend to come by Catahoula to look in once I was out of the Army. Guess that won't be necessary now."

"You can still come to Catahoula anytime you want, assuming it is still there."

He grew serious. "You ain't been home yet?"

I shook my head. "On the way there now."

A nearby steamer blew its whistle. "I think that's me." He grabbed my hand and shook it vigorously. "I pray you find all's well at Catahoula when you get there."

"Where you headed now?"

"New York to see my sister, then maybe I'll head back to Texas. Haven't made up my mind yet. Good to see ya, Ethan, and you too, Miss Rachel."

"Bye, Tom. Remember my offer."

"I will. You take care."

After Tom was aboard his northbound steamer, Rachel turned to me and smiled. "Well, looks like one ghost has been put back into the grave."

I could only nod and smile.

After we crossed the Mississippi, we purchased a wagon and two mules in Vidalia to transport all of Rachel's baggage, paintings, and studio equipment and began the final leg of our trip home.

We passed the burnt shells of plantations along the way. Big Cypress was still standing, but no one about, and it looked abandoned. I began to fear for Catahoula, but as we rounded the last bend and came upon the avenue of oaks to the Big House, we saw it was still standing, in need of paint and some repairs, but still standing.

I reined in the mules near the house and expected my mother to come out any moment to welcome us home, but no one showed, and I grew apprehensive again.

Rachel touched my arm. "Ethan?"

"It'll be all right. Let me look around. You two stay here." I took a Colt with me and slowly climbed the steps to the gallery, moving quietly and cautiously.

I found the front door unlocked, slipped inside and paused to listen for sounds but heard none. I eased down the hall and heard a noise from the parlor. It sounded like a shuffling foot or something I was unable to identify. That was followed by the unmistakable clicks of a Colt being cocked.

"Mother, that had better be you."

"E-Ethan?" she called out.

"It's me, Ethan."

There was a pause. "I don't believe you. Show yourself."

"Put the gun down, Mother. I look a bit different from the last time you saw me, and I don't want you to shoot me." I stepped into the doorway and lowered my pistol, slipping it under my belt behind my back.

My mother was partially hiding behind the sofa. She stared at me, squinting as if unsure who I was, the pistol still pointing in my direction. Slowly, recognition swept over her, and she bit her lip as she lowered the pistol, and her eyes filled with tears. Struggling to speak, she said, "It is you! They said you were dead."

"I am happy to report they were mistaken, Mother."

Still not fully believing it was really me, she walked cautiously in my direction, stopping within reach and staring at me as if her eyes might be deceiving her. I reached down and relieved her of the pistol then let the hammer down to half cock and smiled at her. With that, she was in my arms and squeezing me for all she was worth, sobbing the whole time. "Some of the boys from the 1st Louisiana passed through and told me you were killed near Washington last year."

"Come close, but not quite. Are you all right?"

"Tolerable, I suppose. This war has been awful! Thank God it's over!"

"I know, but I'm home now, and everything's going to be better."

"I am so glad I have my boy again!" she said as she pulled away.

Her hand went to the scar on my nose and cheek and gently traced it. "Oh, baby!" And the weeping started over. "Where have you been?"

"Spent most of the last year in a Yankee prison."

"What about Rachel? Did you find her?"

"I'm right here, Aunt Analee," I heard her say from behind me. As was her style, she had not obeyed her husband's instructions to remain in the wagon.

She rushed forward and the two women very nearly slammed into each other with what seemed to me like enough force to break bones. An ocean of female tears issued forth from the both of them. I could only stand back and marvel at the spectacle with my own eyes full to overflowing.

Finally they let go of each other. "You two married?"

Rachel grinned. "Want to see the marriage certificate?"

"I trust you, but this has to be an incredible story, and I want to hear all about it." She turned to me, her expression pleading. "Ethan, your father? I haven't heard a word from him since the summer of '63. Did he find you?"

"Well, Mother, as it turns out, I brought something back from the war for you."

I whistled, and Pernell stuck his head in the door. Analee gasped and both hands went to her mouth

He removed his hat, nodded, and as if uncertain of his reception, walked slowly down the dogtrot toward us. Likewise, my mother hesitantly made her way in his direction.

"Pernell," she said politely.

"Analee, so nice to see you again," he replied just as politely.

Rachel shook her head and rolled her eyes. She had had enough of that foolishness. "You two going to stand on ceremony all day? For goodness sake, kiss her!"

That was all Father needed, and he took my mother into his arms.

Rachel turned to me. "And what about you? You going to just stand there weeping, or are you going to give me one of those kisses? You know which ones I mean."

5 July 1865

Yesterday was July 4, and as is the tradition at Catahoula, we celebrated, but this time we celebrated the "rebirth" of our nation. It was both joyous and sad at the same time, and all of us experienced the same conflicted emotions concerning the celebration.

We dread the occupation that comes with defeat and imagine all manner of evils associated with it, but we will have to wait and see just what the future will actually bring. Whatever that may be, we give thanks to God that a long and terrible war is behind us.

As I look around Catahoula and see so much we must do to get it repaired and profitable again, I feel overwhelmed and excited at the same time. Excited, because I see a new beginning where Ethan and I can rebuild our lives together and turn Catahoula into a home filled with love and laughing children.

END BOOK TWO

Catahoula Book Three — The Avenging Angel follows their story after the war into Reconstruction as the young couple attempts to begin their lives together at Catahoula Plantation in the shattered economy of the postwar South. A free excerpt from Book Three follows.

Chapter 1 – Carpetbaggers

From Rachel's Diary
28 July 1866

I knew, by the hard expression on my husband's face, that he was nearing the limits of his patience. Listening to Mr. Waldo T. Pettigrew expound upon how he had been sent by Washington to repair the broken South and lead it from its wayward rebellious ways back into the Union fold was not sitting well with Ethan. In Pettigrew's tone you could hear the man's utter contempt for people like us, southerners, whom he considered to be beneath his station.

Four years of war tends to change a man, and I knew it had affected my husband in ways I was yet to fully understand. But I was sure his tolerance level for carpetbaggers, like this one who came to bring us the way, the truth, and the light of his enlightened existence, was much diminished.

"Can you swim?" Ethan asked him in a dry, matter-of-fact manner.

Upon hearing that, I looked over the rail of our riverboat at the swirling, muddy waters of the Mississippi passing below. I knew exactly what he had in mind to do. "Ethan, please don't."

As this pompous ass pontificated on his considerable swimming ability, being as he was from the Atlantic Coast of New Jersey, Ethan noted my pleading expression punctuated by my arched eyebrow expressing my displeasure, a trick I learned from his mother. Thus admonished, he tipped his hat to Mr. Pettigrew and excused himself from his company.

I lingered for a moment only because Pettigrew inquired of me, "Why did he suddenly leave? Did I say something that offended him?"

I smiled. "I believe he found your attitude toward the South offensive, as did I. And I would advise you to temper your speech during your stay in Louisiana—unless you fancy wearing tar and feathers."

Mr. Pettigrew's shocked expression indicated he clearly understood my meaning. "But—why did he ask if I could swim?"

"Because you, sir, were about two seconds away from him grabbing you by the scruff of your skinny neck and the seat of your store-bought trousers and tossing you overboard. You are not treading water right now only because I asked him not to do it."

His expression went blank as he took a deep breath and sighed before replying barely above a hoarse, stuttering whisper, "I–I lied. I can't swim."

I shrugged. "Then I just saved your life."

Nearing New Orleans, we stood alone at the rail as our riverboat churned downriver passed the many magnificent homes in the Greek revival style that graced the shores of the Mississippi River, grand homes, homes more opulent than our own. But in my mind, none of these were as beautiful as our Catahoula Plantation, a simple home in the Creole style along the Red River.

My heart was heavy with concerns for my husband. He had suffered terribly during the war, and he was still feeling its effects more than a year after its conclusion. He had spoken to me about some of what he experienced, but I sensed he was holding back, not wanting to upset me with gruesome details. From the corner of my eye, I looked at him as he stared off at the passing riverbank. His face was expressionless, but his eyes often narrowed, and I knew something was bothering him.

"Are you all right?" I asked.

"Tolerable." His usual reply when he wished to be non-committal.

"You weren't really going to toss that man overboard, were you?"

"Yes I was. Until you stopped me."

"Suppose he would have drowned?"

He looked away as if afraid to face me, but as he turned back, a frown spread slowly across his face. "He would have deserved it."

"For merely speaking as he did, which I will admit was thoughtless. But is that enough to kill a man?"

He shook his head and looked down at the brown waters of the Mississippi boiling past. "No, it's not."

"Ethan, I'm worried about you. Your temper has gotten worse."

He looked at me with sad eyes. "I—I don't know what to do. People like Pettigrew seem to easily get to me and arouse the anger inside."

"The question is what is the real source of your anger. It isn't Pettigrew or people like him. Such never seemed to bother you before."

There was a frustrated look in his eyes. "Before? Before the war, you mean?"

"Yes. The war changed you. You weren't this angry, and the man I now see sometimes frightens me."

He became pensive before answering. "I would never hurt you, Rachel. I love you too much."

"I know that, but what about those you don't love so much?"

He shrugged. "I reckon they're on their own."

"You can't just blow this off that easily. Your temper can get you into serious trouble."

He turned to fully face me, and his eyes flashed with anger. "Rachel, I don't think I want to talk about this any longer."

And I had to agree. I could see he was becoming quite agitated. But somehow, I must get him to talk about his pain inside. That may be the only way he can get it out of his system. For a while right after the war, he would talk, but soon he began to resist speaking of his experiences. I know the war was terrible for him. Living in Gettysburg when the war found me there, I experienced some of it myself, especially the truly awful aftermath of a recently abandoned major battlefield and the incredible damage and death associated with it. It was months before we could get a breath of fresh air that did not reek of corrupting animal and human dead.

For Ethan, it was far worse. He went through many battles. He was an aid to General Dick Taylor in '62, during Jackson's Valley Campaign in places like Winchester, and Port Republic. After that, it was Sharpsburg, Fredericksburg, then Chancellorsville, and Gettysburg. He was badly wounded after Gettysburg and was a year recovering from that. He returned to duty only to be captured during the late war campaign against Washington and spent the final year of the war as a prisoner in that awful place, Fort Delaware, where he was tormented and nearly killed by a sadistic guard.

He has seen things that would bring many of us to our knees, and he has done things he does not wish to even think about, much less speak of. To all those horrors, I believe we should add a deep-seated guilt that he survived the war while so many of his friends did not.

Should it not be expected that such would change a man—even damage him?

Sadly, there are thousands of men just like Ethan who went through that terrible war and survived it only to be left suffering the effects of what is called "nostalgia." These veterans came home, expecting to return to a normal peacetime existence, but they themselves were so utterly changed by their wartime experiences that they see their world in ways they did not see it before the war. Often for them, everything becomes a threat, and unchecked anger and frustration drive these men to do truly awful things in a vain attempt to regain what was before the war their "normal" lifestyle. This may, in some way, explain, though not excuse, some of their actions after the war.

Somehow, those of us who love these men must find ways to help them find relief from their mental torment—before they destroy themselves.

While many men came back damaged mentally, many also came home damaged physically with missing legs or arms or blinded. This often leaves them unable to earn any sort of a living in the trade they practiced before the war and no chance for a new one after. Families are starving for want of the means to feed themselves.

Those are the wounded in body and soul who came home, but many did not come home at all. Some estimate that the South lost 300,000 men in that war. These were the men who would have worked the farms, run the plantations, built the cities, healed the sick, and hundreds of other professions and occupations—and help rebuild the South. But, they are not here. Instead, they rest in graves all over this country, some marked, and some known only to God.

Our men were not the only casualties of this long and brutal war. The southern economy is also badly broken. Many southerners held Confederate script or bonds which are now worthless. It is hard to conceive of it, but there is simply very little money in circulation in the South. Without cash there can be no investment in a recovery.

The planters had their fortunes tied up in land and slaves. With many of the latter gone or unwilling to work, the land has became a tax burden for its owner or to be forfeited to creditors holding the notes.

On the boat coming to New Orleans, Ethan spoke with some travelers, and they told of areas of the South, like in Georgia and South Carolina, that were little more that blackened scars on the land with broken fences, fields burned, and the once majestic homes naught but burned rubble. Only the tall chimneys remain as forlorn reminders of a once proud plantation's former glory.

Yes, the South is broken, and a rebirth seems a long way off.

We managed to keep Catahoula operating by the hardest. Ethan borrowed money from his father, money he had made from the sale of his properties before the war. He had wisely hidden it away in gold and Yankee dollars in case things went badly for the southern cause, and it did.

Labor is nearly impossible to find, and many days Ethan was in the fields behind a mule, cutting the earth to receive the seeds of life. He used his wits and his father's investment to find ways to entice freedmen to come work for him. Had he not been successful in getting help, he would surely have died attempting to save Catahoula. He got enough planted and harvested that first summer after the war to risk hiring more freedmen. And it is only because of Ethan's reputation for fairness and the way he pays his laborers did they come to work for us. Because of his hard work and his father's generosity, we are now able to live a reasonably comfortable lifestyle many others only dream of these days, but we employ only as many as we absolutely need. Still, it is nothing like before the war when profits flowed. Men who earned $100,000 a year then must now get by without any house servants and may even be compelled to sell honey on side of the road to feed their families.

Even the freedmen are suffering. Before the war they may have been slaves, but they had food, clothing, and a roof over their heads. No, I am not defending slavery. Neither Ethan nor I believe it was wise for America to enslave others. He freed his before the war as soon as he had the authority to do so. Now many of the freedmen think freedom means not having to work for the white man, or they have simply picked up and left for the larger cities, like Baton Rouge or New Orleans, to look for work there, any kind of work other than picking cotton or cutting cane. But they aren't finding any jobs, and they are themselves starving and depending on the government and the Freedman's Bureau to help them.

Indeed, that terrible war changed everything, and so far, it appears to be only for the worse.

CHAPTER 2 – NEW ORLEANS

We arrived in New Orleans on the afternoon of 28 July after our two-day trip from Catahoula Plantation in Catahoula Parish. I secured a carriage to carry us to the home of my parents on Dauphine Street at Orleans. This visit was a bit unusual, since we were coming during the hottest months of the year in New Orleans, a time when many, who are able to do so, vacated the city for cooler, less humid climes with fewer mosquitoes. My parents had planned to spend their summers at Catahoula and reside in New Orleans only during the cooler months, but having been away from New Orleans for the four years of the war, Pernell, my father, seemed unable to extract himself from the Crescent City. "I have too much business to attend to here. Perhaps we will spend next summer at Catahoula," was his excuse. We had not seen them since Christmas when Rachel and I had spent a month visiting. Of late, we had been far too busy at Catahoula getting fields prepared and crops planted, all of which prevented us from returning to New Orleans any sooner.

Indeed, my father did have much business to attend to. He had wisely seen the war coming and sold most of his properties, keeping only the Vieux Carré house in which they resided. With the war over, he found himself with ample cash and was busy investing, a financial condition few could claim after the war.

Ester Legendre, a Creole servant who had been in my father's employ since long before the war, met us at the door of my parent's Vieux Carré home. "Miss Rachel, Cap'n Ethan, so glad to see you again. Please, come in."

My mother was right behind her and enveloped me in one of her all-consuming hugs. Then she turned her attention to Rachel and swallowed her in like manner. "Pernell!" she fairly yelled, "They are here!"

I heard his footfalls on the stairs. "I'm coming! I'm coming! And how is my favorite daughter-in-law?" he said as he embraced Rachel and kissed her on both cheeks.

"I'm your only daughter-in-law, and I'm just fine, thank you."

"But you would be my favorite even if I had twenty." He turned his attention to me, a broad smile on his face. "Ethan, my boy, you look fit. Hard work agreeing with you?"

"Doesn't much matter if it does or not. Help is expensive these days, and I must do many things for myself now."

While the rest of us went through our greetings, my mother stepped back and remained quiet. Her finger rubbed her chin with a questioning expression on her face as she studied Rachel. Slowly a smile spread over her lips and her eyes lit up.

"Something bothering you?" I asked.

That famous Analee eyebrow went up as she continued taking her daughter-in-law's measure, her smile growing ever larger. After a few moments, she pointed to Rachel, and barely able to contain herself, she announced, "Pernell, we are going to be a grandparents!"

Go to www.catahoulachronicles.com and sign up for notices about this book and others by the author.

"Nostalgia" aka PTSD

Post Traumatic Stress Disorder was officially defined and named in 1980 to describe the mental issues suffered by Vietnam veterans. But it existed long before that, at least as long as war and trauma have been visited upon mankind. It was known by other names during different periods of history. It was called "shell shock" in WWI, and during WWII, it was called "battle fatigue." In the mid 19th century, during the American Civil War, it was called "nostalgia."

That term was coined by a 17th-century medical student to describe the anxieties displayed by Swiss mercenaries fighting away from home. It was described as a form of melancholy.

The Greek origin of the English word is *nóstos álgos*. *Nóstos* is usually translated "homecoming" but carries the idea of returning home after a long journey to find that everything is the same, yet just a shadow of what it had been before. *Álgos* refers to pain. Literally, we have "homecoming pain."

I think that 17th century medical student had in mind the pain of a soldier returning home after a war to find that while everything may look as it did before he left, he sees things differently, because stressful wartime experiences have changed his life perspective, usually not for the better. Depression, nightmares, and anger are often symptoms.

I believe nostalgia is related to the saying, "seeing the elephant," often used by soldiers during the American Civil War and since. The idea behind "seeing the elephant" is that of the profound disappointment and disillusionment associated with having one's "grand" notions about war dashed by the brutal reality of the killing fields. It suggests the soldier has seen enough, and he is sick of all the misery, pain, and death. He has "seen the elephant," and it was an exceedingly ugly beast.

Nostalgia, or known by its current title, PTSD, is not limited to veterans of war. It can be caused by any manner of stressful conditions, such as rape, witnessing something terrible like an accident or death, a near death experience, or really anything that can leave a profound and lasting impression of fear or anxiety. Ethan suffered his first bout of nostalgia as a result of his witnessing the death of Cornelius as a child of three, and later as the result of losing Rachel, followed by what he saw and did during the war in places like the Shenandoah Valley, Sharpsburg, Chancellorsville, and especially Gettysburg and its aftermath. Rachel also "saw the elephant" and it affected her as well.

Both Rachel and Ethan had come from a comfortable lifestyle of plenty in a time of peace to one of horror and death in a time of war, a war described by author Paul Fussell as "long, brutal, total, and stupid." Should we not expect such might affect a sane person?

Dear Reader,

I cannot express how grateful I am that you spent a few hours reading this book, and I hope you enjoyed it.

If you liked this book, please take a few minutes to leave a review on the site where you purchased it. Indie authors need your support to be able to continue writing. Other than purchasing our books and telling others about it, the very best way you can show support is to write a review.

For more information and to discover other books available for purchase, please visit my blog at www.catahoulachronicles.com and sign up for email notifications.

My pledge to you is I will never sell your email address and NEVER spam you. The only time you will hear from me through email is if I am about to release something new or to tell you about some offer you may be interested in—and that may be only a few times a year.

My blog is where I will be giving background information on the Catahoula Series, telling a few tales that will eventually become another book, and where and how you can contact me. If you follow *Catahoula Chronicles* (click the "follow" button on any page of the site), you will receive an email notice of every new post.

I would love to hear from you and will do my best to answer your questions in a timely manner.

Thanks again,
Lane Casteix

Author's Biography

I was born in New Orleans under a curse: I like to draw, which was forever getting me into trouble in grade school and high school. My grandfather, an educator, thought he could take advantage of that and prepped me to study architecture. So, I studied fine art with a minor in beer instead—or maybe it was the other way around? My grandfather gave up.

I came to my senses and realized making a living in fine art was an iffy thing, or really more of a not-very-likely thing. I heard about a great program in advertising design at the University of Southwestern Louisiana (now the University of Louisiana at Lafayette), and that sounded professional and maybe even profitable. So I transferred and changed my major to advertising design—but I kept the minor in beer and doubled down by joining a frat, Kappa Sigma.

Eventually, I graduated and married my high school sweetheart. Almost 50 years and two kids later, she is still putting up with me.

After four years in the Air Force, I landed a job in advertising in New Orleans where I had the privilege of working with people much more talented than I am, designing many award-winning packages and product promotions. I am still there. Only instead of being a graphic designer, the other inmates let me think I run the place.

Hobbies? This is where it gets confusing. I had my painting period. Most of them are hanging in my home. Then it was my pistol-shooting-competition period, followed by my rifle-shooting-competition period, followed by my deer-hunting period. In there somewhere was my Jeep-riding period, when my elder son and I would trash my Jeep on the weekends in the Bonnet Carré Spillway. After that, came my Bible period. I am still in that one.

All my life I have made up stories in my head to entertain myself, and since I'm an incurable romantic at heart (eyes water during chick flicks), my stories usually have a romantic plot. Lest my head explode, I decided the folks inside needed to come out, thus my writing period. Since my other minor in college was history, I like writing historical fiction.

I live just outside New Orleans with my wife, and sometimes my two granddaughters, by younger son and daughter-in-law who live nearby, spend the night. Elder son, daughter-in-law, two more granddaughters and a grandson live in West Texas. And should I even mention I have four great grandkids, too?

Pets? I have four useless feral cats (make that five, a new one just showed up), one of which doesn't even like me.

That's about all I can say about me, except I like writing and I hope you enjoy reading what I write.

Lane Casteix

57219305R00229

Made in the USA
Lexington, KY
09 November 2016